Good Evening Merry Gentlemen

by

Robin Kruger

Published by Robin Kruger Books

ISBN: 978-0-6399865-2-4 (epub)
ISBN: 978-0-6399865-3-1 (mobi)
ISBN: 978-0-6399865-7-9 (print)

Robin Kruger Books

Courting Justice
Dear Scarlett
Good Evening Merry Gentlemen
Shabeni
Suffer the Little Boys
Kruger Park – Heaven on Earth
How to Make (or Not Make) Money Trading Online

www.robinkrugerbooks.com

SMALL BEGINNINGS

CHAPTER 1

Who can ever forget the magic of that first kiss? The embarrassment of your voice breaking up at that inopportune moment when chatting up the love of one's life? The awkwardness of sprouting more arms and legs than one bargained for? Or the horror of discovering in front of the mirror a sudden explosion of acne? Defining moments of growing up! I knew one such moment arrived the instant my father pressed that cold steel into the nape of my neck. Life would never be the same again!

It was the end of my lazy summer of '68 spent lying on the beach, listening to short wave radio and drinking orange soda with a warm sun on my skin. A time when people in unforgettable fashions danced to rock 'n roll and talked of peace and love and sexual freedom. But also a time when youth came of age and authority was under attack, with *Life* magazine depicting images of assassinations, peace marches against a divisive war, women's lib and civil rights movements. Exciting, revolutionary and turbulent times when possibilities seemed endless.

And although at the time I knew little of this — I was only 12 and very naive — like the first heart transplants beating new life into old I could sense the dawn of a new age. Or was it the lull before the storm!

As I sat in that chair on our back verandah with a cold shiver running down my spine, between wriggles and squeals I vaguely heard a transistor radio warbling something about going to San Francisco and wearing a flower in your hair, and I wondered, 'What hair?'

School holidays were over and the gnarled finger of high school beckoned. Instead of San Francisco, I was to go to boarding school the next day so Pa set about shearing me with a pair of old rusty hand driven hair clippers. Had them before the war, he proudly claimed. Which war I was never quite certain, but it obviously made a huge impression on my father because everything was either dated before or after that war. Perhaps the hard times of that momentous occasion explained why he still seemed so intent on challenging Scrooge for all-time cheapskate.

Mostly Pa spent Sunday afternoons in his rocking chair on the verandah of his modest house blowing on his heirloom saxophone, but that day, rather than spend a bob at the local barber, he insisted that *he* cut my hair. The hair clippers were definitely before the war! Frequently they jammed, so he cut them away from my head with a pair of scissors, leaving irregular tufts and holes in my hair, prompting Cocky, my only friend at junior school, to tease, 'Have rats been eating your hair again?'

Looking back, I think it was Pa's obsessive frugality and eccentricities that made my mother desperate for me to go to boarding school in the city — some three hours' drive away — a place I had never even been to. She feared that someday I would turn out to be just like my father and even though I was her only child she would do anything for me to escape his clutches.

'All the great statesmen of the world went to boarding school!' she would dream aloud.

I didn't really want to go but I also didn't want to go to the local high school. Miriam was going there and I hated her with a passion. I had attended a missionary convent primary school, not because we were Catholic, but simply because it was the only school in our small country town. I worshipped Mother Superior. Thought she was a saint. She normally selected a head boy and a head girl from the final year of junior school, but since there were only two boys, myself and Cocky, Mother Superior decided to have only a head girl that year and she would be boss over all. And that was she, Miriam, the spindly bug-eyed future librarian that bossed over the school like a tyrant. I hated her. Especially when she tattled on Cocky for saying the 'eff' word — a word I never even knew the meaning of — and the German nuns, being so strict on morals expelled my only friend. I hated Miriam. I hated girls.

Boarding school was the lesser of two evils. My mother visualised Eton, Pa grudgingly settled for Windsor House. It was the cheapest!

SECOND FORM

CHAPTER 2

'Hey, you!' a loud voice called.

'Huh!' I wondered out aloud, an expression my mother detested as much as me calling her Ma instead of Mum. Having only just entered Windsor House, the boarding establishment for the school Windsor College, I turned around to confront an adult man with straight red hair on his head and straight red hair all over his body. Lots of it. 'Who, me?' I enquired tentatively in a small high-pitched voice.

'Yes you, you poop!' the man answered. With his eyes popping out of a reddening oblong face, he ordered, 'Go and fetch my suitcase and take it to my dormitory.' A puzzled expression on my face prompted him to swat me across the head and bellow, 'Fucking mooove!'

Dazed, I scrambled around looking for a spare suitcase but found none. People scuttled about me, each carrying their own suitcase, seemingly not wanting to be disturbed. What suitcase? Which dormitory?

I searched the entrance hall in vain. Perhaps it hid outside. Suddenly I spotted a lone trunk lying unattended in the courtyard. I took hold of the side handle and turned to go back to the overgrown barn-like building.

Huh! It would not budge. I yanked the handle but the stubborn trunk, seemingly glued to the ground, jerked me back.

'Oh, gee!' I cried out with dismay.

Before me lay an immovable box-shaped black metal trunk, large enough to be a coffin for my slight scrawny body. Wary, I circled the trunk, suspiciously surveying the obstinate creature. Noticing two metal hoops on each end, posing as handles, I decided to use both hands, reached out to grab them, only to find that my arms were not long enough. I quickly came to terms that this trunk was designed to be carried by two stalwarts so I looked around for help, but everybody walked with purpose.

Back to the side handle. I tried pulling it again but it rooted to the tarmac like a large granite rock. Blood rushed to my head and my throat tightened. I felt lonely. Come on, you sod! But that trunk had a mind of its own and a very disagreeable one at that, simply refusing to be drawn into any reasonable debate.

What if I go and tell the mango pip man that I can't manage on my own, perhaps ask him for help? I quickly dismissed such thoughts. His

3

volcanic breath still lingered in my nose. The muscles in my neck grew tight. Desperate, I decided to see if I could lift just one end. I took a deep breath, braced myself and tugged.

Yes, yes, yes, it lifted! No, no, no! The thin metal handle tore into my tender flesh and slowly slipped out of my sweaty hands, the beast crashing down on my toes.

'Ouch!' I yelped.

Reacting spontaneously, I quickly summoned unknown strength to jerk it sideways off my aching foot. Aah! Unwittingly I had managed to move one end of the trunk, albeit just a smidgen. So I went to the other end of the trunk. Inhaling and straining, I managed to swivel the case just a tad, scraping it with a metallic sound on the tarmac.

Against the sun sinking behind the red brick building, casting a gloomy shadow, with my newfound strategy of alternatively dragging each end of the tenacious suitcase, I marshalled every ounce of my being and inched my way to the side door.

Suddenly my heart sank and the blood drained from my face. Across the hallway I saw stairs, stairs and more stairs! I felt ill. A lump grew in my throat, but still that hot breath haunted me.

With a feverish pounding in my head, my eyes blurring and the thin metal handle pressing hard into my bruised sweaty hands, I heaved one end of the trunk up the first stair. Then the second. Then the next. Using one leg to anchor my progress, I pulled on the other end of the trunk. One step. Two steps. Three steps. Using this strategy, I tugged, trembled and tugged.

Just on negotiating the first landing, a boy whizzing past in the other direction bumped into me, sending the trunk crashing all the way down the stairs and crushing my heart beneath it.

I looked to the boy with forlorn eyes, desperate that it would solicit help.

'Mind the fuck where you're going,' scowled the boy, swatting me sharply on the head. Thwack!

To this day, my only explanation to the mystery of how I ever managed to single-handedly hoist that monstrosity up two flights of stairs and down a long corridor into the prefects' dormitory, is that some kind of delirium numbed my pain.

§

'Where the fuck have you been?' roared the mango pip man as I entered the prefects' dormitory. He sat on a bed in the far right corner from the door.

4

I kept quiet. Breathless.

'Unpack my clobber!' he ordered with a slight nasal tone, just before blowing his red bulbous nose.

Next to Mango stood a wooden double-door locker. I assumed that I should unpack his belongings from his trunk and repack them in the locker. So I opened the trunk, grabbed a handful of items and placed them on the top shelf.

Thwack! Mango swatted me on the head, surging it forwards, causing my upper lip to connect against the timber shelf. It burned.

'Were you born in a bloody pigsty? Shirts go on the second shelf!'

With trepidation, I dutifully arranged his shirts on the second shelf.

Thwack! My head swirled.

'Darker shirts on the bottom, lighter ones on top!'

Thwack! Again he swatted me on the head.

'Fold them again!' his coarse voice ordered. Mango removed the shirts and strew them across the bed. 'See this,' he demonstrated with two fingers, 'this size gap between shirts and the sides of the locker. No more, no less!'

Taking a deep breath, I tried to etch the finger gap in my numbed mind and repacked the shirts. Then shorts, longs, underpants, socks and shoes. Same procedure.

As I finished, Mango stood up from his bed, towering over me when a bewildered look creased his face, as if he had noticed me for the first time. Ma would say I was young looking, maybe even good looking, with straight dark brown hair parted at the side, striking blue eyes and a straight nose in a face of fresh clear tanned skin from spending all my time outside.

'Why are your eyes so red?' he asked. 'Have you been smoking weed?'

Not understanding his question I kept quiet. Nor was I going to explain to him that at the age of seven I had developed a recurring bout of conjunctivitis, causing my eyes to itch and turn red at the slightest irritation. Since Pa made me stand on my head for half an hour each day in the belief that the blood would drain down to my eyes and heal them, I would sooner forget that I ever had an eye disease.

'And this?' he asked, grabbing a tuft of my hair. 'Have rats been eating your hair? Who the fuck are you? Do you have parents or are you some kind of tyke from the orphanage down the road?' Then, ignoring his own questions he continued, 'You're my fag. You fag for me. You look after me and you look after my shit! When I park a brown bear in the porcelain chamber, you wag your tail and go and plant your arse on the toilet seat to warm it up for me. Got it?'

I tried to nod my head but it remained motionless.

'Got it!' he roared, the hot air from his mouth blowing into my face.

'Yes,' my voice trembled.

'Yes, sir!' the drill sergeant bellowed.

'Yes, sir!'

I left his dormitory shell-shocked. With so many orders swirling around inside my head I wondered if I would ever be able to remember them.

§

Such was my introduction to life at boarding school. My mother, my dear innocent mother thought it was in my best interests to attend boarding school, ostensibly to become cultured. A place where, on my first day, a mango pip man deemed that I should be called Tyke! A place that was to be my home for the next five years!

CHAPTER 3

As I left the prefects' dormitory, the bell rang, a loud clanging sound. On cue, everybody converged downstairs to the dining room for supper. I immediately spotted the new boys. Apart from being the smallest, we were the quiet ones, the ones with the thousand yard stare. And we followed everyone else.

We all gathered in the large dining hall and took our appointed places. The head boarder master, Mr Frank Sherman, whom we called Bum Lump due to his rather large backside, said grace.

I looked to the boy standing opposite me, the spitting image of a mole. He closed his eyes and bowed his head, so I did the same. Then after opening grace, we all sat down, the 10 second formers — first year at high school — all at the same long wooden table, five on each side, with a monitor at the head of the table. His name was Pygmy, the shortest of the fifth formers.

Supper comprised a bowl of onion soup and a plastic mug of milk. I hated onion. Not with good reason, though, since I had never eaten onion before. Never even tasted it to see if I would like it. So I pushed the soggy brown onion rings to one side of the bowl and spooned the liquid into my mouth.

'You eat all your food at my table,' ordered Pygmy, breaking the deathly silence at our table. 'Leave any and I'll personally ram it down your gullet!'

My tummy heaved at this news, made worse because I had drunk all the liquid, so was unable to wash down the onion rings. I gingerly placed a spoonful of solid onion in my mouth and wrestled between an inability to swallow them whole and the ugly taste of masticating them into a puree. I opted for the latter, though not without nearly gagging on many occasions. My stomach heaved too when I looked down at the plastic mug of milk. I hated milk. Too sticky!

Knock! Knock! Twice Mango banged loudly on his wooden table with a metal gong to signify the end of supper. Just before saying closing grace, he made an announcement.

'All new poops are to go to the prefects' dormitory after supper!'

§

I followed the herd of second formers on the way to the prefects' dormitory. First we alighted a flight of stairs, turned right at a landing

7

and right again for a second flight of stairs. As we reached the top I peeked through a doorway immediately to my left, noticing that all traffic up and down the stairs passed the masters' office.

Immediately at the top of the landing were three doors. The one on the right opened to the junior dormitory for second and third formers, the left served the middle dormitory for fourth formers and half the fifth formers, with a box room, where we stored our trunks, sandwiched between the two dormitories.

Leading off the top landing were two corridors. One led to the left and straight into the senior dormitory, housing the sixth formers and the remainder of the fifth formers. We turned down the corridor in the opposite direction, past the resident master's bedroom on the right and headed towards the prefects' dormitory at the end.

Standing congregated outside, I sensed no good lay beyond that door. The tallest of the second formers opened the door and led us in like sacrificial lambs to the slaughter.

The prefects' dormitory was small, housing only three beds, one in each corner, the entry forming the fourth corner. A locker accompanied each bed. Between the two lockers on the far right side stood a wash basin and between the third locker and the doorway sat a gramophone. Although there were only three beds, there were five prefects in total. One monitored the middle dormitory, the other the senior dormitory, with all the prefects except the head prefect rotating each week.

As we gathered in the dormitory, waiting in anticipation, I observed the prefects. All huge, bruising and domineering. But two, in particular, stood out. My prefect, the redhead Mango who brooded alongside his bed. And Grizzly, scratching his black frizzy hair with a vacant look on his face as he sat on the window ledge with his feet on his bed, the one closest to the record player.

We all faced Mango.

'We are the prefects. I am the head prefect. And you second formers are poops,' belittled Mango. 'So we can get to know which poop is which, for the next two weeks you are to wear a big cardboard sign around your neck with the word poop on it followed by your name! Got it!'

Silence.

'Got it!' shouted Mango, brandishing a stick.

Some second formers mumbled.

'What? I can't hear you!' the head prefect bellowed with his hand cupping his ear, his face turning red.

'Yes!' we sang in unison.

'Yes, what?'

'Yes, sir!'

'You do as we say,' Mango continued. 'When you enter our dormitory, you knock, and then you wait for a prefect to say come in. As you enter, you greet us. Good morning, merry gentlemen! Or good evening, merry gentlemen! Or whatever. You poops got it? Just walk in here and you get clobbered!'

With that he swatted the head of the second former who stood closest to the front, the one who led us into the dormitory.

A thought briefly flashed through my mind about a conversation I had with my father that morning, the only advice he gave me. 'Never be in the front,' advised Pa. 'Never at the back. Don't even stand in the middle. Go somewhere between the middle and the back.' Being of average height I easily melted somewhere between the middle and the back of the group of second formers.

As Mango cuffed him on the head, the well-built second former, who looked twice the size of any other second former, swung his head back defiantly. Mango's eyes bulged and his face turned an even brighter shade of red.

'Oh, yes!' exclaimed Mango, his anger changing to a smirk. 'We have one of these! What's your name?'

'Edward,' the second former replied confidently with a voice that had already broken.

'Sir!'

'Edward, sir!' replied the second former, his defiance melting away.

'Eddie, Eddie, Eddie!' sneered Mango, shaking his head to the slow timing of his voice. He took a fistful of the second former's short wavy blond hair and spoke deliberately, 'You have the manners of a cunt! No, not a cunt, that's too classy for you. A spare arsehole! And we don't need any more spare arseholes,' the head prefect continued, looking at the rest of the second formers, 'because we have enough of them right here!

Still holding Eddie by his hair, Mango slapped his face with an open hand, the second former's large oval shaped head snapping sideways on his short neck, sending beads of sweat flying. Then a backhand. All second formers stood rigidly to attention, shocked and on edge. I was particularly careful to keep my mouth shut.

Mango shoved Eddie back into the herd of wide eyes, and continued, 'Like I was saying, you—'

'Atishoo!'

'Who was that?' demanded Grizzly in a deep goofy voice. This prefect was all muscle, even between his ears.

Silence. It was so hushed you could have heard an amoeba mate!

'Who the fuck sneezed?' yelled Grizzly.

'Me,' wailed a soft, tremulous voice, emanating from behind Eddie. The short kid tried to raise his hand, but it vehemently resisted.

'Come here!' ordered the prefect, getting off his window perch, looking for the source. 'What are you, wailing like that? A fucking dog!'

As the second former emerged from behind Eddie, the muscle bound Grizzly picked up a cake tin lid and buckled it over the kid's head and growled, 'This isn't a pound where your parents can keep their dog, and judging by the look of you, not so much a dog as a mutt.'

'I feel sick,' the kid complained, but in a voice so trembling it was unintelligible to muscular ears.

'What?' yelled the scowling prefect.

'I feel sick,' repeated the kid, now visibly shaking.

'Great! Just what we need, a sick mutt! Go to the matron and get a bucket!' the prefect ordered.

The kid, from that moment on known only as Mutt, quickly left the dormitory.

'Thank you, merry gentlemen!' yelled the prefects in chorus.

Mutt quickly returned, poked his head through the doorway and wailed, 'Thank you, merry gentlemen!'

Mango continued ordering us, 'You poops must close the windows at night. Ring the bell. Make tea for the master on duty.'

There followed a list of instructions, ad nauseam, of a thousand and one items we second formers had to carry out as duties.

'In addition, you will all fag for a prefect. Two of you to a prefect.'

'But there are only nine of us!' exclaimed Eddie from the front, proudly trying to help.

'You fucking douchebag!' spat Mango, shaking his head, a smirk curling on his lips. He again grabbed Eddie by the hair. 'You think I'm some kind of imbecile?'

'No, no!' protested Eddie, suddenly wary of Mango's mood.

The head prefect swung Eddie's face, crashing it into his locker. Blood spurted from the second former's large rounded nose, staining his white shirt with red polka dots.

Mango swivelled Eddie's head around to face the rest of us and asked, 'How many poops do you count?'

'Er, er, eight. Eight, sir!'

'And counting you?'

'Nine, sir!' Eddie sang through a full lipped mouth, his face lighting up.

Knock! Knock!

'Come in,' yelled a prefect.

'Good evening, merry gentlemen!' wailed Mutt, entering the prefects' dormitory.

'And Mutt makes ten!' Mango completed with a satisfactory smile.

Eddie's sweaty face visibly deflated.

'Fetch that bucket,' Mango ordered the bleeding Eddie, 'and wash down my locker!'

Mutt handed Eddie the bucket, then slipped in between the middle and the back, standing next to me. He learned quickly.

'And you poops are to answer the telephone,' the head prefect went on. 'It must not ring more than three times, so move your arses.'

The bell rang for lights out.

'Fuck off, now, and remember what I told you.'

'Thank you, merry gentlemen!' we sang as we left the prefects' dormitory.

§

Along with my peers, I entered the rectangular junior dormitory and hurried down the aisle that divided a sequence of bed, locker, bed, locker, stopping at the fifth bed on the right. Observing the third formers who resided in the far end of the dormitory, I opened my single door wooden locker, took off my evening clothes and dressed in a pair of homemade powder-blue cotton sleeping shorts, a royal blue towelling dressing gown and a pair of flip flops.

'Attention!' called the fifth form monitor from the door.

Copying those around me, I stood in the aisle at the foot of my bed, dead quiet. Waiting there, I gazed at the sorry looking bunch around me, a conglomeration of fallout from dysfunctional families, brightened only by the array of different coloured towelling gowns. Though similar in age, all appeared older than me. I stood in a row of boys whose beds backed up against a windowless wall that also served the corridor on the other side that led to the prefects' dormitory.

Standing next to me on my left was Basil, a short guy we called Spazz instead of Bazz due to him looking like a cartoon caricature of a plumpish mole. You get shades of what people commonly refer to as black hair — various hints of dark hair until on the one extreme it can get no more black. Spazz had that black hair. Straight with a long fringe that came right down his forehead, which itself seemed to slope into a long pointy nose along which a pair of low set eyes sighted through spectacles. He stood with his feet pointing at ten to two.

Next to him stood Perve, who had the dubious distinction of being named after his kinky looking dick. It appeared to have knuckles, resembling a crooked finger that seemed intent on curling around under his ballbag to inspect his backside. Mutt would one day accuse him of being perverted, and so 'perve' would become both a nickname and part of hostel lexicon for anything perverted.

Next in line, Goofball, a laid back case so dozy he appeared permanently high on grass.

Lastly, by the door, Beanie. He wore one of those heads that sat off centre on his neck, a flat face leaving most of his head protruding behind him, resembling a dried butter bean.

We faced another row of boys, only a pace away, whose beds backed up against the window wall that overlooked Windsor road. Directly opposite me, I faced Mutt, the short guy with a large squarish head that now gave the same shape to the prefects' cake tin lid. Mutt had so many freckles the puppet-like figure positively resembled the curdled offspring of a mixed marriage.

Next to him on his right stood Eddie. Eddie Alcock, the territorial male. Strangely, the only boy at hostel not known by a nickname. Perhaps his surname sufficed, because he was definitely all that!

Then Hog, a fatso who suffered the indignity of looking like a pig, right down to a nose so upturned that you could see right into his nostrils. No matter how long or short, or dry or wet, his light brown hair stood to attention like porcupine quills, making his large head seem even bigger. A big pig head. Right off the bat he gave me the creeps. My father intensely despised fat, perhaps because it cost too much money to get that way. I was skinny.

After him, Gecko, a boy so white a network of visible blue veins made him appear translucent.

And finally, Flake, an anorexic looking specimen that would float to ground like a dried leaf if ever he jumped out of a plane without a parachute. He had the unenviable honour of sleeping next to the fifth form monitor, whose bed lay in the corner opposite the entrance door. Flake and I were to share Mango's fagging duties.

Past Mutt and me on the other end of the dormitory lived the third formers. Immediately to my right slept a scumbag with short emaciated arms and legs, a tragic victim of thalidomide. With tufts of motley brown hair on a scrawny head that jutted forwards on rounded shoulders, he looked the spitting image of a moth-eaten vulture, so everybody called him Vulture.

Opposite Vulture, and therefore standing next to Mutt, Vulture's best friend, Chief, a character straight out of a spaghetti western movie.

In the distance, I heard a distinct clapping of footsteps start in the masters' office, growing louder and louder until finally Mr Percival Dawkins, dressed in a beige three piece polyester suit, entered the junior dormitory.

'Good evening!' he greeted, the first cultured voice I had heard all day.

'Good evening, sir,' we mumbled.

'Before prayers, let me introduce myself,' continued the master with refined facial features and light brown hair combed backwards from a high forehead.

As with the second formers, this was also his first day at hostel. Tall, perhaps in his forties, he appeared aristocratic, prim and proper and laundered with starch, and quickly became known as Duke. Unmarried, he was the resident boarder master, whereas Bum Lump and Mrs Bum Lump lived without children in a separate house at the back of the hostel premises.

Duke then prayed, as was custom every night before lights out.

'Good night, gentlemen!' greeted Duke, in a deep, learned judge's voice.

'Good night, sir,' we mumbled.

Soon after the dormitory monitor switched the lights out, I took off my gown, hung it on a brass hook attached to the side of my locker and climbed into bed, mounting the tall black metal frame, somewhat like a hospital bed with grey army-type blankets. Lying down on a pitifully thin mattress, coir knots prodding into my back, I struggled to find comfort in a pillow as lumpy as a sack of potatoes.

Long into the night I wondered what I had done to deserve this, longing for my bed at home. It was hellishly hot. In stifling humidity, each time I tossed and turned my sheet clung to me, wrapping me into a claustrophobic cocoon. Amongst 50 boys at hostel I felt so alone. The place seemed foreign. So, so foreign. Every wall of every room was the same colour, public works department pale green. And like a hospital with its own distinctive odour, hostel smelled of an eternal conflict between industrial disinfectant, the smell of burning bodies from the crematorium next door and the stale body odour of boys, boys and more boys.

§

'Hey, Tyke! Come on, man, wake up!' a voice urged.

I woke to see Spazz tugging at me. Exhausted from lying awake much of the previous night, I had slept through the bell. With the sad realisation that my nightmare was indeed a reality, I donned my dressing gown, showered, got dressed and then set off to attend to Mango.

As I approached the door of the prefects' dormitory, I noticed it was

13

open. I knocked on it softly. No answer. It had gone 6.40 am. I wrestled with what to do. Do I knock again? I reasoned not, so I walked in and as I got near my prefect's bed I said in a low voice, 'Good morning, merry gentlemen.'

'Keep quiet, poop,' mumbled Mango from under his pillow.

Eddie entered the dormitory and tiptoed to his prefect.

'Good morning, merry gentlemen!' quipped Grizzly, cuffing Eddie across the head as he rose from his bed.

Mango carried on sleeping. I looked at my watch. Only 15 minutes for the head prefect to shower, get dressed and be ready for breakfast at seven o'clock. Damn! What should I do? I tugged at his shoulder.

'Fuck off!'

I stood and gazed at him, feeling utterly helpless.

'Sir!' I pleaded.

'Fuck off!'

'But sir,' I said hesitatingly, 'it's gone 6.45!'

'What, you poop! Why didn't you wake me up?' the head prefect demanded, swatting me on the head as he arose.

§

After breakfast we all headed off to school, some five minutes' walk from the hostel, for the second formers, our first day at high school. As I exited the gates of the boarding establishment and turned right, a hand leapt out from nowhere and swatted me on the head.

Huh! I turned around to see Vulture, a third former no bigger than me, scowling at me.

'Go around the tree!' he squawked, flapping his arms.

Oh yes! I had forgotten one of the many rules dished out the previous night. When commuting between hostel and school, instead of simply turning right and treading off on the normal pathway, second formers had to navigate around an oak tree on the verge some 10 paces to the left before returning to the path and joining the rest of the boarders.

CHAPTER 4

Five weeks later, the bell rang at 5.45 in the morning. Same time every day, routine the glue that held the place together. Along with the other second formers, like a zombie I climbed out of bed, took off my sleeping shorts, slipped into my gown and flip flops, slung a towel over my right shoulder and headed off downstairs to the junior showers, used by second, third and fourth formers.

Despite boys being tagged with 'frogs and snails and puppy dog tails', nobody could accuse us of being unclean. Just the slightest hint of uncleanliness aroused passionate condemnation. Never leave a pair of dirty socks lying at the bottom of one's locker. Electing to skip a shower broke an unwritten law held in high esteem in the sanctity of hostel cleanliness.

The term 'mouldy' stuck like a supermarket price tag to the person least inclined to be clean. One of a trio of unwanted labels. Therefore, we showered twice a day on weekdays and three times on weekends, always an eventful occasion.

I entered the junior ablutions through a swing door. On my immediate right stood six basins and past them three toilets, each in its own cubicle but with walls that fell well short of a high ceiling. On my left a separate enclosure housed eight showers and beyond them, opposite the toilets, lay two baths. At the back of the ablutions, 30 wire lockers stood to attention, one for each boy.

First port of call, the piss trough, as we called the urinal. It backed on the side wall of the first toilet, allowing enough space for only two. Ahead of me decanting the night's build-up were Eddie and Spider, a tall fourth former with a short torso that sprouted long spindly limbs.

'Hey, you bloody dribbler! Are you the jerk who always leaves a piss trail?' a miffed Spider asked, then without waiting for a reply, cuffed Eddie across the back of the head, sending the second former crashing into the piss trough. Spider then demonstrated the art of how to end off a piss. 'When you're finished, you give your dick a shake and then you squeeze it like this,' coached Spider, milking his own equipment, 'then another shake! Got it!' With that demonstration done, Spider went to shower.

I stepped up to the urinal, mindful of the technique of how to avoid being a dribbler. Careful, too, not to step too close to the piss trough for fear of treading on the drip of the previous dribblers, which, as the day progressed, meant standing further and further away. I relieved myself, shook my dick with vigour, squeezed and shook again.

After undressing and placing my gown and flip flops in my wire locker, I slung my towel over the wall of the dank, steamy shower enclosure and entered it. Damn! All eight showers were occupied so I walked to the far wall, turned around and waited for a shower, second in the queue behind Hog.

There were four showers on each side with only narrow side walls separating each into a cubicle, the open front making it easy to spot a vacancy. Spider stood in the best shower, third on the right, the only one without a rose, simply a solid flow of water blasting out of a steel water pipe. Another fourth former, the portly Scrote, barely squeezed into the cubicle of the next best shower, second on the left, the rose with the most pressure. Two third formers occupied the next two showers with the most pressure and four second formers filled the remaining showers, those with the least pressure.

A shower is a shower is a shower. Not at hostel! As with everything else, each shower embodied a ranking. It all had to do with an artificial pecking order that insidiously entrenched itself into hostel life. Any senior could and did assert a myriad of rights over any person junior to him.

So a scrawny runt of a third former had full right to kick out of a shower a much bigger second former with the confidence that, should the junior resist, the third former would have the full backing of his peers. Were these boundaries ever tested? Yes, and that's how they evolved. But in order for the pecking order to function there had to be the best and worst of everything and a ranking of everything in between.

Somehow we all got caught up in it. Absurd, perhaps, but it had something to do with survival. It would have been easy to simply go to the worst shower — after all, you still got clean — and abandon the drive to strive for the best. Indeed, initially most of us probably preferred the spray of a shower with a rose to the blast from the pipe without one. But to let go would be to give up the constant struggle to be someone. Incredibly, therefore, our tastes moulded according to likes and dislikes formed over time, as if we were systematically channelled through the same mincing machine.

Amongst our peers, though, it was different. The accepted code was one of first come first served, though this was frequently challenged by those with greater strength, which in turn had to be countered by wit. But the battle to strive for the best still existed.

Chief entered the shower room. Damn! I now lined up third in the queue. For a moment he just stood there surveying the eight showers and assessing his options. A round head covered with soft, straight, blond hair that always settled into the shape of a straw hat, sat directly on a strong thickset body, the lack of a neck giving the impression of someone deeply suspicious of all around him. Below he wore a foreskin so long he could practise birth control by tying a knot in it. Jaw jutting out, blue eyes closed to slits, he made his choice, walked over to the shower having the most pressure held by a second former and touched Beanie on the shoulder who, without a word spoken, vacated his shower. Still full of soap he rejoined the queue but, luckily for him, first in line having already occupied a shower.

Waiting there, I continually estimated the progress of each person in the showers. We all did. My heart momentarily sank when I spotted an apparition of Vulture dragging his bones across the open doorway of the shower enclosure, believing I had slipped further back in the queue, but then I suddenly remembered that Vulture never showered. Always hovered near the baths.

Both a third former and Goofball left, so Chief quickly abandoned his shower and took up residence in the one previously held by the third former. It had more pressure. Being first in line, Beanie chose the shower vacated by Chief and the always clammy fair-skinned Hog entered the other, first on the right, making the fatal mistake to face the back wall.

'Cockshy!' Scrote mocked, pointing a finger at Hog.

Scrote was a fat fourth former. His seniors and peers called him Scrote because he had a bloated red scrotum that made his small dick appear even smaller, but his double chinned red face grunted if anyone junior called him by that nickname. Rumour was that he was a cry-baby and would break if resisted. Normally such resistance across the pecking order was taboo, but exceptions that involved an act of courage standing up to someone disliked were sometimes overlooked, such as when Mutt dared to call him Scrote. When confronted by the grunt, the dog argued that it was not on account of his small dick or large scrotum but because his character lay somewhere between a prick and an arsehole. I was not up to the challenge. Not yet!

All eyes turned to Hog accompanied by a chorus of sniggering. Never shower facing the back wall lest you be labelled 'cockshy'. Cockshy ranked alongside mouldy.

'I'm not cockshy,' mumbled Hog as he turned around. Dribbling through fat slobbery lips he continued, 'I just turned to fetch some soap.'

'You calling me a liar?' asked Scrote, angrily.

A forlorn Hog with droopy brown eyes and a sprinkling of large faded freckles on his upturned nose shook his head.

'Then you *are* cockshy!'

Unsure, poor Hog looked at Scrote.

Just then Eddie poked his nose around the side wall that separated his shower from Hog's.

'What are *you* looking at?' Scrote asked Eddie.

'Uh,' paused Eddie. 'I'm just checking to see if he's cockshy.'

'Why? Don't you believe me?'

'I do!' Eddie retracted.

'Then you're a rabbit!' Scrote accused.

Never be cockshy but also don't show over-enthusiasm in another person's equipment lest you be accused of being a 'rabbit', hostel's term for a homosexual. Mouldy. Cockshy. Rabbit. The lowest of the lows.

Suddenly, Scrote issued the dreaded, 'You both see me, tonight!'

Eddie knew what that meant. His fair-skinned face washed as red as the carbolic soap he held in his hand, his nostrils flared and his dark brown eyes looked menacing.

I felt tension in the air. Hmm! I looked at Eddie, then at Scrote, then back at Eddie. What have we here?

But Eddie just stood there and glared at Scrote. With muscular calves shaped like chicken drumsticks and barely able to wash his ears for biceps, I suspected that Eddie could make an easy meal of Scrote but for his second form status. Scrote seemed to bloat like a puffer fish in his shower cubicle, an unsure defence mechanism.

Aggrieved, Eddie broke the stalemate, retaliating in a manner he knew best. Keeping his eyes fixed on Scrote, he thrust his pelvis forwards and deliberately lathered his dick, drawing Scrote's attention to it to make a point. Whilst all other second formers sported worms, Eddie flaunted equipment beyond his years, giving credence to his name, Eddie Alcock! A donkey dong, dropped balls and a veritable bush of brown pubic hair. Despite his fourth form status, Scrote owned little more than a spare belly button, hidden below a huge roly-poly paunch. Hog appeared a carbon copy and I suspected that Scrote was once accused of being cockshy when in second form. Scrote never picked on Eddie again.

A five minute wait. Aah! Mutt finished rinsing, so my turn next. Nope, false alarm! The mongrel stayed on, enjoying his absolute right to remain in the shower so long as nobody senior usurped his position.

Dragging his lip, Scrote left, causing a reshuffling of the showers, third formers upgrading. That left a vacancy for me so I entered the fourth best shower of the eight. No sooner had I started showering when a third former's hand touched my shoulder and pushed me out. No words spoken. None needed.

Thankfully, though, I was wet. That meant I could soap myself, if one could call it soap. Using a large carving knife, the matron cut up huge blocks — two by fours — of red carbolic soap. The so-called soap had a decided acid quality and just as well, too! With so many boys showering twice a day, the scummy rough concrete floor barely had time to dry, so fungi flourished and the tart dip probably helped to keep them at bay. We used it for everything. Body, feet, bum, genitals and face. Oh, it also served as our shampoo and we washed our clothes with it, too!

I lathered myself from top to toe and waited. Body pink with soap, eyes peeled for the slightest sign, just a hint that someone may leave his shower.

Aah! Mutt leant his long body over his short legs and shook his head violently, instantly drying his coarse hair, smacked his lips, then firmly nodded his head with a grin of satisfaction. That signature pronounced himself done.

Damn! A fourth former entered and shoved Chief out of the best shower, stopping me dead in my tracks because Chief then walked over to the shower Mutt had vacated and assumed his entitled spot.

Between such cat naps of wetting and soaping myself in a complex game of musical chairs, I eventually managed to rinse myself.

§

Late, I grabbed my towel, quickly dabbed myself dry, slipped on my gown and ran upstairs into my dormitory, entering to the blast of Goofy's heavy handed strumming on a tinny guitar drowning out the ubiquitous dormitory transistor radio. Despite weeks of effort, our fifth form monitor still struggled to play the introductory chords of *Proud Mary*.

We lived for music. It became our lifeline to the outside world. Our main diet was an offshore radio station on AM playing 'all the hits all the time' to those who would call in and make requests and dedications. We'd listen to everything. Well, nearly everything! From romantic schmaltz to the sweet sound of the Carpenters to the popular Hollies, Bread and Bee Gees. Lots of Bee Gees. Petula Clark was more for our parents, though some of us whose tastes had not quite moulded to that of hostel had secretly not quite let go of her. We loved the beautiful harmony of Art Garfunkel and the raw sound of Creedence Clearwater Revival. Heck, we would even listen to the odd Tom Jones number. But Elvis was out. The Beatles were fading, as were the Rolling Stones, though every so often one of their songs would revive our interest in them. And there was always time for The Beach Boys.

The radio seldom played the 'heavies' like Led Zeppelin, Pink Floyd and The Who, but occasionally someone would lay his hands on a cassette tape containing an album like *Tommy* and we would listen to it over and over again. Songs like *Pinball Wizard* and *See Me, Feel Me* would become favourites until the novelty wore off. Only Perve listened to the Moody Blues and Bob Dylan. The rest of us thought that was weird. Well, mostly.

And then there was music from the movies like *Ballad of the Green Berets* and *Raindrops Keep Falling on My Head*. And instead of whistling *Colonel Bogey March* from the movie *The Bridge on the River Kwai*, we sang to the same tune:

> Hitler had only one big ball,
> Göring had two but they were small.
> Himmler had something sim'lar,
> But poor old Goebbels had no balls at all!

That morning, Goofy's rendition, 'Da, da, da, daaaaah. Da, da, da, daaaaah,' a not too dissimilar variation of scratching one's fingernails on a blackboard, soured my attempt at whistling along with the radio's sweet sounding *Jesamine*. Whereas my father could always be found playing his saxophone in his spare time, I whistled. If Mango had not been so quick to nickname me Tyke, I might just have been called Whistler.

As I walked down the aisle, Mutt scampered off in the other direction. Damn, he was already dressed and on his way to comb his hair in front of the small mirror that hung near the door of the dormitory, to be shared by all. Well, brush his hair in *his* case. Whilst all others used a comb, Mutt used a brush.

Hanging up my gown, I noticed Vulture reach into his laundry bag, extract a pair of dirty socks and start to drag them over his carcass.

'Phoof!' I exclaimed, waving the air with my hand as a nasty odour of smelly socks permeated the dormitory.

Vulture turned around, looked at me with his dark beady eyes and was about to squawk when a third former who slept on the other side of him interrupted, 'Vulture, you mouldy creature! How can you even put on those socks? They're so stiff you can stand them up against your locker, whistle, and they'll come walking to you!'

All the third formers except Chief started to whistle. Like a wild animal in a cage, Vulture swung his moth-eaten head this way then that. Laughter broke out. Returning from the mirror, Mutt wailed, always a high pitched howl with a wide grin baring his teeth, sometimes combined with unintelligible sounds as he tried to speak at the same time.

'Hey, Mutt!' Eddie called as the pooch passed his bed. 'What's that fly shit on your teeth?'

Like his parents and four sisters, the brown-eyed Mutt had freckles everywhere. Freckles all over his square head. Freckles on his rectangular shaped body. Freckles on his arms and legs. Freckles on his bum and dick. Even seemed like freckles on his teeth, though he disputed that, claiming that the borehole water they drank in the Masai Mara, where his father used to work as a game ranger, had stained his teeth. If he weren't so clearly mongrel he would definitely pass for a Dalmatian.

'It's not fly shit, man!' defended Mutt, his eyes rolling back with impatience. 'I've told you before, it's from the water we drank.'

'Couldn't you buy toothpaste in the jungle?' teased Eddie. Then alluding to Mutt's thrifty trait, he asked, 'Or were you too stingy to buy some?'

'Aay!' dismissed Mutt. 'What would you know!'

'Woof, woof!' Eddie continued teasing. 'When you've learned to clean that fly shit off your teeth you can go back to the jungle because we don't need foot and mouth disease here!'

'You don't need to tell me to go. When I'm finished school, there're two things I'm gonna do. Grow my hair and set sail and never come back,' Mutt announced, referring to the yacht he often claimed that his father was building to sail around the world, though nobody ever believed him.

'You call that hair!' Eddie teased. 'And why do you always use a brush?'

'Because a comb won't go through his shaggy fur coat!' dribbled Hog.

'You're right!' Eddie exclaimed. 'At the dog squad in my dad's army camp they use a brush to give the Alsatians' coats that extra sheen.'

'Aay!' wailed Mutt, shaking his head in disbelief, but handling his teasing in good spirits as he applied the finishing touches to his salt and pepper coloured hair, hair so coarse it resembled steel wool.

Suddenly Eddie snatched Mutt's hairbrush out of his hands, and being so much taller than the short Mutt, easily held it high out of reach.

'Hey, give me back my brush, you fucking lover-boy!' yelped Mutt, repeatedly jumping up at Eddie.

'I just want to see what it's like to brush my hair instead of combing it,' Eddie smirked. 'Maybe I can also get it to shine like a dog's.'

As Mutt climbed on Eddie's bed to salvage his brush, Eddie called to me from across the aisle, 'Hey, Tyke! Catch!'

Whilst bending over and putting on my socks, I shook my head. Apart from sensing Mutt's increasing agitation, I was late and still needed to polish my shoes.

'Aw, you spoil sport wimp!' complained Eddie, then turning to Hog, shouted, 'Here, catch!'

'You fucking blubberguts!' Mutt called. Walking purposefully to Hog's bed he demanded in a raised voice, 'Give me back my brush!'

The hound went after Hog, prompting the plump pig to quickly seek sanctuary by throwing the brush back to Eddie, who caught it and made the fatal mistake of putting it to his hair. Hair that had a tendency to curl and go frizzy at the ends, so he would plaster it down with Vitalis to give the appearance of only a slight wave.

Suddenly Mutt went wild. He jumped up onto Hog's bed and made a flying dive, head first into Eddie, both crashing into Eddie's locker, slamming the door shut with a loud bang. Though small, the wiry Mutt fought like a terrier, wrenching the brush in a frenzy from a dazed Eddie.

All eyes turned to the bundle of flailing arms and legs. Tension.

Having retrieved his brush, Mutt stood up and quickly climbed over Eddie's bed to reach his own domain. Once there, he wagged his finger and, in a high pitched voice laden with emotion, issued the order, 'Don't *ever* touch my stuff!'

Eddie gathered himself. His eyes grew wild, his forehead sweaty, his face red and his nostrils flared. He jerked his head a few times in defiance, but he said nothing. He never teased Mutt again.

Just then, Flake, with whom I shared fagging duties for Mango, reminded me, 'Tyke, remember it's *your* turn to fag today!'

I looked at my watch. Damn, I was five minutes late! Neglecting to polish my shoes, I hurried to the prefects' dormitory.

'Good morning, merry gentlemen!' I said hesitatingly.

'Tyke, you're late!' exclaimed Mango, before turning his head over on his pillow to continue to sleep.

Just how he knew from the depths of slumber that I had arrived late mystified me. Always did. So began the interminable drag before he finally rose. Eventually he sat up on his bed.

'Why'd you wake me up so late, you poop?'

Ignoring his question, I grabbed hold of his gown and held it out for him to slip into. But first he stood up, displaying a monstrous morning glory with his dick piercing hard against his sleeping shorts.

'Shit! Now I remember, I had this wet dream last night,' he announced, lifting his sleeping shorts over his dick to remove them. 'No wonder there's dried cum all over my dickhead!'

'Fucking liar!' Grizzly growled, still lying in bed. 'You've been screwing your hand again, you horny bastard!'

'Peel it off!' Mango ordered me, with a deadpan face.

Huh! With the eyes of all the other fags turning to face us, my heart quickened.

'Peel the cum off!' his voice grew louder.

Unsure what to do, I stood there glued to the spot. Hesitatingly, I looked down at his dick but didn't see anything different. Just his usual frisky weapon donning a purple helmet.

Mango took a step closer to me, pointed to his dick and commanded, 'Listen, Tyke, peel that cum off. But I'm warning you, if it hurts I'll bang you on the head and stamp noughts all over the floor with your arsehole. Now, peel it off!'

My heart thumped. Always this dilemma. Like having the unenviable honour of choosing to be hit on the head with a brick or be hit on the head with a block.

'It's twenty to seven, sir!' Spazz informed Grizzly.

'What!' responded Mango, overhearing my friend.

Suddenly forgetting his wet dream dried cum dilemma he snatched his gown from me and left for the showers.

Seizing my prefect's towel from its hook on the side of the locker, I nodded my head in appreciation to Spazz, dashed out the door, stopped, returned, poked my head through the doorway, quickly said, 'Thank you, merry gentlemen!' even though by now there were only second formers in the prefects' dormitory — but that was the rule — then ran past Mango, down one flight of stairs, onto the landing and into the senior ablutions, a replica of the junior ablutions directly below.

Phew! A toilet was free. Quickly unbuckling my belt, I pulled down my trousers and underpants, sat on the toilet and waited. After awhile Mango popped his head in the doorway so I got off the toilet, pulled up my underpants and trousers and buckled up my belt.

The head prefect disrobed, handed me his gown and sat down on the toilet for his clockwork morning evacuation. He liked his toilet seat warm! Body temperature!

6.45 am.

After arranging Mango's gown on a bench and hanging his towel over the front wall that enclosed the showers, I exited the senior ablutions and ran off towards the prefects' dormitory when the telephone, situated back on the first landing, rang. Damn! In a quandary, I looked down the passageway behind me but there were no second formers to be seen, so I decided I had better run for it.

'Tyke! Running in the passage. Two black marks!' exclaimed a prefect returning from the showers.

I nodded acceptance, then slowed down to a fast walk. One ring. Two rings. Three rings ... and ... four rings! Damn!

As I picked up the receiver, Grizzly peered through the doorway to the ablutions and growled, 'Don't you fuckers learn. The phone mustn't ring more than *three* times! Tyke, two black marks!'

Again, I nodded acceptance but a lump grew in my throat as I tried to digest the absurdity for being punished simply because I was closest to the telephone, though far away enough not to be able to answer it before it rang three times, especially if I were not allowed to run! I took a deep breath and sighed, then answered the phone. Damn! A wrong number!

Back in the prefects' dormitory, whilst the prefects' radio played the latest number one hit, *Build Me Up Buttercup*, providing a welcome respite from the woeful endeavours of Goofy, I first made Mango's bed. Hospital corners. Then, from his locker, I withdrew and arranged neatly on his bed a white long sleeved shirt with a striped navy blue and gold tie, white cotton underpants, the type with speckled holes, grey trousers complete with belt and grey socks before black shoes. It all looked like a dressed up Mango lying on his bed sans the body!

Grizzly suddenly burst into the prefects' dormitory, took one look at me and got out the black mark book, penning two black marks against my name. Prefects were not allowed to cane us, that pleasure was reserved for the masters only. To avoid continual harassment of the masters for minor infractions, prefects would issue us with black marks which would accumulate during the week and for every black mark we would get caned one stripe on Sunday evening.

'I also get two from him, sir,' I owned up, pointing to the other prefect in the dormitory, hoping that honesty would pay. It didn't, my plea for clemency falling mute on muscular ears.

Turning away from Grizzly, I suddenly realized that my prefect's shoes looked a sorry sight. Having forgotten to polish them the night before, hands working feverishly, I grabbed the polish kit, fumbled for the tin, prised it open, applied polish and shined and shined some more.

6.55 am.

Mango returned from the showers, peeled off his gown from a damp hairy body and sat on the freshly made bed for me to dry him. Same routine every day. Head, shoulders, back, stomach. That done, he lay back on the bed and lifted his legs up into the air. Whilst I dealt with his legs, feet and in between his toes, with the other end of the towel *he* dabbed his bum and genitals.

After hanging up his towel, I turned around to confront the head prefect with his arms held high. Deodorant time! I reached into his locker, found his *Mum* roll-on deodorant and scribbled on each bushy armpit. Next I held up his shirt for him to slip into. *He* buttoned up his own shirt!

'Shoe!' he demanded.

The left shoe, today. Yesterday it was the right.

'Comb!' he ordered.

In the reflection of the shoe he held up to his face, with his silver-coloured metal comb he attended to his red mango hair.

7.00 am.

On time the bell rang for inspection. Damn! I knew I was going to be late.

Whilst Mango flung back on his bed, endeavouring to slip on his trousers, I tried with shaking hands to capture his wriggling feet to put on his socks. Next shoes. Lastly, his laces.

'Thank you, merry gentlemen!' I sang on leaving the prefects' dormitory before bolting down the passage.

'Tyke! Two black marks for running!' Grizzly shouted from the prefects' dormitory. 'See me after breakfast!'

Disconsolately, I turned around and nodded the cursory acceptance. As I walked the last few steps of the passage, behind me I felt the presence of Duke leaving his bedroom and bearing down on me. Scampering into my dormitory, I opened my locker door and took up my place at the end of my bed, ready for daily inspection.

'A, a, attention!' Goofy sang in time to the opening chords of *Proud Mary*.

Damn! My shoes! I quickly hooked one shoe behind the other leg of my grey flannel trousers and zealously rubbed it to a shine. But suddenly Duke entered the room giving me no time for the other shoe. I gingerly glanced below. One shoe reflected light, the other looked mournfully mottled.

'Good morning, gentlemen!' Duke sang with gusto.

'Good morning, sir,' we mumbled.

Dressed in a dark brown polyester suit with perfect crease lines, not a hair out of place, Duke slowly marched down the corridor between beds, carefully giving the once over, inspecting shoes, correct dress code, beds with hospital corners and tidy lockers.

Great! He first inspected the side opposite me. After he passed my bed, I feverishly devoted my energies to the other shoe. Out of the corner of my eye, I sensed that Duke stopped suddenly and glanced backwards so I froze and gazed at the floor. Never catch the eye. Moments passed before he continued walking, confirmed by the sharp crack of leather soles on wooden floor boards.

On his return the master on duty concentrated on my side of the aisle. I had no chance to assess my latest polishing efforts so I looked forwards with grim determination. As he neared me, he paused. My heart fluttered when he started to talk and my eyes uncontrollably gravitated towards his which glared down at me through black horn-rimmed spectacles.

Despite my hair conforming to regulation short back and sides with a side parting, Duke, fastidious to the hilt, calmly said, 'Make the parting in your hair more defined, young man.'

I nodded but felt my face flush for being singled out. I hated that. Hated it ever since my father made a pair of goggles for me to use when swimming. Chlorine in the water was bad for my eyes and I would go blind, Pa had said. So he fashioned a pair of goggles from glass lenses glued into cut-out jam jar bottle tops, themselves glued onto a mask cut out of rubber tubing from car tyres. The problem was that the brown Pliobond glue had smeared onto the lenses so I could barely see where I was swimming. And since the rubber strap was fixed to the mask with green tennis court wire, to prevent the goggles leaking the wire had to be twisted again and again until I felt like the top of my head was about to pop off, rather like ratchet torture of medieval times. But to add insult to injury, to prevent the goggles from slipping off when diving, I had to ask for special permission during galas to enter the water first and gently push off the edge. I didn't like to be singled out.

As Duke continued down the passage, I quickly gazed down at my shoes. Both reflected a relieved face!

CHAPTER 5

Whilst Duke inspected both the middle and senior dormitories, we stampeded downstairs to the dining room for breakfast. Always awaiting us at our station was a piece of fruit. Either an orange, a banana or an apple — always low grade quality. To outsiders, each piece of fruit probably looked alike. Not to us! All 50 oranges laid neatly on a side plate in that dining room looked decidedly different!

Second to reach my table, I quickly picked up my orange without giving it much of a glance — in my hands it would be safe — all the time my eyes quickly scanning the other fruit. Damn! Hog swapped his for the best at our table. My hand shot out for the second best.

'That's mine!' shouted Eddie, shouldering me off balance.

Snatching an orange at the far end of the table, I quickly compared it with my piece of fruit only to discover mine to be superior, so I replaced the other orange. Damn! Without a gain that day, I glanced over at the fruit arranged on the fourth formers' table. Having never dared to before, I listened carefully for footsteps, estimating the fourth formers to be crossing the landing, and decided to go for it. With my heart beating in time to my quick footsteps, I scurried to the fourth formers' table, assessed for size and quality, made a gainful swap, but on returning to my table noticed that the fourth formers had already entered the dining room. I quickly looked towards the floor as if gazing absentmindedly into another world. It worked! Perhaps because the fourth formers were so intent on rearranging their fruit.

In a weird way, in just moments, 50 pieces of fruit shuffled around a thousand times or more, rearranging into a reverse pecking order where the prefects got the worst and the second formers the best, or so we thought! The window of opportunity was small, a minute or so, but it worked because a tight breakfast schedule before school did not allow the seniors to check up on us. In some small way we got back at the seniors.

The dining room filled with all the boys except for the prefects. They stood just outside the entrance, in the foyer, waiting for Duke. The second formers' table was on the immediate left as one entered the long dining room. All other tables seated seven, growing in seniority further down the dining room.

Duke arrived with his customary loud footsteps and marched like a king into the dining room, followed down the aisle by a procession of prefects. They turned off at their table like jet aircraft in a manoeuvre, whilst Duke stepped up a platform to the masters' table. Perched at his raised table, Duke said grace and we all sat down to breakfast.

All second formers immediately looked to Pygmy. *He* controlled the milk! That ill-tasting slop of day one had become a totally new species. Perhaps because it was rationed, it suddenly tasted good! It was a hot commodity, liquid gold, and even doubled as currency. One milk meant a glass of milk. All other items or actions in the boarding establishment could be reduced to numbers of milks. 'I'll wash your under-rods for three milks!' one boy might offer to another. 'Two milks for your next bread pudding!'

'Pass!' ordered Pygmy.

As usual, our eyes turned to the aluminium jug containing the milk. I sat halfway down the table on the side away from the aisle. As the jug passed my way, I judged immediately from its weight the quantity of milk we would each receive. Just under half a glass today!

Pygmy poured himself a glass of milk. With a gloating face he slowly emptied it down his gullet. Burped! Then another glass. We all watched with longing eyes. Damn! Today he went for a third glass before his porridge. My estimate of just under half a glass now reduced to a third.

In came Babalas with a tray of porridge. Babalas, the black skivvy of all hostel trades, now a waiter, so named because a lurching gait causing him to appear constantly inebriated. Babalas meant hangover in his mother tongue. First he went to the prefects, then to the sixth formers, then to all the fifth form monitors spread throughout the dining room.

Pygmy took his plate of porridge and drowned it with milk before ordering, 'Glasses!'

We passed our tumblers, once transparent plastic, now clouded with use. Pygmy shared the remaining milk with our eyes glued to the operation, carefully assessing which received the most. As the tumblers returned down the table, those closest to Pygmy kept the ones containing just a few drops more, precipitating a daily argument.

'Hey, Mutt, that's *my* glass!' Hog moaned from the far end of the table.

'Aay!' wailed the dog. 'Prove it!'

'I can!' asserted Hog in a triumphant voice. 'I scratched it underneath with a fork. Look underneath the glass.'

'You what?' cried out Pygmy, looking up from his milk drenched porridge. In a slow deliberate voice he questioned, 'You scratched a glass at *my* table?'

'Er, not really,' Hog dribbled from a slouched mouth, his body slowly sinking in his chair.

'Then you fucking lied to me!' Mutt piped up.

'Shut up, you hound!' Pygmy ordered, then turned to Hog. 'I'm gonna check under your glass and, if you've scratched it at my table, I'm gonna fart in it and hold it over your pig snout! Mutt, pass the glass!'

Mutt did, and sensing it to be more trouble than the few drops of milk he might gain, he quickly retrieved his own glass.

Pygmy held up Hog's glass, turned it over and poured half the contents into his own tumbler. Taking his time, he drank the remaining milk before turning the glass upside down to inspect it.

'Fuck it, you *did* scratch it!' Pygmy accused, looking at Hog with mean eyes.

Hog must have wondered how he could tell. After many years of use, every plastic container was scratched so many times it resembled a patchwork of hieroglyphics.

Then Pygmy uttered the dreaded, 'See me, tonight!'

As the remaining glasses passed my way, I assessed the level of milk and made what I thought was a gainful swap, quite sure that after the Hog incident no one would challenge me. A third of a glass of milk! It would have to suffice for our porridge and the balance for drinking. Not that we ever went thirsty. We could drink as much water and coffee as we liked. Such fare was freely available during breakfast, hence we coveted milk!

I poured just enough drops of milk on my porridge to maximise drinking the remainder. My first spoonful netted a glutinous lump lurking deep in the murky porridge. As I lifted the spoon, the lump dragged a thick skin, resembling a swamp monster rising up to haunt me. Time for our tried and tested defence against gastronomic flops. Syrup! Whatever matron couldn't cook properly, we disguised with huge dollops of industrial grade syrup from the bottomless tins she supplied to each table.

'Spazz,' I called across the table, 'After you!'

I deposited four huge spoonfuls of dark syrup onto my porridge, twirling it into ever rising turbans before it spread over the porridge skin. Like a concrete mixer, I mushed the goop into one homogenous mix, masking any existence of hostel porridge.

Next course, omelettes. Again Babalas delivered plates of food down the classes of tables. I inserted my fork into the square yellow rubbery blob imitating egg, it rebounding with interest, giving me a fine understanding in science later that day of *Newton's Law* that for every action there is an equal but opposite reaction. Aah! Another candidate for syrup.

'Mutt, after you,' I said, waiting my turn.

'Aay!' replied Mutt, shaking his head resignedly.

Finally the coffee tray arrived. Matron brewed her coffee in hell, boiling it in a massive pot on a huge stove, which somehow always seemed hotter than water boiled in an electric kettle. Babalas packed his tray of coffee cups tight like survivors of a shipwreck in a lifeboat, braced for a rocky journey. It was heavy and hard work. And hot! As the steam rose from the piping hot coffee, so he sweated from a face hunched over the tray due to curvature of the spine, dripping torrents of droplets from his forehead back into the coffee cups. And with one leg shorter than the other, causing a severe side kick with his longer leg as he walked, Babalas would frequently catch the leg of a chair, slopping sweaty coffee from one mug to another.

'Coffee?' Spazz asked disinterestedly from across the table.

I examined the tray. Needless to say the seniors had taken those mugs furthest away from Babalas. By the time the tray arrived at our table, only those mugs hiding underneath Babalas's hunched sweat beaded head remained.

'Uh, no thanks!' I replied, suddenly losing my appetite for coffee.

CHAPTER 6

With all that syrup for breakfast, I squeezed a huge worm of *Vote* toothpaste from a soft plastic tube onto my toothbrush, turned on the tap, placed the brush under running water and started brushing my teeth.

Thwack! Scrote's heavy shoe sank deep into my bum with such a force it sent shock waves reverberating up my spine and into my head, giving me an instant headache.

'Don't leave the tap running when you are brushing your teeth!' he ordered, shaking his head. With a shrug of his shoulders as he turned to leave, he issued, 'You'd think water just falls out of the sky!'

If Scrote's comment left me somewhat confused, there was no doubting my next intentions. From the bathroom, I marched purposefully upstairs to my dormitory, opened my locker and saw it. My homemade goggles, hidden in a brown paper packet at the back of the bottom shelf. Peeking inside for one last look at the hideous *Heath Robinson* job, I quickly disposed of them in the dormitory's waste paper basket. Shedding that monstrosity felt good!

Not all monsters were so easily discarded. Some boys used satchels to ferry their homework books to and from school, others a suitcase. Mango used a suitcase. Damn, it was heavy! A smaller brother of his travel trunk, but still huge and packed solid with books, which I suspected he seldom used since he hardly did any homework. So, day after day, week after week for the whole of that year, I lugged his timber-laden suitcase just for the sake of it!

Grabbing my own suitcase from my pigeon hole in the prep room, I donned my straw basher, left hostel, walked out the gates, turned right to stride the pathway to school looking like a Chinese water carrier, when I suddenly remembered. Oops! The tree! On navigating the infamous oak tree, I joined a group of second formers also heading off to school.

Despite our school residing on the same block as hostel, some daft idiot at the town-planning division with a macabre sense of humour saw fit to separate the two with the city's cemetery and a funeral parlour called Pushin' Daisies. Maybe it was an omen to all that were sent to Windsor House.

'I think we should ring bark this darn tree!' I suggested aloud.

'No way, man!' replied Mutt. 'Then next year the second formers won't have anything to walk around and we'll have a useless bunch of weeds on our hands.'

Whilst Mutt was yapping, I overheard Eddie asking Spazz if he would bring Grizzly's suitcase to his classroom after school. The two of them fagged for the same bear.

'What class are you in?' Spazz asked.

'The A class!' beamed Eddie. 'The class with all the boffins.'

Whilst Eddie carried on and on, I looked at him with utter disbelief and chuckled quietly.

'Hmmph! What are *you* looking at?' Eddie asked me in his deep voice.

'Nothing!' I replied.

'What's your case, Tyke?' Eddie persisted. 'Or would you even know, since you're in the, er, what's it, er A, B, C, D, E, F, yes, that's it, the F class! That's way down the alphabet, man.'

Yeah! Yeah! I thought, smiling ruefully, knowing full well that during the first term the school streamed the second formers alphabetically according to our surnames. Lacking the courage to speak aloud, I whispered to Spazz in pidgin talk, 'Sinclair, end of alphabet, you go bottom class. Eddie Arsehole, you go top class!'

We both chuckled.

'Wipe those smiles off your faces!' Eddie ordered us.

I suspected Eddie sensed I knew the truth. His eyes glared with fury, his nostrils snorted and he jerked his head with defiant aggression. Not trusting him, eyes not leaving him, I ran a few steps back to the path leading to school and bumped heavily with my two suitcases into Bum Lump.

With a large head squashed down onto a short, thickset body, the head boarder master with no visible neck reminded me of a bulldog. His once close cropped blond hair turned grey framed a face of ruddy complexion sporting cross eyes and a long crooked nose, the type that would give a field day to a caricature artist. Always in a safari suit with short trousers, always with a double vent so that the back flap could hang comfortably over his large backside, only the colour changed. That day it was grey. The long socks, too, were grey, into which he tucked a metal comb, but whatever the colour of the suit and socks the *Grasshopper* shoes were always light brown.

'Sinclair!' bellowed Bum Lump through a pencil-thin moustached mouth, with the same snorting nostrils of Eddie, as if they were a family trait.

'Sorry, sir!' I apologised, quickly suppressing my giggles.

'Behave more like Eddie, here!' the master commanded, pointing to the well-built blond second former, whose face transformed angelically.

Eddie passed Bum Lump and walked briskly up the path to school.

'He walks like he has a carrot up his bum,' I suggested to Spazz in a low voice. 'Like he owns the place!'

'I wouldn't worry,' consoled Spazz. 'Barking dogs seldom bite!'

CHAPTER 7

When the bell rang at 2.30 pm for school to end, I grabbed my suitcase, scampered off to my prefect's classroom to fetch his case of unread tomes and set off on the path back to hostel. There I joined a group of other second formers also lugging their twin packs.

We walked briskly. As we passed the cemetery, I looked sideways at Mutt. He glanced back at me, stole a quick look at Perve on his left, then quickened his pace. Eyes darted backwards and forwards. An air of agitation set in much like wild animals just before a storm.

I thought I heard footsteps behind me, so I turned my head to investigate and noticed Eddie some 20 paces away, closing in fast. Suddenly out of the corner of my eye I spotted Mutt's move, the hound breaking loose from the pack. The chase was on!

Like the massive wildebeest crossing of the Mara river in Mutt's old homeland, we consumed the path that led back to hostel in a cloud of dust, around the tree, inside the gates, up the stairs that divided the air-raid shelter, into the building and straight into the bathroom. Fumbling for my keys, I opened my wire locker, snatched my towel and raced for the showers. Yes! I was first for a change, quickly hanging my towel on the shower second on the left as viewed from the entrance, the one without the shower rose.

On that day, it was *my* towel that hung on the pipe that called itself the best shower. And it would be mine from that moment until later on that afternoon when, of course, it might be a different story! Besides there was good reason to shower quickly, though not so quickly that you might be labelled 'mouldy', so why not shower in the best shower!

Behind me, the rest of the pack booked the other seven showers in quick succession according to pressure. Two second formers stood aimlessly, towels in hand.

§

It was my duty that week to deliver cake and milk to the prefects, so whilst the other second formers headed off for tea, I made my way to the prefects' dormitory.

Knock! Knock! Knock!

'Come in!'

'Good afternoon, merry gentlemen!'

So far, so good.

'Were you born in a fucking pigsty?' Mango asked, irritated.

I did not answer, simply feigned ignorance.

'When you knock on a door, you knock twice!' he explained, then formed a sharp knuckle and knocked twice on my head. 'How would *you* like to be knocked three times?'

'I wouldn't, sir,' I answered, quiet enough for him not to accuse me of shouting, but loud enough not to come across as a wimp. And of course, I thought to myself, I also wouldn't like to be knocked twice, either!

He left me alone.

'Thank you, merry gentlemen!'

§

Each afternoon, matron provided tea and bread on the kitchen verandah. Three huge aluminium jugs of ready-made tea — same sweetness for all — and a Manhattan skyline of piles of old bread.

I lifted a jug and judged by its weight to be empty. Second jug, also empty. Damn! Because I had delivered cake and milk to the prefects, the tea was already down to the dregs.

I tried the last jug. Aah! A dark mud-like liquid trickled into a plastic mug. Suddenly, gadoosh! The giant teabag, a homemade job of tea leaves tied into the foot of one of matron's old stockings, crashed into my cup and splashed what little tea I had onto the floor. Damn!

I took the last three slices of sun-dried bread, smeared them with melted margarine, and tucked into them whilst filling my plastic mug with water from an outside tap.

CHAPTER 8

After dressing in navy blue boxer shorts and a pale green T-shirt, I wondered where everyone was and foolishly poked my nose out the back door of the ablutions. Damn! My heart sank at the realisation that it was Monday — Scrote's gauntlet day!

In the grass clearing immediately behind hostel, fat Scrote sat in a chair like a Zulu king surrounded by his subjects, the second formers. 'Harvest thorns!' he ordered them from the chair. 'The thorn bag is running low.'

Oh, no! As I walked disconsolately towards the chair, I looked at the tall veld grass that stretched from the short grass clearing to the fowl run some 30 paces away and heard the cries of the second formers as they set about their task. The vegetation spawned a devilish thorn with four sharp points. Whichever way the thorn landed on the ground, three needles sank into the soil, anchoring the landmine, the fourth pointing upwards, sadistically inviting, 'Stand on me!' Harvesting thorns meant walking barefoot to the fowl run and back again, collecting each thorn stood upon to top up Scrote's thorn bag.

'Tyke, you're late!' shouted Scrote.

Thwack! From his seat the fourth former again booted me up my tender bum and sent me on my way. I stepped into the undergrowth and treaded gingerly. Hmm! So far, so good … ouch! I bent down and pulled a nasty looking devil thorn out of my bare foot, held it gently in my hand and continued. Ouch! Another prick, another thorn collected.

Ahead of me I heard a chorus of ouches! I soon caught up with Hog, his forlorn looking eyes drooping towards his upturned nose. Alongside him I heard rustling so I parted the long grass and discovered Eddie on all fours rummaging in the undergrowth.

'Tyke, how many devils have you got?' Eddie asked.

I looked to my hand and replied, 'Five!'

Displaying his loot, Eddie's face lit up with a devilish smile and boasted, 'Fifteen! That should be enough. Enjoy the harvest!'

After reaching the fowl run, I retraced my steps. By the time I neared the clearing I looked to my hand and counted twenty thorns so I quickly discarded five of them. Too many caused further pain in the next stage of Scrote's gauntlet, too little and the sadist would force me to repeat the harvest. Fifteen seemed about right. I looked to my hand again and decided to risk only fourteen, throwing away another thorn.

'Tyke, you're late!' complained Scrote as I exited the long grass, his fat foot again striking up a relationship with my bum.

Somewhat surprised, I looked around me and counted all other second formers to be gathered around the chair, including the notoriously slow Hog. Suspecting some chicanery, I wondered how *he* had got back so quickly?

'Right! All thorns in the thorn bag!' ordered Scrote from his seat, opening a leather drawstring bag.

Like an elder in church with a collection plate, Scrote held out his bag to each of us to deposit our harvest of thorns. Protected by sandals, Scrote stood up and meandered the well-worn earthen path that snaked through the long grass, scattering the prickly balls as a peasant sows seeds.

Time for the dreaded gauntlet! A series of time trials running barefoot on the thorny pathway, eliminating the winner of each round.

'Tyke, you know my law. Last out the grass, first in the gauntlet!'

Damn! Not only had I to set the pace, giving the others a target, but being first, I had to run the gauntlet when it was most densely littered with devil thorns.

'On your marks, get set, go!' announced Scrote, clicking the *Omega* stopwatch he hung around his thick neck.

The race was on. I decided to run with long strides. Apart from giving me a faster time, it would minimize the number of times I would have to step on the thorn infested path. Ouch! The first thorn punctured deep into the sole of my left foot. The pain hit immediately, causing me to stop dead in my tracks. I bent over, pulled it out and threw it aside. Ouch! Another long stride, another deep puncture.

My good intentions soon melted away. Losing courage, I changed to a lighter hopping motion. One thorn! Not as deep with the guarded tread, so I gritted my teeth to carry on for a fast time. Two thorns! Three thorns! My feet crying out in pain, I succumbed, bent over and removed the triplet of barbs from my pin cushion soles with trembling hands.

With the intervals between stopping growing shorter and shorter, the chance of setting a good time quickly evaporated. Feeling desperate, my throat tightened but without a choice in the matter, I inhaled a deep breath and summoned the courage to push on, eventually reaching the sanctuary of the clearing.

'Sixty seven seconds!' Scrote read off his stop watch, setting the bench mark for the other second formers.

'Spazz, you're next!'

Whilst the gauntlet tortured Spazz, I sat down and rubbed my aching feet, mentally willing a slow time for my friend. Spazz emerged from the long veld grass, feet splayed in his inimitable duck gait, grimacing face squeezing his eyes to thin slits.

'Seventy nine seconds!'

Great, I was twelve seconds faster. Spazz's face deflated. He knew he would have to go again whereas I still had a chance.

'Hog! Get moving!' bellowed Scrote with glee.

Good, *he* was slow. Hog emerged from his torture session with his mouth drooling, collapsed, then crawled to Scrote's chair.

'Ninety eight seconds!'

Yes! My time still the best.

'Next, er, Eddie!' called Scrote, holding up his stop watch, then giving him the cue. 'On your marks, get set, go!'

Whilst Eddie bolted into the long grass, I sat behind Scrote and counted Eddie's time in my head, willing the seconds to pass by. Sixty three ... sixty four ... don't you dare come out ... sixty five ... Oh, no! The muscular second former emerged, nostrils snorting. But maybe, just maybe, I hoped optimistically, I had counted slowly!

'Sixty four!' Scrote announced, dashing my hopes.

Damn! I might have groaned out aloud, I certainly did inside. Eddie beating my time meant I had to contest at least another round, regardless of the times of the rest of the second formers.

Perve, Mutt, Goofball, Flake, Beanie and Gecko each took their turn before Scrote announced, 'Okay, Eddie, you're out. See you next Monday!'

Eddie jumped to his feet, beaded sweat flicking off his forehead. Pain forgotten, he broke into a broad sadistic grin as he looked back at us before disappearing into the building through the back door of the ablutions.

Scrote spread a few more thorns on the pathway, then called, 'Next round!'

For round two we ran according to our previous times, slowest first, which meant they had to deal with the greater number of thorns. Mutt beat me by a ball hair. Then Flake upset the formbook by winning round three. Damn! I was normally faster than him but I reasoned he was lucky. Being so light I suspected the thorns were no more than just an irritation to him.

Not for the first time and certainly not the last, a lump grew in my throat. I felt desperate. Long strides hurt like heck but hopping just prolonged the agony for another round so I bit my lip and ran with grim determination. Yes! Round four was mine.

I limped away like a wounded dog and sought out a spot on the side of the grass clearing to lick my wounds. I hated Scrote. I hated his gauntlet. Since we were not allowed in the dormitories in the afternoon and just hanging around meant falling prey to Scrote's sadism, I decided that I would have to take up sport, something I could not do in my old school for lack of boys. I opted for cross-country, not only because I liked running, but I had a sneaking suspicion that training was held on Mondays — Scrote's gauntlet day — and even if not, cross country training ought to help me never lose another time trial!

From the side of the grass clearing I glanced back to the gauntlet. Round by round another second former was eliminated. Poor Hog, always last. So, in the final round, fat Scrote sat in a chair and watched fat Hog suffer with tears in his eyes. I couldn't help but feel that Scrote was once in the same boat and that Hog would one day take over as keeper of the thorn bag.

'Hog, put the thorn bag in my locker!' ordered Scrote. 'See you next Monday!'

CHAPTER 9

From the gauntlet, I limped towards the ablutions to sip some water to wash the dust down my strained throat. Just on entering the back door, a voice yelled, 'Tyke!'

Damn! Against my better judgement, I peered around the door and saw Bull, a towering sixth former, perched on a wooden platform built in an avocado pear tree that bordered on the edge of Bum Lump's property.

'Pull the rope!' he ordered.

A long rope dangled from a pulley that ran on a cable strung high over the long veld grass, stretching left from the pear tree to a guava tree near the fowl run, some forty paces away. We called it the Hurdy Gurdy ride. I tugged the rope, sending the pulley up towards the platform but it fell short by an arm's length.

'Pull the fucking rope!' Bull shouted.

I tried again. Short again.

'Come on, you wanker. Jerk it like you pull your wire!'

Sensing Bull's increasing frustration, I mustered every ounce of energy I could and yanked the rope but with no success.

Bull glared down at me and with his nostrils flaring like a prized specimen in the bullring, he bellowed, 'Puuuuullll!'

The earth shook, yet I stood still. With my strength sapping, I knew I couldn't send the pulley up to Bull. By now a queue of boys senior to me snaked up the ladder to the platform, all impatient, all shouting. With my head clouded in confusion, I clung to one ray of hope, that they were halfway up a tree and I was down on the ground out of harm's way.

'Tyke, if you don't send that pulley up here I'll jump down and stretch your foreskin from this tree to that one and use *it* for the ride!'

Oh, no! Not now! Just then a sneeze started to brew, caused by dust puffing up from the dirt pathway that formed in the long veld grass after years of sending the Hurdy Gurdy up to the platform. Remembering Mutt's sneeze on our first day at hostel, I knew, whatever else, not to sneeze now! I tried biting my tongue. Phew! Fortunately, the sneeze subsided. But just as I thought it was safe to address the impending problem of my foreskin stretching to match that of Chief's, the itch of the sneeze returned so I bit my tongue again. Harder, this time. Despite tasting blood, the sneeze loomed close to the point of no return. Desperate, I pinched my nose and then all hell broke loose.

'Are you telling me I stink?' yelled Bull, smoke seeming to pour out of all his orifices. 'Are you telling me that I fucking stink! See me, tonight and *I'll* tell you who stinks!'

My heart sank. The dreaded, 'See me, tonight!'

A movement caught Bull's eye. Mutt poked his snout out of the back door, only to smell trouble, then darted back in. But the bellow of a raging Bull brought him back out again like a dog on heat.

'Help that miserable wimp and send the Hurdy Gurdy up to me!'

Together, Mutt and I ran the pathway through the overgrowth, oblivious of any devil thorns, yanked the rope and sent the pulley racing up towards Bull. It reached.

'Now, you wankers remember to anchor me!' ordered Bull.

The cable was strung taut. A free flight would dispatch the rider smack into the guava tree with dire consequences to the second formers on the ground whose role it was to prevent this. Bull leapt off the platform whilst Mutt and I held on to the end of the rope and ran for our dear lives, racing after the flying Bull. About 20 paces before the guava tree we stopped and anchored ourselves on the ground to act as a parachute for a drag car. But a ton of Bull hurtling straight towards the guava tree jerked us into the air, arms and legs flailing wildly, then threw us back down to earth with a thud and dragged us along the ground in a cloud of dust.

Lying there in a crumpled heap, Mutt and I looked up with great trepidation as the dust settled. Phew! Bull had stopped just in time. My friend and I rose slowly and inspected our bleeding roasties caused by friction with the ground.

'Fuck, that was great! Feels like more!' exclaimed Bull with a wide grin.

§

Much later that afternoon, after Bull had enjoyed his last race, he invited, 'That's me done. You wankers can have a ride!'

Mutt and I looked at each other in utter disbelief, then shrugged our shoulders, scampered off to the avocado pear tree and climbed it. With one yank of his hand Bull sent the pulley flying up to the platform. Mutt grabbed it.

'Both of you together!'

We both grabbed onto the handles of the pulley.

'Jump!'

We did, acting on command. The ride was great, some reward for an afternoon of hard work. But suddenly we jerked in mid-air, catapulting wildly like two trapeze artists before coming to a stop two stories high off the ground.

Below us, Bull held the rope and guffawed. He walked back towards the avocado pear tree, slowly pulling us along, wound the end of the rope around the trunk of the tree and tied a knot, leaving us stranded some ten paces along the cable with our dangling feet treading air high over a patch of devil thorns.

'Tyke! See me, tonight!' Bull snarled before disappearing.

A few moments later, a host of curious boys appeared out the back door. Needless to say they laughed at our predicament.

'Untie us!' I pleaded.

Nobody moved. A few moments later all but Chief and Vulture remained.

'Come on, you blokes. Chief? Hey, Vulture? Let us down!' Mutt appealed to the third formers.

Vulture squawked, shook his head violently, then flapped his arms and disappeared. Chief jutted out his jaw and closed his eyes to thin slits. He looked to the right, then to the left, surveying the scene. Suddenly he looked up to us, turned around and vanished, knowing the price to pay for helping us would be the dreaded, 'See me, tonight!'

'Aay!' Mutt wailed, shaking his head. 'Tyke, what the fuck are we gonna do now?'

CHAPTER 10

At 5.00 pm the bell rang for evening shower time. As I barged through the swing door to the ablutions, I noticed my towel hanging over the front wall that enclosed the showers. Damn! The price to pay for aiming for the best. Oh, well, at least it was *my* towel that hung over the best shower that afternoon. Besides, *I* won the race to book the best shower and winning was food for survival.

Behind me, Eddie burst through the door. With him bearing down on me, I quickly disrobed, hung my gown up in my wire locker and beat Eddie to the showers.

First in queue, I stood against the far wall and observed the shower status. Four third formers stood in the best ranked showers, Chief in the shower that I had booked, the remaining four occupied by second formers. Hog, Mutt, Flake and Gecko all hurried and with good reason, though not too fast to get tagged mouldy. Who would finish first? I wondered. Not Mutt! He lapped up the sensation of warm water running down his skin. Probably Hog, I surmised, first shower on the left.

Perve entered and wedged himself between Eddie and me at the back of the shower enclosure, third in line. Out of the corner of my eye, I spotted Hog give a subtle nod as he vacated his shower and Eddie quickly moved in.

'Hey, that's *my* shower!' I demanded.

Eddie tilted his head towards the shower rose, water flowing over his head, then lowered his face, opened his eyes and said defiantly, 'So what you gonna do about it?'

For a moment I was speechless. Then tugging at his bulging shoulder muscle, I argued, 'Come on, Eddie! You know it's my shower!'

Eddie ignored me and started to soap himself. With a deep sigh and my shoulders slumped, I retreated to the back wall and waited. I felt cheated. Eddie had broken the unwritten protocol amongst peers of first come, first served. And being twice my size there was little I could do about it.

Suddenly, the flash of the brown gown. Spider! One sensed the collective groan of the second formers. It became an art to shower long enough not to be tagged mouldy, but as quickly as possible to avoid the impending doom portended by the flash of the brown gown. Hog tried desperately hard, even had a little soap on his body as he reached for his towel to dry himself.

Suddenly Spider appeared in the doorway. With the same stern look in his eye of a father catching his kid with his hand in the cookie jar, Spider tilted his head towards Hog and spoke down to him as if he were his child, 'And where are you off to in such a hurry? Not mouldy, are we?'

Hog did not answer. Simply shook his head, a look of sheepishness morphing into abject disappointment across his porky face. Without another word spoken, he slung his towel back over the shower wall and forlornly joined Perve and me in the queue.

Spider waltzed in and kicked Chief out the best shower, who in turn kicked Eddie out his illegally occupied shower. Goofball, Spazz and Beanie walked in and behind them two third formers, who kicked Gecko and Flake out their showers. Of the second formers, only Mutt occupied a shower.

'Hog!' came the dreaded voice of Spider, causing the flesh on the second former's face to slouch. 'Showering quickly to get out of working? Thirty press-ups!'

Any fourth, fifth or sixth former had the right to 'work' a second former, to make him do press-ups, sit-ups or bunny hops. This commonly occurred during shower time as initiation, though sometimes in the dormitory as punishment. Most seniors never invoked this right. Some worked second formers out of pure sadism. Not Spider. He appeared to derive no pleasure from it. To him, working was simply a yearlong discipline all second formers had to endure to blend our differences into one homogenous mix. Someone had to do it, so Spider took it upon himself to be the task master. Because of his detached approach, we accepted it as our lot to be worked. Hated it, but accepted it.

'Hmm! Who else?' pondered Spider with a jerk of his head. 'Eddie, hogging a shower out of turn. Thirty sit-ups!'

I felt a degree of retribution had been exacted and it must have shown because Eddie looked at me with angry eyes, then sat down and performed his repetitions with gusto.

'Eddie, thirty press-ups!' Spider ordered.

The second former looked peeved that his star sit-up performance should be punished with press-ups. But Eddie never learned, setting about his press-ups with vigour.

'Gecko and Flake, you're clean enough. Bunny hops!'

Great! That meant I jumped to the head of the queue and when Chief left I slipped quietly into his shower, third on the left, tilted my head in the spray and let the lukewarm water cascade down my body. Once wet, I soaped myself. Always the same procedure. Everyone did the same. First lather the genitals. Of course, for Eddie and all non-second formers that meant lathering their pubic hair. The rest of the second formers were still baldies! That done, I rubbed a two by four block of carbolic in my hair until my head frothed pink. Next would be arms, body, legs, bum and lastly face, before rinsing off.

At the leg stage I leant forwards to soap them when I confronted the unmistakable bloated ballbag hiding below a protruding gut. Scrote! Damn! The unwanted tug on my shoulder was imminent.

Body completely pink with soap, I vacated the shower and returned to the back wall where I intentionally looked down. Away from Spider's eyes, away from Scrote's. Instead, I saw in effect a penis parade and discovered that, after just five weeks, I could recognize everyone by their equipment.

A few minutes later Spider found me out and ordered, 'Tyke! You're a quiet one. Go and turn the water temperature up!'

One boiler supplied hot water to all the showers, both downstairs and upstairs. Just as our afternoon tea was the same sweetness for all, so was the temperature of the water since there was only one control dial for all the showers and that was upstairs. This triggered a daily argument between those who liked their shower warm and others who preferred hot. Spider liked his shower piping hot, boiling his pale skin every day to look like a cooked lobster.

'Spazz and Mutt, thirty sit-ups! Hog, bunny hops!' Spider ordered.

Relieved to escape working, I scampered to the upstairs ablutions with just a towel around my waist and turned the temperature dial clockwise, precipitating screams from below, coupled with a loud banging on the exposed water pipe to indicate that the temperature was too hot. So I turned it counter-clockwise. Still more banging. Now the dilemma. Was it still too hot or now too cold. I always surmised that if it were too hot the banging would be accompanied by screams, so I turned it just a fraction hotter. Still banging. A little more clockwise. Two distinct bangs. Got it!

Reluctantly, I headed back downstairs and into the lion's den, trying to blend in amongst the naked bodies, hoping that Spider would not notice me. But even with a jet of hot water pummelling his head and his eyes seemingly closed, somehow he knew. Jerking his head towards the ground, Spider said dispassionately, 'Tyke! Thirty press-ups.'

Twenty two. Twenty three. My arms started to shake, causing the dried crust of soap on my body to crack with the sensation of creepy-crawlies swarming all over my skin. And each time I lifted off the ground, I confronted Hog's voluminous bum wobbling in my face as he bunny hopped, giving me the fortitude to go down again to escape. Twenty nine. Thirty. Inching my way to the back wall on all fours, I groped for the exposed water pipe that fed the showers and pulled myself up.

'Tyke, sit-ups!'

I got down again, sat my bum on the bare concrete floor that swilled with soapy scummy water and set about my sit-ups. One, two, three ... I didn't mind sit-ups that much, they came easily for me. Except that each time I reached forwards, my bum cheeks opened up with a squelching sound somewhere down there and like a drain plunger would suck up mucky water in mini-enemas, squirting it out again as I sat up. No wonder we all suffered terribly from Dhobi's itch! Spider didn't say how many sit-ups. I hated that. I felt a lack of target. After thirty or so, I slowed down and then petered out.

'Who said you could stop?' It wasn't Spider, but the vindictive Scrote. 'Push soap!'

Damn! I hated pushing soap. Despondently, I hunched over on my hands and knees, positioned my nose on a block of red carbolic soap to look like Pinocchio and pushed it from one end of the shower room to the other. Again and again!

Suddenly a jet of water blasted at the wet soapy floor and rebounded up into my face. Instinctively, I jerked upwards to rub my eyes!

'Push soap!' shouted Scrote, gleefully holding a plastic milk bottle aimed in my direction.

Sensitive at the best of times, my eyes burned. Tears mixed with carbolic soap streamed down my face, blurring my vision. Losing all sense of direction, I panicked and started to get up.

Thwack! For the fourth time that day, Scrote's heavy foot booted my bum, sending me crashing forwards, sliding on the slippery floor like a ten pin bowling ball, my head striking the far wall with a jarring of my brain.

'Tyke, 30 press-ups!' ordered Spider. In a strange way, that saved me.

With shower time nearing the end, everyone started to leave so I finally managed to get into a shower, ironically the best shower, the one I had booked earlier that afternoon. No sooner had the dried crust of pink soap on my body melted into a liquid lather when I heard a banging noise on the water pipe upstairs to indicate that junior shower time was up. With any shower operating downstairs, the pressure upstairs reduced to a trickle, and since pressure was all important, it was time to stop. Bang. Bang. Bang. Definitely time to stop! There was one snag, though, I was full of soap but *they* controlled the water temperature upstairs. If banging on the water pipe failed to get the desired results, scalding water would.

Continuing to shower in a race against time, the water suddenly turned boiling hot. Yelp! It scorched so I quickly switched off my shower and waited a few moments. With the pressure restored upstairs and the temperature back to normal, I turned my shower on and rinsed a little. Bang. Bang. Bang. Boiling water! Knowing that this irritated the seniors upstairs, but surmising that they were soapy and wet and in the nude, therefore not likely to come downstairs to deal with me, I finished showering in dribs and drabs.

Suddenly the swing door to the junior ablutions burst open. Uh-oh! Bull stood in the doorway to the shower enclosure. With a piercing glare beneath his single hairy eyebrow, nostrils snorting, he mouthed slowly and methodically, 'See me, tonight!'

CHAPTER 11

'Good evening, merry gentlemen!' I greeted on entering the prefects' dormitory.

'Tyke, you're late!' complained Mango, standing next to his locker in just his underpants. Slowly shaking his head, he said scornfully, 'What a pity you weren't this late when you were still a fucking sperm!'

Not understanding his comment, I walked slowly towards him, careful not to catch his eye.

'Hit me!' he suddenly ordered, standing with his arms to the side. 'Come on, hit me!'

I just stood there, faking ignorance.

'Take your best shot and hit me right there,' he directed, pointing to his solar plexus. 'Hit me as hard as you like and I won't budge!'

Again, the damned if you do, damned if you don't dilemma. If I struck him softly, he would mock me, beat the shit out of me and make me do it again. Hit him hard and he'd really beat the shit out of me. But maybe, just maybe buy some time and hope for a distraction!

'Come on, you poop, punch me!'

Just then, Eddie, fagging for Grizzly, snorted, gleefully enjoying my predicament.

'Eddie!' bellowed my prefect. '*You* hit me!'

Like a bull to a matador's red flag, Eddie couldn't resist. With his well-built body, he charged forwards and pummelled a powerhouse into Mango's gut, instantly doubling him over.

'Hiirrrhhh! Hiirrrhhh! Hiirrrhhh!' gasped the head prefect, adding a new dimension to the bouncy introduction of the song *Eloise* that simultaneously played on the radio.

Chuffed with his accomplishment, Eddie gave me a look of 'after action satisfaction', as if to tell me how I should have done it.

'You fucking cunt!' Mango swore in gasps, his breath slowly returning to a raspy voice. 'You're gonna die for that!'

'But—'

Mango punched Eddie in the eye, the second former's head snapping backwards, his smile of satisfaction vanishing into shock. Another punch to the gut caused him to hunch over, presenting his nose to meet the upward jerk of Mango's knee with a deep thud. Blood spurted everywhere.

'Go and get his laundry bag!' the head prefect ordered me, panting heavily. 'I'm gonna teach this spare arsehole a lesson!'

As I left the dormitory, I heard Eddie protest, 'But, sir, you *told* me to punch you!'

After emptying Eddie's dirty laundry onto his bed, I returned to the prefects' dormitory with his cream linen bag and presented it to Mango.

'Get inside!'

My body froze. Adrenaline spiked. Me or Eddie? I needed to be very careful because Mango was in a foul mood.

Fortunately, he cuffed Eddie on the back of the head and shouted, 'Get inside your stinking laundry bag!'

Still perplexed, Eddie wiped his bloodied nose on his arm and slowly stepped into the bag.

'Right inside!'

Whilst Mango grabbed a handful of the second former's oily hair and shoved him down into his laundry bag, Eddie's eyes threw daggers at me. A look that soon turned to fear as he curled up like a foetus when the head prefect tightened the draw string, kicked the bag, yanked it up onto his bed, tied the balance of the draw string to the mullion of the wooden window frame, then slung the bag out the window and left Eddie to dangle in the evening breeze.

Without a flicker of emotion, Mango took off his underpants, lay face down and naked on his bed, turned his head to me and ordered, 'Massage!'

Quite used to this daily routine, I reached into his locker for a tube of Deep Heat, opened it, squeezed liberal amounts onto his hairy legs and massaged them. Whilst the white cream mixed in with red knotting hair, I rubbed and kneaded, karate chopped, then patted until the cream finally disappeared like some Houdini act, only to reappear when I rubbed again, much like the difficulty we had in getting rid of the evidence when wiping our bums with the low grade toilet paper matron supplied us! Calves, thighs, then bum cheeks, taking one at a time, always careful not to get too close to the hairy crack, since Deep Heat and anus and prefect and fag made for one volatile combination! After ten minutes of this daily practice, Mango put on his gown and went to shower.

No sooner had he left when Eddie called from outside, 'Hey, Tyke!'

'Huh!'

'Let me out, man!'

Climbing onto Mango's bed, I looked out the window from which Eddie hung. Feeling a little sheepish talking to a laundry bag, I replied in a loud whisper, 'I can't!'

'Come on!' Eddie implored.

'I can't!' I reiterated, knowing I didn't have the strength to lift Eddie out of his plight. 'I'm already in trouble with Bull.'

'Aw, Tyke, you chicken! When I get out of here you'll be in more trouble with me than with Bull!'

Ignoring Eddie, I laid out Mango's evening clothes for him. White short-sleeve shirt, beige casual short trousers, fresh underpants, long grey socks and imitation brown *Hush Puppies*. Next to the clothes on his bed, I arranged his metal comb and his *Mum* roll-on deodorant. Aah! His school shoes, I remembered. Polish them now and avoid the bottleneck in the morning.

When Mango returned, he dug his hand into his gown pocket, withdrew a handkerchief, threw it to me and ordered, 'Wash it!'

Great! All my life I longed for the life experience of washing Mango's handkerchief, I thought sarcastically. The crusty crumpled ball went straight into my pocket.

Mango's arms went up. Again, a scribble with his *Mum*. Whilst the head prefect sat on his bed, I towelled him down. Arms. Back. Chest. Stomach. He then lay back on his bed and lifted his legs in the air. As I dried one leg, without warning, Mango ripped a fart.

'Air the dormitory!' he instructed.

'Huh!' I responded, utterly bewildered.

'Don't you fucking huh me!' he shouted, cuffing me on the head as he rose from the bed. 'When I tell you to air the dormitory, you breathe in my fart and go and blow it out the window!'

I didn't say it, but my face must have looked like, 'Huh!'

'Here comes another!' Mango trumpeted. Cocking up one leg like a dog against a tree, he ordered, 'Bend over!'

I did. Mango grabbed my head and thrust it down towards his hairy crack. This sudden movement caused me to inhale just as he exploded, scorching my throat with the stench of burnt rubber. Phoof!

'Now blow it out the window!'

I quickly climbed up on his bed and stuck my head out the window to exhale. Just below me hung the laundry bag containing Eddie, the drawstring forming a pucker hole. Hmm! I suddenly remembered Eddie hogging my shower and calling me chicken. Pursing my lips, I blew a kiss of death into the hole, causing the cocoon to wriggle with great disagreement.

Back to Mango. He sat still as I slipped his shirt on, then underpants, the head prefect flinging his legs up in the air as I wriggled them over his bum. Touching the genitals of others was strictly taboo, so *he* tucked away his dick, to the left. Some were lefties, some righties, some straight down. Mango was a lefty. Of course, for us second formers with our worms, it was a case of any which way it landed! Then his socks. As usual they were trying. With his hairy legs so difficult to dry, unravelling long socks over them always proved a mission.

CHAPTER 12

When we first arrived at hostel food was a means to an end. Eat to live! Around the time our balls dropped, things changed. There arose this obsession to consume as much food in the shortest possible time. Definitely a case of live to eat!

Grace done, we sat down at table in our designated seats and waited for Babalas to deliver our food on his well-worn metal tray, eight plates at a time. First the prefects' table, then the sixth formers, then the fifth form monitors scattered throughout the dining room, right down to the second formers' table. As Babalas entered through the swing door from the kitchen, all eyes strained to see what matron had concocted for us. This allowed for bartering.

'Aay! Looks like chow is some kind of bird, today,' Mutt announced. He could always tell first. We put it down to a keen sense of canine smell. 'And squash, beans and potato.'

'I'll swap my gem squash for your beans,' Perve bartered with Gecko.

'My drumstick for your breast,' Spazz offered me from across the table, in the event that he received a drumstick.

'Uh-uh! You leave my breast alone!' I replied.

Nearing the end of the barter phase, the waiter approached Pygmy, who selected the plate furthest from him, the one he estimated to have the most food. Sitting at the head of the table, Pygmy started eating, ten pairs of eyes staring longingly at each forkful of food he mouthed. Agitation set in. Spazz tapped his feet whilst I played a drum roll on the table with my fingers. Thwack! Pygmy reached over and gave my fingers a sharp tap with the back of his knife. So I joined Spazz in tapping my feet. The restlessness grew. Finally, the last of the third formers got their food.

Suddenly all eyes shifted away from Pygmy and focused on the kitchen doorway. As Babalas entered the dining room some twenty paces away, every second former strained their eyes, quickly ranked each plate according to quantity of food and made their choice.

'Second right!' claimed Eddie through a bloodied nose.

'First left!' declared Spazz.

'I bag middle front!' I shouted.

With only eight plates on the tray, two second formers would have to wait, no matter what their claim. It all, of course, depended on which end of the table the waiter served first. Sitting in the middle on the side away from the aisle, I was guaranteed of getting a plate. Each end of the table waved furiously for Babalas to approach them first. He went to Pygmy's end, so Hog and Eddie who sat at the other end would have to wait.

Perve passed the plates but kept the middle front for himself. Damn! We all shouted at once, demanding our plate of food. With Eddie losing out on his claim to the plate second on the right, I reached over to grab it as it entered the foray, shouting, 'That's mine!'

'No way, Tyke!' complained Eddie. 'You can't steal my plate!'

'Uh-uh!' I voiced, dying to imitate Eddie and say, 'So what you gonna do about it!' Instead I argued my point with logic. 'You know you lose out if Babalas goes to Perve's end.'

'Aw, you smart arse. You'll regret this!'

My heart beat a little louder at Eddie's threat, but was quickly forgotten about when Gecko clung on to my plate and began to complain, 'You're both wrong! It's my plate. I bagged second left.'

'Well, this plate was second right!' I explained strongly. 'Second right as you face Babalas, not the other way around!'

With that I yanked the plate free of his clutches and quickly took a mouthful before scanning the rest of the plates to see how well I had done. Not too bad, I thought!

Like a pack of hyenas scavenging off a kill, we wolfed the food down our gullets as if it were our last meal. Little enjoyment of taste, for there was only one purpose in mind, to get one's plate first in line for seconds! In quick time I gobbled my bird and veggies, lifting my head only once towards the end of my meal to assess the status of the other tables, because seconds for food broke the pecking order. A case of first come, first served for seconds.

Still chewing the penultimate mouthful, I hurriedly gathered up the last scraps of food on my fork and held it airborne as I sent my plate up the table towards Perve to join the queue for seconds.

'Middle front!' we all shouted to Perve when Babalas arrived, and with good reason. But no such luck! Perve put his plate there. Mine landed front right.

We waited, more drum rolls, more foot tapping. When the tray returned, only the front middle plate got extra food, a dollop of mashed potato. Perve kept it for himself and shuttled the rest of the plates down the table, each with two slices of bread drowning in gravy.

'That's mine!' I demanded, again snatching a plate from Gecko.

Lastly, Perve prised the two plates at the back of the tray from underneath Babalas's thumbs, his overgrown thumbnails swimming in the gravy as he pressed down on the edges of the plates to be able to carry an extra two. Never get the back plates on the edge of the tray! They went to Spazz and Eddie.

No sooner had the plate landed in front of me, when I sank my knife and fork into the bread smothered in gravy. A quick, but large mouthful. Then another. Whilst I swallowed these, I quickly cut the balance into the shapes I thought would maximise the space in my mouth, therefore minimizing the time I spent eating. Next forkful. I placed the sopping bread into my mouth, crust end last. A quick suck and the gravy-softened middle disappeared. Chew the crust. One. Two. Swallow. Next piece.

Whilst eating my bread and gravy in the most efficient way possible, I noticed Flake next to me scrape his gravy to one side and carefully deposit the slice of bread into a brown paper packet before sending his plate up to Perve for thirds. Hey, that's cheating, I thought, though I reasoned he needed it more than most, but quickly forgot about it to focus my energies on the task at hand.

Chewing one mouthful, fork suspended in the air with another, I sent my plate to join the queue and demanded, 'Front!'

It landed back left. Babalas returned with only seven plates. Poor Spazz lost out. Judging that matron's supply of food had come to an end, I tried to eat my last piece of bread and gravy at leisure, savouring every morsel. Well, every bit except the spot contaminated by Babalas's thumb nail. But my intentions fell short. Somehow the rush still flowed through my veins. Only Mutt slowed down, smacking his lips as he relished each mouthful.

As Eddie rose to leave the supper table, he glanced towards me and spoke in a nasal tone caused by a stuffy swollen nose. 'You're a different kind. A brownnoser who likes to stay out of trouble. But mark my words, I'm gonna get you!'

I carried on sitting at the table, feeling queasy. Not because I'd eaten too much, nor because of Eddie's threats, but because I had to pay Bull a visit, the dreaded, 'See me, tonight!'

CHAPTER 13

At hostel we had two kinds of 'working'. The Spider type where all second formers participated in initiation workouts during shower time and the punishment type, the dreaded, 'See me, tonight!'

I knocked softly on the door of the senior dormitory, which housed all the sixth formers and about half of the fifth formers.

'Come in!'

'Good evening, merry gentlemen,' I greeted before walking over to Bull's bed.

'You miserable little shit! How dare you tell me that I stink!' the burly sixth former accused, then instructed, 'Forty press-ups!'

Thwack! His cuff on my head knocked me over and onto the wooden floor, straight into the starting position for doing press-ups. Twenty five. Twenty six. Twenty seven. My work rate slowed and my arms started to shake. Twenty eight. Twenty ... I struggled for the next, but couldn't lift off, my body still aching from the workout in the showers. I tried again but failed, always hoping for sympathy.

'Get up!'

I did, very shakily.

'Hang!' Bull commanded, pointing to his locker.

I had not hung from a locker before, but rumour had it that this simple looking act was plagiarized straight out of the torture manual. I clung onto the top of the square locker with my hands, fingers on top, palms in front, pulled my legs up off the ground and simply hung there. At first it seemed easy. I could cope with this. Perhaps my light body could handle this better than those who had spread the rumours.

After a few minutes my arms weakened a little. But, so far, so good! Then little beads of sweat spotted my hands. Suddenly my arms started to shake. A little at first, then violently. The air surrounding me heated like a sauna, even my breath against the locker was hot. With my hands sweating profusely, my grip weakened and at the same time my legs grew heavy and started to drop, desperate to touch the floor to relieve my arms.

Thwack! The instant my legs reached solid ground, Bull cuffed me on the head, banging it against the timber locker door, pain spiking into my brain.

Face grimacing, teeth clenched, I quickly clung onto the locker again and pulled my legs up. The brief respite lasted only a moment. The shakes returned, uncontrollable shakes. A black cloud seemed to envelop me and a lump choked my throat. I felt lonely. Sharing a workout with others during shower time seemed to lighten the load. Now all centred on me and I felt terribly lost in a dark hole.

Unintentionally, my feet touched the floor. Thwack! Again my head crashed against the locker, swirling my brain in my skull like milk in a jug at breakfast time. So I mounted my wooden horse again, but with my hands perspiring heavily, I immediately slipped off. Thwack! A quick wipe of my hands on my shorts. Thwack!

Desperate, I decided to clutch onto the locker from the sides. For a moment it seemed easier, but the pain, the shakes, it all returned and rose to a climax. Despite hugging the timber box for dear life, I reached breaking point and collapsed to the floor in a crumpled heap. Tears welled up in my eyes. I slowly rose to my feet but wobbled. With my legs unsteady, Bull pushed me on the chest, sending me crashing to the floor. Body broken, my mind gave in and I cried.

But there was no sympathy. Instead Bull bellowed waves of hot air. 'You fucking cunt. Pinching your nose at me, telling me I stink, eh! Who's the little shit that stinks now?'

I opened my mouth to apologise, but no sound came out.

'Forty press-ups! Count aloud!'

The prep bell rang out with its distinctive loud clanging sound, the sweetest music to my ears. Relieved, I stood up.

'Where do you think you're going? Press-ups!'

I got down again. Twelve. Thirteen.

Just then Mango walked in and ordered, 'Tyke, go to prep.'

Phew! I never thought I would ever be so pleased to see my head prefect.

As I got up to go, Bull pointed his finger at me and snarled, 'Don't you ever dare pinch your nose whilst I'm speaking to you! This was just foreplay to the good fucking up you'll get next time. Now fuck off!'

§

Every weekday, starting at 7.00 pm, we did two hours of homework or prep as we called it. Juniors in the dining room, seniors in the prep room, a replica of the dining room across the foyer.

Heartbroken, I wobbled downstairs. On entering the dining room, I felt 30 pairs of eyes turn to stare at me. Of course, we all lifted our eyes to anyone or anything that entered during prep, just to break the tedium. Head down, eyes to the ground, I walked over to my designated prep table in the centre of the dining room. We sat three at a table, usually in mixed forms.

'Cry baby!' Scrote whispered from the opposite side of the table, a gleeful look on his face.

Having said that, he placed his elephant feet on my lap. Every day of every week, I sat in prep as a footstool to Scrote's heavy legs. There was nothing I could do about it, he was senior to me.

Feeling numb and unable to read, I stared vacantly at my book. Damn! I hated that place!

CHAPTER 14

After prep, whilst getting dressed in my sleeping shorts and gown to get ready for prayers before bedtime, I noticed a bulge in my pocket. Damn! Mango's handkerchief!

With time running out like water draining from a basin, I hurried to the downstairs bathroom, filled a basin, threw the crusty handkerchief into the water and watched it melt into a soft cloth. After a minute of soaking, I lathered the cotton handkerchief with red carbolic soap, rinsed it, held it up to the light and sighed with dismay on finding it still stained yellow and green.

'Aay!' wailed Mutt, shaking his head whilst brushing his freckled teeth. 'Mango got you plucking oysters from his snot-rag again!'

I rubbed furiously and again held it up to the light. Still soiled. Come on, damn you! Pursing my fingers around one blob to trap it, I pulled the tenacious slimy globule loose. Aah! Got you! More rubbing, more plucking and a final rinse before placing the handkerchief in my wire locker to dry.

§

'Good night,' mumbled Bum Lump, on completing lights out.

'Good night, sir!' we sang loudly.

After Goofy switched the lights off, I hung up my gown and climbed onto my bed to slip under the covers, but half way in my legs hit a dead end.

'Damn!' I cursed softly.

Someone had apple-pied my bed, doubling the top sheet back on itself. I heard faint giggles coming from opposite me, but I was so tired I ignored them. So tired, instead of remaking the bed, I just curled up my legs against my aching body and fell asleep like a baby.

Screech! Bang! Huh! I woke abruptly. Feeling terribly disorientated, I gingerly put my hand out to feel my way in the pitch darkness, only to discover I was trapped in a cage. Claustrophobia set in, but each attempt to escape met with a dizzy spell, causing me to fall over. I started to panic when suddenly I found myself swinging through the night air as if on a rollercoaster, landing with a crash to discover I was still in bed, in my dormitory at hostel.

'Tyke! You didn't lock the back door!' Grizzly said nonchalantly. 'Two black marks!'

As I got out of bed to go and lock the back door, I watched agog at Grizzly lifting the foot end of Spazz's bed, then pushing it vertically, right up against the back wall, causing the poor second former to experience just what I had only moments ago.

On walking out the dormitory, I quietly cursed Mango. Cursed his red bulbous nose! Washing his handkerchief caused me to forget about my evening duty that week, to lock the back door before lights out. Downstairs, I simply pushed the barrel bolt into place, went upstairs to bed and fell asleep as soon as my head hit the pillow. A deep sleep.

§

Click! The dormitory lights glared down into many sets of bleary and bewildered eyes.

'Who's talking?' demanded Grizzly.

After lights out, talking was forbidden.

'Come on, own up, you fuckers! Who was talking?' shouted the prefect, as he walked down the aisle. Silence prompted his next move. 'Okay, you yellow bastards, go and line up outside the office, the whole bang lot of you!'

Damn! I hated getting punished when a prefect or master could not flush out the guilty. Moreover, Bum Lump was on duty. He always caned hard, the extra oomph in his heavy wrist betraying a touch of vindictiveness. One by one we went into the office and received our punishment, including the third formers who shared our dormitory. Ahead of me, Spazz wore a raincoat instead of a gown.

'What's the meaning of this?' demanded Bum Lump, flicking at Spazz's raincoat with his malacca cane.

'I've lost my gown, sir!' explained Spazz. 'I'm using this raincoat until I get a new one!'

'Hmmph!' grunted Bum Lump. 'Take it off!'

Spazz complied, revealing thin cotton sleeping shorts. Peeved by Spazz's explanation, Bum Lump caned with extra venom. My friend emerged from the office, eyes screwed shut, hands furiously rubbing his bum.

Making sure I did not catch Bum Lump's eyes, I walked in and bent over to offer my backside as a target, praying that his anger with Spazz had subsided. Thwack! Thwack! It hadn't! There always seemed to be a delayed reaction between cane meeting flesh and the emergence of pain. About half way to the door the pain suddenly hit me, with a strong urge for me to rub my bum. Don't do it, I exhorted myself. Not until I'm out of the office. Don't give Bum Lump the satisfaction.

'Thank you, sir!' I called through clenched teeth, as was the expected protocol when leaving the masters' office, even after having received punishment.

'Sinclair!' called Bum Lump.

Damn! Desperate to give my rear end attention, but equally determined to hide my pain, I turned my head around to face the head boarder master with a passive face.

'Tell the raincoat man I want to see him!'

'Huh!' I responded. Wrong response!

'Don't you huh me!' Bum Lump erupted, his face giving way to anger. 'Come back here at once and bend over!'

I did. Thwack! Thwack! After standing up, I turned to face Bum Lump and waited for him to repeat his request. But we both just stood and stared at each other, except in my case my hands fidgeted, desperate to rub my burning bum.

Long moments passed before Bum Lump spelled out his request in a deliberate voice, 'I said, tell the raincoat man I want to see him! He needs another two for losing his gown.'

'Yes, sir!' I replied, finally realizing that he meant Spazz.

As I reached my bed, Spazz peeled his thin cotton shorts away from his bum to reveal two red hot welts and ranted, 'I hate that Bum Lump! Just because I was wearing a raincoat he blows his top!'

'Talking of raincoats,' I interrupted with a heavy heart, 'Bum Lump wants to see the raincoat man! Something about getting another two for losing your gown.'

Spazz opened his eyes fully for the first time since he was caned, betraying a look of horror. When he returned from the office, having received another two stripes across his backside, my friend came over to my bed and let it all out.

'I've had it with this place!'

'Sshh!' I said softly.

But with a new sense of bravado, Spazz said even more firmly, 'I'm sorry, but I've just about had as much as I can take of this place!'

Other second formers heard him and listened with interest to someone mouthing their own thoughts. Some gathered around.

'Bum Lump canes me for nothing!' Spazz complained. With his voice rising, the son of a reverend crossed a threshold. 'And the others, Spider, Scrote, the bloody prefects, they think they're … they're … they're … God!'

In my mind I agreed with my friend, adding Bull to the list.

'What're you gonna do?' asked Hog.

'I dunno!' replied Spazz. 'But I've had a shitload full!'

Flake broke a long moment of silence when he asked what everyone must have been thinking, 'Have you ever thought of running away?'

'Every living moment I'm awake!' replied Spazz. Echoing our adopted theme song by the group called the Animals, he continued, 'I've just gotta get out of this place, if it's the last thing I ever do!'

With that Spazz got into bed and the others dissipated.

Click! The lights glared down again.

'Who's talking now?' demanded Grizzly, scratching his frizzy hair.

Eddie immediately pointed in our direction. 'It's those guys over there.'

Spazz, Mutt, Flake, Goofball and I put up our hands and had already started trudging off to the office before Grizzly commanded, 'Line up outside the office! You too, Eddie! My fag shouldn't be such a blabbermouth!'

As I passed Hog's bed I noticed his head buried in his pillow pretending to be asleep. Spazz glanced back at me, his face conveying the same pent up feelings of rage in me.

After another of Bum Lump's hit parades we returned to bed. Lying on my back, my body aching as it lay on the thin, lumpy coir mattress, I cradled my head in my hands, dog tired, but unable to sleep. I thought about hostel life. About running away.

Where would I run to? Back home, perhaps. But what would I be going home to? I thought of my parents. Conservative. Old Fashioned. Strict on morals. Neither of them communicated very much. Fifteen years older than my mother, scruffy Pa dominated in his tactless manner and prim and proper Ma just bottled up.

I can only imagine that she must have threatened to leave to get her way and have me go to boarding school. Perhaps Ma was right. If I stayed at home I would turn out to be just like my father. Live all my life in the same country town and work in a trading store from eight until five. Never change jobs just in case there were to be another depression. Perhaps boarding school did offer me more hope, though I was convinced it would not assist in me becoming the great statesmen my mother envisioned.

According to Pa, children were neither to be seen nor heard, and were to go outside and play, since that's what he had to do when he was a kid. I'm not sure Ma always wanted that but she had little say so she kind of gave up on me and apart from her once a week meeting at Women's Institute I think she spent most of her time wishing she had a daughter. Wishful thinking. A daughter would cost money!

So I went outside and played, mostly with Cocky, but after he was expelled he also went to boarding school. And that left Miriam. I could just imagine the monster teasing me incessantly about being a scaredy cat and running away from the big boys. And now that I knew what the 'eff' word meant and would mostly likely use it, no doubt Miriam would tell on me, have me expelled and sent back to boarding school!

Hostel versus home? The choice seemed bleak.

§

It seemed that each of us had a reason to not run away, or surely we would have done so. So what lurked in each person's background to keep us in this crucible of conflict?

I knew Spazz had a brother at hostel two years older than himself and a sister two years older than the brother. Their father was a dominating and autocratic reverend who reared them with a strict religious upbringing and took his role as head of the household to the extreme. His sweet *Stepford* mother submitted herself totally to her husband, with his sister a carbon copy of the mother, a *Stepford* daughter.

But the boys were different. At first they were typical Sunday school goody goodies. However, the enormous demands on the reverend's time by the church unintentionally caused the parents to see less and less of the boys. Increasingly, they subconsciously let the boys pretty much run their own lives and to gain even more free time to devote to the church, they sent them to boarding school, convincing themselves that the boys would have a spiritual influence on the kids they met. Besides, they would see them at church every Sunday.

Once Spazz and his brother had tasted the forbidden fruits of the outside world, they wanted more. So when the idea arose to send them to boarding school, the boys readily agreed. Developing dual lives, one of gaining freedom, but quickly falling into line when in view of the parents, taught them to be sneaky, adventurous and fun loving.

Having an elder brother at hostel also made it difficult for Spazz to run away. If he were to escape, how could he ever look his brother in the face again, knowing that his brother had the courage to see it through.

Apparently Mutt's father was a game ranger who worked on contract in the Masai Mara National Park in Kenya, an itinerant loner who was married to the great outdoors. But late in life when the opportunity arose, he accepted that a wife to look after him as he grew older would be slightly more advantageous than not having one. So when he met an old plain Jane sitting with her parents in a bar in a camp in the game reserve, he proposed to her and hitched up before their holiday was over, much to the relief of her parents who did not want her back on the shelf at home in the United Kingdom. Grateful for marriage, Mutt's mother became a dutiful wife and accepted her somewhat lonely lot in life. Making up for lost time, they begat Mutt and then four daughters to keep Jane company.

They belonged to the old school of father is boss, mother rears children and tends to the house. Boy children must grow up to be like their father and girl children must be like their mother. Mutt, therefore, followed his father and spent much time in the bush with him, learning the ways of the wild with the expectation that he, too, would one day become a game ranger.

Living in the bushveld, with no school nearby, Mutt's mother taught her children at home. Although it was expected that the mother would teach her daughters at home until the end of their school days, the parents decided that a woman teacher was not good for a boy, so at the same time when Mutt's father decided to retire and build a yacht to sail the world, Mutt was sent to boarding school.

Though confined at hostel, Mutt accepted it as a temporary hiccup before sailing off in his dad's yacht.

The easiest to understand was Eddie. The major influence in Eddie's life was his father, a sergeant major in the army. As a boy Eddie's father also attended Windsor College where he excelled at rugby, getting his national school colours and was rewarded by being made head prefect of both the school and hostel.

After school he joined the army for a career in the military. It became his life and led to a bitter divorce, his high standing in the community and his ambitions for his only child allowing him to retain custody of Eddie.

From a young age Eddie was surrounded by male adults who doted on him, partly because he was the sergeant major's son, but also because he was strong and physical, and participated in army activities. He became their mascot and Eddie revelled in the adulation. He especially liked the fact that his large dick was an endless source of amusement amongst the army recruits, who constantly asked him to haul it out and show it off.

Because of sergeant major commitments, Eddie's father gave him little time, though he tried to make up for it by doting on him when they were together and buying him presents. But his expectations for Eddie were high. Born to continue the family lineage. Born to go to Windsor College and become head prefect of both school and hostel, play in the first rugby team and then go on to become a sergeant major in the army. Eddie soon learned that success pleased his father.

Eddie couldn't run away. He had a huge burden to prove himself to his father.

Hog's case was the most perplexing. Continually picked on, he seemed the most likely candidate for running away, yet so far he hadn't and I wondered why. I knew so little of him I could only imagine Hog's life at home.

I saw a father who lived in his cousin's shadow, a loser who sought solace in food, married a woman who was a food provider rather than the good looking girl his cousin got, and the family became fat.

I imagined Hog's father to be a bank clerk, with little influence on Hog in the way of sparking ambition. Returning at five everyday to a home in disrepair, he would put his feet up, drink beer, wait for his food and after supper he would smoke and whittle wood on his soft sofa until it was time to go to bed. On weekends he was master of the barbeque, taking over from his wife as the cook, the only area he felt superior to his cousin.

Housebound, because she never learned to drive a car, Hog's plump mother took to cooking. She baked cakes for the family and for others, making pin money to fund further baking.

As to Hog, bored out of his mind, he lounged around a lot and filled his time by reading lots of comics. He found pleasure in bossing over and tirelessly teasing his plump younger sister, often by stealing or doctoring her food, causing her to whine and run off to the kitchen to be with her mother where she would learn to bake.

Wow! I couldn't imagine why Hog was at hostel and except for the unfathomable protection he enjoyed by Eddie, even fewer reasons why he stayed. An odd couple, those two. Fat Hog hiding in the shadow of Eddie, the obvious contrast showing Eddie to glow even more brightly. What secret lay there?

§

I lay awake a long time. Oh, Ma! You sent me to hostel to broaden my horizons. What have you done?

Just as I drifted off, a shrill alarm shattered my flimsy sleep. Next to my bed, Vulture reached out, switched off his alarm clock, sat up, and in the dark of the night he reached into his laundry bag and got out a half-smoked cigarette and a box of matches. He lit the smoke, dragged on it twice, stubbed it out, put the cigarette and matches back into his laundry bag and went back to sleep.

Fuck you, Vulture, I seethed under my breath. Fuck you, cigarettes! Fuck you, hostel! Fuck you, …

§

'Huh!' I exclaimed aloud the following morning, whilst waiting for the master on duty to arrive for inspection. Noticing an empty bed and suddenly remembering the incident the previous evening of the anorexic apparition packing a slice of bread in a brown paper packet, I announced in a loud whisper to the rest of the second formers, 'Flake's run away!'

A murmuring amongst my peers grew to a loud excited chatter.

'Aay!' wailed Mutt. 'The Biafran's got more brains than I thought!'

'Shut up!' shouted Goofy, the dormitory monitor.

Spazz looked at the empty bed, then at me. He said nothing, nor did I. I looked at Hog, then back at Flake's bed. Perhaps it took more courage to run away!

We never saw, nor heard from Flake again. And only then it dawned on me. Damn! With Flake gone, I would have Mango's fagging duties all to myself!

CHAPTER 15

End of first term break came and went all too quickly. Under a pall of gloom hanging over the dormitory just before lights out, when he wasn't looking I switched off Perve's radio that was playing *Crimson and Clover*, opened my locker and marked off on a calendar the number of days left before our midyear holiday.

Spazz entered the dormitory, trudged over to his bed and greeted me in a downcast voice, 'Hi, Tyke. Parole didn't last long, eh!'

'Yeah!' I answered, but my dejection could not cloud the one ray of sunshine in an otherwise dark day. Pulling my cotton sleeping shorts down over my dick, I announced to my friend, 'Hey, Spazz, look! Ball hairs!'

'Hey, man, where'd they come from? What've *you* been eating?' Spazz asked with a hint of jealousy, looking despondent as he examined his own bald patch whilst undressing.

'I dunno. This fluff just grew!' I beamed proudly, stroking my short curlies.

Not to be outdone, Spazz's despondency suddenly gave way to a mischievous grin as he turned the tables on me and asked, 'Have you done it, yet?'

'Done what?'

'You know, wanking.'

'Huh!'

'Have you pulled your wire?'

I hadn't and obviously betrayed a look of confusion.

'You must try it. It's good stuff, man. Just get a boner and away you go!' Spazz coached, animating a pumping action near his crotch.

The bell rang, so we all moved to the end of our beds, ready for lights out. Standing opposite Spazz and myself, Eddie overheard our conversation and, perhaps feeling threatened by the start of our new journey, hauled out his dick and displayed his ware.

'Aw, you guys are just winkie wankers,' Eddie teased us. Looking around to select just the right moment, he boasted, 'I banged a bird this holiday!'

Stunned silence.

Eddie carried on, 'I went on a fishing holiday and—'

'You screwed a girl?' Spazz interjected, deliberately and with not a small hint of disbelief.

'That's right, man! Anyway, there was this—'

'A girl?'

'Yes.'

'How old was she?'

'Old enough!' Eddie beamed proudly. 'She looked just like Susan George!'

Susan George! Our bewildered minds salivated.

Then, cupping his hands to his chest, Eddie described, 'She had these monstrous tits, man! Huge cans out to here that make Raquel Welsh's look like bee stings!'

Raquel Welsh!

'Yeah, but how old was she?' Spazz persisted.

An irritated Eddie snapped, 'Old enough, man! Old enough to fuck you out of your mind! Man, what's wrong with you?'

'Because if she was old enough,' retorted Spazz with a grin, 'you'd think she'd have the good sense not to let you screw her!'

'Aw, she was turned on, man. So turned on she was begging for it!' claimed Eddie, bending his arm at the elbow and demonstrating a cocked forearm. 'When I put it in, she was wet, man!'

Silence.

Still wet behind the ears, I looked down at his dick and concluded that he did indeed have the equipment.

'Tell them what else happened, Eddie,' Hog butted in, a look of pride on his face.

We all looked to Hog and wondered what *he* knew. Eddie hesitated, turned to Hog with unsure eyes when the fifth form monitor broke the silence and shouted, 'Attention!'

'Welcome back, boys. I trust you've all had a restful holiday!' Duke greeted us. He then prayed and sang, 'Good night, gentlemen!'

'Good night, sir,' we mumbled.

As soon as Duke left, Eddie quickly took off his gown to climb into bed, but we quickly congregated around him like flies to a horse's backside, eager for more juicy details. But Eddie remained quiet. Hesitant.

'Nothing else happened,' Spazz commented, breaking the silence. Baiting Eddie, he added, 'Because obviously nothing happened in the first place.'

Not wanting his major news story to peter out, Eddie stole a quick look at Hog before regaling, 'Yeah, well, you won't believe this, man! After I finished banging this bird on the beach, this huge wind blew in and washed in this gigantic tidal wave. We didn't know what to do so we ran under the pier. And then, man, you should have seen it. This wave dumped this giant octopus on top of the pier with its testicles dangling over the—'

'Tentacles!' Spazz corrected, with a grin, shaking his head.

'No, man!' Eddie protested. '*She* said they were testicles! They were massive and, dangling over the edge of the pier, made it dark. This bird was so scared, man, she kept grabbing onto me so I switched on my torch to find a way out, but the wind blew the beam all over the place and—,' Eddie paused as he saw the second formers dissipate and return to their beds. 'Hey, where're you guys going?'

'You *are* right, Eddie!' Spazz called from his bed. 'We *don't* believe you!'

After lights out I climbed into bed, lay in the dark, reached down into my sleeping shorts and stroked my new treasured ball hairs. My dick grew. With a vivid picture of Spazz's pumping action, I wondered at his question, 'Have you done it, yet?'

Feeling somewhat guilty, I propped my legs up slightly to give myself room, ever careful not to draw attention, clutched my dick and emulated Spazz's pumping action, waiting for something to happen, but nothing did. Not much to wanking, I thought.

Just then the door flung open with a bang and the lights switched on. I nearly swallowed my heart. Quickly dropping my knees, I lay rigid, eyes shut, pretending to be asleep.

'Where's the bloody wanker?'

Damn! The unmistakable bellow of Bull. What's *he* doing here? My heart beat like a caged bird. How did *he* know I was wanking? Trembling, I debated if I should own up. Damn! Another working by Bull. And the longer I leave it, the worse my punishment. On the verge of raising my hand from the dead, I opened my eyes to see Bull and a host of other seniors gather around Eddie's bed.

'Grab him!' Bull ordered as he pulled back Eddie's sheet. 'Hold him down!'

With Eddie pinned to the bed, Bull pulled the second former's sleeping shorts down to reveal his adult equipment. Without looking away, Bull held out his hand and another senior handed him a set of electric hair clippers.

Eddie's nostrils flared and snorted as he wriggled in vain and protested, 'What're you doing? What're you doing, man?' Then he realised. 'No! No!' he vehemently protested. 'You can do anything else. Shave my head if you want, but please leave my ball hairs alone!'

Bull flicked the switch on and shaved Eddie's pubic area as smooth as the pate of a new army recruit. In doing so, he diminished Eddie's sexuality, returning the second former to prepubescent status as best he could, holding off the challenge.

'Screwing a bitch at your age!' Bull spat, shaking his head. The burly sixth former broke into a deep belittling laugh. As he turned to leave, he caught my eye and shouted, 'What're *you* looking at?'

I quickly lay down on my pillow.

'Oh, what the fuck, *you* wouldn't have anything to shave!' Bull sneered at me before leaving the dormitory with his barber attendants.

I breathed a huge sigh of relief, forgot about wanking, and turned over to go to sleep, anxious that I not lose my new and prized curly possession. Instead, my mind turned to those clippers that Bull had used. I had never seen electric clippers before, and remembering the hand-jobs Pa gave me, I coveted them.

§

As I rose wearily from my bed the following morning, Spazz looked straight into my eyes with one question in mind. 'And?'

'Huh!'

'What was it like?'

It took a moment for me to realize what he was asking about. Embarrassed to admit that wanking seemed like, well, nothing much, I lied, replying, 'Uh, not bad.'

I felt my face flush red so I quickly turned away and walked off to the ablutions. Damn! I felt terrible about lying to my friend.

§

At the piss trough I hauled out my dick to urinate, but instead of one spray, two sprays emerged, one to the left and the other to the right at an oblique angle, hitting the sidewall of the piss trough, ricocheting back onto Spider.

Thwack!

'Mind the fuck where you're pissing, you jerk!' growled Spider, cuffing me on the head, sending me crashing into the piss trough.

Mindful how to end off a piss, flip, flip, squeeze, squeeze, flip, flip, I suddenly spotted the cause. Aah! A stray ball hair had caused the divergent spray!

As I walked into the shower enclosure I was shocked to see Vulture standing in the first shower on the right as he usually cleaned himself in one of the baths. A new term resolution, I surmised. Eddie and Mutt waited ahead of me in the queue at the back wall.

I looked at Vulture. Scruffy head on a seemingly long body supported by only two bones for legs, splayed out at the knees, and a third bone for a dick. Somehow he always appeared to have a partial erection, as if held up by cobwebs. Vulture rinsed his mangy hair, then stood, his beady eyes darting this way then that.

Sensing that Vulture was finished, Eddie moved in, placed a hand on the bird's wing and tugged. Vulture resisted. All eyes turned to them. A second former challenging a third former, albeit, seemingly, the weakest.

'You *are* finished, aren't you?' Eddie remonstrated.

'I'll finish when I want to finish!' declared Vulture, standing his ground.

Eddie looked peeved and couldn't resist teasing, 'Vulture, if you stay in that shower any longer you'll catch pneumonia!'

'Watch it!' squawked Vulture, flapping his featherless wings.

'Oh! So what you gonna do about it?' Eddie challenged, jerking his head up in defiance.

'Meet me this arvie under the guava tree!' Vulture asserted, the spot near the fowl run at the back of the property where all differences were settled.

'Hmmph!' snorted Eddie, surprised at Vulture's courage.

Suddenly Chief stepped out of his shower, walked over to Eddie, and with a piercing stare through furrowed eyebrows, simply issued, 'Back off!'

Eddie retreated with his tail between his legs whilst Mutt, like a scavenging jackal, darted into the shower vacated by Chief.

As Chief left, Eddie looked to Mutt, then to the rest of the occupied showers, then back to Mutt, dropped his lip and just stood there.

I looked down to Eddie's dick. Devoid of ball hairs, it seemed even larger than usual.

'What are *you* looking at?' snarled Eddie.

'Eh, nothing,' I replied, careful not to arouse his anger. But after a moment I suddenly plucked up enough courage to deliberately put a two by four block of carbolic down to my ball hairs and, whilst proudly lathering them, I thrust my pelvis forwards and chimed, 'Yep, I'm looking at nothing!'

CHAPTER 16

Whilst seated and waiting in the school hall for assembly to begin that morning, I idly perused the honours boards in the school hall, noticing the name Edward Alcock several times. Head prefect of school. Head prefect of hostel. National school colours for rugby.

'Must be Eddie's dad, eh?' I whispered to Spazz sitting next to me. 'I wonder why Eddie never boasts about him.'

A procession of staff walked up the aisle followed by the headmaster, a Mr Windsor, great-grandson of the founder of the school. Whilst the two dozen or so staff members duly sat on chairs on the stage, the tall, thin headmaster stepped up onto a lectern to address over 500 restless boys. Clutching the corners with his crooked fingers, draped from the shoulders in a long black academic gown, he stooped forwards before speaking, dwarfing the lectern. No wonder we called him Batman! And the longer he spoke the more his gaunt face would project forwards on his long gooseneck, with a pair of beady eyes looking over a pair of wire-rimmed spectacles that hung on the end of a long, thin, crooked nose.

'During the holidays,' the headmaster addressed us, 'a young second former, playing up two age groups, excelled at the interschool rugby festival.'

Sitting in front of me, Eddie proudly sat up in his chair, blocking my view of Batman.

'Our rugby coach has asked me to make a special commendation and award this badge to him, so please give a big hand to Edward Alcock III.'

Before his name was even called, Eddie stood up, pouted his chest and walked tall towards the podium.

'Edward Alcock III, hey!' I whispered to Spazz. 'He has a title!'

'Yeah,' my friend responded, 'but he still walks with a carrot up his bum!'

After presenting Eddie with his badge to resounding applause, the mostly bald headmaster announced, 'Will the second formers please remain behind to be assigned to your new classes, which, as you ought to be aware, will be based on your end of term test results.'

Whilst we waited for the other forms to exit the hall, along with others I held out my hand and congratulated Eddie and said, 'Well done!'

'Sit down and keep quiet!' Batman commanded before reading a list of names allocated to classes. 'Class A first!'

Second on the list, Eddie.

'Hmm! So he has some brains after all!' I whispered to Spazz.

Eddie turned around to gloat. He caught my eye and smirked. 'The boffin class!'

A few names later, Spazz. I nodded a look of mock surprise to my friend. Batman droned on and on, so I drifted off. Next thing, Spazz dug me in the ribs.

'Ouch! What's that for?' I whispered, annoyed.

'For getting into the A class. Not bad for a tyke!'

'Huh!'

Eddie turned around, looking peeved.

Before he could comment, I quickly chimed in, 'Boffin class, eh!'

'Last one in, man!' he gloated.

'Class B next!' Batman continued. 'By the way boys, the list for each class is in alphabetical order.'

'Eddie Arsehole!' I whispered aloud, causing Eddie to squirm in his seat.

§

When the headmaster finished reading out the new class lists, he announced, 'It is the beginning of rugby season. All second formers must turn out for rugby practice this afternoon. Now go to your old classroom, fetch your books and proceed quickly and quietly to your new classrooms.'

I walked back with Mutt to the prefab section of the school, set aside for the dunces, and packed my books.

'What's the meaning of this babel?' admonished Duke, peering into the classroom. 'The headmaster asked you to proceed quietly. Now line up, the lot of you!'

Like cattle getting branded, Duke caned us two stripes each with his trusty old wooden ruler.

As I turned to leave, I looked back at Mutt who was to remain in the F class.

'Work hard!' I counselled. 'Work hard and you can get out of here!'

Mutt said nothing, but acknowledged my advice with a slight nod of his head.

I headed off to the A class, saw Eddie sitting on the far side, so I looked for a seat on the near side and got a desk at the rear of the classroom. Good, I can swing on my chair against the back wall! I liked that.

Due to his poor eyesight, Spazz sat in the front. It suddenly dawned on me that nearly half the class seemed to have poor eyesight, wearing bottle-bottom glasses. The boffin class!

'What's the meaning of this babel?'

Oh, no! Not again!

Duke entered the classroom and reprimanded us. 'The headmaster requested that you proceed quietly. More is expected from this class. Now line up, the lot of you!'

§

Afternoon arrived, Monday afternoon. Dressed in a pair of blue running shorts and a white vest, I sat on a bench pulling on my trainers.

'Rugby practice!' Spazz reminded me.

'But I have cross country training,' I moaned, my strategy for escaping Scrote's thorn gauntlet.

'Uh-uh! You heard Batman. Rugby's a bloody religion here and it's compulsory for all of us to turn out this arvie.'

I went to the rugby field and approached Rhino, the school's short, stocky rugby coach, also my maths teacher, and said, 'Sir, please may I be excused. I have cross country training on Monday afternoons.'

'You what?' questioned the coach in a gruff voice, the long hairs sprouting out of a wart on the tip of his nose vibrating as he spoke. With a tweed flat cap pulled low over his eyes, cigarette butt hanging from his lips, clouds of smoke puffed out of the short man's head like a steam train as he spoke. 'There's no such bleedin' thing as cross country training on rugby practice days!'

'But, sir—'

'Cork it, blighter. Are you any good at cross country?'

I both shrugged my shoulders and nodded my head before saying, 'I think so!'

'So you're a runner, hey! Then you'll play fly-half. Now move!'

Damn! It was true that rugby practice would also mean no more of Scrote's thorn gauntlet, but I had come to really enjoy my cross country. Oh, well, maybe if I played badly he would let me off.

I had little clue about rugby, just a vague idea that a fly-half stood somewhere behind the scrum, and that the object was to catch the ball and run to the other side of the field.

The ball came shooting out from the base of the scrum. I caught it, but before I could run, Eddie, playing flank, charged like the coach's namesake and flattened me down to the ground, knocking every last molecule of air out of my lungs. I rose slowly, gasping for air.

'Fine tackle, Eddie! Bleedin' fine tackle!' Rhino praised, then turned his attention to me. 'When you get the ball, don't just stand there. Mooove!'

Same move again. The ball torpedoed out from the scrum. I caught it, but immediately Eddie bulldozed me! I felt extra venom in the tackle.

With his arms still embracing me from his tackle, Eddie mocked me, 'Aw, is this a little rough on you! Well, get used to it because rugby's a real sport, not like that sissy stuff you do.'

I stood up and immediately bent over to catch my breath to get ready for the next assault. My one consolation was that Rhino must have got the impression that I was better suited to cross country. But if the crash tackling lasted any longer, I may not have had a body left with which I could do cross country. Besides, Eddie was getting on my nerves.

Third move. As I caught the ball, I quickly dummied, pretending to throw it to my left. Eddie stopped dead in his tracks, glaring at me. I darted to the right.

'Play the ball, Eddie, not the man,' Rhino bellowed. 'Play the ball!'

With Eddie leaning the other way, I quickly dashed around him and ran off down the field.

'Pass the bleedin' ball!' the coached yelled at me.

I looked around to see if Eddie was behind me, and unsighted, ran straight into an opposing player.

'Oh, you bleedin' idiot!' lamented Rhino.

It took six weeks of bumbling rugby to convince Rhino that I was better suited to cross country!

CHAPTER 17

'Scraps! Scraps! Scraps!' I called out during midmorning break at school the following morning. So did Spazz. So did Eddie. For some bizarre unknown reason, matron did not provide us anything to eat or drink for mid-morning break. So we bummed food from the dayboys.

Scraps and scratch! That separated the boarder rats from the day dogs. Bumming food and scratching our balls. So sorry did the mother of the dux of our class feel for us, that every day she packed a separate lunch of sarmies for Spazz, Eddie and myself. But we still bummed more.

'Scraps! Scraps!'

After tea break and back in class, Rhino, our maths teacher, gave us a lesson on reciprocals. A law unto himself with a foul mouth to match, he waved a cigarette in one hand and a piece of chalk in the other as he explained animatedly about inverting one number with another, then turned around to the board and proceeded to write with his cigarette.

We laughed. He turned to face the class and said in a slurred accent, 'I've got a shitload of bleedin' marking to do.' Whilst tapping the one end of another non-filtered Lucky Strike cigarette on the cigarette box, he more specifically addressed Spazz and myself, 'Do you blighters care for a free period?'

'Yes, sir!' replied Spazz without hesitation from his desk at the front of the classroom.

'Well, you hostile boys know the drill! Up you come!' Rhino announced, affectionately referring to those from the hostel, though Eddie never volunteered.

I got up from my chair, went to the front, faced away from Spazz, bent over and placed my backside up against my friend's. Rhino lit his cigarette with a match from a book of matches from his favourite pub, pulled out Ol' Faithful, as he called his famed Perspex ruler, and swiped it down between our bum cheeks for one of his infamous bacon slices. Because he was still inebriated from the night before, his hand shook, so it mostly connected only one of us. Fortunately for me, Spazz took the brunt of the ruler that day. He jerked up, grimaced until the pain subsided, then looked at the maths teacher and nodded his approval. A bizarre and painful ritual that seemed to absolve Rhino from the guilt of giving us a free period, but worth every ache of it.

Moments later Rhino's voice bellowed. 'Whoah! What have we here? Some vermin in the class!'

The maths teacher came marching up to my desk at the back of the classroom, threw my homework book onto my desk and demanded, 'Who's the bleedin' cheat?'

'Huh!'

'Don't you huh me!' he shouted. 'Which one of you is going to rat on the other?'

I still wore a bemused face.

'You yellow bellies. I'll bleedin' well test you.'

Rhino suddenly turned to face Eddie on the other side of the classroom. The second former's face drained of colour as if bleached by the sun.

'What's an arsehole divided by zero?'

Eddie shrunk in his seat, but Rhino's gaze held his look of terror.

'I can't hear you!' shouted the maths teacher, cupping his hand around his ear.

In a faltering voice, Eddie offered, 'Er, er, one!'

'One what?'

'Er, one … arsehole,' Eddie eventually replied, his voice tapering off.

'You bleedin' dipstick! I ought to wrap my foreskin over your head and fuck some brains into you!'

'Sinclair!' Rhino bellowed, turning to vent his venom on me.

I squirmed in my seat, thoughts swirling between Rhino performing his brain enhancing deed on Eddie and trying to determine what one arsehole is when divided by zero. All I knew was that it couldn't be one. Eventually I decided to come clean and own up.

'Can't do it!' I admitted sheepishly.

'Well, how about that! A fucking rat with brains!'

His comment was lost on me, not realising at that moment that I had unwittingly given him the correct answer.

The maths teacher turned to Eddie again. '*You* of all people!' he spat. 'I'm so disappointed in you that I'm liable to kill you, so it's best that I write a letter to your parents. It's only fair that they see what a yellow rat they spawned!'

Trying to worm his way out, Eddie said, 'Sir, I'm in the hostel!'

'Then you can give the note to Mr Sherman. He can have your arse!'

Eddie's face again went pale and I wondered why.

'Sinclair!'

'Yes, sir!'

Rhino's finger beckoned me out of my chair and up to the front.

'Can't do it, eh!' he smiled, before cackling. 'You mean you *couldn't* fucking do it!'

I nodded my head.

'It's because you *can't* fucking do it. You can't divide anything by zero!'

'Oh!'

'What is an arsehole divided by two?'

'Um!' I thought this one out carefully before responding. 'Half. Er, half an arsehole,' I replied, getting increasingly less confident in my answer.

'And I'll demonstrate it to the class. Bend and I'll divide *your* arse in two!'

I did, and he did too!

§

On the way back from showers that evening I answered the telephone, just making it before four rings. Whilst speaking, I spotted Eddie standing next to his dad alongside a military vehicle, munching a large slice of cake. Eddie's dad appeared larger than life with an expanding girth as he grew older. A large oval face, much like a rugby ball perched on his shoulders without benefit of a neck, with a reddish hue on a light complexion betraying a liking for booze. Beneath his military hat a balding crown invaded his once blond hair, now turning white. Dressed in full sergeant major regalia, he handed over a parcel and a huge tin to Eddie, then shook hands and parted. This occurred every Wednesday. Eddie's Wednesday present and chocolate cake.

In the dormitory, Eddie placed the cake tin on his bed and shouted, 'Cake, every one!'

Every one meant mostly third formers and, of course, Hog. Whilst a throng of third formers descended on his bed and scavenged every last crumb of cake, Eddie approached me and held out a very large slice of chocolate cake.

'Hey, Tyke!' he called, beckoning me to a quiet corner of the dormitory. Then depositing the slice into my hands he offered, 'Have some cake!'

I was dumbfounded. I would suspect that I would normally be the last person on Eddie's freebie cake list, so I was extremely suspicious, but a piece of cake in the hands would definitely overcome that feeling!

'You've gotta help me out, man, cover me for my maths! Mr Sherman knows my dad. They are both old boys of the school. If he tells my dad—'

'In your dreams!' I interrupted, handing back the cake.

Eddie wouldn't take it. Instead he pleaded with me. 'Please, man, uh … you don't know what my dad will do to me!'

'Piss off!' I replied. I was tempted to draw out Eddie's grovelling, but my anger spilled over to spoil the occasion. 'You crib my homework, you don't own up when found out, now you're trying to buy your way out. Go to hell!'

His eyes grew misty with tears, which shocked me.

'Come on, Tyke. I'll owe you. Big time. Anything you want!'

Spazz entered the dormitory and informed us, 'Bum Lump wants to see both of you. Be careful, because he looks like he's having a wobbly!'

'Here Spazz, have some cake!' I offered to my friend, his eyes nearly popping out of their sockets. 'I've lost my appetite.'

Eddie and I marched off to the office. I knocked on the door. Bum Lump's voice bellowed. The foul mood was obvious so I stepped guardedly into the office. Eddie followed.

'What's this nonsense I hear about cheating in maths?' demanded Bum Lump, his nostrils flaring.

Silence.

'Answer me. Quickly!'

I felt awkward. I glanced sideways at Eddie. Beads of sweat lined his forehead and a look of terror on his face prompted my voice. 'I cribbed, sir. From Eddie.'

Waving his cane, Bum Lump looked to Eddie and dismissed him.

'Bend!' he ordered me.

Bum Lump caned me six of the best, slap bang on top of where Rhino gave a practical demonstration with his Ol' Faithful that morning on how to divide an arsehole by two.

As I left Bum Lump's office, my mind was a blur between pain and a puzzled wonder at the terrified look on Eddie's face. What's up with him?

CHAPTER 18

As usual, Pa dropped me off early on the day we returned from midyear break. I sat on top of Mutt's locker and watched out of the sash window as each boy arrived back. Spazz and his brother kissing their mother goodbye and vigorously shaking hands with their reverend father. Mutt and his hillbilly family, all so freckled that when they alighted from their car it appeared like peanuts pouring from a paper bag. Four look-alike sisters, just different heights. All the boys dropped off by their parents except Chief. He seemed to just walk in from the distance.

That night with no prep between supper and lights out, a heavy atmosphere hung over me. As others returned from their holiday, some quiet, others regaling their exploits, I again flipped through a calendar pinned on the inside of my locker and counted the number of days left until the next holiday.

Eddie and Hog both arrived late, bursting into the dormitory to quickly get dressed into sleeping shorts and gowns for lights out.

'Hey, you guys!' Eddie announced, attracting everyone's attention. 'I made a lady pregnant!'

'Well she's no longer a lady then, is she!' Spazz commented with a deadpan face.

I just looked ahead towards Eddie and remained quiet. Spazz, Perve and Goofball gathered closer.

'It's true, man. The officers' club had this party and invited all these women over. Shit, you've never seen so many just hanging around wanting it. So later that night I snuck into the club via the kitchen and there was this spare bird, pissed out of her mind. She grabbed hold of me and just wouldn't let go. So we went into the pantry and did it!' boasted Eddie.

'And now she's pregnant!' exclaimed Spazz indignantly, again with no small measure of disbelief.

'Yeah!'

'How do you know?'

'She told me, man!'

'When?'

'She asked me if I had a rubber, and when I said no, she said something about always wanting to have a baby. Then she takes a swig and she bloody well passed out.'

'And then you screwed her?'

'Yeah, I gave her what she wanted, man!'

The bell rang for lights out. As we lined up at the end of our beds, Hog said, 'Tell them Eddie. Tell them what you told me.'

Eddie looked towards the third formers, then to the monitor standing at the door, then lowered his voice to impart a big secret.

'She's a sex change!'

No one responded.

Not happy, Eddie asserted, 'Man, she's a sex change!'

'What's a sex change?' I asked, my curiosity overcoming any embarrassment I may suffer at showing ignorance.

Eddie looked at me with disdain and responded in a belittling tone, 'She was a guy, but she had her penis removed and made into a vagina.'

'You're a fucking rabbit!' Mutt chimed in.

Eddie ignored him and continued, 'It's true! I've read about them in a magazine at my dad's army camp.'

'Oh, come on, Eddie,' I interjected, 'a person can't change sex. It must have been some ugly chick that looked like a guy!'

Eddie grew angry at my doubt and questioned me, 'Aw, what do you know, Tyke! Have you ever banged a bird?'

Well, I hadn't, so that shut me up for a moment.

'How do you know she was a sex change?' Spazz tested.

'She showed me these scars under her tits where they put in these, like balloons, man!'

'Was this before or after she passed out!' Spazz teased.

'Aw, you're just jealous, man. These were cans to die for. I just buried my head in them and went for it!'

'You're a fucking rabbit!' Mutt repeated.

Eddie looked to Mutt, peeved, then back to the rest of us, beseeching endorsement.

Early that July morning whilst packing the car to return to hostel, I eavesdropped on Pa and Ma listening to the transistor radio on the back verandah. Pa sat in his rocking chair and said nothing. Ma was engrossed.

'That's one small step for man, one giant leap for mankind!' she repeated with wonder in her eyes. 'A miracle! Those Americans are getting so clever with their inventions. And it's all because of those wonderful boarding schools they have.'

Man landing on the moon was indeed a giant leap for mankind, a miracle, but a sex change? I had grave doubts.

'What are you shaking your head about?' demanded Eddie.

'A sex change!' I said questioningly, unable to remain quiet.

'That's fucking right!'

'And you made her pregnant?'

Eddie breathed in deeply, his nostrils starting to flare. Just then the master on duty entered the dormitory for lights out.

§

Not long after I had dropped off to sleep, the door burst open and the lights glared down into my brain.

'Where's the bloody wanker?' sounded the familiar bellow of Bull.

I kept my head on my pillow, careful not to attract too much attention. With my eyes closed, I heard Eddie's protests.

'No! No! Not again! You can do anything else. Please, man, please leave my ball hairs!'

CHAPTER 19

Whilst escaping from hostel consumed us in the first few months of the year, there literally came a moment for each one of us when our thoughts changed radically. Around this time, over a short period, one by one our balls dropped and, with it, a whole new interest consumed us — sex! Calendars that mark the number of days left of term were joined by pictures of the female persuasion cut out from magazines. Saturday night movies were viewed under a new light. Heroes like Steve McQueen, Charles Bronson, Robert Redford, Paul Newman and Clint Eastwood had to share the limelight with new sex-goddesses. Sure we still argued about which of Levis or Wranglers were better, or if Jimmy Hendrix was indeed the best guitar player on the planet, cassette versus reel tape, stove pipes or bell bottoms, but inevitably our conversation would return to sex.

Then one evening that bubble of conversation burst when a disk jockey broke into the song *Sugar, Sugar* and announced that Sharon Tate had been murdered.

'What retard would murder a sexy babe like that?' Spazz lamented.

He went to his locker and removed a picture of Sharon Tate stuck with cello-tape on the inside of the wooden door. Holding the picture of the ravishing movie star dressed in a silver bikini, he looked into her haunting eyes darkened with eyeliner and mascara and kissed her pale lips.

'Goodbye, my candy girl,' he whispered before crumpling it up and throwing it in the waste paper bin.

Feeling sorry for Spazz I opened my locker, pointed to a picture of Hayley Mills and offered, 'You can have this one if you like.'

The rest of the boys laughed at me. Spazz quietly said no thanks. Hayley Mills was never in. Marilyn Monroe was out, so was Twiggy. The bombshells that adorned the inside of our lockers were Britt Ekland, Racquel Welch, Susan George and Bridgette Bardot. And for me, my prize picture of Julie Christie with her captivating eyes.

Our dejection soon dissipated as our conversation once again turned to sex.

'You're all sexual rookies!' accused Goofy, strumming his guitar, still trying to master the opening chords of his beloved *Proud Mary*.

Huh! The indignation in the air was thick.

'I'll ask you a question and I bet you'll all screw up!'

'You're on!' Eddie responded.

'Okay, but if you're wrong, you make my bed for a week,' Goofy challenged.

'Go for it,' Eddie said eagerly.

'What does masturbation mean?' Goofy asked during a brief though welcome interlude from his guitar.

We all appeared dumbfounded. That put us in our place. We, the great wanker converts, did not know the meaning of masturbation!

'I, er, I,' hesitated Eddie at first, but desperate to prove a superior knowledge of all things carnal, he grew in false confidence until he beamed proudly, 'I know! It's when a woman gets the curse!'

Huh! What woman gets a curse? I wondered.

'No, you dumb shit! That's menstruation!' ridiculed Goofy, packing away his guitar to leave the dormitory. 'Eddie, my bed. You can start by straightening it out now!'

'Hmmph!' Eddie protested after Goofy left, trying to restore the wind in his sails, 'You guys probably don't even know what the curse is. It's when a woman bleeds the first time she has sex. You know, when she's a virgin.'

Huh! I had heard of the Virgin Mary at my previous school. Now bleeding virgins. It all seemed like a curse to me. And with my mind still wondering about curses, I returned to my bed to pack away my shoes, but mistakenly passed into third form territory.

Vulture woke me up from my reflections with a sharp clip on the head.

'Huh!'

'You know you must knock before you come past my bed!' scolded Vulture.

Because there was no physical door, second formers had to say out aloud, 'Knock! Knock!' and wait before entering third form territory, coupled with the usual merry gentlemen greeting.

'And don't you huh me!' Vulture reprimanded as he reached over to clip me on the head again.

The reach was a touch too far. His unstable bird legs gave way under him, causing him to crash into me, landing on top of me as I fell to the floor.

'Phoof!' I cried out after tasting a mouthful of mangy hair. I got up quickly, spat out a few tufts, then instinctively asked, 'Don't you ever wash your hair, you mouldy creature?'

Lying on the floor, Vulture grabbed my foot. To make up for his emaciated limbs, Vulture compensated with a fierce determination. I tried to pull away, but no such luck, his talons clamped around my ankle like a pair of handcuffs.

With no option but to distract him, I stuck my elbows out, flapped them, and yodelled a fine rendition of a squawking bird.

'Cluck, clu, clu, clu, cluck!'

Vulture grew wild and in an attempt to reach up and wrestle me down to the ground, he temporarily had to let go. Not wanting anymore scarecrow embraces, I seized that fleeting chance and jumped out of the way. But Vulture wasn't done yet. He hauled himself up and came after me. Knowing he could not jump, I quickly improvised by climbing onto my bed, then hopping onto Spazz's, then Goofball's, vaulting from one bed to another down to the end of the dormitory. Restricted to the aisle, Vulture followed me with steely resolve. Try as he might, his flapping arms just wouldn't allow him to fly, so he dragged his bird legs down the corridor between the beds, squawking for my blood. But just as he reached me, I turned around and bed hopped back to my bed. This new athletics event occurred over and over until finally the prep bell saved me.

Goofy put his head through the doorway and shouted, 'Shut up, now, and get to prep!'

As I jumped off the bed to go, Chief stepped in my way, gave me a piercing look and said sternly, though quiet enough to be out of earshot of Vulture, 'Leave him alone!'

Whilst walking downstairs, I bumped into Mutt. Somewhat surprised at Chief's comment, I criticised him. 'Chief is weird. How can he stand up for a mouldy creature like Vulture?'

'No, man, Chief is one of the good blokes. Not like those other city lowlifes,' Mutt tried to educate me.

'Huh!'

'Hang on, Tyke. Can't talk now. My piss bag's so bloody full it's gonna rupture. I've gotta take a leak before prep.'

Mutt ran off, leaving me bewildered about his observation of Chief. As I approached the bottom of the stairs, Spazz caught my eye by rolling his eyeballs to the left before he, too, also headed off to the junior ablutions. Acting innocently, I followed him.

'Let's spy on matron bathing!' Spazz suggested, his eyes beaming.

'What?' I gasped, before thinking that Spazz's balls, too, must have dropped! 'I don't think you're operating on a fully furnished brain!'

'Come on, it's a dare!' Spazz challenged me.

Normally I would have shrunk away from this challenge, but surrounded by the constant thought and talk of puss 'n boobs as adolescent hormones danced like wild flames of fire in our bodies, Spazz's dare pushed me over the edge.

'I accept!'

We entered the junior ablutions to gain cover, and waited to see if any prefect noticed that we were absent from prep. Apparently they hadn't.

Spotting Mutt at the piss trough with his trousers unzipped, we walked over to him, and feeling safety in numbers I invited him, 'Hey, Mutt! Want to join us spying on matron bathing?'

'Aay!' wailed Mutt, shaking his head in disbelief. 'Now how do you propose to do that?'

'We're gonna climb up the drain pipe outside their bathroom!' Spazz informed.

'Sshh! Not too loud. There's some fucker bogging in the shithouse!' warned Mutt.

'Damn!' I whispered to Spazz, hearing a strained grunt emanate from the first toilet. 'He could spill the beans on us.'

'Who is it?' Spazz asked quietly

Mutt shrugged his shoulders and put his forefinger to his lips, urging quietness before whispering, 'I'll flush him out!'

With a mischievous grin warming from ear to ear and little whimpers whistling through his freckled teeth, Mutt stood back from the piss trough, thrust his pelvis forwards, and aimed his spotted dick skywards. Mutt's piss power would become legendary but here we witnessed it for the first time, a practical demonstration of Bernoulli's principle studied that day at school.

Pinching the end of his dick, Mutt strained until his face washed red like a constipated baby. Then it happened. A steady stream of piss rocketed upwards, over the toilet wall and towards the high ceiling, hitting the light bulb that presided over the first toilet, the single light for that area of the ablutions. Pop! The bulb shattered and rained shards of glass down into the toilet cubicle.

'Hey!' a slobbery voice lamented from inside. 'I can't see what I'm wiping!'

'It's Hog!' whispered Spazz, recognising his fat lip mumble. 'He'll be too shit scared to give us away. Come, let's go. Mutt, are you coming?'

'No way, man!' Mutt replied emphatically, shaking his head. 'I've gotta go and graft!' Having said that, he marched towards the door, on his way to prep and with his head still shaking, he mumbled, 'You randy fuckers are sex starved, man!'

Spazz and I walked quietly to the back door, opened it carefully, exited the building and headed towards the matron's bathroom. Two drainpipes flanked the sides of the bathroom window. Spazz shinnied up one, myself the other, squatting on joints in the pipes and hanging on for dear life.

'I hope Ma Betty baths first and not Coughballs!' whispered Spazz.

The bathroom light switched on.

'Sshh!' I cautioned.

'Shit!' cursed Spazz. 'See who it is!'

'Should at least be good for a laugh!' I consoled him.

Coughballs was an old matron who had been at hostel for a long time, probably since before the war, Pa would say. She smoked like a chimney, had developed emphysema and coughed those deep wheezie coughs like Scottish bagpipes. The matron ran the bath water and slowly undressed. With each item of clothing removed, our curiosity changed to amusement. Finally she stood in her underclothes and started to unbuckle some strange contraption that masqueraded as her bra.

'Definitely before the war!' I commented.

As the Victorian accessory gave way, two wrinkly bags unrolled flat against her chest. Spazz started to laugh.

'Shut up!' I said in a staged whisper, trying to mask my own giggles.

'Ol' Coughballs could store her cigarettes in those empty saddlebags!' laughed Spazz.

Then she removed her panties. Damn! Below a soft droopy stomach we caught only a fleeting glimpse of a dark patch.

'Where's her pussy?' I asked Spazz, feeling somewhat cheated.

'Buggered if I know!'

'Then how does one know where to put it in?'

Spazz shrugged his shoulders and counselled, 'Well, with Coughballs you wouldn't want to.' Then after a brief moment, a wicked grin creased his face where the corners of his mouth curled upwards, bunching his cheeks into rosy apples and closing his eyes to thin slits, and between giggles he continued, 'But for those nutcases who do, sprinkle Coughballs with Enos, and where it bubbles, that's where you stick it in!'

I laughed at his suggestion, then asked my friend, 'How do you know these things?'

Spazz's eyes went skew with puzzlement at my ignorance.

Coughballs stood naked next to the bath, resembling a ball of plasticine with two match sticks stuck into her bottom for legs. She turned the tap off, stepped into the bath, splashed a little here and a little there, then got out.

'She's mouldy!' exclaimed Spazz.

I started to laugh, which set my friend off. Fearing the rusty drainpipe would give way under my shakes, I quickly got down and ran for cover behind a tree. Spazz joined me.

§

Not long afterwards, matron's bathroom lit up again.

'Ma Betty!' I exclaimed excitedly, pointing to the light shining from the window.

Spazz's eyes lit up with renewed vigour.

As we reached the bathroom window, Ma Betty was already in the bath, lying back, unwinding from a day of tending to her horde of boys.

Neither Spazz nor I spoke a word. In truth, the fair-haired Ma Betty looked as dashing as a preliminary sketch faded over time, but in front of us we saw puss 'n boobs. The matron soaped herself, slowly, starting with her arms, followed by her chest, carefully massaging each breast, then down to her tummy. Finally she lathered her brown pubic hair, turning it frothy.

Spazz fidgeted, I got a boner, and in front of us the window steamed up from the outside!

Just then, Ma Betty looked up towards the window. Spazz and I jumped in a flash, hitting the ground with a thud.

'Do you think she saw us?' I asked Spazz.

'Yeah, but it was worth it!' my friend replied.

'Yeah!'

§

As we entered the prep room, Grizzly demanded, 'Where have you two fuckers been?'

'We've been watching matron taking a bath!' replied Spazz with a deadpan face.

My heart palpitated. Spazz's brain was definitely not fully furnished!

Disbelieving Spazz, the prefect on prep duty disinterestedly washed his hands of the matter with a dismissive, 'Bunking prep. Go to the office!'

Great! Spazz's ploy of hyperbole worked like a charm. By going to the office, the master on duty would interpret a minor misdemeanour in prep.

Thwack! Thwack! Duke caned us two each.

Walking back to the dining room, feeling well satisfied, Spazz commented, 'It was definitely worth it!'

I nodded, but reminded my friend of our real worry. 'I just hope that Ma Betty didn't recognise us!'

'Perhaps she enjoyed it, too!' Spazz countered.

For the next hour or so, Spazz and I occasionally glanced at each other during prep, sitting on tenterhooks, awaiting a bellow from the office should matron have reported us. It never came.

'I suppose she didn't see us after all,' I surmised.

'No way!' Spazz disputed. 'Those old fogies are as horny as a rhino. Well, not Rhino the rugby coach! I'll bet she's hoping we'll try it again!'

§

At lights out, Mutt eagerly asked, 'So what did the sex starved spy ring see?'

'Well,' I got the ball rolling, 'first Ma Coughballs waddled in and—'

'Aay!' wailed Mutt, clapping his hands on the bed frame behind him. 'Tyke! Spying on ol' Coughballs! Man, you've been locked up in here too long.' But despite his accusations he was still intrigued to ask, 'So what does the antique look like in the flesh?'

'Bit like a beanbag!'

'But you should have seen Ma Betty!' Spazz butted in.

'Yeah!' I agreed quickly.

The rest of the second formers quickly congregated around us.

'Mmm! She's got nice boobs, man,' said Spazz, describing the episode with zeal, cupping his hands to his chest. 'She soaped them, sliding up and down, and over and around. And then,' Spazz said, lowering his tone, 'she lathered her pussy!'

'Oh, and she's not a real blonde!' I exclaimed, thinking this to be a newsworthy item.

'How do you know?' asked Eddie, up until now quiet and unsure.

'Because her, um, er, her ball hairs are brown!' I announced.

'Her badge of womanhood!' Perve interjected.

'Huh!'

'That's what my mom calls it!' informed Perve.

'Aay, you pervert! More like an unhealed wound that smells like last week's prawns!' piped up Mutt, falling over backwards on Spazz's bed as he pumped his hands with laughter.

'Huh!'

'That's what my old man calls it!'

'Your dad said that?' I asked, incredulous that Mutt or anyone for that matter had discussed the private parts of a woman with their parents. Except for my very existence, I sensed that Pa and Ma never even knew about sex!

'Hmmph! So they're brown, eh,' mused Eddie calmly. 'She's blonde but her box hairs are brown. I've seen birds like that. Maybe she's not really blonde, but just dyes her hair!'

Suddenly Chief, standing near the end of his bed, interjected, 'Ma Betty would never dye her hair and you shouldn't talk about her like

88

that!'

§

Lying in bed that night, knees propped up and absentmindedly fondling my dick, I thought of Ma Betty in the bath. I thought of lady teachers at school with new meaning, young and old, always undressing them, especially the one that always scratched herself on the corner of her table. In an all boy school, all boy hostel, it was all consuming. In our minds, we reduced women to little more than life support machines for pussies.

Lost in thought, lost in time, without much warning, my groin grew tighter and tighter until, quite by accident, it happened, shattering my train of thought and bringing me back to earth with a bang!

Wow! I sheepishly looked around in the dark to see if anyone had heard, if anyone had seen this amazing happening. But everyone appeared to be asleep. Sure, it was a blank cartridge, but wow! With a deep grin of satisfaction from ear to ear, I lay down on my pillow and purred like the cat that got the cream.

CHAPTER 20

Whilst walking with Mutt on the way back from school, both of us lugging two suitcases, my heart sank as I heard the unmistakable voice of Mango.

'Tyke! Wait up!' he ordered, before adding, 'You too, mongrel!' After catching up to us he continued, 'You two poops go around the neighbourhood and collect everyone's dog bog!'

'Huh!'

Thwack!

'You heard me. Do the neighbourly thing and offer to remove dog bog from their lawn! And put it in a packet which you can get from matron.'

Mango walked off. I looked at Mutt and slowly shook my head. No wail this time from my friend. He was simply stunned.

§

After dressing into our afternoon clothes, T-shirt and shorts, we set about cleaning up the neighbourhood of dog bog. An hour later, heading down the lane that led off from Windsor Road, directly opposite the driveway to hostel, I wearily knocked on the door of the house second on the left. To our utter surprise, a young girl answered the door.

'Hello!' she said, sleepily.

Gobsmacked, I just stared at her. Barefoot, she wore a red low cut tight fitting blouse and a white mini skirt with a gold chain-belt at the waist. And a handcrafted headband of multi-coloured beads that highlighted her blue eyes adorned her ruffled blonde hair.

'Hello!' she repeated. 'How may I help you?'

My heart thumped. I looked to Mutt, but he was too busy gawking at her cleavage, so I turned back to address the girl in a very shaky voice.

'I, er, I—'

'You're from the boarding school across the road, aren't you?'

'Uh-huh!'

'I can tell,' she commented, her eyes scrutinising our clothes. 'You all dress the same!'

With my mind elsewhere, such criticism went over my head. Instead, her magnetic allure captivated me, so I continued staring at her as if in a trance.

'What can I do for you?' she asked.

'Huh!' I woke from my stupor.

'You knocked on the door. I presume you want something.'

'Er, yes,' I replied, suddenly feeling self-conscious. 'May we, er, may we collect your dog, er, er, your dog, er—'

'My dog?' she queried with surprise.

'Yes! Er, no,' I stumbled, then pointed to the garden, again looked at Mutt for help but he was still in a daze, then back to the girl. 'Your dog, dog mess!'

It was her turn to go quiet, a look of bewilderment creasing her face.

'Er, er, we're cleaning up the neighbourhood,' I explained.

'Oh, yes, sure. Go ahead, if you want, it's all yours!'

The girl went inside whilst Mutt and I searched for dog bog, starting in the front garden, combing the property from one side to the other. As we neared the front porch, the girl emerged from the house, sat on a parapet that enclosed a porch, propped her knees up and leant back against the corner pillar. She licked an orange ice popsicle.

As we bent down to gather a log of dog bog, I whispered to Mutt, 'I swear I can see her panties!'

Whilst I held the packet open, Mutt bent over and simultaneously tried to scoop the piece with a makeshift cardboard spade, all the time with his eyes straining upwards towards the porch, but careful not to draw attention.

'Mutt!' I whispered, 'Your hand is dunking in the bog!'

Mutt didn't hear me, his mind in another world.

'Whoah! Those *are* her panties!' I whispered excitedly out the corner of my mouth.

'Would you two like a popsicle?' the girl suddenly asked, her tongue sensuously mouthing her own flavoured ice on a wooden stick.

Her voice prompted my heart to skip a beat and I wondered if she had caught us looking at her panties. Though dying for a popsicle, some inhibition in me caused me to reply, 'Er, no thanks!'

Mutt was not so reserved. He stood up and raised his hand to indicate that he would like one. The girl's eyebrows rose questioningly.

'Mutt, your hand!' I whispered in a low voice out the corner of my mouth.

On spotting the dog bog mushed on his hand, my friend quickly withdrew his paw and groaned, 'Not for me!' then buried his head in his task and mumbled, 'Shit!'

We scoured the garden, but found little else. Our good deed done, we returned to the porch to bid farewell to the girl.

'We're finished!' I said.

'Oh, thank you very much. Do I pay you? Is this one of those bob-a-job things?'

'No,' I replied. 'We don't want anything.'

'Are you sure? It's a very smelly job?'

Damn! Could she smell us? I wondered. We tried desperately to put our best foot forward, but we failed dismally, what with me carrying a packet of dog bog and Mutt's hand dunked in it. Whatever did she think!

'Well, thank you very much. Come again, anytime!'

As we left, out of sheer habit I said, 'Good bye, merry gentlemen!'

I never turned around. She would have mistaken my red face for the setting sun!

§

On our way back to hostel, though, our speech grew in excitement and we became increasingly animated.

'She wanted us, man!' yapped Mutt. 'I mean, she even asked what she could do for us!'

'Did you see her panties?' I asked.

'Then she says we can come again anytime! She wanted us, man!'

'Did you see her panties?'

As we approached the front gate of hostel, Mango shouted from the balcony upstairs, 'Where have you poops been? Get up here quickly and bring the dog bog!'

'Welcome back to the real world!' I mumbled despondently to Mutt.

We met Mango in the corridor leading to the prefects' dormitory and followed him in, me carrying the booty of dog bog.

Knock! Knock!

'Come in!'

'Good afternoon, merry gentlemen!'

Thwack!

'Get that stench out of here!'

With a spaced out Goofball breathing in his prefect's fart to air the dormitory, I wondered if Mango meant that I should do the same. So my face said, 'Huh!' looking for confirmation.

Thwack!

'Put that dog bog in your locker and then come back here. Mutt you switch the radio on.'

Just as I entered the prefects' dormitory, Mango turned a brown paper packet upside down, spewing out row upon row of firecrackers onto the floor

'Aah! Guy Fawkes night!' I exclaimed excitedly.

'Shut the fuck up!' groused Mango, thankfully breaking his nasal accompaniment to the radio's *Sorry Suzanne*. Handing me a couple of his razors he ordered, 'And take the gun powder out of all these crackers.'

I looked at him with another, 'Huh!'

Thwack!

'Mongrel, help him!' the head prefect ordered Mutt.

Mutt and I dutifully removed the blades from the head prefect's razors, cut the wrapping from the hundreds of crackers and extracted the gun powder, forming a mountain of it on a sheet of paper in the middle of the dormitory floor.

'Fetch some bog-roll!' Mango ordered.

Acting on orders, I reached into his green gown pocket where he always kept a roll of toilet paper.

'Now go and fetch your shoes! Both of you,' the head prefect directed us. 'And your shoe polish!'

Mutt and I complied, still awfully perplexed.

'Listen carefully, you poops,' Mango spelt out deliberately. 'Take out your shoe laces, tie them together into one long lace and smear them with polish.'

The loss of our shoe laces seemed trivial as such commands grew more and more intriguing. Whilst we set about our task, Mango went over to Grizzly's locker, withdrew a can of *Shield* deodorant and proceeded to wrap a few layers of toilet paper around it, followed by several layers of cellophane before sealing the one end. He extracted the can, leaving an empty tube-like container.

'Tyke, get that newspaper, tear off a page and make a funnel!'

I did.

'Mutt, pour the gun powder into this fucker!' the head prefect growled, his eyes growing in menace.

Mango held the container, I inserted the funnel and Mutt poured in the gun powder.

'Now put the fuse in!' Mango ordered.

Mutt and I looked at each other, baffled.

'The fucking shoelace!'

I grabbed the polish-smeared shoelace and inserted the one end into the container held by Mango. With his other hand, the head prefect clamped the container shut and bound it with more cellophane tape.

Suddenly Mutt realised the potential of the bomb we had just been privy to make and started wailing.

'What the fuck, have you got rabies or something?' Mango asked, bemused but peeved as usual. 'Shut up, and go and fetch the dog bog! Tyke, you clean up all this mess.'

Mutt scurried from the dormitory with a high pitched, 'Thank you, merry gentlemen!'

When Mutt returned with the packet, Mango handed over a shoe box and issued further instructions to us. 'You take this box and pack it with dog bog. Then you bury this fucker deep in it,' Mango ordered, holding up his crudely made bomb. 'Make sure you pack the shit tight!'

'Yes, sir!' we sang in unison, a shit job, but one with potential explosive consequences.

'And keep it in your locker!' he ordered, giving it to me.

'Yes, sir!' we both sang again.

'You do it, Tyke! Mutt, you breathe in this stench and blow it out the window!' he ordered, wafting the air. 'And fucking hurry up!'

§

Back in my dormitory, just before supper time, Spazz asked, 'Hey, Tyke! Where've you been all arvie?'

'You're not going to believe this, but Mutt and I collected dog bog from the neighbourhood and—'

'Dog bog!' Spazz interrupted with bewilderment. 'Why would you do that?'

'Mango made us.'

'Oh shit, man! What's this place coming to!' Spazz lamented, throwing his hands up and shaking his head.

'No, it's okay. The dog bog was to make a bomb!'

'A bomb?'

'Yep! A dog bog bomb! But that's not all.'

Just as a drowsy looking Mutt entered the dormitory, more second formers gathered around.

'We went to a house up the road,' I continued, 'and we met this chick. But not just any chick. You dream of chicks like this!'

'Aay!' wailed Mutt.

'What?' demanded Spazz, impatient.

'She looked like she was on heat!' Mutt announced.

Spazz looked to me for confirmation.

I nodded my head. 'She sat on this porch wall with her legs up, sucking a popsicle. And she even offered us one.'

'And?' Spazz asked excitedly.

'Um, we collected her dog bog,' I replied, shrugging my shoulders, deflating the story.

'Oh, what a retard!' Spazz chided us. He was dumbfounded. 'Don't you know that offering a popsicle was her way of inviting you in. She was saying come and get it, and instead you collected her dog bog!'

'You talk shit, man!' piped up Eddie from the corner of the dormitory where he had just finished plastering his hair down with Vitalis in front of a mirror. After a quick flex of his biceps to admire his muscles, he turned and walked towards us. 'You really talk shit! There's no bird at any house. You're dreaming!'

'Of course there was this chick!' I asserted in a piqued voice. Pointing towards the window, I continued, 'Right there across the road, second left as you go up the lane!'

We all went to the window wall, climbed on Mutt's bed, perched at the window and strained our necks to see the house.

'She sat on that small brick wall,' Mutt said, pointing to the parapet. Indignant that Eddie wouldn't believe him, he raised his voice, 'Then she leant up against the pillar, and put her legs up for us to perve! She wanted us, alright!'

'Then how come haven't we seen her before?' Eddie questioned.

'I dunno. Maybe she's just moved in!' I replied.

'You talk shit, man!'

'I'll prove it to you,' I said. 'I'll show you the dog bog bomb!'

Extracting the shoe box from my locker, I opened it to reveal a well-packed mass of dog bog with a long shoe lace smeared with polish piercing through the one end. A vile stench quickly permeated the dormitory.

'There was no bird. You talk shit, Tyke! Shit, alright! And you smell like shit!' Eddie criticised, walking away.

'And you smell greasy with all that shit in your hair!' Mutt yelled at him. 'You fucking lover-boy!'

I turned to Spazz and said in a low voice, 'Something is going down tonight!'

CHAPTER 21

The bell rang for supper. I sat at the table waiting with an air of anticipation. As Babalas entered the dining room, a chorus of howls erupted.

'Why? What's going on?' I asked aloud, the dog bog bomb flashing to mind, but quickly remembering that it still lay in my locker.

We looked to Pygmy.

'Vulture's sweat soup!' exclaimed our table monitor with a gleeful look on his face. We all looked puzzled.

'It's Ma Coughball's special brew. You'll find out!'

Nobody knew what ingredients the old matron put into it, but some chemical reaction would inevitably take place in our guts. The first time, of course, we were unaware of what was to come, but all the seniors appeared overtly delighted at this magical brew.

§

Later that evening between supper and prep, Mutt and I waited in anticipation. But nothing happened. During prep, I kept on looking across to my friend, but his remarkable work ethic got the better of him as he buried his head in his books.

Eventually, the pocket money register came around. Our parents paid in a certain amount of money each term from which we were allowed a weekly allowance. Each Wednesday we were to record the amount we wished to have paid out on Saturdays, subject, of course, to a limit depending on seniority. As usual I wrote a zero. And then I heard his wail. Same time every week. I looked up to see Mutt making faint whisper wails as he rubbed a curled finger up and down his snout, teasing me of being tight with my 'start' as he called it. What money? Pa coughed up the minimum amount required and expected it to be paid back to him each term.

Just then, a flash by the entrance of the dining room caught my eye. Inexplicably, the bell rang. Prep had been on the go for only half an hour, so all eyes looked up in confusion.

Anticipating an evening of Guy Fawkes entertainment, I exclaimed loudly, 'Yes!' at exactly the same time Grizzly entered the dining room.

'Who the fuck rang the bell?' the mutant demanded, looking at me.

Then everyone looked at me. I grew wary and shrugged my shoulders.

'*Who* rang the bell?' he asked in a raised tone.

'Where *is* the bell?' Mango asked, also entering the dining room.

Silence.

'I dunno,' I answered before gingerly proffering my opinion, 'but just after the bell rang, someone ran out of the building!'

'Those bloody douchebags! They've gone and swiped our bell!' Mango accused, referring to the boarders of our rival school, King's College. He then asked, 'Which second former does cross country?'

I held up my hand.

Mango gave me a disbelieving look, ignored me and looked around for someone else.

'I play rugby!' Eddie interrupted, envious and desperately keen to get involved.

'Well, I didn't ask for rugby, you poop,' Mango scowled, clobbering Eddie on the head.

Without any other hands raised, Mango's eyes returned to me. 'You're not bullshitting me are you?'

I shook my head.

Thwack!

'No, sir!' the head prefect snapped.

'No, sir!'

'See me after prep!'

§

During the remainder of prep, everyone seemed a little agitated, a restlessness growing in the air. Was it the bomb? I wondered. For myself, I was more concerned about my stomach, which at first seemed a little tender, then literally boiled, bubbles of gas churning up inside.

I was so grateful for the end of prep, desperate to frequent the toilet, but as I left the dining room, I suddenly remembered that Mango had asked to see me so I headed off to the prefects' dormitory and knocked on the door.

'Come in!' replied Mango in a strained voice.

'Good evening, merry gentlemen!'

As I walked in, Mango presented me with a cigarette lighter.

Yes! Time to light the bomb!

But no such luck. Instead, the head prefect stripped naked, climbed onto his bed, knelt on all fours, pouted his bum in the air just as the radio appropriately played *Bad Moon Rising*, and with his head buried deep in his pillow he ordered in a muffled voice, 'Hold a light to my arse!'

'Huh!'

With a major stomach affliction griping on the one hand, and deep disappointment that I was not asked to come to the prefects' dormitory for something to do with the bomb, I was totally baffled. Now I had to hold a flame to my prefect's backside!

'Hurry up, you poop!' Mango shouted.

I flicked the lighter and cautiously held it some distance from Mango's derriere.

'Closer!'

As my hand neared his rear end, Mango proceeded to strain, and the sight of his pink thing emerging deep from within caused me to falter and lose my grip on the lighter and the flame went out. Suddenly he ripped this deep resonating fart. Instantaneously, a vile smelling sulphurous fog engulfed me, and I nearly fossilized on the spot. Matron's brew had begun to speak.

'You cunt!' shouted Mango, waking me from my comatose state by clobbering me on the head. 'You let the bloody flame go out!'

A look of deep anger clouded his face due to this lost opportunity. I cowered, expecting the worst. But just then, he broke into a devilish smile, turned over and again pouted his bum into the air.

'Don't let the flame go out this time or I'll fart in your face!'

That threat galvanised my conviction. With his stench still scalding my throat, I held the naked flame up really close and with grim determination, utterly convinced I was about to enter hell. The ill wind erupted, igniting a flame that shot into the room from an angry dragon. Startled, I jumped out of the way. Incredibly, instead of a sulphuric fog, the smell of singed hair permeated the room.

Quite expecting Mango to thump me again, I backed off. Instead, he emerged from his burrowed hole in his pillow with a smile of deep satisfaction.

'Aah! That was goooood!' he purred. 'Now fuck off!'

Grateful to get off so lightly, I scampered off, bumping into Eddie as he entered the prefects' dormitory.

'Hold a light to my arse!' Grizzly growled.

I turned to Eddie, smiled and said, 'Enjoy!' before adding the customary, 'Thank you, merry gentlemen!'

'Tyke!' Mango shouted.

'Huh!' I uttered, poking my nose back into the prefects' dormitory. 'I mean, yes, sir!'

'Come here!'

'Good evening, merry gentlemen!'

'Who else can run?'

'Me, sir!' interrupted Eddie.

'Is your name Tyke?'

'No, sir, but I can run!'

Mango looked at me, questioningly.

'Er, Mutt, sir!' I told him, knowing he also went jogging, though he would never join the cross country team.

Mango looked at me with grave doubt before shrugging his shoulders. 'Well, the poop smells like dog bog already so both of you see me after lights out! Now fuck off!'

As I left the dormitory, out the corner of my eye I saw Eddie holding a light to Grizzly's bum and behind me I overheard Mango address Eddie. 'As for you, after lights out, fetch your laundry bag and come back here!'

'Ouch!' cried Grizzly. 'You burnt my fucking balls!'

Thwack!

Walking down the passageway to the junior dormitory, my stomach boiled like a hot geyser. When I entered the dormitory that evening, I couldn't believe my eyes. Bed after bed depicted flame throwers! By the time I reached my bed, I was about to explode so I quickly undressed, climbed onto my bed, sunk my head into my pillow and pouted my bum in the air just like Mango had done. Like the proverbial moths to a flame, peers quickly warmed to my backside.

'Doo, doo, doo, doo, doo!' sang the bubbles like water poured from a bottle, rising up the musical scale as they journeyed their way out through the bowels of hell. Suddenly the volcano erupted, shooting forth long tongues of fire.

'Aah! That felt gooooood!' I sighed, relieved.

Without a bell to ring to signal lights out, Goofy shouted, 'Shut up! Time for lights out!'

Duke entered the dormitory to pray. His nose twitched this way, then that, before his face broke into a wry smile. Without another word, he left the dormitory, returned with a can of *Right Guard* deodorant and sprayed the room as if at some imaginary bug, causing some boys to snigger at his fastidiousness.

Duke prayed, then greeted with gusto, 'Good night, gentlemen!'

'Good night, sir,' we mumbled.

'Mutt!' I called to the dog opposite me, 'Mango wants to see us.'

'Why? What have we done wrong, now?'

'I haven't a clue, except that he asked me who else is good at jogging!'

Eddie piped up, 'Aw, you two are just arse creepers!'

We knocked on the door of the prefects' dormitory.

'Come in!'

'Good evening, merry gentlemen!'

'So you poops can run, eh!' Mango said disparagingly.

We both kept quiet.

'Get dressed in dark clobber, put your gowns on and pretend you're gonna do extra prep. Then meet me downstairs. Now fuck off! Oh, and bring the bomb!'

Mango turned his attention to Eddie, who had just entered the dormitory with his laundry bag, and in time to the slow shake of his head, the head prefect uttered, 'Eddie, Eddie, Eddie!'

CHAPTER 22

As we skipped down the passage way, leaving the prefects' dormitory, Mutt and I looked to each other and pumped our fists with a great, 'Yes!'

After dressing in dark clothes, we passed the masters' office before Duke finished with the lights out procedure in the middle and senior dormitories, probably taking longer than usual, fumigating each dormitory. After 10 minutes, Mango came down stairs, peered into the senior prep room and whistled. All sixth formers stood on cue and gathered around. He peered into the dining room at Mutt and me.

'Follow us!'

Together, all sixth formers, including the prefects, Mutt and I set about on foot into the dark of the night, me carrying the bomb! Mango had obviously done a fine job in convincing Duke that he ought to recover the bell. My guess is that he revealed little else.

We briskly marched for half an hour until we came upon King's College, the only other school in the small city. Unlike ours, their hostel was contained within the school premises, the front door overlooking a rugby field some five tiers of concrete terraces below.

Standing under cover below the terraces, Mango clicked his fingers to get my attention and nodded towards the front door. 'See if it's open!'

Me? I wondered why, before quickly surmising, of course, me! Just in case there's an ambush!

I started to walk towards the front door.

'Crawl, you poop!' Mango whispered loudly, agitated.

'Huh!'

'Leopard crawl!' the head prefect growled.

I got down to the ground and inched forwards to the front door, got up and guardedly tried the door handle. The solid timber door would not budge so I looked back towards the terraces, ten faces and a dog peering over the top terrace. Unsure, I shrugged my shoulders.

Mango's hand pointed upwards.

Huh!

He shook his hand with vigour, betraying annoyance. My eyes followed until I caught sight of an open window on the second floor. Oh, yes! And how am I supposed to get up there? As if he possessed mental telepathy, Mango's hand drew a line in the night sky, tracing a drain pipe.

I crawled to the drain pipe and started to climb it. Damn! It was rickety. My heart pounded. Deciding that I should spend minimal time on the precarious drain pipe, I shinnied up like a West Indian coconut picker, each creak doubling the flutter in my chest. Finally I made it to the open window, but as I pushed off to climb through it, I felt the drain pipe creak away from the building, hanging aimlessly in the night sky. Damn! Now I'm going to have to find another escape route!

Inside the building, I stood in near darkness, in what vaguely appeared to be a corridor. Now where do I go? I wondered. I inched ahead, came to a T-junction and chose to go right. As I proceeded down a dark passage, a door creaked open, and someone appeared in the corridor so I quickly drew up against the side wall and prayed.

My pulse quickened but fortunately the night apparition proceeded down the corridor in the same direction I was headed. I peeped into the room he exited and vaguely made out a small dormitory of sleeping bodies.

Suddenly, a weird thought struck me. What the heck was I doing there in the middle of the night standing at the entrance of a dormitory of another boarding school? What if I'm caught? Damn that miserable excuse for a mango! As if to test my thoughts, a toilet suddenly flushed and disturbed the silence. The boy emerged and headed back down the passageway in my direction. With no time to escape, I had no option but to enter his dormitory and quickly duck under a bed.

The body entered. A silhouette of his legs edged closer and closer then flopped onto the same bed I was hiding under! Great! I had to choose *his* bed to hide under! Give him a minute or two, I estimated. Moments later, above me, I heard a snore. Phew! My cue to move on.

About to extricate myself from under the bed, I suddenly froze. The boy sleeping in the opposite bed thrashed around, removed his sleeping shorts, threw them to the floor and, whilst turning over to carry on sleeping, he mumbled, 'Aw, what a pity she wasn't real!'

I crept out from under the bed, exited the dormitory, tiptoed down the corridor in the opposite direction and discovered a flight of stairs. As I reached the bottom landing I saw the front door, and just as I was about to try to open it, I spotted a large metal triangle hanging on the door handle.

'Aah! That's our bell!' I exclaimed aloud.

I shifted the dead bolt, opened the door and triumphantly held the bell aloft for an anxious group of heads peering over the top terrace. After waiting a few moments to make sure the coast was clear, Mango and the rest of the sixth formers joined me on the brick paved porch.

'Tyke, you're late!' Mango scolded, then asked, 'Are you sure no one saw you?'

I nodded my head.

Mango gave me a steely look.

'Yes, sir! I mean no one saw me, sir!'

'Where's the mongrel?' Mango asked, turning around. Spotting Mutt, he held out his hand and simply said, 'Bomb!'

Mutt handed him the evil looking shoe box.

'What's it look like in there?' Mango asked me, but not bothering to wait for an answer, anxious to perform his deed, he entered the foyer. The rest of the prefects and sixth formers followed him. Mutt and I followed them.

Mango placed the shoe box on the floor in the middle of the foyer. A dozen faces congregated around it like a pride of lions at a kill, bruisers closer to the action. Mango struck a match and put it to the end of the lace that protruded through the cardboard box. As quickly as it ignited, we dashed outside. Mutt and I followed the rest of the pack to hide behind the top terrace.

The anticipation was tangible. I pictured the burning polish smeared shoelace, slowly entering the shoe box's backside, through the pack of dog bog on its journey to the mini-limpet mine.

'We should have rung the bell,' growled Grizzly, 'and timed the bomb to shit in their faces!'

Mango nodded his head slowly, his brain scheming, stole a quick look at Mutt and I, then finally back to Grizzly and shook his head. 'Too late!'

As the minutes ticked by, the excitement grew to impatience.

'Did you poops put enough polish on the shoe laces?' growled Mango, his piercing eyes locking onto Mutt and me.

We nodded our heads, then sang in unison, 'Yes, sir!'

'Then why is the fucker taking so long to shit?' he asked. 'Tyke!' he simply said, his head nodding in the direction of the foyer.

Damn! I glanced at Mutt, then back to Mango with pleading eyes.

'Fuck off, both of you!'

Mutt and I nervously rose from behind our safe haven and skulked towards the hostel entrance. As we reached the top of the stairs leading to the front door, a blinding light flashed, coupled with a deafening thunder clap. I instinctively ducked for cover that did not exist and felt a tornado of wind whoosh through the front door, splattering dog bog in all directions.

A moment of stunned silence.

I looked up from the ground to see a huge smile crease Mutt's face accompanied by a triumphant wail, shit splash lost amongst his freckles.

'Mutt! Run for it!'

I led the way, the dog snapping at my heels. We dived for cover behind the top terrace, turned to face the building and waited. After a few moments, I developed the sneaking feeling that we were alone. Looking first to my left and then to my right confirmed my suspicions. Damn! The seniors had vanished and deserted us at the outpost.

'Tyke!' Mutt cried out, sniffing their whereabouts. 'Mango and his cronies are on the other side of the field!'

A cacophony of excitement erupted in the foyer, followed by a spewing of bodies through the front door. Mutt and I leapt into action. We scurried down the terraces and sped across the field with our hot tempered rivals in hot pursuit. My heart pounded. Thoughts flashed through my head about the consequences of being caught. Nearing the edge of the field, we hurdled over the hedge and sped off in the direction of our own hostel. Never was I so keen to get back to Windsor House!

Ahead of us, I vaguely saw our sixth formers also running, some filtering off into side lanes.

At my heels, Mutt moaned, 'They set us up, Tyke!'

'Huh!'

As we ran past a side lane, I spotted two sixth formers waiting behind the corner of a boundary wall. Phew! At last a comfort zone, I thought, confident in the strength of our sixth formers. I turned down the lane to join them.

'You poops carry on straight to hostel!' bellowed the unmistakable voice of Mango.

Huh!

So Mutt and I continued running along the main road. A quick look over my shoulder confirmed that not thirty paces behind us was a posse of half a dozen or so charging greyhounds.

'They set us up, Tyke!' wailed Mutt.

Not comprehending my friend, I ran my hardest, my cross country training coming to the rescue. As we passed the next lane, I sensed the presence of more sixth formers lurking in the dark. The urge to join them and seek refuge was overwhelming, but Mango's bark carried a lot of bite.

'They set us up, Tyke! They used us as bait!' whined Mutt.

Back on the run, I turned my head to assess the chase and began to see Mutt's point. They had used us as decoys. As we lured the pack past the side lanes, our sixth formers picked off the stragglers one by one. The bastards!

At least the longer we ran, the more the pack diminished. Another two blocks, then suddenly no one! Mutt and I slowed down and stopped opposite an open park, panting heavily as we tried to catch our breath.

'Careful, Tyke! You never know what other stunts these fuckers might have up their sleeves!'

Like antelope in the bushveld, we looked this way then that to sense any danger that lurked in the darkness. All I could hear were crickets and the odd frog.

But Mutt put his hand up. A warning. He whispered, 'There's someone hiding in those bushes!'

Moving deftly from tree to tree, we stalked the hiding body, came up from behind and prepared to ambush. I looked to Mutt, he at me. Summoning up the courage, I pounced, suddenly hoping like crazy that Mutt had the same idea as me. Fortunately, he had. We hit the body with an Eddie-like rugby tackle. Mutt clamped his arms around the waist whilst I went for the jugular, wrapping my arms around his neck, squeezing for dear life. To our utter amazement, the body turned out to be someone no bigger than ourselves. Much relieved, Mutt and I quickly pinned him on the ground.

'Whoah!' the boy responded, 'Go cool, man! Go cool!'

'Get up!' ordered Mutt.

The boy rose to his feet, the streetlight revealing a boy with red hair. He started to dust himself down.

'Hey!' Mutt uttered with bravado, clutching the boys arm. 'You come with us!'

The boy protested, but Mutt would have none of it. I looked to my friend, but his eyes were fixed on his prey. Totally at a loss for what to do, I followed Mutt's instincts and clenched the kid's other arm.

'What smells?' the redhead dared to ask, clearly suffering the fallout of our dog bog bomb.

'Shut up!' Mutt barked.

Together, we frogmarched the kid back to hostel, oblivious that across many lanes in the city, so others were herding their quarries to the same destination. As we climbed the stairs to the front door, a certain swagger grew in our gait. By this time it was late and hostel seemed subdued. Mutt and I looked to each other and shrugged our shoulders, somewhat at a loss as to what to do with our prey.

'As we came up the stairs I noticed that the light in sickbay was on with quite a few shadows moving behind the curtains,' I informed. 'Perhaps that's where Mango and the others are.'

As we made our way down the corridor past the matrons' quarters to sickbay, a buzz emanating from beyond the door grew louder and louder. I knocked. No answer. So I guardedly opened the door and, together with Mutt, herded the boy inside.

No one noticed us. All eyes focused on the body lying on the bed in the far corner, with Bull pinning down the boy's legs and Grizzly embracing him in a bear hug. Beside the bed, Mango triumphantly held in his hands the same set of electric hair clippers that had tormented Eddie. A broad smirk lined his face.

'Take off your rods!'

The boy obeyed, immediately pulling down his sleeping shorts.

Accompanied by a loud cheer from the room, with one flick of the switch, Mango turned the hair clippers on and, with the deftness of an Australian sheep shearer, shaved the guy clean of his ball hairs.

'Next!'

One by one, the luckless boys from our rival school lost their short and curlies.

'That should teach you douchebags not to swipe our bell!' Mango lectured the newly shaven. 'Now fuck off!'

Suddenly Mango spotted the redhead boy at the back of the queue, desperately trying to hide amongst the herd to escape from sickbay.

'Whoah! And who's this little poop?' asked Mango, his eyes quizzical.

Mutt and I were both hesitant and said nothing. But Mango's raised eyebrows prompted my voice.

'Er, we found him in the bushes,' I said. 'He must have joined in.'

The redhead started to protest.

'Shut the fuck up!' ordered Mango. He then turned to Mutt and me. 'Well what are you waiting for! Hold him down on the bed.'

We did, Mutt pinning his legs, me half strangling the boy around his neck.

'Take off your rods!'

Unlike the rest, the redhead wore jeans and a T-shirt. He pulled his longs down, then his underpants.

'Oh fuck! The little poop doesn't have any ball hairs!' Mango mocked. Standing with his hands on his hips and shaking his head he asked, 'Now what do we do with him?' Suddenly his eyes lit up with a depraved grin and he ordered, 'Pass the clippers!'

With my left arm still throttling the redhead, I reached for the clippers on a bedside table and held them up for the head prefect. With the powerful feel of those electric clippers in my hands, a stark contrast to Pa's hand clippers that gave rise to my name of Tyke, my eyes pleaded with Mango.

'Er, you do it, Tyke,' issued Mango. 'I only do ball hairs!'

I switched on the clippers, the vibrations immediately sending waves of adrenalin through my veins. Slowly savouring each moment, under Mango's instructions I shaved off two swathes of hair, leaving the redhead with just a Mohawk tuft.

'Now fuck off with the rest of them!'

'But I'm not with them!' protested the boy.

'Huh!' exclaimed Mango, using my term for befuddlement.

'I dunno, man. I just ducked out of my house for a smoke!'

§

After Mutt and I washed up, we returned to our dormitory, looked at each other before retiring and nodded with satisfaction.

'G'night!' I called.

Suddenly Mutt called in a high pitched voice, 'Hey, Tyke! Loverboy's run away! He's fucking run away!'

My heart thumped in my chest. I looked to Eddie's empty bed and wondered if it could be true. But suddenly I remembered. With a shrug of my shoulders I whispered, 'No, he's still hanging out the window in his laundry bag!'

Lying in bed that evening, I pondered the incredible day I had just had. Inevitably, my thoughts turned to the girl across the road and I instinctively fondled my dick. A vision of her sitting on the porch parapet, tousled blonde hair cascading over her shoulders, boobs pressing against her tight blouse, teasing me with her legs propped up, sensuously sucking her popsicle.

§

I woke with a huge grin and bounced whilst making my bed.

'You look like the cat that's just had the cream!' Spazz commented as he arose.

'I have! Last night I discovered I can become a blimmin' father!' I beamed proudly. 'Now I know why everybody keeps a bog-roll in their gown pocket.'

'Really?' my friend questioned, slightly dejected, before admitting, 'Bugger! I'm still shooting blanks!'

CHAPTER 23

On the last night of the year, matron gave us a slap up Christmas dinner. At the end of the meal, the gong sounded for us to stand up and for the head prefect to say grace. But all eyes turned to Bum Lump and I wondered why, especially when he asked Pygmy to say grace. Afterwards, all the boys congregated around Pygmy and congratulated him. Being asked to say grace at the end of the Christmas dinner was the official announcement that Pygmy was to be head prefect the following year.

'Will all second formers stay on afterwards!' shouted Mango before disappearing into the kitchen.

Whilst all the other boys left the dining room, we sat at our table, waiting.

'What have we done wrong, now?' I wondered out aloud.

The head prefect returned from the kitchen with a huge tub of ice cream and plonked it on the table.

'The prefects have clubbed together and bought this ice cream for you. It's for all the shit you've done for us!'

An excited, 'Yes!' rang out from the second formers.

Despite matron's feast, there was always room for more, especially ice cream. Besides, this was well earned! Nine pairs of hands dug spoons into the tub of raspberry ripple as we devoured its contents. Eventually, the enthusiasm wore off. I groaned and just sat there holding my tummy.

'I feel sick!' moaned Hog.

The fat second former got up and waddled to the toilet whilst the rest of us just sat there, bloated and immobile.

Moments later Hog returned, reeking of vomit, and demanded, 'Pass the ice cream!'

§

The following day after school, I caught up to Spazz on the path back to hostel.

'What's the rush?' I asked.

'I'm free, man!' Spazz whooped with delight. He took the straw basher off his head and punched a hole through it, shouting, 'I'm fucking free!'

'Hey! You poops stop making such a noise!'

Oh, no! The unmistakable voice of Mango.

Spazz and I turned around.

'Two black marks each! And Tyke, before you go home, make sure you pack my clobber and take my trunk downstairs!'

THIRD FORM

CHAPTER 24

To be quite honest, I was a little excited going into third form. I'd be king of the hill. Well, sort of, at least king over the new poops. No more fagging. No more being at the bottom of the pile for all those senior to order us about at their whim.

Whistling to the tune of *He ain't Heavy, He's My Brother*, I walked up the stairs leading to the hostel with spring in my step, remembering with a wry smile the large trunk I dragged up to the prefects' dormitory only a year ago. Yes, I could smile now. No more Mango. No Grizzly. And no Bull.

As usual, Pa dropped me off early in the morning. Since most arrived back at hostel after a holiday as late as possible, usually just before supper, I didn't expect anyone to be there already. I thought I'd take my time, see where in the junior dormitory I'd be sleeping, book my wire locker in the ablutions, sort of check out my new domain. However, as I strolled into the junior dormitory, I unexpectedly found a new boy standing next to his bed, unpacking his clothes.

'Hi! My name's Tyke!' I greeted, curious at this new species.

The first thing that hit me were his eyes. With black hair falling away from a middle parting, his long greasy fringe curling around either side of his pale face to meet dark eyebrows that cowered menacingly over deep set black eyes, the boy stared straight through me for a few moments before saying with a deadpan face, 'My father died today!'

Unsettled by his statement, I recovered sufficiently to offer my sympathies, 'I'm sorry about that.'

'I'm glad he died!' the second former replied without a flicker of emotion, then jerked his head and turned to attend to his locker.

Bewildered, I left him in search of my own locker but not before noticing that he had several scabs all over his body.

'Yes!' I exclaimed loudly, discovering my name on a green Dymo label affixed to a locker that accompanied a bed in the far right corner.

My own corner and my own window. True, it overlooked the cemetery which made me the first line of defence against the smell of burning bodies emanating from Pushin' Daisies, but I liked the idea of having my own window. I quickly read the name tags stuck around me to see where the others would sleep. Great! Spazz next to me and Mutt next to him. Who was in the other corner, I wondered, only to be taken by complete surprise to discover Spider's name. Damn! What's *he* doing down here? I questioned to myself. Normally the fifth form monitor slept opposite the entrance door.

More bad news. At the foot of my bed, but banked up against the wall that led to the prefects' dormitory, would sleep Hog. Opposite him, against the window wall overlooking Windsor Road, Eddie. Good! They can square off at each other during inspection and lights out.

I stood next to my bed in front of my locker, surveyed the whole dormitory, took in a deep breath and felt good. No mouldy Vulture to foul up my air. No more Chief always defending Vulture, both promoted to the middle dormitory. Best of all, a whole new litter of new poops to satiate the sadistic appetites of the bullies.

§

At six o'clock on the dot, the bell rang for supper. I stood at my designated spot, second table on the right as one walked into the dining room. I breathed a deep sigh of relief. Although I was to sit at Spider's end of the table, it could just as well have been Scrote's. Both were table monitors for the two third form tables. I thought of my contemporaries at the table behind me and concluded that they would get no milk for the rest of the year!

Bum Lump walked in, followed by a new set of prefects, headed by Pygmy, the new head prefect. Standing behind the masters' table, perched on a platform, Bum Lump addressed us.

'Forthwith, there will be no more so-called working of second formers!'

Huh! A wave of indignation swept through the dining room.

'And fagging will be limited to the bare essentials such as polishing shoes, making beds and the like. Second formers will no longer be slaves to the whims of the lazy! Is that clear!'

'What the heck is going on?' I whispered, indignant.

'They're getting soft!' Mutt replied angrily. 'Soon they'll think they own the fucking place and it'll go to the dogs! There're gonna be major problems. You mark my words.'

'Yeah, this place is going down!' Spazz lamented.

All the third formers at my table echoed similar comments. We all turned to Spider, our fifth form monitor, demanding some response and interpretation.

He shrugged his shoulders before answering, 'You guys had it soft. You should have seen it in *my* day!'

You could cut the disbelief with a knife! *We* had it soft!

Spider continued, 'Probably one of you guys squealed!'

'Quiet, down there!' Bum Lump rebuked us. 'In addition, we are instituting an arrangement whereby you will be able to earn white marks by doing odd jobs, and these white marks can be used to cancel out black marks. If you want white marks, come and see me in the afternoon.'

As we sat down to supper, the others continued to moan.

'I was never gonna work the guys anyway,' Spazz enlightened, 'But Bum Lump mustn't take away my right to work them. I've earned that right!'

'Yeah!' we all agreed.

'Aay!' wailed Mutt. 'I mean, look at them. Look at that dodgy bloke with scabs. You'd swear he's been used as an ashtray. You can tell he's up to no good!'

But while the others continued to moan, my thoughts wandered off to the last announcement of Bum Lump's. Something about white marks.

§

We may not have had the power to work second formers, but being a year ahead, we still had the entrenched right of first choice. One evening, a few weeks into first term, I entered the showers. They were full, with four second formers waiting at the back wall. The best shower containing a second former was second on the right so I walked straight to it, waved the new guy out and, as if I possessed magical powers, he responded. It felt good!

I grabbed a two by four, turned around to face the shower room and surveyed the scene, especially the new poops. It struck me how much smaller they were, how much we had grown. And not just our bodies. Where we sprouted a bush, they displayed bald worms, just as we had a year earlier. All except Scab, the boy who seemed ambivalent about his father's death.

No sooner had I soaped myself when Chief entered the shower enclosure, asserted his right and kicked me out. That's okay, I thought. I simply selected the next best shower occupied by a second former. It contained Scab. With his hair full of soap and face tilted up to the spray, I tapped him on the shoulder, but he didn't budge.

Huh!

I tapped again. Still he remained under the shower, water cascading down his face.

Uh-oh! I looked at Scab. He was bigger than me. Stronger than me. Now, for the first time, he threatened my seniority.

'Scab! Get out of the shower!' I ordered.

His gaze dropped to my level, but instead of departing he stood his ground and glared at me with those cold eyes that were like bottomless black pools staring into your very soul. I felt everyone looking at me and a cold shiver ran down my spine. I knew I had to stand up to him.

'Listen here, get out of my shower!' I repeated, summoning up the courage.

But still he glared at me. After a few moments that seemed like hours, he slowly looked up into the shower spray and said, 'I'm full of soap. Just let me rinse it off!'

Against my wishes, I let him, but I took a small step closer to show some assertion of authority. With Scab taking his time, I felt desperate and eventually I plucked up the courage to tug at his arm until finally he grudgingly vacated the shower.

I walked in, relieved, but very annoyed with myself.

With the bouncy gait of an ape, Scab walked over to the shower that contained Quiff, a weedy looking second former, so named because of a huge tuft of hair that hung over his forehead.

'I'm nearly finished. Let me share your shower!' demanded Scab, barging in.

Quiff withdrew and stood in the queue.

Suddenly Mutt appeared in the doorway, assessed his options, went straight to Scab's shower and demanded, 'Out!'

Scab stood still. But Mutt grabbed his arm and yanked him out the shower. I sensed a huge relief from the other third formers.

After a few moments of silence, Zulu, a dark skinned second former, left his shower and Scab quickly filled in ahead of Quiff. Instead, Quiff turned to face the blank wall and soaped himself.

'Hey, are you cockshy?' asked Hog. 'Quiff, I'm talking to you. Turn around!'

Quiff turned his head.

'Right around!' Hog instructed. 'Come here!'

All eyes turned to Quiff.

'Are you cockshy?'

'Er, no,' replied the timid boy, probably unsure of the meaning of cockshy.

'Then don't face the wall and hide your cock!' instructed Hog. He then tested the new boy. 'Do you know what a cock is for?'

Quiff nodded his head.

'What?'

'For peeing,' he said quietly.

'Quiff, where do babies come from?' Hog asked, enjoying his new superiority. 'Where did you come from?'

Quiff's eyes lit up at last. He knew this one. 'Out my mommy's bum!'

Everyone laughed, causing Quiff to skulk back to the far wall and dissipate amongst other naked bodies.

Whilst Hog teased Quiff, I noticed Scab get an erection. Except for a morning glory, displaying an erection was taboo, even embarrassing. This would never have happened before. It would have received taunts of 'rabbit'. But now nobody said anything.

CHAPTER 25

The following morning in class, I sat still, patiently awaiting the legendary performance of our Latin teacher. Scratch was a middle-aged single woman. Tall, athletic figure, with short, dark hair, a face made up with dark eye shadow and plum shade lipstick, and always a short skirt. No doubt single because one sensed she was a man eater, gobbling up men in one night stands only to spit out their bones the following morning as she cast her eyes further afield for her next prey. She exuded sex, rough sex, so she captured our attention! I thought to the words of the song *Venus*, currently on the hit parade, 'She's got it. Yeah, baby, she's got it!'

Then it happened. Head buried in her book, reciting Latin, Scratch sidled towards the end of the table. Psst! Word spread quickly and all eyes rose from their books and stared at her as she rubbed her crotch up and down against the corner of the table.

Knock! Knock!

Damn! Damn! Damn! Not now! We collectively groaned.

'Come in!' Scratch answered, the interruption quickly stemming her flow.

'Er, Miss, the headmaster has asked us to collect your table and take it to the swimming pool to set up for the gala,' a second form boy announced with hesitation.

'Well, alright!' Scratch acquiesced, closing her book with a thud, peeved at the disappearance of her soothing tool. She turned to us and announced, 'Class, under the circumstances you may have the rest of the period off to do your own work, but please remain quiet!'

Bored, I held my head in my hands and switched off, annoyed that Scratch's ticklish performance had been interrupted. My absentmindedness turned to complete engrossment as I observed the dux of my class practise his chosen future career — dentistry! With a compass he drilled holes in his wooden desk, then picked his nose, rolled the mucus amalgam into little balls, then packed them into the holes before polishing it clean with a plastic ruler.

Deeply absorbed, a missile bombarded me on the head and woke me abruptly. I quickly retrieved the screwed up paper ball and looked around to see from where it was launched so that I could send it back with interest. Just then I caught Spazz's eye from his desk at the front of the class. He seemed beside himself.

'What's going on here?' asked Scratch, sitting directly opposite Spazz.

Spazz blushed. 'Er, nothing, Miss! Nothing!'

Out of shear boredom I unravelled Spazz's bomb with the intention of increasing it in size and lobbing it back to the sender. But some of Spazz's scribble caught my eye.

'Major sight! Get your arse here fast!'

I looked at Spazz, but he looked straight ahead at Scratch. Hmm! I raised my hand to draw the teacher's attention and asked her, 'Miss, please may I ask Basil for some help with my work?'

Scratch nodded. I arrived at Spazz's desk, but his eyes were still fixed directly ahead.

'Yes?' I whispered.

Without lifting his gaze, Spazz drew an arrow on a piece of paper on his desk and nodded his head forwards.

I followed his gaze right up to where my eyes had no business going, until I saw it. Wow! Suddenly those eyes grew wide in utter disbelief. In front of us, Scratch sat, without cover of a desk, her short cheesecloth skirt above her knees with her legs apart. But amazingly, she wore no panties.

I was agog, two sex-starved hostel boys gawking at this big hairy thing. It was no doubt true that it probably grew bigger and hairier with our fertile imaginations, but there it was, unmistakably a close-up view of Scratch's pussy.

With my hand absentmindedly scratching my balls, I felt a huge boner pushing out from my rods. Suddenly Scratch looked up from her book. Spazz and I simultaneously raised our gaze and smiled at her with all our innocence.

'Yes?' she enquired with a lilt in her voice.

'Er, nothing Miss!' I croaked.

I felt my face blush. Used to virginal penguins at my old school, not only was I caught red-handed, but my voice suddenly transcended up and down the musical scale in a series of high pitched wheezes and low purrs, the first sign of it breaking. With suppressed giggles behind me and an unconvinced teacher in front of me, I quickly added, 'This Latin, miss, it gets better *all* the time!'

'Well, don't just stand there, now. Get on with your work.'

'Yes, Miss!'

In quick succession she looked down at her book, stole a quick look at me with a sly smile before returning to her book again. Needless to say I instantaneously dropped my gaze to stare at our newly discovered treasure, stopping occasionally to remind Spazz to wipe the steam off his glasses!

CHAPTER 26

That afternoon, no sooner had I got dressed in my afternoon clothes when I felt the urge to go to the toilet. Bad timing! Since the period immediately after school was a popular time to frequent the bogs, they were always booked up, causing queues to form. I lined up behind Spazz and waited.

The toilet next to the urinal became vacant, so Spazz took his turn. Then the end toilet flushed so I walked towards it and waited outside for the door to open. Spider emerged. And since he was now a fifth former, this obviously meant that there was also a long queue in the upstairs ablutions! I entered and just as I turned around to close the door, Scrote tugged at my shoulder. Damn! Seniors had priority in toilet selection, so he kicked me out. Pressure rose in my gut, so I sat down on a wooden bench to dull the urge.

Finally Chief vacated the middle toilet. Clenching my bum cheeks in desperation, I waddled to the toilet, entered, closed the door, pulled down my trousers and under-rods and was about to sit down when I nearly passed out from the smell.

Phoof! Major hostel rule: Never follow Chief in the toilet pecking order. Matron fed us the same food, yet, amazingly, all 50 boys processed her rations with different degrees of efficiency and with a great variety of smells. Chief stored up for long periods, building up a ghastly odour that he evacuated once a week. I opened and closed the window in quick succession to clear the fog.

To make matters worse, if the urinal was fully occupied, the boys would urinate in the toilets, and since many never lifted the wooden seats, they became permanently soaked with urine. I quickly lined my seat with toilet paper and sat down to do my business. Relief!

To my left, Scrote farted, prompting someone to shout from the direction of the wire lockers, 'Hey, Scrote, close your lunch box! You stink!'

Scrote's fireworks and the legacy of Chief! What a concoction! I rather hoped no one was going to light up a cigarette. Smoking was strictly taboo, and therefore often clandestinely done in the toilets. I knew Spazz was not a smoker, and I surmised Scrote would commit suicide if he lit a match, so I reasoned I was safe!

The deed done, I wiped my bum, for what it was worth! The cheap toilet paper matron allocated to us resembled old wartime rations, more like greaseproof paper that smeared rather than wiped. As I reached for another piece of paper I spotted a fleeting glimpse of Scab staring through the window. He quickly ducked.

Huh! What the heck! I shook my head in disbelief, unable to understand what pleasure he took in seeing me wipe my bum. Bewildered, I stood up and started to pull up my under-rods, wondering if I had imagined it.

'Bangled!' I heard Scab shout through the window of Spazz's toilet. 'Pulling your wire!'

'I wasn't pulling my wire!' defended Spazz. 'You're just fucking blind, man. Probably from pulling *your* wire too much!'

'Bangled, Spazz! You *were* pulling your wire! You're a rabbit!' sniggered Scab, before running off to brazenly tell of his discovery, knowing that with Spazz still occupied in the toilet, the third former was unable to do anything about it.

Spazz probably was pulling his wire, especially after class that morning. Everyone masturbated. Everyone masturbated frequently. And everyone knew that everyone else masturbated. But the unwritten rules of masturbation were clear. Do it, or be labelled a wimp, but don't be seen to be doing it or risk being called a rabbit! Except, of course, during a competition.

The action of Scab, a second former spying on a third former in the toilet and then accusing him of being a rabbit was unheard of, transgressing borders which, in the past, would have warranted severe punishment.

Most second formers were wide-eyed at such a flouting of protocol, but deep inside they probably secretly relished the challenge to the deeply entrenched hierarchy. The fourth formers, the most senior in status in the junior ablutions, outwardly ignored the incident. They appeared above it all, and besides, they were not directly attacked. But the air amongst the third formers was tense, except for Eddie. Perhaps because he was stronger than Scab and bigger below, he was unconcerned. I secretly wished to intervene and put Scab in his place but his sheer size and arrogance intimidated me, and I wasn't even sure of backup from my peers. Finally Mutt broke the silence.

'*You're* the fucking rabbit, man! Perving on someone taking a shit! Now get out of here!' Mutt barked. 'They should never have taken away working!'

'Remember Scrote's gauntlet,' piped up Hog. 'That would put them in their place!'

I shuddered when thinking about the previous year and Scrote's dreaded gauntlet. Yet, hard as it may seem, it occupied us and eventually drove me to do cross-country.

Just then I overheard Zulu. Whilst pulling on his cricket boots, the second former who was destined to become one of the most talented sportsmen ever to grace the school sport's fields, mumbled, 'If you're so bored, why don't you play cricket or some other sport instead of watching us wipe our bums!'

'Hmm! He seems an okay guy,' I remarked to Mutt, standing alongside me.

Mutt stopped halfway through tying his shoelaces, raised his gaze and looked long and hard at Zulu. Turning his attention to his laces again, he slowly shook his head and commented, 'Can't trust a beak like that!'

Mutt's comment puzzled me, so I changed the subject.

'Talking of noses,' I said, aware of Mutt's penchant for rubbing his snout with a curled up finger anytime talk centred on money, 'remember Bum Lump mentioned something about white marks?'

Mutt wailed and then cut me short, 'That Bum Lump's a charlatan, trying to get us to be his lackeys. There's no way he's gonna get me to graft just to avoid being caned. No way, man!'

'Hmm!' I thought quickly to convince Mutt. 'But what if we could make some cash from white marks?'

'Aay!' wailed Mutt, rubbing his nose before shaking his head in disbelief. 'Trust Tyke to come up with a plan to build up his coffers from white marks.' Despite the ridicule, with his interest piqued he asked, 'So what's this scheme of yours?'

'I'll explain later. First we need to earn some.'

We walked across to Bum Lump's house, knocked on his front door and waited, feeling somewhat out of place. The door opened and Bum Lump's wife appeared.

'Yes?' she enquired.

Mrs Bum Lump was a librarian at our sister school only a few miles away. Grey-haired bun, stern, spectacles, but with a difference. The boobs on her chest heaved up and down each time she breathed in and out, making it hard to look away from them.

'Er, may we see your husband, please,' I asked, eventually pulling my eyes away from her mammary glands.

Bum Lump's wife left and was replaced by Bum Lump.

'Yes? What do you want?' he demanded in a gruff voice.

'Er, we want to earn some white marks, sir!' I replied.

Bum Lump raised his one eyebrow, as if surprised that Mutt and I would deign to work to avoid being caned. He then issued our tasks.

'You two can wash and polish my car for four white marks each,' he explained. 'Come to the kitchen door and I'll give you a bucket and polish.'

After 15 minutes of slogging away washing and polishing Bum Lump's mustard Vauxhall station wagon, with only the car radio breaking the tedium as I whistled along to songs like *My Belle Amie, Bridge over Troubled Water, Let it Be* and *Who'll Stop the Rain,* Mutt questioned, 'Tyke you'd better have a bloody good reason for us slaving away on Bum Lump's behalf.'

On putting the final touches to our spiffing efforts, I asked my friend, 'Would you have cleaned Bum Lump's car if he offered you 20 cents?'

'Aay!' wailed Mutt. 'For 20 cents I'd offer to clean his fucking backside too!'

'Well, I suspect, come Sunday evening's hit parade, that Hog would pay, say, five cents per white mark to avoid being caned,' I explained.

'You're a fucking genius, Tyke! A skinflint genius!' wailed Mutt like only he could, his eyes lighting up as if he'd seen the way to eternal life. Then feeding the coals to fire his brain, he counted aloud using his hands, 'Four white marks at five cents each ... that is, er ...'

'Twenty cents!' I eventually added, putting him out of his mathematics misery.

'Fuck, 20 cents, and I don't even have to clean Bum Lump's backside!' Mutt sang.

Just then, Bum Lump appeared, his face flushed red and his eyes wild. 'Not only have you forfeited your white marks for talking about me in such foul language, but you come and see me this evening and I'll tan your backsides. The both of you!'

CHAPTER 27

Whilst opening my locker that evening to swap shoes for flip flops, deep in thought about that afternoon's incident, I absentmindedly let rip a fart.

'Hey, Tyke! Why did you waste your bowel breath?' Hog dribbled from his bed, breaking my musings. 'You know the rule. Share your spare air!'

'Okay! Okay! Don't squeal your head off!' I replied, knowing that Hog was collecting farts in his mother's cake tin, professing to make the ultimate fart bomb. 'Relax, here comes another.'

Not that I wanted to give Hog the satisfaction, but for some strange reason we all complied to humour him, so whilst he rummaged through his locker to find the famed cake tin amongst his beloved stash of comics, I walked over to Hog's bed and bent over. He prised open just the smallest crack and quickly covered my bum so as not to lose the countless farts he had captured. At the same time that Hog blew a massive bubble of *Wicks* bubblegum that was to burst over his piggy face, I pushed out the other end, the eruption reverberating in the tin, mixing my brand with all the others.

'Yuck, Tyke! Did a rat crawl up your bum and die?' he asked as he deftly closed the tin. 'It's worse than that pong of burning bodies coming through your window. Er, it's vegetable rack!'

Hog had a brand for every fart. Vegetable rack, burnt rubber, earthy, dog bog, sweet milk, wet washing and to top it off, gravy! You name it, he had it!

As I walked back to my locker to address my footwear, I took comfort in knowing that Hog's mom would repeat the favour one day by reusing the same cake tin to supply her son with her famous chocolate cake. Somehow the thought of my fart being in his cake tin did not seem so bad after all!

Suddenly Mutt broke into a wail that drowned out *Pretty Belinda*, the song that blared out from Perve's radio. We all looked up and saw the mongrel standing on the window sill above Eddie's bed, staring intently out the window across the street.

'What's up?' asked Spazz.

'That chick is parading for us again!' announced Mutt excitedly. Then clapping his hands and wailing as he spoke, he made the claim, 'I swear she wants us, man. Get any closer and she'll suck us up like those Hoover vacuum cleaners!'

We quickly clambered up onto Eddie's and Perve's beds, which overlooked the road, and gawked. Whereas we would once peer out the window to check out passing bikers on their Harley Davidsons, now we perved the girl who lived in the lane off Windsor Road. Barely discernible in the evening light, Hoover, as she became known, sat on the porch parapet, a sight for sore eyes! We panted and drooled, and chanted, 'Hoover, Hoover, Hoover,' which prompted Mutt to wail even louder.

'Shut up, man. She'll think you're on heat!' Spazz jokingly scolded the dog.

Falling on deaf ears, Mutt took his cue from our favourite scene in a movie that was legendary at hostel, *Cool Hand Luke*, the scene when Dragline salivated whilst Lucy washed her car, and started barking. Spazz and I soon joined in, followed by the rest. Perve dropped his rods and flashed a brown eye.

'She's getting turned on!' proclaimed Hog, who scanned through a pair of binoculars that he would only ever share with Eddie. 'Look. She's drawing her legs up!'

'That's the same position I gave that sex change a mango kiss!' Eddie beamed proudly.

Suddenly Hoover upped and disappeared inside.

'Man, she fucking heard you, Loverboy, and ran away!' Mutt complained.

Shoes off, but still needing to put my flip flops on for prep, as I returned to my locker I asked Spazz in a low voice, 'What's a mango kiss?'

'Um, it's a French kiss. You put your tongue inside and drool!'

'Oh!'

Such talk reminded Spazz of the morning's incident. 'Listen, buddy, have you told the guys what happened in class today?

'No. Not yet!'

Beaming from ear to ear, Spazz announced, 'Tyke and I saw Scratch's pussy this morning!'

The dormitory went silent before a throng of bodies swarmed around us like bees at a honey pot.

Spazz sat on the edge of his bed and splayed his legs. 'I swear, she opened her legs like this and there in front of our eyes she showed us her pussy. No panties, man, just a big hairy pussy!'

'Bullshit!' Eddie challenged from his bed. 'I was there in class and no such thing happened!'

'Ask Tyke!' Spazz suggested, looking to me for reassurance.

I nodded my head.

'Aw, what does *he* know!'

'It's true, Eddie, she had no panties!' an agitated Spazz asserted.

'You guys are green, man, as if your balls haven't even dropped,' accused Eddie. From his high chair, his voice laden with scorn, he lectured, 'If a woman sits down you can't see her box, she's sitting on it!'

Everyone grew quiet and I wondered what he was saying.

Just then, Scab wandered in on the third form gathering, prompting Mutt to bark at him, 'Fuck off, you rabbit!'

'It's not like a guy's cock that sticks out in front,' explained Eddie. 'A box lies between a woman's legs. That's why you don't just lie on her to bang her, she's gotta open her legs. I'm telling you, man, she was sitting on her box! You couldn't have seen it!'

Huh!

'Oh, fuck off, Eddie! She sits on her arsehole!' Spazz argued.

'On her box!'

Spazz then grinned from ear to ear and remarked, 'Hey, Eddie! When you've screwed all those chicks you claim to have screwed, maybe you've been putting your dick in the wrong place!'

Eddie's face grew wild, his nostrils snorting.

'Maybe that sex change hadn't changed and he was still a guy!' Spazz laughed with his famed wicked grin.

Eddie marched over to Spazz's bed, red-faced, fists shaking with fury.

'Cut it out!' ordered Spider, our fifth form monitor who had entered the dormitory only a few minutes before. 'All of you know fuck all!'

That shut us up, at least for a moment! But Eddie, the self-proclaimed stud, couldn't stay quiet for long and challenged Spider's authority by proclaiming, 'That's not true. I *do* know. Who else here has even banged a bird let alone a woman?'

Spider glared menacingly at Eddie, silencing him, then turned to the rest of us and advised, 'You guys need a sex lesson!'

He turned around, opened his locker, bent over and with his bum sticking out at us he rummaged through his belongings. For a moment we were baffled, but not for long. Despite his buried head and his muffled voice, we distinctly heard him say, 'I've got a sex book you all need to read.'

A sex book! A stampede converged on Spider's locker. With the fifth form monitor's bed in the other corner, I arrived last at the mêlée. But fortunes changed. To his everlasting credit, Spider threw the book over his shoulder and like an old maid on the shelf, I watched it soar up into the air like a bride's bouquet, up, up, and away, over the seething mass in surreal slow motion before crashing down with a thud into my open hands.

Huh!

Eight pairs of eyes turned around and glared at me so downheartedly

I almost felt guilty. *I* had the sex book!

'Dibs after Tyke!' Hog slobbered.

In quick succession, the rest of the pack booked their turn to read it. All except Eddie, who looked at me and spat, 'Just as well. You need it most. I know all that shit anyway!'

I looked down at the booty in my hands, a moth eaten, dog-eared book without a cover, a book that had been passed down over the years. My heart beat wildly. A sex book and it was all mine! I quickly sought solitude on my bed, but the horde followed.

Thankfully, the bell rang for prep. Not wasting a moment, I hid the book under my shirt and took it with me. Pretending to do homework with a large text book open on the table, instead I held the sex book down on my lap, my wide eyes glued. Hmm! Let's get to the juicy bits, I thought, so I cradled the book on its spine and just let it open to the most frequently read page.

Huh!

Before my eyes I saw a drawing of a couple copulating. Wow! They resembled two dogs mating, I thought, prompting me to look up at Mutt, but he seemed fully focused on rear-ending his homework books.

Back to the sex book! The header at the top of the page read, 'Positions'. Er, maybe I'd better back track, I thought. My hand fumbling, I quickly opened the book towards the front and saw another drawing titled, 'Female Anatomy.' Gee, it looked like Eddie was right, I concluded. A woman's pussy *is* between her legs. Damn! Then what had I see that morning, I questioned myself. Maybe just her pubic hair. Damn! Didn't even see *that* thing, I deduced, on reading an annotation, 'Clitoris'. What *is* a clitoris? I wondered.

Interesting, this anatomy stuff, but desperate for something more juicy, I paged ahead to a chapter called, 'Foreplay.' Placing the book inside my text book, and tilting them both to hide away from prying eyes, I continued reading about things I couldn't have even imagined. Wow! So that's what a mango kiss must be. I looked to Spazz and chuckled to myself. He still had a bit to learn!

So ensconced was I in foreplay, the sharp clap of Duke's leather shoes failed to invade my subconsciousness.

'Hmm! Nice to see you reading, young man!' Duke commented, peering over his black horn-rimmed spectacles as he slowly walked past.

My body went as rigid as a cat dangled over water. Anxious, I tilted the text book a little more and breathed a sigh of relief when Duke walked two paces past me. Good I had escaped!

Suddenly his head turned and, with a beaming face, he commented, 'And history, too! I hadn't realised we have a young historian here at hostel!'

My history teacher reached over and grasped the book at the spine with one hand. 'Let me see what you're interested in.'

As he held up the text book, all eyes in the prep room turned to face the master on duty. At first, he appeared baffled. But that soon changed as his eyebrows rose higher and higher at the same time that his spectacles slid down his nose to reveal a steely glare.

'Good gosh, young man! I see your interest in reading! Stand up and explain this!'

I stood to attention as commanded, but so did my dick, pushing hard against my shorts. Duke's jaw dropped, his spectacles nearly falling off his face.

'Upstairs, at once!'

After waiting in the office for Duke to complete his inspection of the prep rooms, the master caned me four stripes. Were that the punishment, I'd have accepted it with a promise to be a saint for the rest of my life, with one minor exception — I wanted just another hour of reading the sex book before I would commence sainthood. But Duke committed the sin of sins against me. He confiscated the book!

I trudged downstairs with a heavy heart, but worse was to come. As I walked into the prep room I heard the murmuring from my peers. They too, noticed the absence of a book in my hands. I never looked at them, but I felt their eyes piercing into my back like shards of glass.

Sitting disconsolately there in prep, I felt claustrophobic, the need to get out. And it came in the form of a fart. Hostel had this bizarre ritual when, if one farted in prep, you had to go and stand on the porch outside to air oneself. I let rip.

'Who farted?' asked the prefect on duty.

Damn! Before I could raise my hand, Eddie stole my thunder and owned up to my fart.

'Go and air yourself!'

As Eddie rose, he looked at me with a smirk on his face. Fortunately, however, I felt another fart brew. This time I relied on a tried and tested method. I leant over and pressed my left bum cheek on one side of the chair, grabbed hold of my right bum cheek and pulled it across the seat of the chair and sat, stretching my ring like one does a balloon when trying to make it squeak. Holding my breath, I built up pressure and let go, sputtering like a motor bike, causing the loose wooden seat of the chair to vibrate loudly.

Everyone looked to me, especially the prefect, his eyes widening with disbelief. With my bum cheeks still jabbering away, I looked to the prefect and raised my hand, and without a word spoken between us, he nodded his head to give me permission to go outside and air myself.

'Why did you go and lose the sex book!' Eddie groused at me as I joined him on the porch.

'Huh! What's it to you? I thought you knew everything there was to know about sex!'

CHAPTER 28

A sombre mood descended on the dormitory after prep, not helped by the mournful background music of *House of the Rising Sun*. The collective disappointment amongst my peers for having lost the sex book gnawed at me.

'Ouch!' a cry suddenly broke the funereal silence.

Lined up for lights out, we all looked down the aisle at the second formers and caught the furtive movement of Scab's hand reaching over to the second former standing in front of him to nip his balls.

'Ouch!' another second former yelped.

'That's for calling me Scab!' declared the second former. He hated that. Scab then thrust out his pelvis and dared anyone to nip his balls.

'Aay, fucking rabbits!' Mutt cried out. 'What are these blokes starting?' Until then, it was considered taboo to touch somebody else in the genitals, lest one be labelled a rabbit. Mutt continued, 'I told you this place would go to the dogs when they stopped working.'

'Ouch!' I cried out, clutching my groin as the pain seared deep into my gut.

Caught unaware, Eddie had leant over and nipped my balls.

'Fuck, the disease is spreading!' Mutt wailed, shaking his head.

As my breath came back I demanded, 'What the heck was that for?'

'For losing the sex book!'

'Attention!' Spider shouted.

As Duke came in to pray, I knew that Eddie had stolen the high moral ground. I seethed inside. After lights out, I took off my gown and was about to place it on the same hook it shared with my laundry bag when Hog mumbled through his thick lips, 'Tyke, you've gotta get that book back!'

All eyes turned to me.

'Why? What do *you* want it for? Just ask Eddie. He claims to be a walking encyclopaedia on sex.'

'I dare you to go and swipe it back!' Hog challenged me.

'And I dare you to stick your head up your bum!'

'Chicken!'

I took a deep breath. Under pressure, I eventually agreed to. 'Okay. I will! I will!'

'If you have the guts!' Hog retorted.

That did it! I slipped my laundry bag off its hook, swung it in the air like a lasso and clobbered Hog on the head, sending him flying onto his bed. The pig started to bawl. But Eddie quickly came to his defence and swung his laundry bag at me. I ducked. He swung again. I ducked a second time.

'Leave Tyke alone!' Spazz called out.

With a third strike imminent, I spotted Mutt come from behind and connect Eddie on the head with his laundry bag. Suddenly there was a free for all as everyone in the dormitory grabbed their laundry bags and battled it out like gladiators. I stood back and couldn't believe my eyes, my hands beginning to tremble as I wondered what I had started.

Despite all his threats, Eddie had never before laid a hand on me. But this free for all gave him the perfect opportunity. Amidst flailing arms and swinging laundry bags, he sought me out and squared up to me. His menacing eyes betrayed a seething anger from deep within. Believing attack to be the best form of defence, I swung my laundry bag at him, but his strength beat me to it and his laundry bag hit my head like a medicine ball, knocking me out cold.

As I came to, I heard Duke castigating us in his sharp tongue. 'Line up outside the office, the lot of you!'

Thwack! Thwack! We each got two stripes.

Walking back from the office, I noticed Eddie extract a shoe from his laundry bag. My blood boiled. I hated him.

CHAPTER 29

Just as we settled down into bed, the lights switched on. Accompanied by a few of his mates and wearing his infamous brown gown, Spider marched down towards the end of the dormitory. My heart beat a little faster. Was he angry that I started a laundry bag fight in the dormitory whilst *he* was the monitor. Perhaps he had got in trouble for that.

As they neared my bed, Spider instructed his mates, 'Pull his sheets down!'

My pulse quickened.

Glaring at me with menacing eyes, Spider demanded, 'Where are the hair clippers?'

A raging Spider and hair clippers meant one thing. My ball hairs were soon to be history.

'In my locker,' I replied meekly, instinctively drawing my legs up.

'Get them!'

I climbed out of bed with great trepidation, opened my wooden locker and retrieved the clippers that were last used when Mango shaved the ball hairs of those unlucky guys who had dared to steal our bell. After Mango left, I commandeered them and kept them in my locker. As I turned around to give them to Spider, I noticed that his mates had already pulled the sheets off Eddie's bed. When Spider snatched the clippers out of my hands and marched over to Eddie's bed, I felt enormously relieved.

'What's this for?' Eddie demanded, lying there.

'Oh, Eddie! You should know! You're the only one who's ever screwed a chick, eh!' Spider spat in a voice laced with sarcasm. 'The only thing you've ever screwed is your hand! And after tonight it'll feel soft and bald just like the first time.'

'Oh no, man! Why don't you leave me alone!' cried Eddie, drawing up his legs.

'Pin him down!' Spider ordered, before spotting Scab who had made his way down to the third former's area of the dormitory. 'What the fuck are you doing here?' the fifth former asked before planting a fist into Scab's gut, sending him back to his bed with a sick grin on his face.

After Spider and his friends left, having shaved Eddie clean of his ball hairs, Mutt clapped his hands on the side of his locker and wailed, 'The only thing Loverboy's screwed is his hand! That's a good one!'

'Aw, you guys know shit. You probably don't even know how to wank let alone screw!'

'Okay, then let's have a wanking competition!' Spazz suggested.

As we all gathered near Spazz's bed at the end of the dormitory, pulled down our sleeping shorts and proceeded to masturbate, I noted that it was almost always Spazz who suggested a competition and I wondered why. The hive of sexual activity immediately attracted Scab. He skulked his way back down to the third former's end of the dormitory, placed his hands in his sleeping shorts and withdrew his dick, a specimen almost large enough to rival Eddie's.

'Fuck off, Scab!' Mutt ordered the second former. 'This competition is for third formers only!'

And for *all* third formers. Not participate and one risked being labelled, 'Cockshy!' Suggest a competition too often and you're labelled, 'Rabbit!'

No sooner had we started when Goofball finished. He always won the category for ejaculating first.

'You randy dog!' Mutt commented. 'Not a chick in sight and you shoot your load in no time! You're a fucking rabbit!'

For the rest of us there remained the contest of how far to ejaculate. Each ejaculation was carefully scrutinised.

After a couple of minutes Spazz announced, 'I'm cumming!' He did, though he could never win. He still shot blanks.

'Hey, better luck next time!' I consoled my friend.

Spazz took his lot well. At least he had an orgasm, I thought, unlike Eddie who so far was unable to muster any degree of a boner. I couldn't resist teasing him. 'Still soft and bald, hey Eddie!'

'Aw, fuck you!' grumbled Eddie.

Perve, too, had problems. With his dick curled under his ballbag, we just accepted his word that he had an orgasm. Whilst all others ranged about an arm's length, not Mutt. The mongrel started to moan like his wild counterpart on a hill wailing at the moon.

'Fuck off, Mutt! Get away from my bed!' ordered Spazz, clearly agitated that Mutt would ejaculate all over his bed.

I suddenly noticed Scab was back.

'Go back to bed!' I ordered.

Scab retreated to the fringe of the activity, hovered there for a moment, but soon returned like a scavenger at a kill.

'Piss off!' I ordered again.

This time he just ignored me, seemingly salivating at the mouth with the prospect of Mutt about to cum. So I shoved him, shouting, 'Go back to bed!'

Scab glanced at me with his eyebrows furrowed, as if I shouldn't even exist, then looked back at Mutt. His tongue started to twirl around his lips. Just then Mutt climbed onto his bed and went to the window. Like a Roman candle he exploded out into the haunting dark sky that hung over the cemetery, easily winning the competition.

Upon returning to earth, Mutt immediately spotted Scab and demanded, 'What are you looking at, you fucking rabbit!' He marched up to Scab, punched him in the face and shrieked, 'Fuck off!'

Scab slinked away, delighting in licking the trickle of blood running down from the corner of his mouth.

'Aay!' wailed Mutt. 'Walks like a bloody orangutan, just like he owns the place!'

With the competition all but over, Eddie's dick still hardly budged.

'A good lover takes his time!' Eddie maintained.

'Yeah, yeah!' Spazz teased.

'It's true, man. There's just nothing here to excite me!'

'Come on, Eddie,' I said. 'Surely if you can get your laundry bag to get a boner—'

'Aw, fuck you!' responded Eddie.

§

I lay awake until midnight to make sure that all in hostel had gone to sleep, got up, opened Mutt's locker to borrow his torch and set off to recover the sex book.

Inside the office I tried to open the top drawer, but found it locked. Damn! The second drawer opened, but nothing of interest there. In the third, all I found was a packet of Bum Lump's *Rothmans* cigarettes next to a roll of *Wilson's XXX* peppermints and a half-jack of *White Horse* whisky. I giggled a little. Bum Lump's wife forbade him to drink or smoke. So he tried his luck by indulging at hostel, always sucking a peppermint to disguise his breath before leaving the premises to return home.

Desperate to get into the top drawer, I carefully removed both the bottom drawers to give me working room, tilted the back of the top drawer from underneath so that the lock no longer caught, and released the drawer.

Aah! The sex book! I picked it up and kissed it.

Whoah! The punishment book! Curious, I paged through it. The last entry was for the whole of the junior dormitory, the indiscretion being horseplay. The previous entry was for me. Duke's impeccable handwriting indicated, 'Reading inappropriate material during prep!'

I returned to the junior dormitory and, despite knowing that Hog was next in line for the book, I placed it under Spazz's pillow and whispered, 'Dream on, my boy. A blimmin' big wet dream!'

Lying in bed I mulled over having to live with 50 boys. You slept in the same dormitory as boys, you showered with them, ate with them, even schooled with boys only. Sex starved, we called it. Yet we were all at an age when we longed for puss 'n boobs. It was all consuming.

CHAPTER 30

The following afternoon, whilst washing down some stale bread with standard sweet tea, I looked across at Bum Lump's house to see some second formers knocking on Bum Lump's front door. Still peeved that my money making plan died an early death, another idea came to mind.

'Mutt, regarding white marks—'

'Aay! No way, man!' Mutt butted in. 'Your last scheme cost my backside!'

'Just give me two minutes to convince you.'

§

Later that afternoon we approached the two second formers polishing Bum Lump's car and I made an offer to them. 'I'll give you four cents for one of your white marks.'

'Tyke,' Mutt whispered, 'You're off your rocker! What are you doing *paying* for white marks? It's supposed to be the other way around, man!'

I raised my hand to calm my friend down, then continued to trade, tempting them, 'Four cents will buy you an ice cream, a nice strawberry sundae and you'll still have enough for six *Wilson's* toffees!'

After toiling for half an hour the prospect of a cool mouthwatering ice cream seemed to hold sway.

'It's a deal!'

'Okay, make it 15 cents for four white marks,' I offered.

There was a degree of hesitation.

'You *are* going to get four white marks each. That's the going rate for polishing Bum Lump's car.'

The one second former started to protest, 'But that's *less* than four cents a white mark!'

'It's quantity discount!' I exclaimed, having heard my father use that term with regard to the trading store where he worked. 'Fifteen cents will buy you that strawberry sundae every day this week.'

'Tyke, where're you gonna get all that start?' Mutt asked me in a low voice, knowing that he and I never ever withdrew any pocket money.

I nodded my head for him to relax, then looked at the second formers and moistened my lips by twirling my tongue over them.

'It's a deal!' They both agreed.

As soon as they left, Mutt asked in an agitated voice, 'Now you're in shit! Where're you gonna get—'

'We've been back at hostel for five weeks now,' I interrupted. 'I figure that Bum Lump's going to have a haircut check any day, now. And when he does, remember that pair of hair clippers Mango used last year to shave those guy's ball hairs, well, I hustled them at the end of last year and now I'm going to establish myself as the official barber of hostel. Charge, say, five cents a haircut!'

As luck would have it, Bum Lump had a haircut check that evening, and I spent the following afternoon shearing heads, with Mutt cleaning up afterwards. We charged five cents a head. With the money earned, Mutt and I bought white marks at the rate of just below four cents each.

That Sunday evening whilst all those who were doled out black marks during the week lined up outside the office for the weekly hit parade, Mutt and I peddled white marks.

'White marks for sale! Only five cents a white mark!' I sang, walking up and down the line, holding up a chit of paper marked with four white marks, signed by Bum Lump.

Always the queue was headed by second formers, growing in seniority as it led away from the office, the reasoning being that the master's arm would tire during the hit parade. As the first second former emerged with a belting from Bum Lump, eyes screwed up in pain, hands clenching his bum cheeks, most of the second formers quickly raised their hands in unison.

'I'll take six!' one second former said urgently.

'Four for me!' another demanded.

As the chits started running out and the second formers evaporated from the queue, I confronted Hog.

'I need eight,' Hog mumbled.

'I only have six white marks left!' I replied.

'I'll take them,' Hog agreed.

'Six cents each!' I suddenly said, surprising even myself.

'What?' Hog complained, his lips dribbling. 'You sold them to the second formers for only five cents. You can't increase the price for me!'

'I'm down to my last lot. Take it or leave it!'

'Tyke,' called Pygmy, the head prefect who stood just outside the office, marking off the black mark list as each one entered the office to be caned, 'You're next!' Pygmy then turned to Bum Lump and said, 'Four, sir!'

I entered, bent over, received my four stripes and as I stood up I decided to overplay my suffering.

'Phew, he's in a foul mood tonight!' I exclaimed as I left the office and confronted Hog.

'I'll pay the six cents!' agreed Hog.

CHAPTER 31

A new boy arrived at the beginning of the second term. Though in third form at school, being a new boy at hostel, policy dictated that he was to be regarded as a second former for the remainder of the year.

One evening as we lined up at the end of our beds for lights out, the new boy, who stood directly opposite Scab, blatantly announced, 'I'm gonna pull my wire every night until it's as big as Eddie's!'

He drew back his gown, pulled his sleeping shorts down a little and held his dick in his hand.

'I want my cock just like Eddie's!' he said defiantly.

Eddie looked a puzzling mixture between pleased and annoyed. Pleased to be the yardstick, annoyed to be threatened.

'You're a fucking rabbit!' accused Mutt.

'That's okay, so long as my cock grows,' the boy replied nonchalantly.

The boy fondled his penis until it grew erect. Egged on by Scab, he started masturbating. Everyone stood aghast at his behaviour, especially coming from a second former.

'You're a fucking rabbit!' Mutt again accused him, this time in a high pitched voice, the dog clearly agitated.

'Attention!' called Scrote, the dormitory monitor for that week.

The new boy stood at the end of his bed with his gown left open, and his erect dick jutting out. Bum Lump marched into the dormitory to pray. He closed his eyes. We were supposed to, but never did. Instead we just stood there in utter disbelief at this turn of events. After evening prayers, with Bum Lump having marched off, we all looked at the boy, dumbfounded.

Mutt marched up to the new boy, cuffed him on the head and for a third time accused him, this time shouting, 'You're a fucking rabbit!' He glared at him, then at Scab, then again at the boy, and before scampering off to do extra prep, he ordered, 'Tomorrow, you move your bed next to the third formers where we can keep an eye on you. You can sleep next to Goofball.'

The boy neither agreed nor disagreed. Instead he just stared at Mutt with a sick looking grin.

We climbed into bed. As soon as lights went out, the new boy raised his knees under his blankets and a rhythmic sound amongst much giggling could be heard.

§

The following day as we lined up for inspection, the new boy claimed, 'I pulled my wire last night! I'm gonna pull it every day, two, three times a day until my cock is just like Eddies!'

'You're a fucking rabbit!' Mutt spat.

From that moment on he became known as Rabbit!

CHAPTER 32

Amazingly, over the next few months Rabbit's dick *did* grow. One evening as we lined up for lights out, Rabbit started singing his own words in tune to the Beatle's song that had just played on the radio. 'The long and wanking road, has led me to this ...' at which point he flung open his gown to reveal his new status to all in the dormitory. 'See! I told you I was gonna pull my wire every day until my cock looked like Eddie's.'

Whilst a murmur of sniggers emanated from the second formers, my peers waited with baited breath for the inevitable reaction. The air was tense. Eddie looked furious, peeved that his status of largest dick should be challenged. Being a smaller boy, Rabbit's dick appeared even larger. Eddie walked over to his locker, pulled out a plastic ruler and marched over to Rabbit.

'Measure it!' Eddie demanded.

'*You* measure it!' a smug looking Rabbit replied with a soft smile.

Eddie was caught in the cross fire of desperately wanting to prove that he was still king of the dicks, but unnerved at the prospect of having to touch Rabbit. The former won out.

Whilst Scab orchestrated a chanting of Rabbit's name amongst the second formers, Eddie bent down, grabbed the dick of his rival in the most well-endowed stakes and measured it, all the while Rabbit wearing a sick looking grin on his face.

Then Eddie hauled out his dick, pulled it by its cherry and placed the ruler against it.

'Mine's bigger!' Eddie claimed.

'That's cheating!' I said. 'You were pulling your wire. Well, I don't mean pulling your wire, but stretching it!'

Eddie looked at me furiously, his manhood threatened.

Rabbit interjected and announced with confidence, 'That's okay, Eddie. I'll just carry on pulling my wire until it's as big as yours. I want my cock to look just like yours.'

As I looked at Rabbit returning to his bed, shaking my head in disbelief, without me realising Eddie pulled the one end of the ruler back and jerked it, snapping me in the balls.

I doubled over in agony, grabbing my gut and holding it tight until the pain subsided. Damn! I'll get you!

§

The following evening I bided my time. Whilst Rabbit and Scab nipped other second formers in the balls, Eddie's eyes turned to them. I crept low, slowly and quietly, placed my forefinger hard against my thumb until it turned white, aimed and then, with a quick nip action, let rip, the end of my finger smacking plumb on one of Eddie's balls with the cold cracking sound of two snooker balls colliding.

Eddie let out a deep agonizing groan as he doubled over. I revelled in the revenge.

My nemesis raised his head, gasped for air and went down again. He repeated this action a couple of times.

Oops! Had I gone over the edge? I wondered. Staring at Eddie, my skin started to tighten with concern, so at first I did not notice. Suddenly I felt it, a hand by my crotch, gently stroking my balls. I turned around to see Rabbit standing right next to me, grinning.

My body went rigid with shock. Instinctively, I punched Rabbit in the face. His head snapped back. So uncharacteristic was my reaction that I trembled all over. I was shaken, confused and angry, but I stood my ground. Rabbit recovered upright. A slight trickle of blood ran from his nose. He wiped his forearm across his impassive face before breaking into that same sick grin of satisfaction.

'Way to go, Tyke!' Mutt said proudly, nodding his head with satisfaction.

'What's this commotion?' asked Bum Lump in a raised voice as he walked into the dormitory.

Before I had a chance to speak, Rabbit said, 'It's me, sir!'

'See me after lights out!' replied the master on duty.

§

Knowing that I was equally guilty, I joined Rabbit at the office and waited for the master on duty to return from his round of lights out duty.

'Do that again and it will be the last time!' I warned Rabbit.

Again, the same sick looking grin of satisfaction.

'What's this?' the master asked of Rabbit as he came back to the office. 'Horsing around again?'

We followed him in. Bum Lump fetched his cane.

'Bend!' he instructed Rabbit, who was closest.

As Rabbit bent over, he let his gown flap open. He wore no sleeping shorts. And still that same smug look on his face.

Thwack! Thwack!

Rabbit rose, an erect penis proudly projecting from his gown. He turned towards the master and thanked him, a big grin on his face before leaving the office.

Wow! Is Bum Lump blind? I wondered.

My turn next. Thwack! Thwack!

I left the office, not amused. Just outside the office, Rabbit stood with one foot on a bench and held his gown back.

'Check my arse!' he said proudly.

It was black. Bruised with welt upon welt striped across his backside.

'Feel the lumps!' he said, slowly stroking his palm across his bum, his eyes fixed on me.

I returned a steely glare, pointed my finger into his face and threatened him. 'Remember what I said!'

After returning to our dormitory, Rabbit jumped onto Scab's bed, lay on top of the second former and thrust his pelvis in and out. Walking down the aisle, my mind shrugged its shoulders at the lack of resistance from Scab. A new behaviour swept through the hostel and it affected all of us. Like a dog attracted to a bitch on heat, a boy would go up to another boy and thrust in and out with his groin, laugh about it, then go and do it to another boy. It slowly grew on us. What previously would have been unacceptable and elicit severe condemnation and punishment was now tolerated.

'Aay! It's gotta be Thursday night,' Mutt mused, heading off in the other direction to do extra prep. 'Look at those fucking rabbits pretending to bum-rush each other!'

Spazz agreed. So did Perve and Goofball, but not Hog nor Eddie, both of whom kept quiet. But we did nothing. There seemed nothing we could do.

CHAPTER 33

To help keep us sane, every Saturday evening we would rearrange the dining room furniture into our own makeshift theatre and watch a movie. Usually the movies were a few years old and I suspect they were rented at a charitable rate so the choice was potluck. Mostly they were B grade, but every so often a movie tickled our fancy. We especially liked comedies such as *The Party, The Odd Couple, The Love Bug* and the *Carry On* movies, and westerns like *Cat Ballou* and *True Grit.* Obviously we gawked at any movie with our sex goddesses.

But it was the macho movies that achieved almost mythical status. *Cool Hand Luke,* of course! The likeable pair of outlaws in *Butch Cassidy and the Sundance Kid* getting up to mischief against the bouncy score of *Raindrops Keep Falling On My Head.* Steve McQueen's unforgettable motorcycle ride in *The Great Escape.* Richard Burton and Clint Eastwood's death defying cable car fight in *Where Eagles Dare.* Cheering the all-star cast in *The Dirty Dozen* against the overwhelming odds of, 'Dem doity Nazis'. *Kelly's Heroes* gave us both a hero in Oddball with his madcap antics and another song to sing, *Burning Bridges.* And the haunting score in *The Good, The Bad and the Ugly* had us whistling for weeks on end.

'I just wish for once we could get parole on Saturday and go to a drive-in,' Spazz said as we changed our shoes for flip flops to get ready for the movie.

'Yeah?' I responded tentatively, breaking into my whistling of *Cracklin' Rosie.* I had never been to a drive-in.

'Yeah! You get a double feature for the price of one which gives you extra time to pick up chicks.'

Two for the price of one! That piqued my interest. Wishful thinking, though, since every Saturday night was spent at hostel. That night we watched Neil Simon's *Barefoot in the Park.* At least it had Jane Fonda to perve at.

The following morning matron gave us our usual Sunday breakfast treat. Instead of glutinous porridge, we indulged in a treat of a bowl of Rice Crispies or Post Toasties. After breakfast on Sundays, most boys went home for the day. Not Mutt and me. We lived too far away. Usually, on average, five to ten boys remained behind.

'Tyke, next week you must join me and come to church,' Spazz announced as he attended to his tie, making a sloppy parallel knot instead of a Windsor.

'Huh!' I mused out aloud. I knew Spazz's father was the reverend of a church, but it surprised me to hear that not only did Spazz seem keen to go to church, but that he invited me too.

'Sure, it's where you meet chicks. They're a bit prim and proper but they call me their mascot and just seem to fall all over me!'

My skin tingled with mixed feelings at the prospect of meeting girls. I loved the idea, but it also made me nervous. I nodded my head, just enough to show some interest, but short of excitement because of my apprehension.

'That's it, then,' decided Spazz. 'It's a date for next Sunday!'

My heart suddenly beat like war drums. To quell my nerves, my mind turned to food and I suggested to my friend, Mutt, 'Let's go and scout out the guava tree.'

Every boy at hostel had been eyeing the guava tree for weeks.

'No man, the guavas are still green. They'll give you Gippo guts,' Mutt rejected. 'I've gotta go and graft!'

Knowing the dilemma Mutt felt between his work ethic and the chance for a freebie, I tried to sway the balance. 'Come on, you can do your work later. Now's the time, when everyone's away. If we leave it any longer, the seniors will scoff them and we'll get nothing!'

'Aay!' Mutt wailed, nodding his head in agreement.

The guava tree, which also served as the stopping point for the Hurdy Gurdy ride, was laden with green guavas in different stages of turning yellow. We climbed the tree and perched in the fork of two main branches. I picked the only true ripe guava on the tree, opened my gob and sunk my teeth into it.

'Worms!' I commented nonchalantly, then proceeded to take another bite.

'Good protein!' mumbled Mutt through a mouthful of guava. He smacked his lips, held up the guava and commented, 'This is good chow, man!'

'And good to be free of those animals, Scab and Rabbit, even if it is only for one day!' I exclaimed.

'That's an insult to animals!' asserted Mutt. 'There's no rabbit behaviour in the animal world. My ol' man says that if you put rats in a cage they will multiply and eventually their behaviour starts to go to pot. They start bum-rushing each other just like Scab and Rabbit. But you never see that in the wild.' He then shook his head in disgust. 'They're all fucking rabbits. They should never have taken away working. Now they act like they own the place!' After taking another bite, between chewing, Mutt carried on, 'The problem with the human race is that we keep the weak alive. We should cull them. Cull the species at birth.'

Although I did not respond, I knew my life would be better off had Scab and Rabbit been culled at birth.

As the morning wore on, we located in different spots in the tree for half an hour or so at a time, working our way around the tree from the inside to the outside, devouring every guava at an arm's length. Always we ate the guavas in a particular order, from the ripest first down to the greenest.

After lunch we returned, and by early afternoon my stomach griped, so I clutched it for comfort. I looked at Mutt. His face seemed to visibly turn green.

'I feel like you look!' I complained.

But like peanuts, which always taste like some more, my hand went out for another guava, a rather green specimen. I took a bite, mouthed the pulp as a cow chews the cud and swallowed. Then I took another bite, but was unable to muster the strength to chew. Like two bloated sloths hanging in a tree, we had eaten ourselves into submission.

Mumbling with un-chewed guava spilling from my mouth, I confided in Mutt, 'I feel ill! What are we gonna do because there's still cake to come!'

'We can't miss cake!' Mutt jibed, shaking his head, his enthusiasm for cake undiminished despite a day's stuffing himself with guavas. 'But I have an idea, an old remedy of my grandma's! Follow me!'

Slipping off the tree, I followed Mutt to the side of the fowl run where he withdrew a pocket knife from his shorts. He always carried one. Like a skilled surgeon, the artist in Mutt cut two stems from a canna plant, deftly sharpening the pointed end. Too uncomfortable to question him, I simply watched in fascination.

'Fill that bucket with water,' Mutt requested, as he put the final touches to the hollow stems, 'and come and join me in the storage shed.'

I returned with the bucket.

'Take off your clobber!'

My resistance to pursue any activity that entailed undressing inside a storage shed in front of a mad friend with a plan crumbled in the face of a sudden stomach cramp.

'Now get down like a dog and stick your backside up in the air!'

'Your grandma did this?'

'Aay!' Mutt wailed, his face lighting up with a grin for the first time that afternoon.

Naked, except for a pair of underpants hanging below my knees, I knelt down on all fours, stuck my bum in the air as Mutt had ordered and turned my head around just in time to see my friend take aim at my bull's eye before plunging the canna stem deep into my pouting bum. To

142

my amazement, he then poured water from the bucket into the funnel shaped canna stem, the cold water causing me to shiver as it gurgled on its way into every nook and cranny of my gut not occupied by guava.

'You're done!' Mutt announced calmly, as if he'd performed this operation many times before. 'Now my turn. Plug it in and fill her up!'

Like a petrol attendant, I repeated the operation and filled up Mutt's tank.

'Now?' I asked.

'Now we jump up and down!'

Mutt and I proceeded to jump on the spot but, being so full, we were no more effective than two fat seals performing a mating dance.

'Let's use the Hurdy Gurdy!' I suggested.

Dressed only in underpants, we hauled the rope to the platform in the avocado tree and set off together, bouncing along the cable like kids on a pogo stick, crashing at the bottom of the guava tree.

Mutt rose from the ground clenching his bum cheeks together with two hands. 'I can't hold on any longer. I'm gonna fucking burst!' he said, eyes popping. He turned to run to the toilets. He voiced the same feelings I felt. We ran for it. But soon our run turned into a waddle as our liquid insides sloshed around in our bloated guts.

'Mutt, I'm not going to make it!' I cried out. 'I'm getting the squirts!' My friend reluctantly stopped. Maybe desperation blurred my common sense, because I then decided that if I were going down, I might as well go down big time. Looking left, then right to assess the situation, I surprised myself by suggesting, 'Let's feed the fowls!'

'Aay!' Mutt wailed, his head shaking from side to side in utter disbelief. The challenge, though, appealed to a sense of mischievousness, for his eyes lit up when he commented, 'Tyke, you're a good 'un!'

We entered the fowl run, took off our underpants, herded the fowls into the far corner, bent over in their direction and let rip. Guava puree as good as Grandma Mutt could ever have made sprayed out and splattered the fowls with a case of freckles to rival that of Mutt's. To our utter amazement, the fowls suddenly set upon each other in a feeding frenzy, squawking and flapping their wings as they pecked off every last guava seed!

'Phew! Relief at last!' I exclaimed. 'Just remind me to pass next time matron gives us home grown chicken!'

Suddenly a voice yelled above the din. 'What's all this commotion?'

Recognising the voice, Mutt and I immediately stood to attention. Looking rather sheepish, we confronted Bum Lump, his face red, nostrils snorting like an enraged bull.

'Er, er, we're just feeding the fowls!' I said, without any hope of a reprieve.

And a reprieve we did not get. Thwack! Thwack! Thwack! Thwack! Thwack! Thwack! Six stripes each! And we were gated for a term, meaning we could not go out on Sundays. For Mutt and me this was hardly punishment since we never went out anyway. But now I couldn't join Spazz the following Sunday to meet his church girls. I felt a sense of relief!

To calm down we decided to go for a swim in the school's swimming pool. With more than half an hour to go to tea, I sensed that Mutt knew what I was thinking. Without a word spoken, we climbed out the pool, dried ourselves with mangy towels of the absorbency of sandpaper and set off walking back to hostel. A brisk, purposeful walk. I stole a quick glance at Mutt. All seemed fine. Suddenly, like Looney Tune's *Road Runner* he broke away, with me, the coyote, in hot pursuit. We consumed the short cut through the cemetery that led back to hostel in a cloud of dust, past the fowl run, through the devil thorn long grass and into the overgrown barn via the back door, bolted through the junior ablutions, then the foyer and straight into the dining room.

Damn! Mutt just edged me! I lined up behind him in the queue. Still half an hour to wait. Fifteen minutes before tea time, three fourth formers charged into the dining room and jumped ahead of us in the queue. With only five minutes to go, two fifth formers quickly walked in to take their allotted place at the head of the queue. Lastly, on the dot of four o'clock, Pygmy and his deputy calmly walked into the dining room, straight to the plate of vanilla slices and selected a piece each.

As a treat for those few who stayed behind on Sundays, matron would supply cake for afternoon tea, one slice per person. According to seniority, each boy in the queue walked up to the plate, carefully scrutinised and ranked the slices according to size before selecting their choice.

With two pieces of cake remaining, Mutt stood in front of the plate and took his time.

'Come on, Mutt, hurry up!'

But he seemed mesmerized, unable to choose. Desperate for my Sunday cake, I decided to force the issue, made my assessment and pointed to my lesser choice and said, 'I want *that* one!'

'No way, man, that's mine!' Mutt retaliated, picking up the slice and quickly putting it to his mouth.

I picked up the last vanilla slice with my left hand, then dabbed the plate with my right forefinger, squashing every crumb into a growing ball before slipping it into my mouth.

'Aay!' Mutt wailed. 'Cleaning the plate, eh!'

After wolfing down my slice of cake, I watched longingly at Mutt who picked at his, prising each flake of pastry and savouring it with a smacking sound.

'Man, this cake is good chow!' he commented, sucking his lips.

CHAPTER 34

As always, a dark mood hung heavily in the air that Sunday evening. Weekend over meant the return of Scab and Rabbit, Eddie and Hog and also Chief and Vulture. Also, another week of school on the horizon. And whilst the hit parade on AM radio tried its best to cheer us up with *Cha-la-la, I Need You,* hostel had its own hit parade, a welcome back treat of caning due to black marks.

For me though, Sunday evenings had a silver lining. Once again, Mutt and I paraded up and down the black mark queue like scalpers outside a hot concert, selling our ware.

Suddenly, Zulu, a second former offered, 'Four cents a white mark!'

'Huh!' I couldn't believe my ears. The audacity! A second former selling white marks and at only four cents. I was in a quandary for I couldn't very well tell him that he was not allowed to sell them. After all, I was not quite sure how legal the whole affair was. It had just kind of developed over time and I had to be sure not to ruin a good thing. Thinking on my feet, I countered, 'Three cents a white mark!'

Hands shot up. The black mark queue never had it quite so good. Deliberately taking my time, I sold two white marks at three cents each, undercutting my competitor, confident that I had enough stock to see me through. Zulu looked at his white marks in his hands, decided that it was not worth dropping to two cents and reasoned that he would use them instead.

'I'll pay you four cents,' I offered him.

Zulu accepted, then entered the office to be caned.

I turned around to face the queue. Next in line for my wheeling and dealing, Hog! Desperate to recover my loss, I announced, 'My price has just gone up to six cents!' The flesh on Hog's face sagged with disappointment but with no other option available he nodded his head in agreement.

'Hang on!' I quickly told him and turned to confront Pygmy. 'Hog's got eight black marks which he's going to cancel with these eight white marks,' I explained, holding up the chits. 'How about I keep them and take over his black marks, and I get caned instead of him!'

Pygmy looked bemused. The simple black mark system he once knew was not so simple anymore. I sensed black marks and white marks floating around in his brain, and now a new hybrid was on offer.

To sway his mind, I nodded my head and said, 'It's a deal!'

Once the confused Pygmy agreed, I addressed Hog, 'I'm taking over your black marks, so I'll be keeping these.'

'No,' Hog dribbled, being otherwise, knowing he was free from being caned that week.

'Then seven cents next week!' I warned.

'Okay, then.'

So, Mutt and I went on the prowl for more, taking back white marks for resale, though at the expense of a black bum. No matter, our bank balances were healthily in the black, too!

For two hours every weekday evening we were supposed to do prep. But after doing the bare minimum of homework, most of us would wile away the time doing the bare minimum of anything else. At the end of prep, the prefect on duty would sign our homework notebooks, checking that we had completed our work for the day. Instead of waiting in the queue, I found it a lot quicker to forge his signature, so one activity I pursued during prep was practising the prefects' signatures.

During one such practice session, I looked across at the hardworking Mutt. Instead of choosing history as an elective, like I did, he chose art. He insisted that one day he was going to set sail in his father's homemade yacht and paint pictures.

Mutt. Art. Forgery. I slipped my hand into my pocket, retrieved a white mark chit and looked at Bum Lump's signature. The cash register bell rang in my head.

After prep I approached Mutt and suggested, 'Instead of buying white marks and selling them for little more than a cent profit, let's forge the buggers!'

'Aay!' wailed Mutt but his eyes lit up. He was keen. Perhaps it was the artistic challenge!

§

But greed eventually was our undoing, resulting in a new rule that white marks could no longer be bought or sold. After weeks of major profit taking, one Sunday evening, with so many white marks floating on the market, one by one the recalcitrants of the week entered the office and handed in their white mark chits in lieu of being caned.

'Oops!' I exclaimed to Mutt. 'I think we've gone too far because there's nobody left to cane! It's going to look too obvious!' Lowering my voice to a whisper, I continued, 'As a precaution don't hand in any white marks tonight! Instead we'll have to choose to be caned to keep the system alive.'

Duke emerged from his office, a bewildered look behind his spectacles, confronted Pygmy and asked, 'What is going on here? Where

147

is everybody? Can it be true that all these boys have done odd jobs for Mr Sherman?'

Duke never took advantage of the white mark system. One sensed that he, an historian, was against the slave trade.

Pygmy shrugged his shoulders, confused.

Then Duke looked to Mutt and me, the only two left in the queue, ready to be caned. 'Good gosh! You two must be the only ones who don't believe in white marks! Inside!' As he followed us into the office to cane us, he could be heard, 'I'm beginning to believe the whole white mark system is corrupt!

FOURTH FORM

CHAPTER 35

When I arrived back for fourth form, out of force of habit I turned right on the landing, but suddenly stopped, excitedly remembering that I was now to reside in the middle dormitory. After locating my bed halfway down the aisle on the window side, I took in a deep breath and felt good. No more Scab. No more Rabbit. He had failed third form and had to repeat. But my excitement soon evaporated. From being kings of the junior dormitory, we were demoted in the middle dormitory, having to share it with half of the fifth formers, the other half residing in the senior dormitory.

I looked to see who slept next to me. Mutt on the near side. Good! Chief on the other side. Damn! Chief and Vulture. I had been free of them for a year, now their spectre came back to haunt me.

Where was Vulture to sleep, I wondered, hoping not opposite me. I searched the dormitory for his name tag on a locker, but could find none. Strange! Maybe he's in the senior dormitory, I surmised, so I quickly ducked in there but could find no name befitting the mangy piece of poultry.

'Yes!' I whooped with delight. 'He must have left!'

Despite escaping the clutches of Vulture's talons, however, my joy was curtailed by the nagging feeling of having to sleep next to Chief for a whole year. But not if I swapped his name tag, I quickly concluded. After looking around to ascertain that the coast was clear, I carefully prised the Dymo label off Chief's wooden locker and replaced it with another fifth former in the far reaches of the dormitory.

No sooner had I done the deed when I concocted a better plan. Why not promote him to the senior dormitory! On the verge of implementing another name change for Chief, in he walked and put paid to my scheme.

'Howdy, pardner!' Chief greeted in a cowboy drawl to make John Wayne proud, and held out his hand.

§

'Tyke, I met this babe at our church's New Year dance,' my friend Spazz announced later that evening. With a grin that stretched from ear to ear, he trumpeted his *coup de grâce*, 'And I danced the night away with her

149

wearing this big boner!'

'Yeah?'

'Yeah! They put on *Love is a Beautiful Song,* you know, a waltz, so I huddled with her and pushed my dick right up against her leg. Man, it drove her wild 'cos she clung to me like a baby the rest of the night!' My friend then asked, 'Did you meet any chicks?'

'Well, I, er ... not really,' I hesitated, thinking of my boring holiday and the only girl in my hometown, Miriam.

'Why don't you ever speak about chicks? Aren't you turned on by them?' Spazz asked before turning his attention to packing away his clothes.

I felt awkward. Embarrassed.

§

A few weeks into term, I entered the junior showers one morning and headed for the shower without the rose. Scab was in it, washing his hair.

'Out!' I said.

'I'm just rinsing my hair!'

Ordinarily that would seem a reasonable request, but this was hostel. A junior must vacate a shower immediately for anyone senior.

Scab continued to rinse his hair and took his time. Uh-oh! Nervous adrenalin spiked through my veins at this confrontation and I sensed the juniors looking at us, delighted in seeing how far Scab stretched the new frontiers of freedom.

When Scab had mostly finished rinsing his hair, I again ordered, 'Out!'

He opened his eyes to thin slits and blurted, 'Fuck it, Tyke! I can't see with soap in my eyes.'

The third former revelled in taking his time and I didn't know what to do. Standing naked in front of another person showering, feeling like a spare part, was extremely awkward. Each moment seemed an eternity. My only saving grace was that none of my peers were present to witness this onslaught against my seniority.

Eventually, with his hair rinsed, Scab placed me on the horns of a dilemma when he started to soap his pubic hair. With new rules chipping away at entrenched authority, increasingly the law of the jungle of survival of the fittest applied and there was no question that Scab was stronger than me. He could have me for breakfast. Yet, if I succumbed to his challenge and backed off, I would lose all authority in the eyes of the juniors, and Scab would rule over me forever.

I knew I had to act immediately, so I placed my hand on his

shoulders to push him out but, being bigger and stronger than me, he didn't budge. Instead, he stared right through me with those penetrating hypnotic eyes, all the time lathering his pubic area. I felt desperate. I knew that *he* knew that I was angry but his response to ignore you, as if you didn't even exist, enabled him to subtly push the boundary rather than overstep it and risk intervention from a senior who could easily deal with him physically.

With what little remnants of authority I still had, fast eroding, I summoned the courage to grab him by the arm and yanked him out of the shower, emphasizing my action by shouting, 'Get out, Scab!' Reasoning that once in the shower it would be harder for Scab to lay claim to it, I quickly darted in, turned around and nervously awaited the fallout.

Amidst the rest of the second and third formers, Scab stood erect, pouted his chest like King Kong, projected a look of defiance on his face and demanded, 'Who the fuck are you calling me Scab?'

I knew that he hated his nickname, but I also knew that I had to hold my ground, so I retorted with, 'Who the heck are you calling me Tyke?'

'You can only push me out because you're senior to me,' Scab asserted. With his admirers relishing his defiance, he made a fist, pointed to his bulging biceps and said, 'You see this! If I were in the same form as you, I'd fuck you up and take that shower away from you!'

With a voice in my head screaming at me not to, I walked up to Scab, stared in his eyes and said in a sharp cutting tongue, 'Scab, that can never happen,' then pointing to my head, I continued, 'Because you don't have it up here!'

I stood my ground, shaking, quite expecting his first blow. Time passed. Just then, Mutt scampered in and Scab took a step backwards.

'You think you're such a know-it-all, eh!' the third former muttered. Waving his arms, he retreated further, gave the odd defiant but weak jerk of his head, grumbled, and left the shower room.

Phew! I felt relieved. A temporary stay. I turned to grab a block of soap but my trembling hands refused to cooperate. Desperate not to betray my inner fears, I stood a long time in the cascading water to drain away my shakes.

§

As I walked up the stairs to the middle dormitory, I felt relieved that Scab resided in the junior dormitory. But in the middle dormitory it didn't take long to realise that a new phenomenon had entered our lives. Pimples.

After dressing, I joined the mad clamber to comb one's hair in front of the lone puny mirror located at the entrance door, all of us singing *My Sweet Lord* with different degrees of efficacy as it played on the radio. Musical talent, or the lack of it, never prevented a medley of the same song in different keys. The shorties, like Mutt, and the blind, like Spazz, always burrowed under the multitude to get right in front of the mirror. But they were not always so lucky!

As I arrived at the gathering, I noticed that Eddie had finished combing his Vitalis plastered hair, but instead of retreating, he placed his comb in his breast pocket, moved in to take his spot, then with his two forefingers he scrutinised his face, focused on a ripe pimple and squeezed.

Pow! A head of pus shot forwards and hit the top left corner of the mirror. Mutt instinctively ducked, never to use the mirror again. He would hustle a hand held mirror and brush his hair by his locker. Using one's own mirror would ordinarily elicit an accusation of being a lover-boy, yet Mutt got away with it. Looking so mongrel, I guess he could hardly be accused of being a lover-boy.

Pow! Another pus bomb shot forwards and hit the short-sighted and unaware Spazz plumb on the back of the head. Splat!

Pow! Pow! Pow!

I instinctively took a step back and suddenly noticed that all the fifth formers of the dormitory had gathered around the mirror and were engaged in the same search and squeeze operations. All except Chief, who developed a novel way of avoiding the mirror. He had no pimples on his face, just a few on his chest. Not only had he the longest foreskin, his whole skin suit was a size larger than his body, and he used it to his advantage. Clutching with his paws he simply pulled his loose bear-like skin away from his chest, looked downwards, inspected, and squeezed any pimples he found between his two thumbs.

There were pimples, the odd spot here and there, and there were calderas, clusters of pimples. But in each case it was sacrilege to leave a pimple with a head of pus. It simply had to be squeezed. The reason was simple. Puss 'n boobs. And now the elimination of pimples. They were inextricably interconnected. To get puss 'n boobs meant eliminating pimples. Clearasil! Scrubbing! And lots of squeezing!

That morning, the vicinity of the mirror rained pus. Over a few weeks, the mirror would cloud over, making it difficult to know which of the bobbing heads in the dull reflection was yours to groom.

CHAPTER 36

When I entered the shower enclosure that evening, Mutt occupied the shower without the rose and Eddie the next best according to pressure. Scab stood in the third best shower, followed by Rabbit and Zulu in that order. Second formers filled the rest.

To avoid another confrontation, instead of kicking Scab out, or even Rabbit, I turfed out Zulu, who himself showed just the slightest bit of displeasure before kicking out another second former.

Damn! I felt a loser. Instead of striking whilst the iron was hot and imposing the meagre authority I had gained that morning at great cost, I shrunk from the challenge. I wondered what both Scab and my peers thought.

I looked at Scab. He had an empty plastic milk bottle that he always kept in the showers. He filled it with water, poured it over his head to rinse his hair of red carbolic soap, wiped his face clear of excess water, looked at Quiff, a fellow third former, held the container up and said firmly but without emotion, 'Fuck the bottle!'

Huh!

Quiff dutifully took the bottle, but just stood. Scab grabbed him by the head and drew him into his shower.

'Lift your cock up!'

Quiff did, exposing the underside of his dick and his balls.

'Now lean back!'

Quiff did, thrusting his pelvis forwards whilst at the same time Scab pushed the third former forwards so that the water from the shower rose sprayed over Quiff's genitals, quickly producing an erection.

Pushing him out of the shower, Scab ordered, 'Now fuck the bottle!'

Quiff inserted his dick into the neck of the bottle, and proceeded to thrust it in and out. Everybody looked at Quiff, who got on with the job impassively, seeming to neither enjoy nor feel uncomfortable with his ordeal.

I felt awkward. This had never occurred before and I wondered what had been going on in the junior dormitory. I looked to Mutt, but his eyes were fixed on Quiff. I felt powerless to do anything. I wanted to, but couldn't.

The other third formers appeared excited, and as moments passed a restless excitement spread.

'Come on, Quiff, I can shoot my load quicker than that,' teased Rabbit. 'It's just that my cock won't fit in a milk bottle!'

The third formers laughed. Eddie appeared peeved.

Then Rabbit started chanting, 'Cum Quiff! Cum Quiff! Cum Quiff!' stopping only to orchestrate the others into a ritualistic chant.

Within a few minutes, accompanied by a loud cheer, Quiff ejaculated, squirting the bottom of the plastic bottle milky white.

Quiff wiped back the tuft of hair that hung over his forehead and looked to Scab.

'Quiffy boy! You don't shoot blanks anymore.'

Quiff's face broke into a broad grin.

'Pass the bottle!' ordered Scab.

Quiff slid the bottle off his still erect penis and passed it to Scab who held his booty up to eye level and just smiled. He then placed the plastic container under the shower, half filled it with water, shook it like a racing car driver does with a champagne bottle, then poured the contents over his chest, beat on his chest with his fists and let out a wild whoop.

'Who's next?' he asked, his eyes surveying the second formers for prey.

'Giblet! Fuck the bottle!'

Giblet, a second former, stood in the corner. He was small, shy and still immature. His balls had not yet dropped and his dick resembled a little blob, so although his name was Gilbert, he inevitably became known as Giblet. He looked petrified.

'Come here!' ordered Scab.

Giblet walked hesitantly to Scab, head lowered, but his sad eyes fixed on Scab's.

'Come on, get a boner!'

Giblet stood there, unsure.

'Aw,' Scab imitated in a mock sympathetic voice. 'Have we still got a little wee wee?'

Scab grabbed Giblet by the shoulder, turned him around, leant over him from behind, put his thumb and forefinger on his tiny dick and pulled the foreskin backwards and forwards over Giblet's small limp penis.

All eyes looked at them. Silence. Scab continued, but nothing happened. No erection. And Giblet looked frightened.

Eventually Scab gave up, pushed the second former away, saying disgustedly, 'You're a fucking wimp!'

As Giblet fell away from Scab's body, it revealed Scab's dick, erect and threatening.

I finished showering, dried myself and joined Mutt by the wire lockers where we put on our gowns and flip flops.

'Phew! Am I glad that Scab lives in the junior dorm!' I commented.

'Thank goodness we only have to endure him during shower time.'

'They're all fucking rabbits!' spat Mutt, disgusted.

'I feel for the second formers. Not being in the same dorm I guess we don't know half of what goes on. But from what we've just seen, he obviously rules the roost. Got them by their short and curlies. I hope it's not worse than what we know. Giblet looked really petrified.'

'I warned you blokes!' Mutt exclaimed, wagging his finger. 'They should never have taken working away. Nobody knows who's boss anymore. This place is going to the dogs!'

Eddie overheard and laughed at us, revelling in my dilemma. 'Poor little Tyke is worried!' Never one to have much concern about those junior to him he continued with glee, 'He's nothing in my life. Nothing. But if he ever threatened me, I'd beat the shit out of him.'

A catchy tune that reached number one on the hit parade earlier that year, *A Summer Prayer for Peace*, told of three billion people living together forever. I wondered what I had done to deserve living with both Eddie and Scab. And I so wished that John Lennon had changed the words for the new number one that week to:

> Imagine there's no Eddie
> It's easy to pretend
> No Scab amongst us
> Around us only friends
> Imagine all the people
> Living life in peace ...

CHAPTER 37

Returning from the showers, I heard a strange grunting emanating from outside.

'Huh! What's that?' I asked of Mutt and Eddie.

'Sounds like a stuck pig!' Mutt said, a bemused look creasing his face.

Curious, I poked my head through the window and looked over to Bum Lump's house.

'You're not far wrong!' I uttered back to Mutt, suppressing my laughter. 'Bum Lump's stuck up a tree!'

'Aay! This I've gotta see!' said Mutt, sticking his head out the window. 'Oh man, he's barely off the ground but he can't get down. And look,' he shouted, breaking into a giggle as he pointed to the head boarder master's wife's beloved cat, Kit Kat, 'Mrs Bum Lump's pussy is perched over him. She must have ordered him to rescue it!'

'Come check, Eddie!' I called, but with no reply I turned around and noticed he had quietly disappeared.

'Aay!' wailed Mutt, shaking his head before leaving.

It was not often that we witnessed something like the fat, vindictive Bum Lump stuck up a tree, so I stayed on awhile to enjoy the spectacle. When the telephone in the masters' office rang and stirred me, I decided it was time to share my discovery with my friend Spazz. Excited, I ran up the second flight of stairs, and nearly bumped into Duke as he exited the office.

'No running up the stairs, young man!'

'Sorry, sir!'

'Would you please find Philip and ask him to go over next door?' Duke asked of me, pointing in the direction of Bum Lump's house.

'Huh!'

'I beg your pardon!' Duke rebuked me, his head tilted forwards, hazel eyes looking over his glasses. The boarder master repeated his request.

'Oh, Philip!' I exclaimed, finally realizing that he was referring to Chief's first name.

'And better you hurry up. Mrs Sherman has just telephoned and asked for him. And she sounded desperate. Goodness knows what for!'

I had a good suspicion and started to cackle.

'What's so funny?' Duke asked.

I quickly recovered my composure and uttered, 'Uh, nothing, sir!'

But as I turned to leave, Duke's voice called me back.

'Have you much homework tonight, young man?'

'Uh, no, not that I'm aware of,' I replied shrugging my shoulders.

'Well, then, when the prep bell goes, I want you to come to the office, please! Now go and find Philip.'

'Yes, sir!' I replied, vaguely wondering what Duke wanted me for. Had I done something wrong? I wondered. Perhaps laughing at Bum Lump's predicament. Damn!

I entered the middle dormitory, walked to the far end and relayed the message. 'Hey, Chief! Mrs Bum Lump wants to see you.'

'Whoah!' the dormitory uttered and laughed in unison.

'Careful, Chief!' Mutt warned. 'Bum Lump's stuck in a tree trying to rescue Mrs Bum Lump's pussy. It's all a plot by the Mrs to get you in their house alone. She has the hots for you!'

Chief looked to me and asked, seriously, 'What does she want?'

'I dunno. She probably wants you to help get Bum Lump down the tree!'

After dressing in supper clothes, the usual white school shirt, a pair of shorts, shoes and long socks, I climbed onto the window sill that overlooked my bed and gazed out the window to while away the time before supper. With Perve's radio playing *Butterfly*, lost in thought, I imagined my butterfly to be that of Hoover when suddenly I saw a sight too good to be true.

'Hey, guys! There're *two* Hoovers!' I trumpeted excitedly.

'You're dreaming!' Spazz responded with a broad grin.

'You talk shit, Tyke!' Eddie said snidely.

'I'm serious,' I commented with an increased tone. I turned to Spazz and Mutt imploring them to come and see for themselves.

'Well, then this I have to see,' Spazz said, climbing onto my bed, followed quickly by Mutt. 'Fuck it, Tyke! Eddie's right! You *are* talking shit!'

'I'm not talking shit! Are you blind? Maybe you need new glasses!' I defended myself angrily, then turned to view my newly discovered prize.

Huh! In the poor evening light I caught just a glimpse of one Hoover as she rose off her beloved parapet and walked inside into her house.

'I'm serious,' I insisted, pointing to the house down the lane. 'There *were* two Hoovers, right over there.'

'Tyke, admit it! You're the one who's going blind. Probably from wanking too much over Hoover!' Spazz claimed as he got down from my bed.

'Aay!' wailed Mutt. 'Tyke, you're hallucinating. You're sex-starved, man!'

Huh! Could it be? Were my eyes failing me? Was my eye disease returning? Or was Mutt right that I was making things up?

Later that evening when the prep bell rang, instead of ambling down to the prep room, I stopped at the office and knocked on the door.

'Good evening, sir!' I greeted, wary of my calling to the office.

'Aah, there you are,' Duke remarked, peering over his spectacles from behind the office desk. 'If you haven't much prep to do, young man, I'd like you to clean my books for me!'

'Er, sorry sir,' I responded, totally baffled. 'I thought I heard you say clean your books!'

'Indeed, that *is* what I said,' replied Duke, rising from his chair.

'Huh! How does one clean books?' I asked, face confused. 'And why?'

Duke walked past me, a look of mock indignation. Beckoning with his forefinger he said, 'Must I teach you plebeians everything! Come with me.'

I followed Duke into his bedroom where the master walked straight up to his easy chair, appeared to straighten it, though it seemed not to move, and bemoaned about Babalas the cleaner. 'Must he always leave my room crooked!'

That little grumble done, he picked up a cloth, walked to the wall opposite his bed, which resembled a library, and said, 'I'd like you to remove each book from the shelf, dust it with this cloth and replace it where it belongs.'

'Okay!' I replied with a shrug of my shoulders, grabbed a book off the shelf and started to wipe it down just as Duke had asked.

'No, no, no!' Duke cried out, his face contorting into one of despair. 'You don't manhandle a book.' Then he coached me, 'Follow my example. This is what I want you to do!'

He carefully placed his forefinger on top of the book and gently released it from its book brethren. Cradling it in one hand as if it were a new born baby, with a soft cloth he gently wiped what seemed to be a very clean looking book before placing it back on the shelf.

'Can you manage that?'

I nodded my head, somewhat bewildered.

'Then I'll leave you to it,' Duke said, before returning to the office.

As I set about cleaning Duke's books, all boring history, my head started reeling. I looked around and I saw Duke. Not Duke the person, but Duke the room. They were the spitting image of each other. Well, not that he looked like a room or that the room looked like a person, but both were fastidiously neat and groomed to be square! Books were arranged according to height in bookshelves that resembled the study of a learned judge. On his desk sat a leathered executive pad, all square, as if measured equidistant from the corners of the desk and two gold fountain Parker pens neatly laid next to the pad. In each back corner of the desk sat a picture of some old lady, framed in silver. Probably Queen Victoria, I surmised. With just a hint of the smell of mothballs wafting into my nose, my abiding thought was that Duke was an island of culture in a sea of riff raff and I wondered why he chose to be a boarder master.

After an hour, just as I was wiping the last book, I heard the clap of Duke's shoes grow louder so I stood a little straighter.

'How are we doing, then?'

'Last book, sir!'

Duke took the book out of my hand, inspected it, nodded his head with approval and placed it back on the shelf. He then turned around, dug his hands into his money pocket and fished out a few coins.

'Here's your remuneration. I trust it'll be satisfactory to you!'

'Er, no thank you, sir!' I replied.

Duke tilted his head in mock indignation, 'What do you mean no thank you! It's yours, young man, you've earned it!'

'That's okay. I don't want it.'

'Well, there's no argument about it. You *are* to be rewarded!'

'But I got out of prep, sir. That's reward enough!'

'Tyrone, I'm not having you work for me for nothing. That is slavery. Don't you know that from your history lessons. Perhaps you ought to listen more in class!'

'But, sir,' I summoned the courage to criticise, 'you have Babalas clean your room! Isn't that slavery?'

'No, young man, he is a paid servant.'

Duke put the money into my hands.

'Er, thank you, sir!' I commented, then surprising myself, said, 'But I still don't think it's right!'

'Well, as long as I am boss over you, you'll do as I say!' Duke argued.

I turned to leave.

'Now that's settled, a cup of tea?'

'Er, no thank you, sir!' I declined, feeling awkward that I should have tea with a member of staff.

'You *are* otherwise, aren't you,' remarked Duke with a questioning look on his face. 'Go and fetch the tea tray from the office and we'll discuss this over a cup of tea!'

About to pour tea from a metal teapot into hostel teacups, Duke changed his mind, stood up, went into his walk-in wardrobe and returned holding two sets of cups and saucers.

'Tea always tastes better in fine bone China!' Duke remarked, causing my mind to do a huh. 'We'll let it draw just a little more. Meantime, tell me Tyrone, is all alright here at hostel?'

'What do you mean?'

'Are there any problems? Any untoward behaviour that perhaps I should know about.'

Wow! I found that a difficult question to answer. I couldn't exactly tell him that Scab made Quiff screw a milk bottle in the showers that evening! But I found it interesting that he should ask such a question and I wondered what he knew.

'I'm not sure,' I replied evasively, shuffling in his soft chair, then turning the tables on him, I questioned, 'Why do you ask?'

But Duke was equally evasive in saying, 'As your boarder master it is my duty to enquire as to your welfare.'

Feeling uncomfortable about this line of questioning I changed the subject. 'Sir, have you read all these books?'

'No, not all,' Duke replied, somewhat surprised at my question.

'Then why do you have them?'

'Books are like companions, young man! Each of these books has its own character and contains a vast wealth of knowledge. It's reassuring to know that at any time I can delve into them with the trust that they will help me become wiser.'

CHAPTER 38

The following day, as we returned to hostel for lunch, my head automatically turned to Hoover's house and my mind drifted back to the events of the previous evening. Two Hoovers! I thought how I would love to be with just one of them. I looked at her porch, but it was empty. No doubt she was at school. I sighed a deep breath of desire.

As we entered into the red brick building, all the boys clambered around a letter board in the foyer just outside the linen room where matron attached the daily post. I never bothered, having never yet received a letter, not even from my parents. A satisfied grin creased Spazz's face as he skipped away from the letter board.

'It's from Wendy!' my friend said. 'The babe I met at the New Year's dance.'

'Yeah!'

Spazz put the letter to his long pointed nose, breathed in deeply and confirmed, 'Yep! It's from her alright.'

I felt somewhat jealous.

§

That afternoon I put on my cross country togs and was about to exit the front door when I spotted Spazz in the dining room. Huh! It was not like him to do extra prep in the afternoon, I thought. Intrigued, I walked in to discover Spazz performing what appeared to be a science experiment.

'We don't have science for homework, do we?' I asked just as the song on the portable radio Spazz had borrowed from Perve changed from *Rose Garden* to *You.*

'Nope,' replied Spazz, as he proceeded to mix red ink with perfume and set about replying to Wendy. 'But chicks dig this. They think you're all mushy and it drives them wild. Just like this song. Listen to it, Tyke. Sing that to a chick and they go weak at the knees. And that's what you want. A chick that is weak at the knees.'

I listened to the words of the song. *Girl, I want to tell you something that I've never told to any other girl before. No, not to any other girl, I really love you. And I'll always love you. Always. Only you.*

Just then I heard a raucous roar from outside. Curious, I went to investigate. Under the spotlight of the afternoon sun eerily shining through darkening storm clouds that gathered in the west, Scab and his growing followers had circled around Kit Kat in the open grass patch, closing in on her like a tiger hunt. Each time the terrified cat tried to escape, she confronted an approaching mass, clapping their hands and chanting.

Eventually the cat bolted and scurried between the legs of Quiff. But just as quickly, Scab grabbed her tail, pulled her back and amid a loud squeal from the cat accompanied by a contorted hissing face, he rendered her immobile.

Pinning Kit Kat to the ground, Scab asked Rabbit to place a crudely made crucifix underneath the cat and issued further instructions. 'I'll hold the fucker, you tie the feet. Back legs first!'

Huh! I knew Scab scraped the barrel when it came to niceties but this crossed all borders.

Back legs tied, Scab pulled a front leg sideways and placed it up against the cross piece whilst Rabbit secured it with string.

'Okay, last leg then we set fire to the fucker!'

'Hey! Leave Kit Kat alone!' I said in a raised voice, but nobody took any notice of me.

As much as Scab tried to pull the other front leg across to the other side of the wooden cross piece, the cat's legs just wouldn't splay. Instead it hissed with terror, so Scab pulled a little harder causing an almighty squeal.

'Hey, Scab!' I shouted, desperate. 'Scab!'

The third former glanced up at me, a fiendish look on his face that unnerved me. Nevertheless, with emotion rising in my voice, I shouted at him, 'Leave the cat alone!'

After giving me that infamous look that pierced right through me, Scab ignored my pleas and returned to the job at hand. This time he yanked the cat's leg causing it to shriek.

'Come on, cat,' he yelled, 'or I'll break your fucking leg!'

Incensed, I broke through the crowd that gathered around Kit Kat, grabbed Rabbit by the collar, pulled him off, and seized Scab by the shoulder.

'Aw didims!' Rabbit uttered with a smile on his face, before teasing me, 'Are you a friend of Mrs Bum Lump's pussy? Tyke to the rescue! Trying to kiss Bum Lump's arse.'

'Fuck off!' I swore at him and turned my attention to his leader. 'Scab, you do as you're told. Now untie Kit Kat and let her go!'

Scab got up slowly but deliberately, as if he meant some mean business. For a moment he just stood there, equal to my height but far stronger. Arms dangling at his side like an ape, he eyeballed me with his black eyes, forehead furrowed in disbelief that I should have the gall to interfere with his fun.

'Who the fuck are you, telling me what to do, hey?' Scab demanded, stalking closer to me. 'You just don't learn, do you! Fuck sake, I'm gonna teach you not to mess with me.'

My heart beat like a jackhammer and fear paralysed my body as I expected the worst. For the first time Scab was going to strike a senior.

Suddenly a blur. Chief appeared out of nowhere and punched Scab in the face, sending him sprawling onto the ground. Dazed, the third former looked at me, stunned, unaware of Chief's intervention. As he staggered to his feet, Chief stepped closer and planted his clenched fist into Scab's gut, doubling him over. Grabbing a handful of hair with his left hand, Chief pummelled the junior's face with short arm punches. Then a sharp upward jerk of Chief's knee and Scab's head snapped backwards, gasping for air with loud sucking sounds.

I felt a flood of adrenalin rush through my body. With every blow I found myself whooping quietly under my breath. Scab was well and truly beaten up.

Only that morning we heard commentary on the radio of Smokin' Joe Frazier beating Muhammad Ali in 15 rounds at Madison Square Garden in their famous 'Fight of the Century'. Now I witnessed the real thing.

But Chief did not let up on his vicious attack. As Scab's head lay ripe for the plucking, Chief repeatedly head butted him. Finally, when Chief cocked his arm, even I felt concern. He's going too far, I thought! But, in what seemed like slow motion, Chief let rip and delivered his knock-out blow, sinking his fist plumb on Scab's nose, crushing it, sending the boy reeling to the ground as a torrent of blood spewed from his nose and mouth.

Everyone was stunned.

Without a word spoken, Chief bent over, released Kit Kat from crucifixion and walked off, cradling the cat in his hands.

Most dispersed quickly. Only Rabbit went over to Scab and asked, 'Are you okay, man?'

There was no reply, so he turned towards his cronies, shrugged his shoulders and together they skulked away. Only Scab and I were left at the scene. I walked a couple of paces towards Scab, noticed that he was still breathing, decided that was enough concern from me and left to practise my cross country.

I ran past the cemetery, past the school and up towards the hill that brooded over the small city. At the top, I took in a deep breath and gazed at the view below, all the while my mind transfixed by the rumpus that had just transpired. The callousness of Scab. The vicious attack by Chief. And why was *he* so concerned? I wondered.

Chief, the mysterious lone gunman. I could just imagine it, when asked his name in second form. Chief, no doubt, kept quiet, just stared with his Clint Eastwood squint. 'Oh, the man with no name,' growled his version of Mango, referring to the *Dollars Trilogy* movies. 'So you think you're a fucking cowboy. Well, you're a fucking red Indian, just like the rest of the douchebags here. Except, in your case you can be chief of them all. The chief douchebag. Got that, hey Chief!'

To clear my mind, I decided to return to hostel via the solitude of Paradise Valley, a stretch of indigenous bush. I loved running on the dirt path through the trees, ducking under the occasional branch.

Suddenly a creature dropped down from a tree, ambushing me. I stopped dead in my tracks, my heart beating wildly in my chest.

'Chief!' I cried out, after recognising the creature. 'Damn, you gave me a fright!' Then after a few moments to let my breath subside, I said, 'Thanks for helping me out earlier.'

Chief ignored me. Instead he said, 'Come and look! Follow me!'

Chief walked to the trunk of the tree he had jumped out of and started to climb it.

'You want *me* to climb *this* tree?' I asked.

Chief put a finger to his lips to indicate that I should keep quiet. Like a leopard, he disappeared up the tree with consummate ease.

After some time of negotiating the gnarled trunk, I reached Chief, perched in a fork between two branches.

He pointed to a bird's nest. In it lay a lone baby bird.

'Its one leg is broken,' Chief informed me in a quiet voice, before picking it up to show me the useless leg that dangled aimlessly. 'Every time it tries to stand, it just falls over.'

'How did it happen? How does a bird break a leg?'

'I found it on the ground down there,' Chief said, pointing below. Suddenly, he placed the ailing bird in my hands and said, 'Hang on to it. I'll be back!'

In a flash he descended the tree and disappeared in the undergrowth. Who is Chief? I wondered. He seemed so different from everybody else. One sensed he came from a farm, though nobody knew where. Nobody knew if he had brothers or sisters. Nobody had ever seen his parents.

I suddenly found myself wondering what the heck I was doing sitting half way up a tree cradling an injured bird. I looked to the chick. It looked so helpless so I patted it on the head like one would a dog, then gently stroked its feathered wing in my hand, all the while an empathy growing inside me.

Suddenly Chief appeared next to me out of nowhere, startling me.

'Are you some kind of wild man? Tarzan of the apes?'

Chief said nothing. He removed a reed from his mouth, broke off a small segment, split it open with his finger nail, clamped it around the broken leg and tied the makeshift splint with a thin piece of veld grass.

'Is that going to work?' I asked, staggered at his handiwork.

Chief shrugged his shoulders, his eyes still fixed on the baby bird.

'Why don't you take it back to hostel and, er, see what Ma Betty can do to help?' I suggested.

Chief shook his head. Then after a while he said softly, 'Its mother will be coming back soon. Won't want to find an empty nest!'

That shut me up. After ten minutes of complete silence, the first bolt of lightning struck and the heavens opened up.

'Time to go,' I said to Chief, 'Besides, it's getting late. The shower bell is probably ringing right now. I'm going back. Coming?'

'You go. I'll stay a little while longer.'

As I jogged back to hostel I thought of Chief and the comments Mutt had made about him, and decided that perhaps my mongrel friend had been right all along.

That evening at supper time, Bum Lump announced that Scab had been found unconscious lying on the grass at the back of the hostel.

'Does anyone know what happened?'

A lot of murmuring took place, but nobody spoke. I looked at Chief, but his mind seemed elsewhere. Then I looked at Rabbit and the rest of Scab's cronies, but they were the quietest of all.

FIFTH FORM

CHAPTER 39

On returning to hostel in fifth form, I walked straight to the senior dormitory and looked for my bed and locker, but could not find my name tag. Huh! I checked the middle dormitory and discovered my name on the locker next to the bed in the far left corner.

'Damn! Just my luck! Why am I still in the middle dorm?' I wondered aloud, peeved at no promotion to the senior dormitory.

I quickly checked to see who slept next to me. Chief! He must have failed. Oh, well! He's not such a bad guy. I checked further. Mutt next to Chief. A prefect monitor next to Mutt in the other corner.

I checked out the rest of the dormitory. Great! No Eddie! No Hog! Both moved to the senior dormitory. But also, no Spazz! Damn! And a real bummer, Scab was in the fourth form section of the dormitory. And Rabbit, too!

Hmm! Far left corner is not too bad as I always like to sleep in a corner. But arriving back early, as usual, gave me the opportunity to enhance my bed position so I carefully prised off the Dymo name tag and placed it on the locker paired off with the bed in the far right corner, the one that would overlook Windsor road, and therefore give me a chance to peek at Hoover's house.

§

That evening I popped into the senior dormitory to visit my friend Spazz. No sooner had he arrived when he sat on his bed and started writing a letter to his girlfriend.

'Another perfumed letter to Wendy from her love-struck boyfriend?'

'No way, man!' Spazz said, writing as he spoke. Reflecting the sombre mood of *Mammy Blue* playing on the radio in the background, he announced, 'This is a grovel letter.'

'Huh!'

'Yeah!' Spazz said, then looking up from his letter pad he admitted ruefully, 'I tried to jump her, you know, as a going away present, but I reckon she's too straight.'

'Really?'

'Yeah.'

'You mean you've never done it!'

'Nope, and its driving me wild. So my goal is to relax her. See if that works.'

§

That night as I lay in bed, I wondered why I couldn't have a chick to write to, even if it were a grovel letter. Damn! How did Spazz get Wendy? The only person of the opposite sex I knew was Miriam, but one would hardly call her a girl. And because I never went out on Sundays I never even got the chance to meet a different girl. So the only real girl I sort of knew was sleeping across the street from me. The girl with tousled blonde hair cascading over her shoulders, wearing a tight red blouse and a white mini skirt, sitting barefoot on a parapet and sucking a popsicle. Hoover!

Boy I would love to dance with her and press my dick against her leg like Spazz did with Wendy. But, in reality, it seemed an impossibility. So I dreamed of Hoover. Dreamed a lot.

§

As a fifth former, I showered upstairs. Mutt and I entered the senior showers one morning at 6.30 am, the time for junior showers to end. I turned the stop cock for the best shower, the one in the far right corner, only to discover a trickle.

'Damn! The guys are still showering downstairs,' I informed Mutt, as he turned on his shower.

No problem! Mutt reached for the dial of the temperature gadget and turned up the heat. In moments the dog and I heard yells and screams from downstairs, and immediately the pressure in our showers returned to normal.

'Aay!' Mutt wailed. 'Works like fucking magic.'

No sooner had I got wet when Stooge, the head prefect that year, entered the showers and kicked me out. Damn! But with six showers still unoccupied, I simply went to the next best shower.

On returning to the dormitory, I passed Scab sitting on Rabbit's bed holding an orange to his chest, fondling it suggestively, whilst Giblet, a third former, made his bed.

Just then the prefect monitor walked past to go to the showers.

'Hey, what's this? You're not allowed to have a fag!' the prefect asserted.

Scab said nothing, just gave that eerie stare of his.

'Did you hear what I said?' the prefect questioned.

'He's not fagging, he offered to make my bed,' Scab defended.

The prefect looked to the third former and asked, 'Is that true?'

Giblet nodded his head.

That seemed so implausible. There must be some other reason and I wondered why. Unsure of the ruling on this new twist, the prefect shook his head and left for the showers.

'Giblet, when you're finished making my bed you can polish my shoes!' Scab ordered.

I finished dressing, and as I left to go to the mirror to comb my hair, I caught Mutt's eye and shook my head.

Mutt stood at his bed brushing his hair in front of his own hand held mirror and wailed, 'Aay! He's a fucking rabbit!'

As I walked down the corridor to the beat of, 'A-wimoweh, a-wimoweh!' from *The Lion Sleeps Tonight*, I noticed Scab still lying on Rabbit's bed. With a large blade knife he punctured his orange, deftly cut open a hole, put the piece of fruit to his mouth and sucked the contents.

CHAPTER 40

That night, just as the bell rang for lights out, having just reached 'the day the music died' part of the song *American Pie*, the radio faded to give way to the 9 o'clock news, which started with the item that Evel Knievel broke 93 bones after successfully clearing 35 cars on a motorcycle. We all cheered.

'Switch the radio off,' the prefect monitor shouted.

Whilst waiting for Duke to arrive, Scab sidled up to Rabbit and, with a sharp snap of his finger, flicked him on the bum. Rabbit opened his gown at the front, reached into his sleeping shorts and clutched his posterior with both hands.

'You cunt!' Rabbit yelled, but with a masochistic smile.

'Quiet!' the prefect shouted.

With Rabbit's hands preoccupied and his privates peeping over his sleeping shorts, Scab quickly cupped his hands over his sidekick's genitals, pushed Rabbit up against the end of the bed and held them.

'Now I've got you!' Scab sniggered.

Suddenly Duke entered the dormitory for prayer.

'I beg your pardon. What's this cavorting around? Both of you see me in my office after lights out!'

Scab sprung around, his gown flapping open, and wearing no sleeping shorts he revealed an erect penis. He looked back at Rabbit and laughed.

'Go to the office, right now!' Duke issued with a stern voice.

Whilst the master marched out the dormitory with a sharp clap of his shoes, Rabbit quickly took off his sleeping shorts and joined Scab, giggling their way to the office.

He caned them both.

Thwack! Thwack!

As the sound of cane smacking bum reached the dormitory, many of the fourth formers jokingly clutched their own bums, as if they'd been caned, and mockingly grimaced. They delighted in this affront to authority.

Scab and Rabbit entered the dormitory, giggling and snorting. They walked down the aisle, gowns open and erect dicks sticking out. Most, like Quiff, laughed. A few, like Zulu, kept quiet. After writing up the incident in the punishment book, the master on duty returned, we prayed and he left.

Scab quickly pushed Rabbit face down on his bed, jumped on top of him and went through mock motions of sexual thrusting, causing a round of hilarity at their end of the dormitory.

'Aay! Look at them. It must be Thursday night 'cos they're fucking bum-rushing again!' commented Mutt. 'I'm outta here. Off to do extra prep! See you, Tyke!'

After lights out, we were to be strictly quiet.

Stooge entered the dormitory and ordered, 'Scab and Rabbit. Go to the office!'

Both walked to the masters' office, giggling. As soon as Duke returned from doing lights out in the senior dormitory, he caned them another two stripes. The two returned to the dormitory still chortling.

'Quiet!' a sharp voice emanated from the office.

Scab and Rabbit got into their beds and every one settled down. Just as I was about to drift off to sleep, a loud crashing noise startled me. Scab ran and jumped onto Rabbit's bed, again simulating sex, causing another round of laughter in the dark.

The lights switched on and Stooge quickly asked, 'Who's making a noise?' Spotting the two offenders he ordered, 'Office!'

Thwack! Thwack!

No sooner had they returned and the lights went out when the same procedure repeated itself.

Fed up and unable to sleep, I got out of bed and decided to join Mutt and go and do extra prep.

As I walked passed the office, Rabbit was bent over with a sick grin on his face, being caned by an exasperated master on duty, an erect dick peering out from his gown.

CHAPTER 41

Only five boys had chosen to do extra prep, including the 'always present' Mutt, his head buried in his books. As I walked into the prep room, my friend looked up and spotted me.

'Aay, Tyke! What are *you* doing here?' Mutt asked, as if he found it strange that I should ever deign to do extra prep.

'Those guys have gone berserk!' I remarked. 'And the bad news is that they will probably be gated so we'll have them on Sundays too.'

Shaking his head, Mutt whined, 'They're fucking rabbits! The whole lot of them.'

'So what does one do in extra prep?' I asked, but with Mutt's attention already back to his book, he refrained from replying.

As we sat in the prep room, every 10 minutes or so, I heard bedlam upstairs. Mutt looked to me and I returned the gaze. We shook our heads.

I opened a book in front of me to pretend to do some prep, but gazed at Mutt. As he read his book you could almost see the tumblers of his brain tick over as he moved his finger one word at a time. He was a picture of concentration, only disturbed every so often when a clamour erupted from upstairs, at which point he would shake his head, wail and comment about fucking rabbits.

Intrigued, I asked Mutt what he was reading.

'Art, man.'

'Is art *really* a subject?' I teased my friend, but Mutt ignored me.

Bored, I walked over to his table to see what he was doing. 'Huh!' I exclaimed aloud. 'That's not art. Here I am thinking you're working your butt off but you're doodling nude drawings!'

'It's life form,' Mutt responded with a hint of annoyance.

'Looks like blimmin' pornography to me! Let's see more of it!'

'Fuck off, Tyke. I can't waste time. I need to be good enough for when I sail around the world in my dad's yacht,' Mutt told me. Then he looked up at me, added a grin and wailed, 'I'm gonna earn my start by sailing into port and doing nude portraits of rich chicks.'

I walked back to my table, sat down and visualised Mutt making his living. I hadn't even thought of what I wanted to do for a career. Except that I did not want to be a clerk in a trading store.

'Chips! Here comes Duke!' Mutt warned without lifting his head.

Although there were no prefects on duty for extra prep – the reasoning being that any boy who chose to do extra study was deemed to be responsible – one was still to be quiet and on best behaviour. Not that anyone was doing anything inappropriate. It was just a reflex warning call, in case somebody was doing something illegal, much like monkeys in the wild warning other animals of a stalking leopard.

'How do you know?' I whispered.

'He always checks up on us, even if he's not on duty. He's so clockwork you can use him to tell the time,' replied Mutt, head still buried in his books.

Hearing the familiar clapping sound of leather on wooden floors like a time-bomb ticking away the seconds, I asked in a low voice, 'Does he come down often?'

'No, just once an evening!' Mutt replied. 'Bum Lump hardly ever comes down to check, but when he does, with his soft shoes, he's suddenly there without warning!'

Duke entered the prep room walking briskly, posture upright, tapping his pen in the other hand to the timing of his steps.

'Sir, will you please sign my homework notebook?' I asked, remembering that I had not forged a prefect's signature earlier.

'Certainly, young man!'

Duke reached to his breast pocket and withdrew a gold fountain Parker pen.

'Why the special pen, sir?'

'This pen belongs to the school,' he explained, showing me the yellow plastic Bic pen in his left hand. 'I've been marking with it.'

'So?'

'Why, it would not be proper to use a school pen for home use!'

As he walked away I slowly shook my head, confused at his explanation. I looked down at his signature. And what a fancy signature! Oh, and he made a comment, too! Such distinctive elegant handwriting, like calligraphy, I thought.

After 15 minutes of whiling away the time practising Duke's signature, in case one day it came in handy, I again repeated my question, 'So Mutt, what does one do in extra prep?'

Still Mutt desisted from replying.

I started tapping my pen on the desk, utterly bored, when my stomach rumbled.

'I know, let's go and see if we can raid the pantry!' I suggested.

The pooch looked up from his books, wailed, then buried his head again, struggling to find the word that his finger had left.

'Come on,' I said. 'By barricading the pantry, matron has virtually dared us to try.'

'Aay, Tyke,' Mutt wailed, 'You're a fucking skinflint.'

That said, he returned to his book.

'I'm serious!' I said to Mutt.

My friend lifted his head to betray a face creased with dilemma. Once again a work ethic second to none versus a chance for a freebie, for if I were a skinflint it took the master to recognise one. He uttered strange whimpering noises, expressions of both pain and delight.

Unlike stealing, which resulted in automatic expulsion from hostel, raiding the pantry was akin to taking something out of the fridge at home without permission, with punishment a standard two stripes on the bum. Just that, at hostel, matron locked the pantry, and after a spate of raiding some years back, she created a fortress, boasting that the pantry was impenetrable.

I stood up and walked to the kitchen, opened the swing door, tiptoed down the passage, through the kitchen and towards the pantry. I tried the door, a one in a million shot that matron might have forgotten to lock it. No such luck. Bending one point of a fork at right angles I stuck it into the lock and tried to pick it.

Just then the swing door opened. The hair on my skin stood to attention. Too late to run and hide, I went rigid in my squat stance, hoping not to attract attention. But my heart beat loudly. I heard every thump in my chest. Shut up, heart!

'And what are you doing there?'

At first, adrenalin spiked through my body, but it soon melted away as I recognised the familiar voice of Mutt. The chance for a freebie had obviously got the better of him!

'Shh!' I cautioned, then beckoned him to join me.

'Any luck?' Mutt whispered, trying the door handle.

'No! It's a damn cylinder lock. It looks as though it is pick proof!'

I stood up and took a step back from the door and was about to give up when I pointed to the fanlight above the door and said to Mutt, 'There's the key!'

'But the fucker's blocked with burglar bars!'

'Here, help me shift this table over!'

Mutt shook his head, 'Aay, Tyke! You won't stop at anything to get a freebie!'

Together we shifted the kitchen table, butting it up against the door. I climbed up and tested the burglar bars.

'Damn! They're pretty solid! And it seems as if they're welded to the frame so we can't unscrew them.'

'Come, Tyke! Let's fuck off!'

'No wait a minute! I have a plan!'

I got hold of my gown cord, looped it and fed it through the burglar bars. Then holding both ends, I tried to hook the cord over the cylinder knob on the inside.

'What're you fishing for?' Mutt said, climbing onto the table to join me.

'I think I've got it!' I announced, pulling the cord taut, then applying a little more tension with my right hand to turn the round cylinder knob.

'Mutt, try the door handle!'

He did, and the door opened.

'Fuck, Tyke! You're a genius. A skinflint, but a genius skinflint!'

We entered the forbidden pantry like two kids in a toy shop.

Food! Food! Food!

Mutt and I sat on the pantry floor and gorged ourselves on the cake that was meant for the prefects the following afternoon.

'You realize that if Duke walks into the kitchen now, we're dead meat!' I said.

'Who cares?' replied Mutt dispassionately shrugging his shoulders before feeding his face with more cake. 'Besides he won't be back. More like we need to worry about Stooge.'

'Want some milk?'

'Mmm!' Mutt replied with his mouth full. 'Good chow, this!'

I stood up and opened the fridge. There were three large vats of milk.

'Damn! They're heavy!' I commented with despair. 'And the cups are in the scullery!'

No sooner said when I spotted a box of macaroni. I climbed up the shelf extracted a couple of stems, handed one to Mutt and we both sucked huge mouthfuls of lovely cold milk through pasta straws.

Satiated, we both returned to the prep room. Mutt carried on working whilst I just sat there, too excited with my discovery to want to go to bed.

At eleven thirty on the dot, Mutt snapped his book closed with a thud and said, 'Time to crash!'

I joined him, walking upstairs and into the senior bathroom. I was just about to get my toothbrush out when Mutt handed me a plastic cup.

'What's this for?'

'Coffee!'

'But aren't you full from all that grub we've just had?'

'Yeah! But I always end extra prep by having a cup of coffee!'

'Really! How do you make it and where do you get the hot water from?'

'I just have it with bath water,' Mutt said, running the bath tap. 'If you're lucky you can get some hot water. Mostly it's lukewarm or cold from all those fuckers who hog the showers.'

A fire was lit only once a day in the boiler room. Hot water for our coffee depended on how much was used in the showers and the temperature outside. Luck would have it that on a cold winter's day, in need of a hot cup of coffee, the likelihood of hot water diminished.

'What's it like tonight?' I asked Mutt, as he held his hand under the running water.

'Piss warm!'

Mutt only had one plastic mug. I held it up as he spooned in coffee, sugar and powdered milk, to which I added the bath water and stirred. I took a sip.

'Yuck!' I complained, looking at the globule infested liquid in his cup. 'This tastes like I'm licking the scummy bath ring after Vulture's weekly dip!' Handing the cup to Mutt, I said, 'It's all yours, mate!'

'Aay! I wonder where Vulture is now?' Mutt asked, sitting on the edge of the bath and cupping the mug in two hands, savouring the coffee as if it were piping hot from a coffee shop, licking his lips after every sip. 'He's probably—'

The door to the ablutions swung open and Mutt's eyes closed in despair. He put his fingers to his lips. But footsteps grew louder until the head prefect entered the bathroom. Stooge, once Larry, Mo and Curly-Joe all in one, a slapstick character with one-liners, now just a Bum Lump stooge with the whole head prefect thing having gone to his head.

'Bangled again, Mutt!' the head prefect announced. 'Oh, and I see Tyke has joined your coffee club. Go to the office, both of you!'

Mutt just shook his head as he and I trudged off to the office where it appeared that Duke had just finished writing up the record book for the day.

'*You* again!' Duke scolded when Stooge reported us. 'Must you persist with flagrantly disobeying orders!' Then he spotted me and commented with a tone of disappointment, 'Oh, and you too!'

Mutt bent over first.

Thwack! Thwack!

My turn next.

Thwack! Thwack!

I stood up, walked to the door and waited whilst Duke sat down and got out his updated record book to note the latest misdeed.

He then looked over his spectacles and asked, 'And what are you waiting for, young man!'

'Um, I just wanted to see which pen you'd use!' Before he had time to react, I quickly chimed, 'Thank you, sir!' and disappeared, cantering down to the ablutions.

Stooge came in after me.

'And what are you two doing now?' he asked in an irritable voice.

'I just want to brush my teeth!' I replied.

'You should have brushed your teeth before lights out!'

'I did!'

'Then why are you brushing them again?'

'Well, you see, Stooge,' Mutt said snidely, betraying a long build-up of resentment, 'We've just raided the pantry, chowed your cake for tomorrow and got our teeth all mucky. And besides, we've just had coffee!'

'Yeah, well, two black marks for brushing your teeth now!' Stooge issued, then stormed out the ablutions.

A deep sigh betrayed my anger.

'It happens every night,' Mutt complained, shaking his head. 'Every fucking night. For three, four years, now, I do extra prep and all I want is a cup of coffee before I go to bed. But these cunts can't understand! Scab runs amok but all we have is a cup of coffee and get treated the same!'

Mutt went straight to Stooge's wire locker, expertly worked the head prefect's tube of toothpaste to the edge, retrieved it through the wire locker and dispensed some toothpaste on his toothbrush.

'It's my way of getting back at these fuckers!' he smiled. 'Here, have some!'

We traipsed upstairs, entered the middle dormitory and walked softly down the aisle between the two rows of beds. As we walked past Rabbit's bed I noticed it was empty, looked straight across to Scab's bed and with my eyes adjusting to the dark, I saw them both in the same bed, sound asleep.

'Pssst!' I whispered, shaking my head resignedly whilst tapping Mutt on the shoulder.

'Fucking rabbits!' Mutt responded with disgust. 'I'm gonna teach them a lesson and give them a frothy to remember!'

Whilst I climbed into bed, Mutt walked over to Chief's locker, the outside street lights revealing a look of glee on his face. He retrieved a bottle of Enos, marched over to his intended victims, opened the bottle and sprinkled some in each of their exposed ears. As I lay my head on my pillow, Mutt scampered back to his bed with uncontrollable wails emanating from between his lips, whilst in the background a lot of mumbling and cursing grew louder and louder.

CHAPTER 42

As much as Daniel Boone tried to cheer us up on our return from midyear break with *Beautiful Sunday*, he failed.

'She dumped me, Tyke!' Spazz announced, mournfully.

'Huh!'

'She fucking dumped me! And I got nowhere. All this time I could have been doing it with some other chick, but instead I'm still a fucking virgin!'

'Join the club!' I said despondently. At least, I thought, Spazz had danced the night away with Wendy and he had got to write perfumed letters.

'I might just as well have gone after Hoover all this time!'

Huh! A sudden pang of jealousy came over me when Spazz mentioned the name of *my* girl.

§

A week later Eddie returned from a rugby tour and was presented with an honour's blazer in assembly for making the provincial school side. Afterwards he strutted around the classroom parading his navy blue blazer with special gold braid trimmings and a present he had received from his father for his achievement.

'You think *you're* bright,' Eddie said to the dux of the class sitting in front of me. 'Look what this thing can do!'

He proudly held up a Texas Instruments 'Datamath' handheld calculator, the first we had ever seen.

'It can add, subtract, multiply and divide, just like that!'

Suddenly a crowd formed around the dux's desk.

'You enter five, press the multiply button, then six and press the big orange equals button and—'

'Thirty!' the dux answered quickly.

'Aw, that was an easy one,' Eddie said, peeved that the dux had beaten him to the answer. 'Let's try eleven times twelve—'

'One hundred and thirty two!' the dux shot back.

'Aw, fuck off, man!' Eddie moaned, annoyed that his new toy didn't elicit quite the response he was looking for, so he upped the ante by keying in the number 58008. Then with a snort he continued, 'Hmmph! You may be the boffin of the class but I bet you've never laid your hands on these!'

Eddie turned the calculator upside down and instead of the number he had just keyed in, the bright red electronic display indicated the word BOOBS.

I strained my neck to see the display and giggled, thinking it was genuinely funny.

'Aw, what are *you* laughing at!' Eddie said snidely, turning to face me. 'You wouldn't even know what a boob is!'

Thinking quickly on my feet, I grabbed the calculator from Eddie, keyed in the number 7734206 and held it upside down for him to read. With the Datamath electronic display of 'go2hell' conveying my feelings for my nemesis, I looked at Eddie's face to see his response and got quite a shock.

'Huh! Are you okay?' I asked Eddie. 'Have you got chicken pox?'

Eddie gave me one of his famous wild looks. Only then did I realise that he had a major outbreak of pimples. To compound matters he had developed cauliflower ears from the rugby scrum. As he turned to go back to his desk with a swagger instead of his earlier carrot up the bum walk, I realised for the first time that I was now taller than him.

§

Whilst whistling the tune *Morning has Broken* as I walked back to hostel after school, Spazz, Mutt and Goofball rushed up to confront me.

'Tyke! Listen, buddy, we want to discuss something with you!' Spazz informed.

'Uh-huh! What about?'

'Um,' Spazz hesitated, looked at the others then back at me before awkwardly mumbling, 'About *you* being head boarder prefect next year.'

'Huh!' I exclaimed with my typical response when I had either misunderstood or misheard something.

'We're serious!' Spazz said with more authority, but looking to Mutt and Goofball for support. 'We want *you* to be head prefect!'

'You're mad!' There was a moment of strained silence before I asked, 'Besides, what do you mean you want *me* to be head prefect?'

Spazz looked to Mutt, then to Goofball, then back at me. 'Well,' he hesitated, 'it's not that we exactly want *you* to be head prefect,' my friend said, before he quickly consoled, 'though we wouldn't mind,' adding emphatically, 'it's just that we don't want it to be Eddie! He would be insufferable!'

'He'd be a bloody tyrant like that Idi Amin creature!' piped up Mutt

'Trust me,' said Spazz, 'I'd sooner have that retard as our head prefect than Eddie!'

'I agree with you on that, but I'd lay my cock on a chopping block that it will be Eddie.'

'Mmm,' Spazz uttered resignedly with a look of despair, but then added, 'What we're suggesting is not to be so cocksure and at least your dick ought to quiver some before placing it on the block!'

'And how do you plan I do that?'

'That you make a run for head prefect.'

'That's crazy! You don't *try* to be head prefect. Well, I guess you don't try not to be, either, but ... damn, I don't know! I guess Bum Lump, Duke and the headmaster just selects someone. Probably based on academics and sporting achievements and character, though when you look at past choices those traits have been in short supply! Besides, why me? Why not *you?*'

'Won't work! The only sport I'm interested in is putting my end away!'

'And you, Mutt?'

Mutt just flashed his speckled teeth in a vacuous stare, but the rolling backwards of Spazz's eyes with a not so subtle tap on the head to indicate the mongrel was once hiding in the kennel when the gifts of academic intelligence were being doled out, gave me my answer. I looked to Goofball, but didn't bother asking, he was so spaced out. Suddenly I thought what a sorry bunch we were.

'We think, under the circumstances, you are the best choice!' exclaimed Spazz.

'But it's a done deal,' I said, then reminded, 'You're forgetting Eddie has pedigree. Born to be king!'

'Maybe not,' Spazz said with a sly look on his face. 'You're good at cross country. You've got some brains and we'll give you character. So you've got all three, but,' he hesitated, then broke into his inimitable grin, 'They just need working on!'

§

If it were the intention of Spazz to sow a seed, it worked. Just after lights out, whilst lying in bed that night, instead of thinking about Hoover my mind turned to the conversation I had with Spazz, Mutt and Goofball earlier that day. Hmm! Head prefect. I had never thought of it before. I just assumed that, come sixth form, Eddie would automatically be made head prefect.

Now the thought horrified me. I remembered Miriam and the misery she caused. And that would be mild compared to how unbearable Eddie would be. I thought of me being head prefect, but kept on dismissing it as absurd.

Suddenly there was an almighty crash as Scab ran and jumped onto Rabbit, his bed giving way and crashing to the floor. The dormitory erupted with laughter.

Click. Stooge walked in.

'Line up outside the office. All of you,' the head prefect ordered.

Bum Lump caned us two each. As I lay my head back on the pillow, I felt angry. Angry that Stooge had us all caned instead of flushing out the guilty. I hated that. Angry that Scab and Rabbit were tearing hostel apart, tearing my home apart. And angry that when made head prefect, Eddie wouldn't even care.

I took a deep breath and made a decision. I wanted to be made head prefect of the boarding establishment.

Academics, sport and character. Well, I could work on sport. Cross country meetings were mostly held in the third term so this would give me a chance to shine. I set my sights on getting national school colours.

§

The following day I togged out in running clothes and set off training. As I ran past Hoover's house I noticed her sitting on her porch. My heart fluttered and I quickly looked away, almost embarrassed, but I stepped up my pace and ran with spring in my step, feeling my sinewy muscles tighten and glisten with perspiration.

That night whilst lying in bed, thoughts of Hoover consumed my mind. I imagined her calling me as I ran past. Dressed in her red top and white mini skirt with her tousled blonde hair blowing in the warm breeze, she would beckon me into her house where we would make passionate love.

Hoover's house became a regular on my route. Every day I would run past, just to be near, always putting in a burst of speed, imagining I would impress her. And every night as I lay in bed I would think about her and make love to her. A love affair from a distance. And more and more it drove me insane.

§

After two months of solid training, feeling fit and strong, towards the end of third term I knocked on the door of the office.

'Come in,' Bum Lump answered in a gruff voice.

'Sir, um,' I started hesitatingly, 'I was just wondering if it were possible to have a cross country tour.'

180

'Hmmph!' he snorted, before asking disparagingly, 'What on earth for?'

'Well, um, I dunno,' I responded, caught off guard, 'Rugby has a tour every holiday and I thought maybe we could also have one for cross country.'

'Sinclair, cross country is not a sport!' Bum Lump stated emphatically. 'Windsor College was built on the fine traditions and results we have achieved over the years in rugby. What kind of school do you think we would have if we had devoted our time to cross country? You can run around like a fool all you want but you are wasting your time. The sooner you apply yourself to rugby the better. Now stop wasting *my* time.'

As I left the office my heart sank. Eddie would definitely be made head boarder prefect.

CHAPTER 43

Returning to hostel after another boring holiday, constant thoughts of Hoover drove me insane. I could imagine Spazz say that I should just go and ask her out. But what if she said no? What if she laughed at me? After all, I once picked up her dog bog! But pent up feelings reached bursting point so I decided then and there that I would go over and introduce myself the following afternoon. Suddenly my heart rate soared.

Remembering her comment that we all dressed the same, I put on my home made orange tie-dyed T shirt, made from washing it twisted with an empty pocket of oranges, a pair of blue running shorts and shoes and set off for her house. I kept reminding myself to stay calm, that the worst she could do is say no. Oh, and that I should definitely not say, 'Good afternoon, merry gentleman!' The closer I got to her house, the more my heart beat. I tried practising an introduction, but no voice came out. Oh, shit! I suddenly imagined myself knocking on her front door and as she opened it she would see me as a guppy sucking air. So I decided to first run the nerves out of my system.

After ten minutes of jogging I started perspiring. Damn! Now I was too sweaty to visit her, so I decided to postpone my rendezvous until the following afternoon. Feeling somewhat relieved, I settled into a good stride back to hostel, turned the corner leading back to the overgrown barn and ran slap bang into Hoover, the two of us sprawling onto the pavement.

'Sorry, Miss!' I apologised, referring to her as I would a female teacher, then felt my face burn red and quickly scampered back to hostel.

§

The feeling of abject embarrassment and dejection dissipated the closer I got back to hostel. Okay, so I hadn't got a date with Hoover, but I did land on top of her boobs. Who else had done that?

As I entered the hostel gates I spotted Spazz at the front door and ran up the stairs bursting to tell him the news.

'Spazz, you'll never guess who I've just bumped into?'

'With the way you're frothing at the mouth it must have been Hoover!' he guessed.

Huh! For a moment I was gobsmacked. How did he know?

'You're right!'

'Are you serious? What do you mean you bumped into her?'

'Well, I was cross country training, and jogging back I turned around the corner and bumped slap bang into her. She fell over and I fell on top of her and … gee, my face landed right in her boobs!'

'Yeah! Is she okay?' my friend asked with concern.

'Yes!'

'She's definitely okay?'

'Yeah!' I answered, a little puzzled at his question. 'Why do you ask?'

Spazz's eyes lit up with a mischievous face, 'I'm taking her to movies tonight!'

'You're … her … what?'

'You won't believe it, man. I just went up to her door, knocked on it, she answered it, I asked her if she wanted to go to the movies and she said yes!'

'Huh!'

'Yeah! To think that all these years we've been dreaming about her and all we had to do was ask!'

I left Spazz to go and shower. Damn! Why didn't *I* ask her? Yeah, when I bumped into her this afternoon. Damn, why is Spazz going out with her and not me!

§

That evening during prep I looked to where Spazz would normally sit. His vacant chair sent shards of jealousy through my heart. Hoover was mine! Why Spazz? It should be me going to the movies with my girl. How can a plump mole just go and ask a pretty chick for a date?

As we got ready for lights out and *The First Time Ever I Saw Your Face* played on Perve's radio, I thought back to the first time I saw Hoover and how the sun rose in her eyes. But there would be no first time I kissed her mouth or lay with her because Spazz had stolen her from me.

Just before praying, Bum Lump spotted Spazz's empty bed and demanded in a gruff voice, 'Where is he?'

'Sir, he, er, … er …' I hesitated, my heart fluttering. I was confused. Normally I would cover for him.

'What Sinclair?'

'Er, … I don't know where he is,' I said, somewhat downcast, feeling my face flush with shame.

'Hmmph!' Bum Lump snorted, irritated with me.

'He's in sickbay, sir!' Mutt piped up, knowing that Bum Lump was so lazy he would not even bother to check.

As soon as Bum Lump left, Mutt asked me, 'Where is Spazz?'

'He's bunked out,' I replied in a lowered voice. 'Gone to movies with

Hoover!'

'Aay!' wailed Mutt. 'He'd better watch out or she'll swallow him up!'

Word soon spread of Spazz's escapade.

My mind was too consumed with Hoover and Spazz and jealousy to go to sleep. Besides, I was curious to know what happened to my girl so I headed off downstairs to do extra prep.

Just after 10 o'clock I heard a tapping on the window of the prep room.

'That must be Spazz!' Mutt wailed. The mongrel went to the window, unlocked it, and lifted the sash. 'Well, I see you're still in one piece. You must have got off lightly!'

Just as Spazz climbed in over the window ledge, his face glowing with satisfaction, behind me I heard footsteps. I turned around to see Eddie and Hog marching into the prep room. Damn! What do they want?

'Did you fuck her?' Eddie demanded.

'No wait, back up. Start at the beginning!' Mutt suggested, his face eager, for once his work forgotten about. 'Give us the details, man.'

Spazz sat at the head of the second prep table and we all gathered around, anxious to hear the news.

'Well, when the prep bell rang I hid in the dorm and climbed down the drain pipe—'

'Not that far back! Get to Hoover!' Eddie urged.

'Yeah!' Spazz's eyes lit up. 'I knocked on the door and her fucking father answered. He asks me what do I want? I said I've come to take your daughter to the movies. He says bloody hell you're not. Then he tells me to scat.'

'So you chickened out!' Eddie chirped.

'No way, man!' defended Spazz. 'As I left the front porch, Hoover stuck her head out a window at the side of the house and whistled. So I went to the window and she asks me to help her climb out. Fuck, here she sticks her leg out and tells me to grab it!'

'Big deal, so you grabbed her leg!' Eddie quipped.

'Not just her leg! As she jumped down, my hands slipped up between her legs and I swear I must have felt some pussy!'

Mutt didn't say anything, but small little whimpers emanated from his mouth as Spazz regaled his tale.

'Anyway, we quickly left. I asked her what would happen if her father found out, now that he'd seen me, but she said not to worry, her twin sister would cover for her!'

'Huh! A twin sister!' I exclaimed. 'Hoover II!'

'Yeah! Can you believe it!'

'So I *was* right. There *were* two Hoovers.' Suddenly the world lifted from my shoulders. Spazz hadn't dated *my* Hoover.

'Carry on,' Eddie urged, as we all edged closer to Spazz.

'We got on a bus—'

'Not so detailed. Get to the juicy parts!' I suggested, all traces of jealousy having evaporated.

'Well, we're sitting in the movies when—'

'What movie?' Hog asked.

'I dunno! What the fuck does it matter!' Spazz responded, irritated that his story was interrupted. His face soon melted to a grin as he continued. 'Anyway, I put my arm around her like this,' Spazz regaled, placing his arm around me. 'I left it there for awhile, then moved in slowly for her boob but she had this blouse with fucking buttons on and I couldn't get my hand in. It was all the wrong angle. So I went for her other boob, but the more I reached for it, the more it seemed to strangle her. So she just leant closer, like this, turned to face me and kissed me.'

'Hey, piss off!' I said, resisting what I thought was an impending demonstration on me.

'Tyke! Relax! I'm not gonna kiss you. Not after I've had the real thing.'

I nodded my head, accepting his explanation.

'We passed an aniseed ball backwards and forwards through our mouths until it disappeared. Like this one,' Spazz said, showing us an orange ball in his mouth. 'Then I came up for air, saw Jane Fonda flash her boob, had a quick perve, popped in another aniseed ball, then went for the real thing. Her boob was right there. So while I was kissing her I used my right hand and just slipped it in!'

'Wasn't she wearing a bra?' I enquired

'Nope, it was just there for the taking. Man, it was soft like you can't believe, but also firm, you know, like just right. Then I touched her nipple and it fucking grew. Just like a dick.' Then Spazz added with a twinkle in his eye, 'Just like *my* dick!'

I imagined Spazz sitting in a movie house, fondling a boob and suddenly Hoover's nipple growing out into the night air. That seemed weird, I thought.

'Forget about your cock!' Eddie instructed Spazz, breaking my muse, 'What happened next?'

'After I had done her boob I went for her pussy. I slipped my hand under her dress or skirt, whatever it was, went up her thigh, inside her panties and fingered her!'

Silence.

'I fucking fingered her!' Spazz exclaimed.

'Wow, Spazz, *you* fingered Hoover!' I said, mouth agape.

'Yep! Right there in the movie house. And I swear I heard her moan.'

'So, come on, come on!'

'Well, you're not gonna believe it. The bloody movie ended. I was so busy fingering her and she was so busy giving me a love bite, we didn't realise it. Suddenly the lights go on and this old fossil of a woman bangles us. 'Shame on you!' she says and clobbers me over the head with her handbag!' Spazz regaled, his eyes closing to slits as his face lit up with a big mischievous grin.

'And then?' Eddie asked.

'And now I'm here!'

'So you didn't fuck her!' Eddie spat disparagingly.

'Oh, like *you've* fucked her, Eddie!' I interjected. 'Wake up! Spazz fingered Hoover!'

'And nobody else better. I'm warning you, she's mine. Hoover is mine. You can take her sister out, but Hoover is mine!' Spazz declared.

We all looked at each other.

'No, she's not my type,' Hog shrunk from the challenge.

'Yeah! What is your type? A fucking pig!' Mutt chimed in.

Eddie butted in. 'Leave him alone!'

'What about you, Eddie?' Spazz asked.

'No, she's just a young bird,' Eddie belittled. 'I go for women. Broads. They know what to do!'

Eddie and Hog started to leave for the dormitory, chatting amongst themselves. Mutt went back to his table and buried his head in his books, and I stayed behind, still overwhelmed by Spazz's story.

Just then Eddie and Hog turned around.

'Tyke! *You* take Hoover's sister out!' Eddie suddenly suggested.

Huh! My heart pounded.

'You've never been with a bird. Phone her tomorrow arvie or we'll phone her for you!'

They left, chortling.

'That's fine by me!' Spazz said. 'I'll give you her phone number if you want!'

I hesitated. It's true that I had not been with a girl. My closest encounter was that afternoon, a flying tackle into Hoover whilst jogging. I longed to go out with a girl. Dreamt about it every day. But suddenly the nearness of it all overwhelmed me. I looked towards my canine friend, walked over towards him and tentatively asked, 'Mutt, don't *you* want to take her out?'

'No, I go for redheads!'

'Psst!' Spazz called me back, rubbing the love bite on his neck before dropping a bombshell. 'Tyke! I can't cum!'

'Huh!' I exclaimed before I thought I had grasped what he meant. 'Oh, I see. You can't join us because Hoover must cover for her sister!'

'No man! When I wank, I can't cum!'

I was stunned.

'Have you tried going on for a bit longer?' I suggested.

'No, not that. I have an orgasm, but nothing comes out! I'm still shooting blanks, man.'

'Hmm! I'm sure it'll happen one day!' I consoled, but my mind was more on Hoover II. 'Spazz, what's Hoover's sister's name?'

'Buggered if I know!'

CHAPTER 44

The following day whilst waiting for Scratch to arrive in class, I set about carving a heart in my wooden ruler with the blade of a pencil sharpener. In the words of the tune I was softly whistling, *Ben*, Spazz and I 'both found what we were looking for', the Hoover twins. I dearly wished to add the name of Hoover II to my ruler but I didn't even know her name. Why didn't I just ask her for a date when I bumped into her? How did Spazz find it so easy? I looked at him sitting at his desk on my left, where the rebel had migrated to. His head was bent over a small mirror glued to the underside of his ruler, grooming himself, popping any pimple that may have surfaced since yesterday, any pimple which may get in the way of another dalliance with Hoover. The sight of Spazz sent a shard of guilt through my heart. I felt bad for thinking of him as a plump mole. Bad that I didn't cover for him. At least *he* had the courage to ask Hoover for a date. And how was I going to summon the courage to phone Hoover II later that day? And damn Eddie for getting me involved!

I looked across the classroom at Eddie and seethed. I hated him. As I turned my attention back to my wood carvings I spotted a tennis ball lurking in the satchel of the dux, who sat in front of me. Inspired by Bobby Fischer's recent defeat of Boris Spassky for the world chess title, so engrossed was the dux in a chess match on a small magnetic set with the pupil sitting in front of him, I leant over, reached into his satchel and retrieved the tennis ball. Rotating the ball in my hand, I discovered he had drawn the map of the world on it.

Bouncing the ball on my desk, I contemplated where I should send the tennis ball globe. Eddie, of course! Good choice, too, because at that moment he got up and leant out the window, presenting me with a bull's eye target, a target I noticed had grown somewhat fatter of late. Too much cake on Wednesdays, perhaps!

I stood up, cocked my arm and with all my might snapped my wrist, hurling the ball across the room, hitting Eddie plumb in the middle of his backside. To compound matters for him, he banged his head against the sash window when turning around to see who had stung him. Of course, my wide grin gave me away. He grew wild, recovered the ball and sent it back with venom. I ducked beneath the lid of my desk, but the ball stung me on the leg. Ouch!

'Pass the ball!' I shouted to the dux.

He did! As I stood tall in the aisle, trying to get a clear shot of Eddie who cowered behind a large atlas, in walked Ballbag, our English teacher.

Named after a scrotum because of the red, droopy, turkey-like wattle that hung under his chin which flip-flopped around when he walked. The old relic, such an institution at the school one sensed he poured the concrete in the school's foundations, stood still for a moment.

'Sinclair,' he eventually called in a very nasal tone. 'Stand up!'

I was already standing, so I just stood there, trying to suppress my giggles whilst slowly bringing my arm down to my side, tennis ball still in hand.

After a pause he asked, 'What's your name?'

'Sinclair, sir!' I responded in an equally nasal tone and deadpan face, but trying desperately not to laugh.

Ballbag mumbled something, shuffled, then announced, 'I'm going to give you a surprise test the next time I see you!'

'What on, sir?' I dared to ask.

He thought for a moment before responding, 'On the work we did the last time I saw you!'

Oh, well, that was okay, I thought, since the last English lesson was about the only one I ever enjoyed, what with Ballbag cackling like a dirty old bugger whilst reading Chaucer's *Canterbury Tales*.

Suddenly Scratch arrived and walked into the classroom. An embarrassed grin creased over Ballbag's face as he stumbled out the classroom in his doddery manner, ballbag under his chin bouncing around, chuckling as he left, 'Nyuck! Nyuck! Nyuck!'

After a few minutes of reading her Latin book, Scratch left the comfort of the corner of her desk and walked up the aisles between rows of desks. Eventually she headed my way.

Wow! Quite a short skirt today, I thought! Suddenly the thought of Spazz fingering Hoover, the anticipation of a rendezvous with her twin sister and Scratch wearing a mini skirt all set me off.

'Psst!' I called Spazz.

With my head I gesticulated towards the ruler on his desk. Spazz looked puzzled, but eventually he held up his ruler and I nodded. About to pass it to me, he noticed the mirror to be cloudy, quickly wiped it clean on the blazer draped over the chair of the person sitting in front of him, then handed it to me.

With my eyes I pointed to Scratch, then to his desk. Spazz momentarily raised his eyebrows, questioningly, before getting the message.

As Scratch walked down the aisle reading her Latin, Spazz asked her a question. 'Miss, I don't understand what you mean by this word.'

As Scratch bent over to help Spazz, I carefully placed the ruler on the ground, mirror side up, and with my shoe slid it between Scratch's legs.

Damn! Being flat on the ground, the mirror's reflection sent Scratch's crotch straight back from where it came.

The Latin teacher started to straighten. Spazz stole a quick look at me. I shook my head, indicating I needed more time.

'Oh, and Miss, I had this problem with my homework last night. What is meant by *coitus interruptus*?' prompting a ripple of sniggers in the classroom.

Oh yeah! Like you did homework last night, I chuckled!

Desperate to tilt the mirror, I got my eraser, leant over, placed my hand on the ground and finger crawled until I was about a hand's length away from the ruler, my chair precariously balanced on two legs. Damn! I thought about giving up, but all the time the magnetic allure of the mirror prompted me to edge closer. What I dreaded most, then happened. I passed the point of no return. But I figured that if I were going down, I might as well go down big time. So with arms flailing and legs kicking wildly, I contrived to land on the floor with my head between Scratch's legs, eyes aimed up at her crotch.

Without stepping away, her legs still astride my head, Scratch looked down at me, and after a pause, asked sternly, 'And what are you doing down there?'

'Er, Miss, I was just trying to reach for my ruler and my chair fell over!'

With that, she suddenly said, 'Class, I need to attend to something so you may have the rest of the period off. I'll be leaving the classroom, so please behave yourselves!'

'Why'd she walk out?' I asked Spazz, both puzzled and worried. 'Do you think she's gone to call Batman? Spill the beans on me?'

'No, I think she enjoyed it!' Spazz commented with a grin of satisfaction. 'You've probably turned her on so much she has to go and get it off with someone. Probably in the staff room!'

'Yeah! With who?' I questioned.

'Maybe Rhino,' Spazz suggested.

'No, he's too washed up wrapping his foreskin around Eddie's head and trying to fuck brains into it!'

'Bum Lump's so fat he'd squash her!' Spazz said with a grin. 'And she's too whorey for Duke. He's so proper he'd only fuck royalty!'

'What about Ballbag?' I asked with a giggle.

'He's so bloody old and doddery. Mind you, the way he chuckled when reading about that brown-eye kiss yesterday, he's a bit of a dirty ol' bugger!'

'Talking of ol' Ballbag,' I suddenly remembered. 'He's going to give me that surprise test so I'd better get studying.'

'I've got bad news for you, Tyke,' warned Spazz, looking at the timetable on the underside of his desk lid. 'You don't have much time. We have him next period.'

I looked at my watch, and exclaimed, 'Damn!' I thought quickly, my eyes suddenly lighting up as I came up with an idea and shared it with Spazz. 'Suppose we blow away his mind, instead!'

'Yeah?'

'Yeah! I've been thinking of this prank for a long time. Let's tilt the classroom! Being the old relic that he is, when he walks in he'll be so disoriented that he'll forget about my test!'

'Tilt the classroom? I like it! Tyke, you're wicked. Let's do it!'

We proceeded to tilt the classroom. Each person placed a few books under the right side of his desk and chair, and on the back wall where we hung our blazers and bashers, we taped them at a slant.

'Tyke, the teacher's desk, too!' Spazz suggested.

Together we also tilted the teacher's desk and chair perched on the platform in front.

'Chips! Ballbag's coming.'

Spazz and I quickly sat down, my heart racing.

On cue, we all tilted sideways.

Wearing a white shirt, navy blue school tie and grey flannels with suspenders, Ballbag entered the room, looking neither left nor right, marched straight to his desk, turned to face the class and stood up and down on his toes as was his trait.

The class waited with baited breath. A pregnant pause.

Without a flicker of emotion, Ballbag turned and nonchalantly walked out of the classroom, closing the door. We were stunned.

'Damn!' I whispered under my breath. 'What a waste of effort!'

Just then, the door handle turned and a stone-faced Ballbag entered, repeating his entry as before. But as he turned to face the class, he tilted his head to match the classroom. Not a word spoken about the prank, he remained tilted the remainder of the lesson.

Spazz looked at me, a grin lighting up his face, winked and whispered, 'Touché!'

I nodded.

My surprise test long forgotten, Ballbag was in the throes of a lesson on syllables, eyes buried deep in his black book as he paced up and down the aisles between desks, head still tilted.

Flushed with success and unable to resist, I rested my head in my hands, elbows on the desk and the little devil inside me prompted me to mumble, 'Ball!' ending with a lilt in my voice, offering some bait.

Across the room, another pupil responded on cue, 'Bag!'

Ballbag looked this way then that.

Spazz murmured, 'Ball!'

As Ballbag turned around, the other side echoed, 'Bag!'

And so a chorus of chants of 'Ballbag!' slowly built to a crescendo with Ballbag spinning this way then that like a top in a tornado.

To our utter amazement, he walked to the front of the class, head still tilted and, like a conductor in an orchestra, he waved his hands and built our chants to a climax. Then, having taken complete control, with one wave of his hands, brought our chants to an abrupt halt, and with a deadpan face, exclaimed, 'Class, I'm pleased to note that you understand that Ballbag has two syllables!'

With that, to an open mouthed class, he marched out of the classroom, lesson over, lesson learned!

'Not a bad ol' bugger!' I whispered to Spazz.

Just then the headmaster walked in.

'Oh shit!'

CHAPTER 45

Batman, dressed in a black academic gown as always, walked behind the teacher's desk and faced the class, at first looking very disoriented. Convinced that Scratch had spilled the beans, I awaited my fate.

'It's that time of the year when we select three boys from the fifth form to become school prefects. Each will have a turn as acting head prefect, one of whom will be selected as head prefect for next year. This is one of the greatest honours the school can bestow upon a pupil.'

The headmaster paused for a moment before reading from a piece of paper, 'There are two boys selected from this class. Firstly, Edward Alcock III!'

The class was quiet, awaiting the announcement of the second boy.

'Well,' the headmaster urged, 'Give him a big hand.'

We clapped for Eddie and he smugly absorbed every moment of it.

The headmaster then announced the other prefect to be the brainbox of the class.

'I'm not sure why,' Batman commented, looking around with his gaunt face, 'But this classroom looks like it's falling over.' He looked to Eddie and the dux, and ordered, 'Your first job is to clean up!'

As the headmaster walked out, I leant over to Spazz and commented, 'I'd rather he caned me for perving Scratch than Eddie be made a prefect!'

'Tyke, shut up there and get the classroom shipshape!' Eddie commanded from the other side of the classroom.

Damn!

§

Walking alongside Spazz on the way back to hostel for lunch, I heard Eddie's voice behind me, but could not hear what he was saying, so I turned around, held out my hand and offered, 'Congratulations, Eddie!'

'Tyke! I said tuck your shirt in!'

'Huh!' I responded indignantly. 'Piss off, Eddie!'

'Do as you're told, Tyke! You heard the headmaster. We have to clean up!'

Eddie walked ahead of us, his fat bum swagger more pronounced than usual.

I looked at Spazz, he at me. No words spoken, none needed.

After lunch Stooge banged on the table with his metal gong. We all stood. Instead of the head prefect saying closing grace, as was custom, Bum Lump rose at his table and addressed us.

'It is that time of the year when each week we select a fifth former to become acting head boarder prefect for one week at a time. Each fifth former will have a turn. This will help the present head prefect to get on with his studies for the final exams and will help us in the selection for the head boarder prefect for next year. This year we are starting at the bottom of the pile, well, alphabetically speaking, so the acting head prefect for this week is Tyrone Sinclair!'

'Huh!'

Silence.

Eventually Stooge shouted to me, 'Say grace!'

I did, then turned to Spazz who immediately commented, 'Fuck! Head prefect for a week! Just make sure you don't bangle me for anything!'

'Relax. But watch this!' I commented, quickly buttoning up my blazer. 'Time for payback!'

I sought out Eddie and pointed to his blazer, 'Button up, Eddie!'

'What?' Eddie questioned.

'I said button up,' I ordered in a mock voice of authority. 'You heard the headmaster, we have to clean up!'

'Hmmph! You can't order *me* around! I'm now a school prefect.'

'Well, in case you hadn't realized,' I spelled out, 'that's only at school. Whilst we're here at hostel, I'm your boss. See, I can take my shirt out, but you must button up!'

Eddie fumed and fumbled as he buttoned up his blazer.

'Hey, Eddie, relax,' I said, giggling, trying to defuse the situation. After having made my point and unbuttoning my own blazer, I continued, 'I'm only joking! Don't take it so seriously!'

'You're only acting head prefect here for this week. Wait until it's my turn!'

As Eddie stormed away, he turned around in time to hear Bum Lump grouse at me. 'Tyrone! Tuck your shirt in. You must be an example to the others! Try to behave more like Eddie!'

CHAPTER 46

In the break between supper and prep, a whirring noise caught my attention so I turned around to see Eddie and Hog marching up the aisle of the middle dormitory, Hog walking the dog with a Coca-Cola yoyo that he commandeered from Eddie, a Wednesday present.

'Have you forgotten, Tyke, you're supposed to phone Hoover's twin, today!' Hog reminded me with glee, before continuing to chew his bubblegum.

I looked up at Hog. He looked so smug, having weaselled his way out last night.

'Are you chickening out?' Eddie teased me.

'No.'

'Then go and phone her!'

I stood still. Unsure. I wanted to go out with Hoover's twin and sample the opposite sex, but I was scared. Besides, I was now acting head boarder prefect, and bunking out with Hoover II was not exactly what Bum Lump had in mind about setting an example. On the other hand, I felt the whole dormitory staring at me, awaiting a response.

'Okay, I will!'

I walked to the phone, followed hot on the trail by Eddie and Hog.

Looking at the scrap of paper Spazz had given me with Hoover's number, I dialled, and waited, my heart thumping wildly in my chest.

I heard the receiver being picked up on the other side followed by a gruff voice, 'Hello!'

I quickly covered the mouthpiece and turned to Eddie and Hog. 'It's her blimmin' father!'

'Well, go on, ask if you can speak to his daughter!'

'Er, er, sir,' I addressed him, thinking I'd better suck up to him, 'May I speak with your daughter, please?'

'Which one?'

'Huh!'

'Which one?'

Oh, shit! He wants to know which one. I couldn't exactly say Hoover II.

'Um, either one!' I answered quickly, feeling his impatience.

Silence. I dropped my gaze and thought I could see my heart beat out of my chest.

'Hello.'

Aah, that sounded just like the Hoover that Mutt and I met when collecting her dog bog.

'Er, may I speak with your sister, please!'

'Hello.'

Damn! They sounded exactly alike so I decided to test her. 'Um, did you enjoy going to the movies last night?'

'Ooh, yes!'

Wrong Hoover! About to ask to speak to her sister, she asked, 'Can we do it again?'

'Er, yes!' I answered, feeling myself falling deeper into a trap.

'Tonight?'

'Er, okay.'

'See you later!' she said in a low seductive voice, and put the phone down.

Stunned, I stood with the receiver still in my hand and asked myself aloud, 'How did that happen?'

'Have you got a date?' Hog asked.

'Yes,' I responded absentmindedly, then said rather sheepishly, 'But it's for Spazz!'

'Aw, you chicken!' remarked Eddie, before he and his sidekick walked away.

Sitting at the window next to the telephone, I contemplated that on my first day as acting head prefect I had just inadvertently arranged to have my friend bunk out on a date with Hoover! And once again my Hoover had slipped through my fingers. Downcast, I gazed out the window and thought of the words to the latest Carpenter's song, singing them under my breath. 'Time and time again the chance for love has passed me by. And all I know of love is how to live without it. I just can't seem to find it.'

Beep! Beep!

Down in the courtyard I spotted a redhead lady hooting in her little red devil, her beloved VW Beetle. Hotstuff. Duke's piece of fluff.

I walked past the office, put my head in the door to tell Duke that his lady friend was hooting for him, but saw Bum Lump instead, and remembered that it was the head boarder master that was on duty.

On my way to Duke's bedroom, Spazz called from behind me.

'Tyke, did you get a date?'

'Yeah, except that ... it's for you!'

'Yeah?'

'Tonight!'

'But we have a history test tomorrow!'

'If it's any consolation, I'll cover for you. I promise!' I offered, assuaging my guilt for letting my friend down the previous night.

At this prospect Spazz's eyes widened behind spectacles that clouded over with mist. The allure of another rendezvous with Hoover quickly changed his mind. 'Bugger the test!'

Just then, the bell rang for prep. I continued on to Duke's bedroom and knocked on his open door.

'Come in,' Duke called, pacing up and down whilst reading, just as he did in class. Tilting his head with an enquiring look over his spectacles, he asked, 'Yes, Tyrone, how can I help you?'

'What's that cat's chorus?'

Duke looked at me, puzzled at first, then raised his eyebrow with disdain. 'Young man, it's Tchaikovsky. Classical music at its best!'

'Sounds more like Mrs ... um, like Kit Kat on heat!' I declared, whilst Duke removed the vinyl disk from his record player. 'And that looks like the new Concorde aeroplane they're developing. What is it?'

'A B&O,' beamed Duke.

'A what?'

'Bang & Olufsen. Music from one of the world's greatest classical composers on a set that just about broke my bank account, and you say it sounds like Kit Kat on heat,' Duke chastised, somewhat tongue in cheek, then adopting a mock posh face, added, 'You really are a philistine!' He then stood, hands on hips, shaking his head in disdain. 'One tries to bring just a modicum of culture to the boarding establishment, but it's all lost on you boys!'

I decided to leave it at that.

'Young man, have you just come to criticise or is there something I can do for you?'

'Oops! Er, your lady friend is honking her horn for you, sir!'

'Good gosh! *Now* you tell me! You don't want to keep the lady waiting, you know!'

'Er, just before you go, sir,' I thought I'd better ask while he was still around, 'this test tomorrow, sir. Who the heck is Napoléon?'

'Who is Napoléon Bonaparte?' asked Duke in a disbelieving voice, his jaw dropping. My history teacher walked over to his library of books, extracted one and said, 'Methinks you had better get reading. You can start with this one and when you're finished there are a whole host of other books here that you can consult.'

'But sir, what about prep?'

'Forget about prep, young man. Now let's see, your test is on the period between his first marriage to Joséphine, that would be March 1796, until his second marriage to Marie in 1810, which ought to be covered by these books,' Duke said, pointing to a particular period section on his shelf.

I wondered how the historian could have those dates off pat, as if he were once there to experience the events, and judging by the mothball aroma of his room was tempted to tease him about it, but refrained since he seemed in a rush.

'You stay here, read these books and digest!'

Duke left his room in a hurry, somewhat anxious.

The Life and Times of Napoléon looked like, well, heavy history, so I returned it to its shelf and looked for something lighter. Possibly a classic cartoon version! In my quest I spotted a few Mad Magazines tucked away in the far right bottom shelf, read the Don Martins and tried the back page fold-ins. But nothing decent on Napoléon when suddenly my eyes lit up! *The Sexual Exploits of Napoléon*! I quickly opened the book, but found it to be a lot of psychobabble, and surmised, somewhat disparagingly, that it were probably written by an historian!

Huh! What's this, I wondered, skipping through a few pages of *The Female Eunuch*. Whoah! Talk about weird, I thought, concluding that Duke must have bought the book to understand Hotstuff, she being young and looking like a women's libber.

Next I discovered some medical text books tucked away in the bottom left corner of the bookshelf. Good, they have pictures. And boy, did they have pictures! Full colour plates of a woman with eight breasts, a set of photos before and after surgery. Huh! She looks just like a dog. Imagine that, you can fondle eight boobs instead of two!

'Shit, Duke! You're a normal kind of guy!' I said aloud.

I sat down in Duke's easy chair and just as Duke had instructed, digested the book in my hands, well, at least the pictures.

After awhile, I heard footsteps approach, but subconsciously knew them not to be Duke's. Too soft for Duke, too loud for Bum Lump! Someone entered Duke's bedroom, but I was too engrossed in my book to even lift up my head.

'You're a bloody arse creeper! Always trying to kiss Duke's browneye!' accused Eddie.

I ignored him.

'So this is what Duke's room looks like! Hmmph! Like a bloody library.' Then he suddenly asked, 'Where is Duke?'

'I dunno.'

'Come on, I need to ask him something about the test tomorrow!' Eddie said, walking around Duke's bedroom, inspecting.

'Um, he's gone out with Hotstuff!' I added, my mind absorbed on matters in front of me.

Suddenly he went quiet, which suited me, as I was engrossed. It was only after a few minutes that I was aware that Eddie had left the room.

Good!

After awhile, with my head reeling, I closed the book and just sat there, stunned. Suddenly it struck me just how ordered Duke was. His room was identical to a year ago when I cleaned his books. The same leather executive pad on his desk, the same gold fountain Parker pens neatly laid on either side of it, and the same framed pictures of Queen Victoria, just a year older.

My bladder woke me from my thoughts. Not wanting to waste any time – those medical books were so engrossing – instead of traipsing all the way to our ablutions, I decided to risk using Duke's en-suite toilet.

Even in his bathroom, everything was classy and in perfect order. I carefully lifted the seat and was about to piss when I suddenly checked to see if a stray ball hair might cause a divergent spray.

Just as I flushed the toilet, Duke walked into his bedroom and asked, 'How's it going with your reading?'

Uh-oh! My heart suddenly beat a little faster as I had left the medical book on his desk.

'Not too bad!' I answered innocently, but trying to distract his attention away from the medical book, I pointed to the framed picture on the far side of the desk, and faking a sudden interest in history asked, 'Is that old duck Queen Victoria?'

'Young man, that is a picture of my mother!' he replied sternly.

Oops!

'And very queenly looking too!' I added quickly.

'Just how old do you think I am?'

'Um, er,' then diverting the question, asked, 'Well, how old are you, sir?'

Duke was caught off guard, and gave his haughty look of indignation. 'Let's just say I'm not far off halfway to my three score and ten, and leave it there.'

'Which side of halfway?' I teased.

Suddenly his indignant visage morphed into a stern crease.

'And what's the meaning of this?' he asked discovering the stray book on his desk.

'Uh, uh …,' I struggled for an excuse, then came up with the idea to appease him by appealing to his medical knowledge. 'Can people really be born with both, you know, uh, uh …'

'Both genitals,' Duke added. 'Yes, indeed! It is more common than people are aware of. They are called hermaphrodites.'

Full of questions, I asked Duke, 'How come do you know so much about this stuff? And where did you get these books from?'

'My father is a doctor.'

'Hmm!' I responded, satisfied with his answer. Feigning indignation I continued with the questions. 'When I've cleaned your books before, how come I've never come across them?'

'They're not for young eyes!' Duke answered sternly, then looking at me over his spectacles he continued, 'What, with you having been caught reading a sex manual in prep and now this, you are rather prurient, young man!'

'What the heck is prurient?'

'It means that you have an unhealthy interest in matters sexual!'

'Oh!' I responded, somewhat surprised at his comment. 'Then what is the word for a healthy interest in sex?'

'Er, er, I'm not sure,' Duke responded, for the first time at a loss for words. 'Why do you ask?'

'Because that's what I'd prefer to be,' I answered. 'Now Scab and Rabbit, *those* are prurient guys!'

Duke suddenly looked concerned.

'Sit down, Tyrone. Care for a cup of tea?'

'Um, no thanks,' I said, not wanting to be seen to be fraternising with the staff, yet I was fascinated by women with eight breasts so I changed my mind, 'Yeah!' Then remembering who I was with, quickly added, 'I mean, yes, please, sir!'

Whilst waiting for the kettle to boil, Duke asked, 'Do you mind if I get a little more comfortable?'

'Huh!' I wondered aloud, but without questioning, replied, 'Yeah, sure!'

I sat on Duke's easy chair dying to continue reading his medical book, but surmised there was no chance of that, so instead I asked, 'Where did you go tonight, sir!'

'A film.'

'Is that all!' I remarked, faking disappointment.

Midway through undressing in his walk-in wardrobe to put on his pyjamas and gown, Duke poked his nose around the corner and asked, 'What do you mean by that comment?'

'No, nothing! What movie did you see?'

'A film called Klute,' Duke answered from his walk-in wardrobe. 'It's the one that won Jane Fonda an Oscar earlier this year.'

'Oh, the one where she shows off her—'

'Yes, young man!' Duke cut in as he walked over and sat on his bed. 'You *are* indeed, prurient!'

The boarder master carefully removed his leather shoes, then peeled off his socks and threw them into his waste paper basket.

'Uh, sir!' I called, pointing to the basket and simply said, 'Your socks!'

'What about them?'

'You threw them away instead of putting them in, er, … I dunno, your laundry bag!'

'It was intentional! You may like to think we staff are going senile, but I can assure you all is present and in order!'

Duke was going to leave it at that.

'But are you throwing them away?'

'Yes. They're no longer fresh!'

'Fresh!' I exclaimed, astounded.

'I suppose you wear them until they get all those horrid holes!'

'Of course! It's only when they get holes do they start to feel fresh. Natural air conditioning!'

'Oh, you plebeian!'

'Sir, if you're really going to throw them away, I'll have them,' I suggested, reaching into the basket and withdrawing the socks.

Duke looked to me with disdain. 'They're all yours!'

'And any other castoffs you throw away, sir?'

'If you so wish! But why are you so keen to take my castoffs, yet when I wanted to pay you for cleaning my books you steadfastly refused?'

'That's different. You can't let things go to waste!'

Duke just stood for a moment with his hands on his hips and indignantly shook his head.

'Now for that cup of tea,' the master said, pouring two cups of tea. 'My apologies for the stainless steel pot and hostel china but I've had mine sent off to be professionally cleaned.'

'Huh!'

'Now, tell me about your first day as acting head prefect.'

'I guess it's been okay,' I replied, not willing to go into too many details, especially the part of getting Spazz to bunk out.

'Well, if you are not too forthcoming then tell me what you were alluding to earlier.'

'You mean Scab and Rabbit?'

Duke nodded his head and sat down on the edge of his bed.

'I don't know, sir. It's a bit difficult to say.'

'From time to time we, that is Mr Sherman and I, hear rumours about untoward behaviour.'

'Well, sir,' I started, not really knowing how to tell him. 'Ever since Scab arrived, which, by the way, coincided with Mr Sherman announcing that there would be no more working, there's been a general decline in behaviour. Not mischief, but, I dunno, like a sexual …'

'Deviant behaviour?'

'I guess so. Nipping of, er, testicles and so on. That would have been taboo when I first came here, now everybody does it, but, of course, mainly Scab and Rabbit.'

Duke nodded his head.

'And …,' I hesitated.

'Go on,' Duke encouraged.

'I worry about the effect that all this will have on the juniors. Scab is like a hero to them and I'm convinced he's a bad influence.'

'I see,' Duke said. 'You have confirmed a lot of my suspicions and for that I'm grateful.'

'Sir, I can't even give you the full story. I'm not in the junior ablutions anymore so I don't know what goes on down there and in the evenings I escape his antics by going to do extra prep.'

'You mean that's the only reason you do extra prep, and all this time I've thought you were being conscientious!' Duke said with a spot of teasing.

'Actually, sir, I think I'd better go and do some now and study for your test tomorrow!'

'Oh, good gosh, young man,' Duke said, looking at his gold wrist watch, 'I apologise for keeping you. Of course you may go and do extra prep. You may indeed. Thanks for the chinwag!'

I decided to push my luck. 'That's if you're still going to have the test, now that you've kept me for that cuppa tea!'

Duke put on his raised eyebrow look and said sternly, 'Methinks you had better go and study!'

I walked downstairs, into the prep room and no sooner had I sat down when Chief came to me to ask for help with his work. He just plonked his homework book in front of me and gave me a look of despair.

'Chief, you spelt your name wrong!' I exclaimed with disbelief.

Chief looked puzzled. 'Why? What's wrong with it? I've always spelt it like that!'

'Philip starts with "ph", you know, as in phone!'

'Hmm, that starts with, er, er, "f",' asserted Chief with triumphant glee.

'Huh!' A furrowed look on my face deflated my friend's confidence like a burst balloon as I asked, 'Chief how *do* you spell phone?'

'F-o-n!'

'Wow!' I exclaimed. 'What have your family been doing on that farm of yours?'

'Yeah, Chief,' piped up Mutt, asking, 'Is your mom related to your dad?'

'P-h. Phone is spelt p-h-o-n-e!' I spelled out slowly, before shaking my head and exclaiming with utter disbelief, 'Fuck!'

'P-h-u-c-k!' Chief spelled out with newfound conviction.

Eddie suddenly interjected. 'Tyke! Look what I've got, man! It's our test for tomorrow!'

'Huh!' I exclaimed, surprised. 'Where did you get it from?'

'From Duke's room. When I came in earlier, it was just there, man, just lying there for the taking. I made a copy and studied it all, so now you and Spazz can have it.'

'No thanks.'

'Take it!' he insisted, putting it in my hands.

'I don't want it!' I resisted.

'You don't want the test paper for tomorrow?' Eddie asked, incredulous.

'No, Eddie. That's cheating!' I said.

Eddie's face grew red and he snorted. 'It's not cheating!'

Chief and I said nothing.

'Well, it's not like real cheating!'

'Eddie, by looking at that test paper, you're cheating yourself!'

'Aw, you're such a brownnoser!' Eddie accused me. Then he shook his fist at me and threatened, 'You know, one day I'm gonna beat the fucking shit out of you!'

Eddie walked off to the other end of the prep room.

'What's with that guy?' I asked aloud.

'I wouldn't worry,' Chief consoled. 'He looks like a bulldog but behaves like an overgrown poodle. All yap and no bite!'

'But why is he always on my case?'

'He's jealous!'

'Jealous of *what*?'

'You being head prefect!'

'But that's only for this week!'

'Nah! He sees you as a threat to him becoming head prefect at hostel next year!'

'That's preposterous!' I replied, the baffled look on Chief's face prompting me to say, 'Absurd, er, silly, dumb.'

But I respected Chief's intuition and wondered if Eddie was setting a trap for me, setting me up to be caught cheating. Hmm! Perhaps that is why he wanted me to bunk out with Hoover II.

Stooge broke my musings and announced, 'Duke wants to see you.'

'What for?'

'I dunno, but he looks like he's having a cadenza!'

I walked upstairs to the masters' office and knocked on the door.

'Come in, and close the door!' Duke said firmly as he sat behind a desk, his hands clasped together in prayer mode under his chin, arms steepled.

My blood chilled as I slowly approached the master.

'Tomorrow's test paper has been tampered with,' Duke informed me in a sharp tone. 'What have you to say for yourself?'

I remained silent for a moment and felt the blood drain from my face. Damn, Eddie! I shook my head and mumbled, 'I'm not taking the rap for you cheating! Not again!'

'I beg your pardon!' Duke exclaimed from behind his desk, looking austere over his black horn-rimmed spectacles.

I looked him straight in the eye. 'It wasn't me, sir!'

'You were the only one in my bedroom!'

I kept quiet.

'Do I detect from your mute response that you know differently?'

I still kept quiet.

Duke asked sternly, 'Tyrone, did someone else enter my bedroom whilst you were there?'

After a moment I nodded my head.

'Who?'

'Eddie, sir,'

'I beg your pardon!'

'Er, Eddie, sir!'

'Eddie!' Duke said with great surprise.

'Yes, sir!'

'Are you implying that he may have tampered with the test paper?'

'It's best you ask him that, sir!'

'And that I shall do! Please call him!'

Downstairs in the prep room I informed Eddie, 'Duke wants to see you!'

Eddie's face went pale.

He got up from his table, walked up to me and asked, 'What does he know?'

'He knows that somebody has done something with his test paper.'

'Does he suspect me?'

'Er, I don't know. He *did* suspect *me!*'

'Then why is he calling me?'

'He asked who else may have entered his bedroom.'

'Why did you say me?'

'Eddie, I'm not going to suffer your cheating this time!'

'You don't have to,' Eddie dismissed me. 'He's got nothing on me!'

We entered the masters' office.

'Eddie, did you go into my bedroom during prep?'

'Yes, sir, I was looking for you.'

'I had tomorrow's test paper on my desk and I found it in a slightly different position from that which I left it. Did you have anything to do with it?'

'No, sir!'

Damn, you, Eddie! Own up!

'I see. Gentlemen, I am left in a Solomon-like dilemma having to determine which of the two of you tampered with my test paper. Now, unless—'

'Sir,' Eddie interjected, 'There is a third person who may benefit from tomorrow's test paper. Basil.'

'I see. Will you call him please?'

'He didn't enter your bedroom, sir!' I added quickly, desperate to cover for Spazz.

'You're quite sure!'

'Positive, sir!'

'Perhaps he'd better vouch for his whereabouts all the same. Please call him, Eddie!'

'Er, sir, um,' I hesitated, then turned to Eddie, now standing at the door, and used body language to implore him to confess, but he stood impassively. Damn it, Eddie! Don't make me do this to you!

'What is it?' Duke asked.

By bringing Spazz into the equation Eddie put me in an awful dilemma. On the one hand there was a strong schoolboy code of honour not to rat on anyone. Even a rat like Eddie. On the other hand, because of my bunglings earlier on the telephone, Spazz had bunked out and would be in serious trouble if discovered. Besides, I still felt guilty for having been jealous of my friend.

Please, Eddie, please own up, I beseeched. But Eddie kept quiet and therefore gave me no choice so I turned around to face Duke and with a heavy heart said, 'Um, I think you should check what's in Eddie's school satchel!'

Duke looked to Eddie, raised his eyebrow and asked, 'What is in it?'

'Nothing, sir!'

'All the same I think you ought to go and fetch your satchel!'

'Er, may I advise, sir, that *he's* not the one to go and fetch it.'

Duke nodded his head in agreement. 'Will you?'

'But sir,' complained Eddie. 'How do you know he won't plant incriminating evidence?'

'Eddie,' I said, turning to him, 'It's in your own handwriting!'

'Is that true?' Duke asked with an acid tongue.

'But sir, he, he—'

'Eddie, I have Chief and Mutt as witnesses that I never looked at what you copied!'

A stern looking Duke said to me, 'Please leave while I deal with this matter. I want to see you in fifteen minutes.'

As I left the office I heard Duke address Eddie, 'Today of all days. The very day you are made a prefect at school. Have you any idea the honour that has been bestowed upon you?'

In the prep room I reflected on my first day as acting head boarder prefect. A day that I had unwittingly conspired to get Spazz to bunk out! Just then my friend tapped on the window and I opened it for him. His look of 'after action satisfaction' quickly turned to concern.

'What's eating you?'

'There's been shit about Eddie cribbing Duke's test tomorrow!'

'Really!' exclaimed Spazz. 'Oh, shit, the test. I'd better get studying!'

After a quarter of an hour I went back to the masters' office.

'Tyrone, my sincere apologies,' Duke said, humbly, getting up from his chair.

'That's okay, sir!'

'Well, it's not okay with me. In my book one is innocent until proven guilty and I should not have jumped to conclusions.'

'No harm done!' I said, knowing that it was logical to suspect me since I had read his medical books instead of studying Napoléon.

'You have my sincerest apologies,' Duke reiterated with a nod of his head.

There was a moment's silence.

'Sir, why did you leave me in your bedroom when you knew you had left the test paper lying on your desk?'

'Because I trusted you, young man!'

I nodded my head, then added, 'Well nothing's changed!'

CHAPTER 47

On the last night of the school year, matron gave us our traditional Christmas dinner. All the prefects dined at the staff table. At the end of supper Stooge sounded the gong.

'All rise!' Bum Lump announced.

We all stood up. My heart beat like chattering teeth and the room buzzed with anticipation.

'Quiet please!' ordered Bum Lump. The room hushed and after an interminable wait the head boarder master announced in a gruff voice, 'Hmmph! Will, er, er, Tyrone Sinclair please say grace?'

The blood drained from my face, my heart thumped loudly and a myriad of thoughts swirled through my head, so much so that I forgot our traditional grace, causing Spazz to nudge me in the ribs. I suddenly felt I was out of my body looking down at myself. I could see my lips move and I heard myself speak, but it wasn't me. I had totally forgotten the standard prayer and said the first thing that came to mind, 'Rub a dub dub, thanks for the grub!'

The room hushed for what seemed an eternity, then suddenly all hell broke loose.

Chief was the first to congratulate me. He just wore his Clint Eastwood look, and while shaking my hand he nodded his head once, then left.

'Head prefect! Congratulations, Tyke!' Spazz said, grinning.

Next Mutt and all others at my table, including Hog.

But on the same day the dux of our class was made head prefect of the school, Eddie looked as sick as a dog and complained, 'I feel sick!' As he headed off to sickbay he mumbled, 'I think I've eaten too much!'

'Congratulations, son!' Duke said, shaking my hand vigorously. 'You deserve it!'

§

That evening, whilst the rest of the boarders watched the traditional after-Christmas dinner movie, *Psycho*, I went to lie on my bed, still in a daze. As Perve's 'always on' radio played the song, *I can See Clearly Now*, I reminisced over the four years that led to this moment. The powwow of the first night, fagging for Mango, the ogre of Scab, and me living in the shadow of Eddie. Now for the first time I came out on top and usurped the alpha male. And it felt good! But there was still the issue of a girl. I longed for one.

§

After lights out, the prefects and sixth formers woke me up.

'It's our last night here and we can't leave without ever raiding the pantry. Rumour has it you know how to get in!' Stooge said.

I got out of bed, snuck downstairs with them and opened the pantry for them. Still full from Christmas dinner, I stayed outside and just sat at matron's kitchen table while the sixth formers ran amok, climbing up and down the shelves like a troop of monkeys in a banana plantation.

Still lost in thought, I did not hear Duke's familiar clap of leather.

'What's this rumpus down here?' he asked in a loud tone. 'Upstairs and line up outside the office, the lot of you!'

He caned us two stripes each across the bum, head prefect, prefects, sixth formers and head prefect elect.

'Young man,' he called as I was leaving the office, then giving me a disapproving look he continued, 'I trust such hijinks will desist next year!'

'I promise, sir!'

Damn! Somehow I knew that with Duke I'd have to keep my promise.

SIXTH FORM

CHAPTER 48

'Hey you!' I called to a junior.

A young kid turned to look at me, giving me the stare of a rabbit caught in headlights.

After pausing for a moment, I asked, 'Help me take this suitcase up to my dormitory!'

Together we carried my huge trunk to the prefects' dormitory. As I opened the door, I saw my bed, the one in the far right corner, Mango's old bed.

'Open the trunk!'

The junior complied, then looked in my eyes.

I addressed him. 'You're going to be my fag. That means you look after all my stuff for me. You make my bed, you lay out my clothes for me, carry my suitcase to school. You're like my butler. Understand!'

The junior nodded his head.

'I didn't hear you,' I said, raising my eyebrows.

'Yes.'

'Yes, sir!' I corrected.

'Yes, sir!' he sang.

'For starters, you can pack my clothes in my locker. Shirts on the top shelf, shorts next shelf, underpants here, socks there,' I pointed out to him. 'All neatly packed.'

The junior nodded his head.

'Yes, sir!' I instructed, feeling a trifle odd. 'When you address me or another prefect, you say, "yes sir!" Got it?'

The junior nodded his head.

'Yes, sir!' I said in raised tone.

'Yes, sir!'

'Hang my blazer on the right side, then my hanging shirts. Make sure you space them evenly. Oh, and my shoes,' I paused as I picked them up, 'These need to be shined every day. Shined so that I can see my face in them. They go at the bottom down there!'

'You get on with it. I'll be back shortly!'

'Um, what's your name?'

'Michael, sir!' he replied, although the plump fellow with the pink complexion would soon be nicknamed Galoob.

I nodded and left. Walking down the passage from the prefects' dormitory, I peeked inside Duke's bedroom and spotted him cleaning his books.

'Aah, there you are,' Duke greeted, holding out his hand, 'Welcome back, son!'

I noted he shook hands vigorously and with a firm grip.

'Hi, sir!' I responded. 'How was your holiday?'

'Too short! I need at least another month to recuperate from you philistines! And how was your vacation? You're looking very tanned!'

'Okay,' I replied, nodding my head.

'Son, are you all ready for the big year? You have a very responsible job ahead of you!'

'Sir, who are the other prefects?'

'Take a seat.'

'Why? Is there a problem?'

I sat down on his easy chair, whilst Duke sat on the edge of his bed.

'The prefects are chosen by myself, and both the headmaster and the head boarder master. The other four prefects are Eddie—'

'Oh, great!' I responded, making no attempt to disguise my sarcasm.

'Yes, Eddie, whether you like it or not! Also your friend Basil, plus Philip—'

The look on my face prompted Duke to ask, 'Why the look of surprise?'

'No, no reason. Chief's a good choice. I just didn't know if *you'd* know!'

'To be frank, I am not sure! His academic work leaves a lot to be desired, he plays no sport and he's somewhat of a loner!'

I wondered then if Chief got his vote via Bum Lump's wife, what, with him rescuing Kit Kat and so on.

'Don't worry about Chief!' I assured Duke.

'And lastly Hugo.'

'Hog?' I questioned in raised tone.

Duke nodded his head.

'Hog and not Mutt!'

'I thought you'd be upset at that!'

'I can't believe it!' I cried out, standing up from Duke's easy chair. 'I can't believe you would select Hog!'

'I told you, it is a three way decision, and no, I didn't select him!'

'You couldn't persuade the other two?'

'I'm afraid not!'

'Did you discuss it? What were their reasons?'

'I'm not supposed to reveal details of our discussion.'

'But sir!' I cried out, taking a deep breath. 'This is *my* team of prefects and it's been split right down the middle! In order to work as a team I need to know how it was assembled. Come on, why was Mutt not selected?'

'After looking over his record, it was felt that he flagrantly disobeyed instructions.'

'You're referring to his making coffee after extra prep.'

'Principally, yes!'

'Sir, he's not academically bright, but he makes up for it with hard work. Works harder than anyone here at hostel, right?'

'Yes, I would have to agree with you on that.'

'For him, that one miserly cup of lukewarm coffee is his reward! Take that away and he might not even do extra prep!'

'I see your point. Perhaps it's a matter of perception.'

'But now it's a reality that Hog is a prefect and Mutt is not!'

'I'm afraid so.'

'But why Hog and not someone else?'

Duke looked deep into my eyes, then nodded, walked over and closed the door, then said firmly, 'What I am to say is to stay between these four walls.'

I nodded.

'When Eddie cheated in my test at the end of last year, instead of dealing with it myself, I took the matter to the head master. That incident scuppered his chances of becoming head prefect at both school and hostel. I also voted against Eddie being a prefect here at hostel, but Mr Sherman would have none of it. Frankly, he wouldn't believe me about Eddie cheating. He implied I had concocted the incident to get you to be head prefect. Having punished Eddie, the headmaster had to vote against Eddie being made head boarder prefect, but unfortunately he relented and voted for him to be an ordinary prefect. Then Mr Sherman dropped a bombshell and explained that since Eddie and Hugo were cousins it would be unfair if one were made a prefect and not the other.'

'Cousins?' I questioned with bewilderment.

'That's how I reacted. But there's more. He then said that being their uncle, he insisted that they were both prefects!'

'Uncle!' I exclaimed. 'Mr Sherman is Eddie's and Hog's uncle?'

'Yes, well, half uncle. Apparently Eddie's father and Hugo's mother are brother and sister, who share the same mother as Mr Sherman. Do you follow?'

'No, but I believe you because finally I can see all the pieces of the jigsaw puzzle coming together.'

No wonder Hog came to hostel when it seemed so unlikely. Probably persuaded to by Eddie who *had* to go. Perhaps he thought life would be easier with an uncle as head boarder master. It explains why Eddie and Hog have always been so close. But why did they never let on? I wondered. Mind you, who would want to announce that you are a cousin to Eddie or Hog or a nephew to Bum Lump! Such an unlikely couple. Hog the passenger with a ready-made hero for a friend. Eddie shining even brighter next to Hog.

'It all adds up,' I said. 'That's why they've always supported each other. Always ganged up on me. Hog brings back chocolate cake Sunday evenings, Eddie gets the same chocolate cake every Wednesday. Why didn't I see that? Eddie's father probably gets it from his sister. Eddie and Hog, and Mr Sherman. No wonder Eddie wanted me to take the rap for cheating in second form.'

'He also cheated in second form?'

'Uh-huh! But I owned up for him.'

'What on earth for?'

'He said that if his father found out, he'd be in big—'

'I get the point.'

I then asked Duke, 'Who is deputy head prefect?'

'Mr Sherman plumbed for Eddie,' Duke informed. On seeing my reaction he continued, 'Yes, I knew what your feelings would be about that. And thinking of you, I opted for your friend Basil. But Mr Sherman was adamant. So I played Hugo off against Eddie and said to Mr Sherman that it might be unfair if Eddie were made deputy head prefect and not Hugo. That stumped him, somewhat, and to be honest, son, it has not yet been resolved.'

'Oh!' I said, surprised. 'Then I opt for Chief!'

'Chief?' Duke queried. 'That surprises me!'

'It may give Mr Sherman a way out over Eddie. Chief is quite friendly with Mrs Sherman and I think she wears the pants in their household.'

'You shouldn't be saying things like that, though you're probably correct!'

'But more importantly, Chief comes from the other side.'

'The other side?'

'He's not what you might call establishment. Over the last few years there has developed a growing rift at hostel, a divide. With him on my side it may help to control the rabble!'

'I see!'

'Here's Chief arriving now.'

Duke looked somewhat puzzled and asked, 'How can you tell?'

'I can hear him singing his favourite song. Well, his only song!'

I left Duke's bedroom and met the wannabe cowboy on the upstairs landing.

'Hi, Chief!' I greeted, holding out my hand. Then referring to his favourite song, I teased, 'How are them old cotton fields back home?'

Chief gave me his customary Clint Eastwood squint, looked left then right before shaking my hand. 'Howdy, pardner!'

After briefly chatting to Chief, I scampered downstairs to the senior ablutions where I met Mutt.

'Hi!' I greeted, holding out my hand. 'Listen, I've just found out that they haven't made you a prefect. I went in to bat for you, but—'

'Aay! Thanks, but no thanks. That suits me fine. You blokes are gonna have to act like prison wardens to deal with the shitload of crap that's brewing, but I won't have time for that. I've gotta graft my arse off because my dad's yacht is coming on and we set sail at the end of the year, so there's no way I can afford to fail!'

'Okay,' I accepted his explanation, 'But they should still have selected you and given you the choice to turn them down.'

'Fuck them. Who're the prefects anyway? I suppose they chose that albino Idi Amin and Blubberguts!'

'Yes!'

'Aay! Anyone would think they're related to Bum Lump!'

As we walked out the ablutions, I teased Mutt, 'Your dad's yacht?'

'Aay!' Mutt wailed. 'Fuck you blokes, man. You'll see. At the end of this year, I'm off!'

CHAPTER 49

Being head boarder prefect automatically made me a prefect at school and I had missed assembly the following morning performing front gate duty. Whilst waiting in class for our English teacher, Spazz broke into my whistling of *Rocky Mountain High* and leant over and whispered the news he had heard in assembly.

'Ol' Ballbag's retired!'

'That's a pity!'

'Maybe not! He's been replaced by this new chick straight out of college!' Spazz said with his apple-cheeked grin.

Just then she walked into class. We all sat there, our mouths agape. She was no chick, she was God's gift to man. All woman and more. Wearing a long sleeved polo-neck top and skirt, she stood behind the teacher's desk, tall with perfect posture, her honey-blonde hair cascading down over her shoulders and a pair of boobs that commanded our attention.

'Good morning, class!' she said in the most beautifully trained voice we had heard in years. 'My name is Miss Simpson and I'll be taking you for English this year.'

We were spellbound.

She continued. 'And then later on during the year, I will also do some career counselling in the form of one-on-one interviews with each one of you.'

Excited murmuring spread rapidly through the classroom.

'Your last year at school is your most important. The marks you get in your final examination will stay with you for the rest of your lives, so let's get off to a good start. Your Shakespeare set work is *Romeo and Juliet*. Please take out your books and I'll start reading.'

As Miss Simpson read from her book, she walked up and down the aisles between desks, exuding an unbounded enthusiasm for Shakespeare. Instead of listening to her, I was mesmerised by the sweet sound of her melodic voice in rhythm to the bounce of her boobs.

At the end of class she paused and then said, 'For homework I want you to read ahead …' Suddenly, she looked my way and called, 'Tyrone Sinclair!'

Huh! My heart skipped several beats. She singled me out. And how did she know my name? I wondered.

'Don't you recognise me?' she asked.

Me? How on earth would I recognise you, I wanted to ask but my throat closed up, so I just shook my head.

'I was at junior school with you.'

The class sniggered.

'Of course, I was in a much higher class than you. In my last year you were just a tiny tot, but I have this clear memory of you coming to me every tea break to help you tie your shoelaces!'

The class roared with laughter, drowning out Miss Simpson as she said goodbye and left the classroom. I felt all eyes looking at me and my faced blushed red and burned as they wolf whistled.

§

Walking the path back to hostel for lunch, Spazz ran up to me and said excitedly, 'Hey Tyke, she was coming on to you!'

'Huh!'

'That's their way. She singled you out, man!'

'You mean she made a fool of me. I felt an absolute idiot!'

'Yeah, but women don't see it that way. They're all protective. She tying your shoelaces makes her feel all motherly. It's an instinctive thing. She probably made the whole thing up anyway!'

'Huh!'

'To make a connection!'

Just then Eddie joined us and guffawed whilst teasing me. 'Miss Simpson tied your shoelaces!'

CHAPTER 50

Five weeks into term the supper bell rang and all the boys except the prefects congregated in the dining room. We stood outside in the foyer and waited for the master on duty to arrive.

Duke's shoes clapped their way down stairs, but just before entering the dining room the boarder master stopped and invited me, 'Would you accompany me to dinner?'

Duke entered the dining room and marched down the aisle, the prefects following him. It felt good to be in this procession, a feeling of accomplishment. After he said grace, we sat down to dinner.

No sooner had I sat down when I poured myself a glass of milk and gulped it down and, with a growing look of befuddlement on Duke's face, followed with a second and third glass.

'Thirsty?' he asked.

'No.'

'Then why all the milk?'

'It's free!'

Duke shook his head as if clearing his thoughts, then asked, 'I want your opinion on the removal of the black mark system.'

'Huh!'

'Well?'

'I think it's crazy! Why would you want to do that?'

'Don't you think it's barbaric to have to wait days on end before being punished?'

'I dunno,' I answered, putting the glass down on the table. 'But the more we remove traditions, the more hostel is going to tear apart! You know, when they took working away, Mutt warned that hostel would go to the dogs. Now look at it. I'll bet it was Hog who squealed to his uncle!'

'Actually, it was me!'

'What? Then *you're* to blame!'

'There is another way of looking at it. Don't you think hostel is a little more civilised than when we arrived four years ago?'

I shrugged my shoulders.

'Have you forgotten the way the prefects behaved then?'

'No,' I replied resignedly.

'Well, I think the quicker we remove the black mark system the better, and especially that absurd white mark system. And for that I am going to need your support when approaching Mr Sherman.'

Oops! I thought about the white mark system and all the benefits I had derived from it. 'But, sir! How are we going to deal with everyday discipline?'

'We'll find a way.'

Supper was a chop, mash and peas. Ravenous, I proceeded to shovel my peas with my fork.

'No, no, no!' cried Duke, shaking his head in despair. 'You must use both your knife and fork!'

'But then you can't get so many peas in!' I lamented.

'Why do you want so many peas at one time?'

'To get seconds!'

'Hmm! Well, sitting here at the masters' table you can have as much fare as you like,' responded Duke.

'Great! Then you must invite me up here more often!'

As I continued to shovel my peas, Duke lifted his pork chop towards his mouth and said, 'Excuse my fingers please!'

'Huh!'

'I beg your pardon!'

'For what?'

'Not "huh"! It is impolite to say "huh"! You must say "I beg your pardon".'

'I thought *you* were begging your pardon!'

'No, I was simply asking you to excuse my fingers!'

'For what?'

'I'd like to eat the rest of this chop with my fingers and I was, well, asking for your permission to go ahead.'

'Sure. What do I care?'

'Well, young man, we're here to teach you kids good manners, to inculcate some culture.'

'What if I said no!'

'No to good manners?'

'Uh-uh! No to you eating with your fingers.'

Duke put his chop down and tried to explain. 'It's a rhetorical question. You're not even meant to respond.'

'Then why bother asking!'

'I'm beginning to wonder why I did!' responded Duke with a look of resignation.

I shovelled the last mouthful of food into my mouth and eyed the serving platter.

'You are supposed to put your knife and fork together when you're finished!'

Flashes of Duke's ordered lifestyle flashed through my mind. 'Gee! Then I'd be like you, er, er,' I responded before hesitating, then running into deep water I quickly added with a smile, 'All cultured, and then you wouldn't have anyone to teach!'

Duke frowned

'Besides, I'm not finished!'

'Good gosh! How do you manage to eat so much?' Duke asked as he opened a red pack of Dunhill International cigarettes, withdrew one and lit it with a tortoiseshell and gold trimmed lighter.

'Phoof!' I said, greatly exaggerating my hands waving away the smoke. 'Why on earth do you smoke?'

'It helps keep me sane with you lot.'

'Don't you think it's a cheek to cane the boys for smoking when you yourself smoke?'

Duke took a deep breath, sighed, stood up and said, 'Should we adjourn, have a cup of tea upstairs. I'll explain it then.'

'Sir, if you don't mind there are still a couple of chops here. I'd like to finish them off. Don't like to see them go to waste,' I responded, then appealing to his sense of order, quickly added, 'It'll make the plates look all nice and clean!'

'Good gosh!' Duke replied and sat down again.

'No, don't wait for me. I'll be a long time because there's also spare mash! You boil the water in the meantime and I'll see you upstairs for that cuppa!'

Chief, deputising for me, rapped the gong to signify the end of supper and said grace. After I had finished filling my gut I wobbled upstairs, but as I passed the telephone window I heard the familiar sound of a car hooter. I looked out the window and saw Duke's lady friend in her Beetle.

I poked my nose into the masters' office, but Duke was not there, so I carried on to his bedroom. Just as I walked in he handed me a cup of tea.

'Sir, there's a redhead downstairs honking her horn for you!'

'Mind your manners, young man!' Duke admonished, though I swear I could detect a faint smile. 'And don't play around with my emotions like that!'

'I promise, sir! She *is* here!'

The colour from Duke's face drained like sand from an egg-timer.

'Good gosh, that can't be! What is the date today?' he asked, clearly flustered, looking at his watch. 'I make it the 15th.'

'Well, well, well! The Ides of March!'

'Oh, shoo!' Duke said, pacing up and down his room, trying to piece the puzzle together. 'Now, let's see, I asked her to book tickets for tomorrow.'

'Tickets for what?'

'A string concerto.'

'You mean you have to book tickets for a cat's chorus?'

'Yes, young man!' Duke replied, both irritated and with his mind racing.

'Maybe she couldn't get tickets for tomorrow, so she booked for today!'

'But I'm on duty today!'

'Then go down and tell her!'

Duke looked at me with disbelieving eyes, 'You don't understand, you don't just go and *tell* her!'

'Oh,' I said, the penny dropping. 'I think I do understand. You're in big shit!'

'Mind your language, young man!' Duke admonished, but without much conviction, his attention elsewhere. The master finally stopped pacing, placed his hands on his hips and asked, 'What on earth am I to do?'

'I dunno,' I replied, then shrugged my shoulders and added, 'Go out!'

'Go *out!* I'm on duty. I can't simply go out. I've got 50 boys I'm responsible for!'

'Yeah, but you've got a stick of dynamite outside ready to explode!'

'Need you remind me!'

'Relax! You go out to your cat's chorus and I'll look after the place!'

'I can't!'

'Of course you can. How long's it going to take? What had you planned to do?'

'Well, to go to the show and then have a bite to eat.'

'And then?'

'And then come back here.'

'Oh, is that all,' I said, somewhat disappointed. 'Well, you can't listen to a cat's chorus for that long, an hour or so maximum unless you go dilly! And you've already had supper.'

Duke shook his head.

'Don't you trust me?' I goaded him.

'It's not a matter of trust. It's just that I've never done anything like this before.'

'I know!' I said. 'But I'll cover for you. No one will ever know.'

Duke appeared absolutely torn between his honour and his lady friend so I thought I'd better tip the scales. 'Sir, I think your stick of dynamite has already lit her fuse!' Then I added in a hot potato accent, 'And you'd better hurry, sir. She'll think you're tardy!'

'In a word, no!' Duke said, then taking a deep breath, added, 'But I'm going to have to go and face the music!'

Duke left his room whilst I stood drinking a cup of tea. Very shortly he returned, a tormented look on his face.

'Not a word, son! Not a word!'

'Yes!' I shouted, pumping my fist, then assured Duke by pretending to lock my lips, adding, 'My lips are sealed.'

'Good gosh! Have we a megalomaniac here? Has this head prefect thing gone to your head? Do you *so* want to be in charge?'

'No! I just want to see you breaking the law!'

'Is that so!' Duke said despondently, his face dropping. He then looked at me and asked, 'Would you help me get ready please?'

'Sure!'

'First you can fetch me my shoes and socks. The Bally Swiss shoes.'

I walked into his walk-in wardrobe and found them. In one drawer he had around two dozen pairs of socks, all dark brown and all neatly stacked in pairs, folded once.

'Which pair of brown socks?' I asked teasingly.

'Please just hurry!'

When I returned with the pair of shoes and socks, Duke was standing in front of a mirror spraying his hair.

'Huh! Sir, I think you'd better calm down. You're supposed to put deodorant under your arms, not on your head!' I said, proud of some newfound culture.

'This is hair spray.'

'Hair spray!' I exclaimed, disbelievingly. 'Why? Are you trying to hide a bald spot under there from your lady friend?'

'I am not going bald. It just keeps your hair groomed and in place!'

'Hmm!' I said suspiciously. 'It seems to me that you just don't want to look dishevelled when you come back to hostel so as not to arouse suspicion.'

'Oh, you!' Duke replied, too hurried to scold me.

The little devil inside me couldn't resist. 'You know, if I'm not mistaken, your sideburns have got a little longer,' I commented, grabbing a tuft. 'And do I detect that your trousers are a little flared? If I may say so, she's got quite a hold over you.'

'Oh, shoo!' Duke blurted, waving me off and rushing into his walk-in wardrobe where he shouted back to me, 'I've got some grooming to do. Please go downstairs and tell my lady friend that I'll be a few minutes.'

§

As I skipped downstairs I couldn't help surmising that for Duke to bunk out he must be in big trouble with Hotstuff! In the courtyard I confronted an odd choice for a lady friend. A redhead sitting in a red VW Beetle, a symbol of the 'make love not war' generation, tapping her fingers on the steering wheel to the timing of *Aquaruis* blaring out from a red 8-track player.

'Uh, ma'am,' I called tentatively to the lady who wore a face so sharp she could do Woody Woodpecker damage. 'Sir said he will be down shortly!'

'He bloody well better be!' the redhead responded with an icy stare, 'Or his nibs will be in for a good tongue lashing!'

Just then out of the corner of my eye I caught sight of the surreptitious movement of Rabbit disappearing around the corner from the back verandah.

CHAPTER 51

'Hmm! What's Rabbit up to now?' I wondered, leaving Duke's stick of dynamite smouldering in her Beetle.

Walking down the driveway that flanked the boarding establishment, I surmised that Rabbit must have ducked into the weights room. An air-raid shelter ran along the front fence of the property, mostly hidden underground with only fanlight windows on the roadside façade for light and air. The outside concrete stairs leading from the gate to the front door divided the air-raid shelter into two halves, the weights room occupying the one half on the right as you entered the premises. I burst open the door, prompting a wild flurry of attempts to stub out cigarettes. Smoking was strictly taboo.

'Bangled!' I shouted, then ordered them one by one, 'Rabbit, office! Quiff, office!'

I despaired when I saw Zulu. Had Scab got to him, too? I wondered.

'What are *you* doing here?' I asked.

Zulu shrugged his shoulders, feigning innocence.

'Have you been smoking?' I questioned.

Zulu shook his head. I looked him straight in the eye and decided something was amiss so I waited and waited. Finally his face went red, he spluttered, then coughed violently, and out shot a cigarette stub that he had been desperately trying to conceal in his mouth.

I looked at him with huge disappointment, hoping it would unnerve him, shaking my head slowly, and without a word spoken turned my attention to the next and last offender, Scab.

'And you?' I asked him.

He gave me his infamous look. One of insolence, but underneath he is laughing at you, trying to provoke you. I found this extremely irritating.

'I asked you a question!'

Eventually he replied, spitting, 'You've got nothing on me! You can smell my breath if you dare.'

Smelling Scab's breath was the last thing I wanted to do. Besides I had long since learned that they would always suck in their breath. Scab was a difficult case. It's true, I had not seen him smoking. Never did! I was not even sure that he ever smoked, which I always thought odd. But he surrounded himself with the smoking fraternity and I strongly suspected that he supplied his cronies with cigarettes.

'The rest of you, go to the office!'

'What a sham!' Rabbit accused.

'And your problem is?'

'You send us to the office and Duke canes us six, yet *he* fucking smokes! Where's the justice?'

Oops! The mention of Duke's name reminded me that the master had bunked out for the evening and I couldn't let on, and so I had to backtrack. 'Alright. This time you get away with a warning. Next time, you won't be so lucky!'

I walked away from the air-raid shelter amid sniggering, my authority sinking in quicksand.

§

Later that evening I walked past Duke's bedroom and noticed the master had arrived back. I popped my head in the door and saw Duke changing his clothes in a cloud of smoke.

'Phoof!' I teased, waving my arms in the smoke. 'You said you were going to explain to me why the boys are not allowed to smoke when you set such a bad example?'

Duke remained silent.

Pretending to cough, I continued to needle the boarder master by claiming, 'This is going to mess up my lungs for my cross country!' and then asking, 'Are you aware that last year the Surgeon General in America declared second hand smoke to be bad for your health?'

Still Duke remained silent.

'Aren't you worried you're going to catch some disease and end up like Ma Coughballs?'

'Right now, son, this cigarette is my lifesaver!'

'Your evening was *that* bad?'

'Terrible!' he replied in a low voice, with a look that supported what he had just said.

'Why, were the cats off key?'

Duke ignored me.

'You're in a real pickle, aren't you?'

Duke sat on the edge of his bed and sighed before opening up to me.

'We didn't exactly go out on a date. In fact we just sat in the car in the courtyard.'

'Huh! Why didn't you invite her inside?'

'That would not be seemly, son!' Duke replied with a shake of his head.

'So what did you do in the car that you couldn't do here?'

'We had words.'

'You mean you're being dumped, aren't you?'

Duke looked over his black horn-rimmed glasses, a stern look.

'She's pulling the plug on you, isn't she?'

'Mind what you say, young man!'

'No! You're always pulling out our files from their pigeon holes, analysing their contents, and when you're finished placing them back on the shelf!'

'Is that what you think I do?'

I ignored him and said, 'It's time the shrink lay on the couch and got some of his own medicine!'

'I beg your pardon!'

'There's something I've wanted to ask you for a long time. Why did you come to hostel?'

'Why are you so interested?'

'I dunno. It just seems you're, er, you're …,' I hesitated, losing confidence in what I was about to say, but then decided to take the plunge, 'You're so out of place, here!'

Duke looked hurt as he asked, 'What do you mean by out of place?'

'Well, er,' I hesitated, wondering what can of worms I had opened. 'Your interests are so different. I mean, we play sport, you read books. Look at all these books you've got here. None of the boys at hostel read.'

'Young man, I seem to recall you had plenty of interest in them last year!'

'What about movies?' I asked, changing tack, feeling I had a little more knowledge in that direction. 'Do you even like comedies?'

'Of course! Do you really think I am without a sense of humour?'

'Name one.'

'Well, let's try *Funny Girl*,' Duke answered. 'But I presume you would like *What's Up Doc?*'

'Yes.'

'Same actress. Barbara Streisand. So we're not poles apart!'

'I'll bet you don't like war movies?'

'That depends. If you mean films that glorify war, then no. But films like *All Quiet on the Western Front, Grand Illusion* or even Stanley Kubrick's *Paths of Glory*, that demonstrate the futility of war, then yes.'

'I've never even heard of those movies,' I responded, suddenly feeling somewhat out of my depth.

'One you do know, since it was shown here at the boarding establishment, is *The Bridge on the River Kwai*!'

'Yes! But I didn't see it like that.'

'No, I don't suppose you did. No doubt you marvelled at the blowing up of the bridge, but did you not see how two men, who had more in common with each other, allowed blind loyalty to their culture and code to lead them on a path of destruction that was pointless. Or madness as the doctor said.'

'Wow! That *really* happened?' I asked, somewhat stunned before asking, 'Your all-time favourite movie?'

'Sunday Bloody Sunday.'

'Huh! Well that sounds like a good war movie!'

'Not quite!' smiled Duke. 'It's actually a thought provoking film. A sexually-orientated adult drama between a heterosexual, homosexual and bisexual involved in a three-sided love story.'

'Huh! An adult sex drama. I could live with that!'

'Son, are you aware that I select your Saturday night films and although the choice is often bleak I don't foist on you the hoity toity la-de-dah pictures you think are the only ones I watch.'

'Forget movies,' I suggested, feeling I was losing ground. 'What about all those cat's choruses you listen to? Do you even know about Woodstock?'

'August 15th 1969—'

'No, sir! That's history!'

'I'm a *history* teacher!'

'But the music, sir! Do you know any of the songs that were played?'

Duke countered, asking, 'Do you know, culturally, what led to Woodstock?'

'Er, no.'

'And for your information, young man, I *have* seen the film.'

'Huh!' I wondered, feeling my argument was sinking like the titanic. 'I bet your lady friend made you watch it!'

'She did not *make* me watch it, she suggested. And yes, it was not quite my cup of tea, but I watched it all the same thinking that it would allow me to better understand the boys here at hostel. Can you say the same about going to a Beethoven concert?'

'Okay! Okay!' I said, then decided to change tack and soften my approach. 'Sir, we're all here because we have to be here, but you've got a choice. So why did you come to hostel?'

'I'm not sure,' Duke replied, adopting a pensive look. 'Circumstances led to me being here.'

'Well, where did you live before?'

'Er, with my mother,' Duke answered with hesitation.

'Your mother! At your age!' I exclaimed before asking, 'Why?'

'Son, when I grew up my father worked in emergency at a state hospital, so I saw little of him. My mother, here,' Duke continued whilst pointing to the framed photo on his desk, 'who hails from an aristocratic family—'

'So I *was* right!' I exclaimed. 'No wonder she looks like Queen Victoria!'

Duke smiled before continuing, 'She raised me and—'

'And taught you all that cultured stuff like classical music and theatre and manners.'

'You could say that. The finer things in life that she wanted to share with my father, but never could.'

'Just like my mom and dad!'

'Really! I never knew.'

'Carry on!'

'Anyway, with the stress of working odd hours he turned to the bottle and became an alcoholic. My poor mum was highly embarrassed, mortified that her friends would discover her secret. More and more he took out his frustrations on her but she bore it with dignity.'

I sensed deep stuff coming out of Duke, perhaps stuff he had never confided in anyone before.

'One evening my mother arranged a dinner party and my father came home drunk. She called off the party and for the first time she stood up to him. I could hear them from the garden flat where I lived. He stormed off to the pub and, unknown to me, this all set off a major asthma attack for my mum. After a few moments of silence I went to see what had transpired only to discover my mother lying on the front lawn clutching an empty asthma pump.'

Choked up, Duke picked up the framed picture of his mother and revealed, 'She died in my arms.'

Duke fell silent and I felt awkward so I asked, 'What ever happened to your father, sir?'

'I lost contact with him, son. I clearly recall my mother asking him to bring back a new asthma pump from the hospital, but I guess in his inebriated state it just did not occur to him.'

'So you blame him.'

'Yes, I do. He is a medical doctor and he should have known better,' Duke said in an angry tone.

'No forgiveness?'

'I prefer to remember him as a medical practitioner rather than my father. Hearsay is that he is very good at it. That's why I have kept the medical books that he once gave me to convince me to follow a career in medicine. Needless to say I chose history as a reaction, though I was always interested in my mother's lineage.'

'I'll make you a cuppa tea, sir! I promise I'll do it correctly. You know, spot of milk first, boiling water, let it draw and all that stuff!'

I handed Duke a cup of tea.

'Thanks, son.'

'I've got you all figured out!'

'I beg your pardon!' Duke exclaimed whilst stirring his cup.

'It's one of those Freudian things! I read it in one of your books. You know that thing where every son wants to kill his father and make love to his mother!'

'I beg your pardon!'

'Well, I don't mean quite like that, but ... well, you worshipped your mother and you blame your dad for her death, so by breaking contact with him it's like killing him. You would like to marry someone like your mother, but that would be betraying her so you've chosen someone the exact opposite like your lady friend. I mean, sir, you got to admit that she's not exactly your type. But you take her out to cat's choruses and so on to get her all cultured. Meantime, you came to hostel so that you could have a family without having to marry anyone. But now your lady friend's putting pressure on you to make a commitment and you're so scared that she'll be taking the place of your mother! And that's why you are in this sticky situation tonight, hey?' I announced with triumph. 'Wow! I think I've found my calling. I've got to become some sort of psycho shrink!'

'Is that what you really think of me?' Duke asked with the slightest hint of a wry smile on his face.

'Well, sir, really, why *did* you come to hostel?'

'Perhaps I am different, but maybe I can make a difference. Has it ever crossed your mind that I may have come here to help. To help children from dysfunctional families. Goodness knows that some of them need it. I do care, you know!'

'I know! Maybe more than you care to commit to your lady friend.'

Duke grew a sheepish look and after a brief silence asked, 'Is it that obvious?'

'Well, all that stuff was just mumbo jumbo psychobabble but I knew it had to be a major problem. You bunking tonight, even if it was just sitting in the courtyard, is *so* out of character there had to be a major crisis. You know, a woman thing!'

'Talking of crises,' Duke suddenly said, changing the subject whilst emptying the contents of his ashtray into a cellophane bag, 'I see the building is still intact, but what about its contents?'

'Er, actually, sir, we do have a crisis!'

Duke's face crumpled, his eyes tilting back with horror, 'I knew it! The one time I abscond—'

'Relax. It's not that kind of crisis.'

'Then what is it?'

'Zulu has turned!'

'I beg your pardon!'

'I caught Scab's cronies smoking again, and Zulu was with them!'

'Are you sure he was smoking?'

'Yes. But even if he weren't, he's with them now. One by one Scab gets hold of them. A guy like Zulu. He's bright, brilliant at sport, prefect material for next year. But not anymore, because Scab's got him! That's his ultimate conquest! If he's turned Zulu, he can turn anyone.'

'What did you do when you caught them smoking?'

'I gave them a warning.'

'Because I was not here to cane them?'

I did not respond.

'I'm sorry, son. I should never have put you in that predicament.'

'Sir, I'm more concerned about the greater problem of Scab,' I said, exasperated. 'His conquering of Zulu is symptomatic of a deeper problem.'

'What do you mean?'

'When I first came here—'

'Which is when I arrived, too!'

'Yes. Even though I hated the place, eventually I saw that there was a kind of spirit about hostel. But since he came it's deteriorated.'

'And you firmly believe it's him?'

'Yes! He's polarised this place into two camps. One good, one bad. And one by one he's whittling away at us! Can't you see that?'

'Don't think it hasn't come to my attention that a change has taken place. Two years ago I could ask you to clean my books for me and you would. Now I couldn't get a boy to share a cigarette they're so alienated against the staff. But you're right. It has become increasingly difficult to keep a finger on the pulse of goings on. For that I rely on you. Whether you like it or not, son, your job has become an extremely important link at the coalface. What do you propose we should do?'

'I don't know!' I said, shrugging my shoulders, feeling at a loss. 'But I know that if we don't do something, there are good kids out there that will be permanently affected.'

'Exactly what has he done?'

'Oh! Come on, sir! *You* know he's a rotten egg!'

'*I* know that! *You* know that! But what do we tell his parents? The headmaster? That he *looked* at us!' Duke said, referring to Scab's vacant look where you know underneath he's laughing at you. 'Goodness knows they'll look at us and think we're daft!'

'What about the incessant caning after lights out? Isn't there a limit?'

'Horseplay, they will say!'

'You mean homosexual horseplay!'

'How do you prove that?'

I was silent for a moment before I plucked up the courage to say, 'Sir, I hate to say this, but *he's* in control of hostel. Not you, not me, but Scab!'

Duke stood up from his bed and walked towards me.

'Son, I think it's time to consult a professional psychologist. Tomorrow I will speak to Miss Simpson and take it from there.'

Huh! Miss Simpson!

Duke then placed his hand on my shoulder and said, 'Once again, I apologise profusely for putting you in such an invidious position. You have my word that will not happen again!'

Huh! What did Duke know about Miss Simpson? I wondered.

CHAPTER 52

The mention of Miss Simpson reminded me that I had homework to do, so I left Duke's room, switched on the radio which was playing *Killing Me Softly With His Song*, went to lie on my bed and opened my set work, *Romeo and Juliet*. The more I read, the more my mind drifted to Miss Simpson. She was a goddess. I would imagine her riding a palomino horse in the jungle, her long honey-blonde hair flowing in the breeze. Suddenly she would be in mortal danger, but despite being wounded, I would heroically rescue my damsel in distress and together we would ride off into the sunset.

I felt differently about Miss Simpson. I used to wank over Hoover, damn well near blistered my hand over her, but with Miss Simpson my thoughts were more than sexual.

§

As she read Shakespeare the following morning in class, Miss Simpson hypnotised me. I gazed longingly at her. Mesmerised by her mellifluent voice. Captivated by her long hair cascading over her shoulders, causing a few strands to radiate over her heaving boobs as she walked.

Suddenly she caught my eye.

'Tyrone, you carry on reading.'

Huh!

My face flushed red. So caught up with Miss Simpson, I hadn't a clue where in the book she had been reading. The best I could do was look down at my book and hide my face.

Perhaps she knew because she said, 'Take it from the top of page thirty eight.'

I proceeded to read. Stumbled a little at first, but then got the hang of it. After a few minutes I even started to enjoy it, and to impress my heroine I decided to embellish by taking in deep breaths and pouting out my chest.

'No Tyrone,' Miss Simpson cried out. 'Your breathing technique is all wrong.'

Huh!

'Class, it is vital when you read to breathe correctly. I'll demonstrate on Tyrone but I want you all to look and learn.'

She leant over and pressed my stomach back into the wooden chair.

'Firstly, you must sit with correct posture,' she coached. Pressing her hand firmly on my chest she continued, 'Then don't stick your chest out when inhaling. Instead breathe down into your stomach and stretch your diaphragm before you fill up your lungs. Try it, Tyrone.'

I did, but all I was aware of was my heart thumping heavily in my chest and I wondered if she could feel it.

'We'll leave it there for today. For homework I would like you to read ahead, please.'

§

After the last class of the day, I asked Spazz, 'Do you understand any of this *Romeo and Juliet* shit?'

Spazz looked at me as if I was daft.

'This Shakespeare guy didn't exactly write like we speak,' I lamented, and I was acutely aware that every time I tried reading my set work my mind drifted to Miss Simpson.

'Ordinarily, I would tell you to go and see the movie because it's got that beautiful Olivia Hussey babe in it. But you'd be wasting your time when you've got the real deal right here!'

'Huh!'

'Miss Simpson!' Spazz's face creased to his wicked grin. 'I told you, man. She targeted you and now she's reeling you in!'

'Oh, piss off, Spazz. This is genuine. I really don't understand Shakespeare and, this being our final year of school, I'm heading deeper up shit street!'

'Then go and see her and ask her for help. Go now!'

It seemed like sound advice, but the thought unnerved me, so I asked for moral support, 'Are you going to join me?'

'Nope. I don't want to spoil your party. Besides, I've got my own Juliet waiting for me to play find the worm.'

Spazz packed the last book into his satchel and as he walked out of a fast emptying classroom, he turned around and advised, 'Just don't scratch your balls, Tyke. Chicks don't dig that!'

Soon I was the last one left in the classroom.

§

I sat at my desk for ten minutes trying to pluck up the courage to visit Miss Simpson. Eventually I knocked softly on her office door. There was no answer. Perhaps she had already gone home, I thought. I decided to try once more. Harder this time. Just as my knuckle crashed forwards, the door opened and my hand nearly hit my English teacher.

'I'm sorry,' Miss Simpson apologised. 'I've been listening to music with headphones on, so I didn't hear you. Please come in.'

I walked in gingerly and no sooner had I wondered how come she had opened the door if she had not heard my knock, when she said, 'I had a sixth sense someone was at the door.'

Oh, shit! Could she read my mind? I wondered.

'How can I help you?' Miss Simpson asked.

'Miss, I'm having trouble with *Romeo and Juliet*. Trouble understanding Shakespeare.'

'That's not unusual. Many students build up a block against Shakespeare, but are later enriched by the Bard.'

Huh!

'Please sit,' she invited whilst walking back behind her desk.

My English teacher offered advice and suggested I should also read a study guide.

'Do you like classical music?' she suddenly asked.

'Huh!'

'Bach, Beethoven, Mozart, Tchaikovsky. '

I thought of Duke and all the disparaging remarks I had made about his music sounding like a cat's chorus.

'Um, it's not my cup of tea.'

'I'm not surprised. It's an acquired taste. But classical music has stood the test of time so there's no doubting its virtue.'

Miss Simpson stood up from her chair and walked over to a bookshelf, on top of which stood a record player. Thumbing through a collection of records, she asked, 'What music do you like?'

'Um, I dunno. Radio music.'

'You mean pop?'

'I suppose.'

'Do you think pop will stand the test of time?'

'Er, I dunno. Maybe the Bee Gees or the Beatles,' I answered with hesitation.

'Well, we'll have to wait and see about that, won't we,' she said, turning to face me with a record in her hand. 'In the meantime, why don't you take this and try it. You do have a record player at home?'

'I'm at hostel, Miss, but yes, we do have one there.'

'Mmm!' Miss Simpson said in a contemplative voice. 'I've heard about some difficulties going on at the boarding establishment.'

Huh! So Duke had already spoken to Miss Simpson, I concluded.

'I've also heard that as head prefect you have got quite uptight with the situation,' Miss Simpson revealed. 'Well, I can assure you that listening to Beethoven will calm you down and set you at peace.

Beethoven and Shakespeare,' she sighed, 'Enough to cure all your woes.'

As Miss Simpson got up and walked me to the door, she added, 'Anytime you wish to discuss your set work, my door is open. Bye, now.'

'Thanks, Miss. Goodbye.'

Phew! Not too bad! At least I hadn't said, 'Goodbye, merry gentlemen!'

I scampered off back to hostel, but decided to go the back route via the cemetery and slip in unnoticed through the back door. After all, I *was* carrying a Beethoven record.

As I passed the swimming pool, Scab and Giblet exited the ablutions, a look of horror etched on the younger boy's face.

CHAPTER 53

During prep two prefects would always be on duty, one in the dining room, one in the prep room, the remaining two ensconced in their chosen venue to do their homework or study. Eddie chose the box room, sandwiched between the junior and middle dormitories, Spazz the linen room situated deep in the entrance foyer on the right, Hog's pen was the scullery and Chief's pad was the one half of the air-raid shelter. The head prefect always did his homework in the prefects' dormitory.

That evening I waited 10 minutes after the prep bell rang before I felt safe enough to take out Miss Simpson's record. I removed the 7" single of *I Don't Know How To Love Him*, switched the setting from 45 rpm to 33 rpm, placed the LP on the turntable, turned the volume low and sat on Eddie's bed which was closest to the record player. And I felt a fool.

Not five minutes had passed when I heard Duke's footsteps growing louder and louder. Since there was no time to switch off the record player, I quickly turned the volume right down and just as I hid the Beethoven cover between *Sgt. Pepper's* and *Dark Side of the Moon*, Duke entered the prefects' dormitory.

'Going somewhere?' he asked, since I was right by the door.

I shook my head.

'Good, then we can chat,' he said. 'I spoke to Miss Simpson this morning and I thought you would like to know that we agreed that it would be best if she spoke with Stephen.'

'Huh!'

'That would be the appropriate measure to take. She can evaluate him and advise us accordingly.'

'I'm not sure that's wise,' I said, suddenly thinking of Miss Simpson and Scab together.

'And why is that?'

'I dunno,' I said, feeling protective of Miss Simpson, but I couldn't exactly tell that to Duke.

A confused history teacher said, 'The sooner Miss Simpson sees the delinquent the better. I'll arrange for it tomorrow.'

As Duke left the dormitory he stopped to look at the record player. My heart stuttered. By that time the record had come to an end and without an automatic return, rotated endlessly with the arm swaggering in the last few grooves. 'You might want to turn the record player off when you study!'

I sat on my bed and immediately thought of Miss Simpson

interviewing Scab. The thought horrified me and my stomach turned. For the first time I felt I was in love.

CHAPTER 54

The following afternoon I headed off in the vicinity of Miss Simpson's office, taking the Beethoven record as an excuse. Standing down the corridor from her office, I waited 40 minutes, wondering if Scab was in fact in her office. Suddenly the door opened and the orangutan exited and walked past me. He didn't say anything but gave me his infamous vacuous stare. My blood shuddered.

'Tyrone,' Miss Simpson called, spotting me. 'Come inside.'

I entered Miss Simpson's office.

'Did you listen to it?' she asked, nodding to the record I held in my hand.

'Uh-huh!' I acknowledged.

'And?'

'Um, …'

Fortunately Miss Simpson ended my discomfort, saying, 'It takes time. Why don't you go and select another whilst I make a cup of tea for us. I need to talk to you.'

'Okay. Er, thanks,' I uttered, suddenly wondering what she had discovered about Scab.

I walked over to the bookcase and fumbled through her pile of records. Huh! The first five all had Duke's name on them. All in his distinctive handwriting. What is his connection with Miss Simpson? I wondered.

'Take that one at the top,' Miss Simpson suggested, whilst pouring boiling water into a teapot. 'I've only had it three weeks but it's heaven on earth!'

It was one of the records with Duke's name on it. And she'd had it for three weeks! I became deeply suspicious.

'Please sit down.'

We both sat in chairs opposite each other with a desk separating us.

'I guess you know that I've interviewed Stephen and—'

'What did you discover?' I interrupted.

'I'm not at liberty to tell you. That's confidential,' she said, though I felt jealous that Duke, no doubt, would get to know. 'But I must urge you not to worry.'

Sure, that's easy for you to say, I said to myself, noting how elegant and refined Miss Simpson looked as she poured the tea. Don't you know it's *you* that I'm worried about, I wished to tell her.

She handed me a cup and saucer.

'Sugar?'

'Um, no thanks,' I replied, having the good sense not to take, since I feared my hands would tremble and I would spray sugar all over her desk.

I placed the cup to my mouth but my teeth started chattering. Oh, shit! So I returned the cup and saucer to the comfort zone of the desk. But just as it neared the table, the cup and saucer developed a mind of their own, and a disagreeable one at that. With the rattling that followed, one could be forgiven for thinking that a major earthquake had struck. Tea slopped everywhere.

'I'm sorry, Miss,' I said forlornly, feeling extremely embarrassed.

'Not to worry, there's more where that came from,' Miss Simpson giggled.

More tea to slop on her desk was not a sentiment that I relished at that moment.

As Miss Simpson dabbed at the slopped tea with a Kleenex tissue, she said, 'You're shy with girls, aren't you?'

My face flushed red.

'When I knew you as a little boy, you were shy then. Since I've come to know you the past couple of months, I cannot believe how you've grown up and matured into a fine young man but I can see that you're a real clumsy oaf around the fairer sex!'

A clumsy oaf! Oh, the embarrassment! I tried deflecting it off with a bit of humour, 'I think it's because I've been locked up in an institution too long!'

'You needn't be worried,' she consoled. 'You just need to take that first step and all will be fine.'

Then my imagination ran wild. Was she inviting me? I wondered. Was Spazz right? Suddenly I spotted an ashtray full of Dunhill cigarette butts. Huh! Duke's brand! One, two, three, four, five butts.

'Miss, aren't you concerned about someone smoking in your office?' I asked, fishing for information.

'In truth, I don't much like it but in the interests of a relationship it's worth putting up with.'

A *relationship*, I cried out in my head, wondering what she meant by that.

§

That evening whilst doing my homework on my bed in the prefects' dormitory, Duke entered, turned down the volume of the radio playing *Daniel,* and sang cheerfully, 'Good evening, son.'

'Evening, sir.'

'I thought I'd tell you that Miss Simpson has found nothing untoward regarding Stephen.'

'Huh!' I was staggered. 'What do you mean? When did you find this out?'

'I've just come from her apartment now. And, yes, she is quite adamant that whilst ...'

I didn't hear the rest of what Duke had to say. My mind swirled with a bewildering concoction of thoughts of why Duke was at Miss Simpson's apartment to sheer disbelief at her assessment.

§

I lay awake a long time that night thinking about Duke and Miss Simpson. I wondered if, after Hotstuff's ultimatum, Duke had broken up with her and started dating Miss Simpson. The shared interest in classical music. She seemed refined and elegant, whereas Hotstuff drove a Beetle! He had obviously spent a lot of time with her in her office and now at her apartment. Shit, Duke, I cried out in my mind, Miss Simpson is mine!

CHAPTER 55

No sooner had the bell rung at the end of the school day when I stormed off to Miss Simpson's office. I knocked on the door but before I heard a reply I opened it, entered and couldn't believe my eyes. Duke was sitting in *my* chair.

'Tyrone?' Miss Simpson enquired with a tone of surprise. She stood up behind her desk.

I looked at Miss Simpson, then to Duke, then back at Miss Simpson.

'Miss, you've got it all wrong with Scab, er, Stephen!' I announced.

'Young man, control yourself!' Duke scolded me, standing up as he spoke.

'No, it's okay,' Miss Simpson consoled the history teacher. 'Let me hear what he has to say. Tyrone?'

Not quite knowing where to start, I took a deep breath and sighed before saying, 'Miss, I dunno. He's a problem child.'

'Aren't a lot of the boys at hostel problem children?'

'I would be the first to agree that he is a handful,' Duke added.

'Uh-uh!' I said in a voice ladled with emotion, shaking my head in disbelief. 'He's different, sir. *You* know that!'

'How? Tell me,' Miss Simpson asked.

'He's just not normal,' I said, finding it difficult to put into words. 'I don't know how to say it.'

'Then let me help you by telling you what I found,' Miss Simpson suggested. 'Although intelligent he comes from a dysfunctional home. That is obvious. He's boisterous. He's crude. But nothing deep seated. In my opinion he's crying out for attention. That much is obvious from when he set fire to a neighbour's dog kennel this past holiday. When I spoke to his father this morning—'

'His *father?*' I questioned loudly, then pronounced, 'But his father is *dead!*'

'I beg your pardon!' Duke exclaimed puzzled.

'His father is dead. He told me!'

'When?'

'When he first came to hostel. The first thing he ever said to me was that his father had died. In fact, died that day! And that he was happy about it!'

'Tell me more about him,' Miss Simpson asked. 'Let's all sit down.'

'Well, er ... I dunno,' I stammered along.

'How about telling me why you all call him Scab?'

'When he first came to hostel he had lots of scabs all over his body. In fact, for the first couple of years, every time he returned from holidays he would have them, though not lately. But once you have a nickname at hostel it sticks.'

'You mentioned he's not normal. Give me an example.'

'Well, he's what you once said to me, sir,' I relayed, nodding towards Duke, 'Prurient.'

'How?' Miss Simpson asked.

'I dunno. He jumps on other kids. I've seen him in bed with this other guy.'

'However unsavoury you might find homosexual behaviour, the fact is, it happens in places like boarding establishments,' Miss Simpson said, 'even though the participants may not be actual homosexuals.'

'Miss, this has nothing to do with homosexuality. It's more his deviant behaviour that is troubling.' With great difficulty, my voice tight, feeling somewhat embarrassed, I lowered my gaze and said, 'He's got, er, got boys to have sex with plastic milk bottles.'

I looked to Duke. He appeared shocked and asked, 'Did he force them?'

'Not exactly.'

'What do you mean?'

'It's like he has this spell over them. He's become their master!' I sighed, then faced Miss Simpson and continued, 'Miss, when I first came to hostel there was a structure. As bad as things were, we all knew where we stood. There was a certain pecking order. But then things changed.' I again looked to Duke, then back at Miss Simpson. 'Ever since Scab came, hostel has split into two groups, the good and the bad. And more and more he reels the good kids in. He's like an idol to them. They delight in him standing up to authority. He even beats them up, especially when they call him Scab, but they are still drawn back to him!'

'What about those senior to him?'

'That depends. In my case, he's stronger than me, so it's awfully difficult to control him. But for someone like Chief he's not a problem. So mostly he doesn't confront Chief, except for—'

'Yes?'

'Well, two years ago Scab tried to crucify Mrs Sherman's cat and Chief beat him up for it.'

'He tried to crucify a *cat*?' Miss Simpson queried, her voice rising with her eyebrow.

'Uh-huh. And afterwards he was going to burn it at the stake when Chief came and beat him up.'

'I see,' Miss Simpson said, as if registering this information in her brain. 'Anything else?'

'Yes. When I left your office the other day, Miss, after you helped me with my English, I saw Scab and this other kid come out of the ablutions of the swimming pool and, er,' I hesitated, 'It's hard to describe but this kid had a look of horror on his face that, I dunno,' I said, shrugging my shoulders then slowly shaking my head, 'But it didn't look too good. Very disturbing.'

'Was this child, by any chance, Gilbert?' Duke asked.

Surprised that he had guessed correctly, I looked to Duke and said, 'Yes!'

'Did you speak with him?'

'Yes, but he clammed up.'

A look of distress drew across Miss Simpson's face and she went pale as she spoke. 'Gentlemen, I do believe that we have a major problem here. It looks to me, now, as if we are dealing with someone with sociopathic tendencies. When I spoke with Stephen the other day he obviously pulled the wool over my eyes, but that's not uncommon with a sociopath. They have this ability to lie with a straight face,' Miss Simpson informed us. 'Tyrone, when he told you that his father died, that was his way of dealing with his father. I wouldn't be surprised if he had been abused by his father, possibly sexually and—'

'With cigarette burns,' I added.

'Yes. They may have been self-inflicted, but my guess is that it's from the father. And that's why he detests being called Scab.'

'And why he doesn't smoke.'

'Quite possibly,' Miss Simpson said, nodding her head. 'And by coming to boarding school he would escape that abuse, which to him equated to his father dying that first day and why he was so pleased about it.'

Wow! This lady had a brain, I thought.

'But what is deeply troubling to me is the cruelty he has shown to the cat without thought to any repercussions and also this look you say this child had on his face. I would say that Gilbert is in imminent danger.'

'Then that's it!' I exclaimed in a forthright voice. 'We expel him!'

'It's not as easy as that,' Duke added. 'We can't just expel him on hearsay.'

'That's the problem with sociopaths, they are cunning when it comes to covering their tracks,' Miss Simpson enlightened before suggesting, 'We will have to report the matter to child welfare.'

'But, sir!' I cried out aloud. 'Miss Simpson had just said that Gilbet is in imminent danger. We must expel Scab *now*!'

'Tyrone!' Duke rebuked me. 'We will go with Miss Simpson's

suggestion and turn the matter over to the correct channels that deal with this kind of situation.'

CHAPTER 56

Seething at Duke for siding with Miss Simpson, that evening I scampered off down to the air-raid shelter to consult Chief. I couldn't wait for child welfare.

The door was locked. Damn! I was sure Chief was inside because I could hear his Credence Clearwater Revival record playing 'them old cotton fields back home' over and over again on his windup gramophone. So I knocked on the door.

'Password?' came Chief's voice.

'Oh, come on, it's me, Tyke!'

Chief opened the door.

'How did you know the password?'

'Huh!'

'How did you know the password was Tyke?'

'You made the password Tyke?' I queried, surprised.

'Yep!'

'Whatever for?'

'Who the hell would want to be Tyke?'

Shaking my head at his response, I entered Chief's pad. Since becoming deputy head prefect, Chief had commandeered the one half of the underground air-raid shelter and claimed it as his domain. Without electric lights he used a candle for light. In the far corner nearest the small fanlight windows stood a makeshift bed, next to it a table and in the corner opposite the door sat a large wooden box full of Chief things.

Chief went straight back to his bed and with his head on a pillow, knees propped up, eyes glued to his work, carried on reading in the subdued candlelight.

'What're you reading?' I asked, suspicious that Chief could even read anything.

'Geo, geo, geomorph ... or something like that.'

'Geomorphology!'

'Yep! You know, mountains, gorges, things like that,' he responded without looking up at me.

'Bullshit!' I stated, knowing there was more chance of Chief joining MENSA than he would be seen reading geomorphology. 'What's she like?'

I turned his magazine backwards and exclaimed, 'Wow! They *are* mountains and what a gorge!'

'See, I don't lie!' Chief responded with a mischievous glint in his eye.

'Is this what you do all evening? Go gaga at a *Playboy* and wank your plank all night!'

'I told you, I'm studying mountains and gorges! Now what do you want? You're interrupting me!'

'Listen, Chief, I need your help, that's if you can wrest your eyes away from your geomorphology.'

'Why should I help you?' Chief asked, eyes still fixated on his magazine.

'Come on, Chief, not this again,' I complained. Each time I asked my friend for help, it led to a drawn out process of bartering and bantering. 'For starters, you *are* deputy head prefect.'

'I didn't ask to be made deputy. In fact, you owe me for getting me that job,' said Chief, his eyes growing to thin slits before commenting, 'You realise that if I help you I get to rub my foreskin juice on you!'

'Yeah, sure!' I responded, desperate for a plan but also quite confident that Chief's wild desires were all a figment of his imagination derived from the other side of the black stump.

Chief threw down his boob mag, pulled me onto his bed, sat on top of me and pinned my arms to the mattress. As much as I struggled to get free, his superior strength held me at bay.

After a few minutes of struggling, he suddenly said, 'I'm listening!'

'We have to get rid of Scab! This guy is—'

'Set a trap!' Chief interjected.

'Huh!'

He let go of me, squinted his Clint Eastwood eyes, pursed his lips and said, 'We're burning daylight! Let's make a plan. But first, coffee!'

Whilst I poured some water out of Chief's cowboy flask into a black pot and lit his paraffin stove, he retrieved two mugs and coffee ingredients from his large wooden chest and with shadows from the flame dancing on the bagged whitewashed walls, Chief and I set about making a plan.

'Why all of a sudden are you keen to set a trap to get rid of Scab?' I asked of Chief, knowing that with his strength, Scab never undermined his authority.

Chief nodded his head, then added, 'I'm not head prefect but I can see he's eating away at you! Besides, when he's gone then you won't interrupt me when I'm reading my literature!'

'Any ideas?'

Chief squinted ahead. Silence. He looked into the distance. I wasn't quite sure if he was communing with his ancestors, but I respected his instinct.

'We've gotta hit him where it hurts most.'

'That would be his dick!' I joked. 'He seems to like putting it into anything and everything he can!'

'Then that's what we go for!'

'Huh! We go for Scab's *dick*?' I questioned with disbelief.

Chief rummaged through his trunk, held up his booty and exclaimed, 'Bingo!'

'What on earth is that?'

'A rubber!'

'A what?'

'A rubber!' Chief replied, then seeing my puzzled expression, explained, 'An FL! Where do you come from?'

'Oh!' I acknowledged. 'I know a rubber is an FL, but they don't come in tins! Or do they?'

'Well this is a tin, and the last I looked inside there was an FL!'

Chief prised open the round rusty tin that definitely looked as if it came from before the war and indeed withdrew a condom.

'Where did you get it from?'

Chief gave the slit-eyed look before retaliating, 'If it does the trick, it doesn't matter where it came from!'

'What trick?'

'You said Scab puts his tool into anything and everything he can. Well, let him try putting it into this once I've doctored it!' Chief said, the grin on his face giving just a hint of a dimple.

'Chief, you're one bad boy, but I like it!'

'Unravel it!' he ordered.

The deputy head prefect gave me the condom and went back to his bottomless trunk. Holding it by the teat, I slowly peeled back the rubber until it opened to full length.

'Now turn it inside out,' Chief instructed, his head still buried inside his wooden chest of goodies.

I did. Just as I finished, Chief surfaced with a crude looking bottle. He turned it upside down, removed the cork and dabbed the condom repeatedly.

'What is that stuff?' I asked Chief, the air permeating with a strong smell of liniment.

'My all-purpose potion!'

The doctoring process complete, Chief instructed, 'Roll it up again!'

I did, placed it back in the tin that Chief held open and my friend snapped the lid closed and nodded with the satisfaction of a job well done.

'And now?'

'And now, what?'

'What do we do now to get Scab to put this on his dick and how does that help to get rid of him?'

'That's your job. I came up with this idea. I can't be the only brains of this outfit. It's your turn to do the rest. Besides, I gotta get back to reading.'

'And I think I've got it. We need to leave it somewhere so he'll swipe it and get expelled. The problem is, anyone could steal it.'

'Then isolate him!' Chief said.

'Uh-huh! And how do you isolate a guy in hostel?'

'Sickbay!'

'Hmm! That's true, but how do we make him go to sickbay?'

'Offer him some bait!'

'What's he attracted to?' I asked aloud, the answer coming in an instant. 'Aah, little boys!'

'You're learning!' Chief said with a smile, then lay down again and buried his face into his magazine.

'Chief, just one favour. Duke is not to know about this plan.'

'What plan?'

I poured hot water from the black pot into the mugs, added coffee, sugar and powdered milk and stirred, handed Chief his mug, then lay on the bed with my legs on the table and sipped coffee.

'Let me also have a look!' I told Chief.

'In a while,' Chief replied. 'I just want to finish reading about sex myths.'

True, the cover advertised an article by Masters and Johnson debunking the ten greatest sex myths. Also on the cover, a picture of a pretty blonde from the waist up wearing nothing but a Santa Claus hat, her right arm carefully obscuring her nipples. So I wondered what lay beneath. But after fifteen minutes I grew impatient.

'Chief, not even *you* take *that* long to read!'

So I snatched the magazine and sure enough Chief had been ogling the centrefold.

'Wow! Christmas has come early!' I exclaimed, then noticing a green bed sheet strategically concealing the Playmate's pussy, I complained, 'Just a pity the present is all wrapped up!'

'Pretty tightly, too!' Chief said sheepishly.

Suddenly I noticed a worn out spot by the Playmate's crotch and cried out, 'No! Chief, *please* tell me you didn't try to remove the sheet with an eraser?'

My friend looked at me guiltily and muttered, 'Can't blame a man for trying!'

'Chief, fold the magazine where it's stapled and you look at the one half from that side and I'll look at the other half from this side.'

'Okay, but don't get randy or I'll wipe my foreskin juice on you!' he said without a flicker of emotion.

We both lay on the bed sipping coffee, ogling a porn mag from opposite sides.

CHAPTER 57

Just before prep ended I called Giblet to the prefects' dormitory.

Knock! Knock!

'Come in.'

'Good evening, merry gentlemen.'

'Giblet, I need to talk to you about something *very* important, but what I say is between you and me, okay?'

The kid nodded his head.

'Scab has become a major problem for me and I'll say it up front, I want him gone. Expelled. And from what I've seen, he gives you the creeps, too.'

Just the mention of the name Scab and the kid went rigid. For a brief quiet moment I wondered if he, too, had succumbed to Scab's spell but then I remembered those haunting eyes when Scab fondled him in the shower.

'Giblet?'

The fourth former shrugged his shoulders.

'Come on!' I exclaimed, surprised. 'Don't you want him kicked out?'

The kid swallowed then nodded his head.

'Then I need your help,' I said.

Again, there was no response.

'Giblet, I have a plan to get rid of Scab, but I can't do it without you.'

The kid stood dead still.

'Please, my boy. I'm desperate and it will be to everyone's benefit.'

I stared into his eyes, deep brown eyes that misted with tears and betrayed a hidden anguish. What's happened to this kid? I wondered.

He finally broke his silence. 'What do you want me to do?'

I waited a moment, then took his hand and said, 'Tomorrow at breakfast ...'

§

During breakfast I looked over to Giblet at the fourth former's table. Come on, I urged, don't let me down! If the kid did not go through with our plan, he might unwittingly expose it and then pay dearly for it. I looked to Chief for moral support and he gave it, squinting through his eyes and nodding his head slightly.

Suddenly a retching sound emanated from Giblet's direction. Everyone's head turned to see a mouthful of porridge spew its way back into Giblet's plate, splashing the table, the boys sitting at the table disbanding like a swarm of flies swatted at by a horsetail.

'Good on you,' I whispered to myself. 'Now be strong!'

Holding his gut, Giblet stood up, walked past all the tables and into the kitchen.

'Go to the sickbay,' we heard the matron say to Giblet through the swing door. 'I'll be with you in a minute!'

I banged the gong to end breakfast, said grace and then watched carefully to monitor Scab's movements. Damn, he sat down again to continue eating. So I sat down too, as did Chief.

'This had better work!' I said softly to the deputy head prefect, worried that it may backfire. But my friend kept quiet, just sipped at his hot coffee and stared out over the wild plains in his imagination.

Scab burped, stood up and walked down the passage. I got up and quickly followed. He exited the dining room, turned right and headed towards the stairs. Exhorting him with mental telepathy to turn left, like a controlled robot he did and headed down the passage between the senior prep room and the matrons' bedrooms. So far, so good!

I followed some ten paces behind. Entering sickbay, I ignored both Scab and Giblet, opened the medicine cupboard, retrieved a bottle of Mercurochrome, opened it and started to dab it on one of the ubiquitous roasties we all had.

'My stomach is sore,' cried Scab, clutching his gut. 'I feel like vomiting. Must be the same thing that Giblet has!'

'Hmm!' Ma Betty prodded his stomach and asked, 'Is that sore?'

Scab doubled over with pain.

'I think you should stay home from school today!' said Ma Betty which brought a smile to Scab's face. 'A good dose of castor oil ought to fix you!'

Matron went to the cupboard and hauled out her evil potion and administered it.

'And you,' Ma Betty addressed Giblet. 'Castor oil?'

'No, Ma!' Giblet said, looking aghast. 'I only choked! I promise you, I only choked at breakfast!'

Ma Betty prodded her fingers into Giblet's stomach.

'Do you feel anything?' she asked.

'No, Ma!' said Giblet defiantly.

'Well, off to school, then!'

Scab looked dumbfounded.

'Ma, I think I'm a lot better, too!' Scab said, prodding his own stomach. 'See!'

'Is that so!' Ma Betty responded, putting on a miffed tone. 'Pity about the castor oil. And a good dose it was, too!' she exclaimed, then pointing to the toilet, she added, 'I think you'll be spending most of the morning in there! So, back into bed!'

§

I left sickbay and waited for matron in the passage next to her bedroom.

'Come on!' I said anxiously.

Eventually she emerged from the sickbay.

'Well done, Ma. You deserve an Oscar for that performance.'

'I don't know what this is all about, but he's going to start soon because that was a double dose!' she exclaimed.

'Good!' I smiled.

'Now what exactly is it you want me to do?'

'In an hour or two, go to sickbay and replenish the toilet paper. He'll surely need more, but leave your handbag there.'

'Where?'

'Just leave it on the counter below the medicine cupboard!'

'But—'

'It's okay. Empty it now and put this in,' I said, holding up a brown packet that contained Chief's condom tin.

Matron walked into her bedroom and emptied the contents of her handbag onto her bed. I dropped the tin into it plus some loose change, deciding the loss of a few coins would be a small price to pay to have Scab expelled.

'Not a word!'

§

At lunch time I met Chief on the dirt path back to hostel. We both walked with spring in our step, eager to find out if our plan had worked. As we entered the front door and saw Ma Betty's blushing face, I knew immediately that it had.

'Yes!' I cried out aloud. 'What happened, Ma?'

'Well, er, I, er, I had to call the doctor in!' the matron said hesitatingly.

'And?' I asked anxiously.

'I'm not quite sure. The doctor said something about being caught with his pants down!'

I asked emphatically, 'Did he steal the money?'

Ma Betty nodded her head.

'Yes!' I exclaimed, so excited I gave the matron a spontaneous hug, then quickly released her and apologised, 'Er, sorry!'

Whilst waiting in the foyer as the dining room filled, I patted Chief on the shoulder and nodded to him, saying, 'Thanks!'

§

Immediately after lunch, Bum Lump dealt with Scab. He reported the incident of theft of loose change from the matron's handbag to the headmaster who expelled him forthwith. By the time I arrived back from school that afternoon Scab had already left.

'Is it true that Scab has been expelled?' Eddie asked me.

'Yes!' I replied, hardly able to contain my excitement.

'Why?'

'Apparently he swiped some cash from matron!'

'Hmmph! Is that all!' Eddie commented. Before walking out the prefects' dormitory he gave us his opinion. 'You'd think at least he'd have been expelled for sticking his cock into some place it didn't belong!'

I lay on my bed, took a deep breath and sighed before taking a bite of my afternoon cake. Chief lay on his bed and ate his cake too. Together we savoured every last morsel. A celebration. Not a word spoken in a silent bond of triumph.

Suddenly Chief jumped off his bed and asked, 'Are you gonna beat your meat tonight in celebration?'

'Huh!'

'Probably not, seeing as you'll prefer to wank over Miss Simpson.'

'Huh!'

'I know how you feel about her!'

'Huh!' I felt my face blush.

Chief jumped on top of me and pinned me down on my bed.

'What you really need is for me to rub my foreskin juice over you!'

After a few moments of holding me in a vicelike grip, without another word spoken, Chief let go, walked out the dormitory and left me wondering if my love for Miss Simpson was that obvious.

CHAPTER 58

Two weeks after Scab was expelled, as I walked down the aisle of the senior prep room to hand back a book I had borrowed from Perve, each footstep reaped an echo, a tap of a ruler on a desk or a click of the tongue. The faces of the boys looked gloomy.

'Eddie, you need to exert more control in prep,' I ordered the prep monitor.

'*You're* the head prefect, *you* sort it out.'

It suddenly dawned on me that a new problem had surfaced. As I left the prep room, I resisted looking back to see who was making the noise because that would play into their hands. Upstairs, I knocked on the masters' office door.

'Sir, I sense there's a major problem brewing,' I started.

'Son, must you always be the bearer of bad news!' commented Duke from behind his desk. 'Sit down and give it to me gently.'

'When Scab was expelled, I thought everything would return to normal, but it hasn't.'

'Explain.'

'When he was here, you knew where you stood. He was the bad guy. The rest just followed him. Now there's no leader. Nobody has filled the gap and there seems to be an undercurrent of, um—'

'Rebellion!'

'Uh-huh.'

'Good gosh! When I teach you boys about the French Revolution I don't expect you to act it out!'

I nodded my head in resignation.

'Before heads start to roll, what do you suggest we do?'

'I dunno. The place lacks spirit. They seem disinterested. Nobody plays sport. I'm not even sure Zulu does anymore. All they do is sit around and vegetate.'

'Idle and without their leader. A volatile combination!'

We both just looked at each other, stumped. Harbouring mixed feelings, I felt awkward in Duke's presence. Betrayal when I so desperately wanted Scab expelled. Guilt for going behind his back. Jealousy over Miss Simpson. Yet he still called me son and believed in me to ask for my suggestion. I shook my head to rid myself of these feelings.

'Why the shake of your head?' Duke asked.

'Not to worry,' I replied. 'Sir, can't we force them to play sport?'

'Even if we could, it wouldn't help. And listen to the word you've just used. Force. That would be the spark to ignite the rebellion!'

'Then we need to occupy them with something they find appealing,' I thought aloud. 'And I think I've got it. A trampoline!'

'I beg your pardon!'

'Yes, a trampoline! I was once at King's College and saw that they had one and I've always wondered what it would be like if we did too. It's fun. It can be competitive. They can fight it out for turns amongst themselves. It might even bring back some old time pecking order.'

'Son, you may just have a point!' Duke acknowledged. Then just as I was about to leave he asked, 'When were you ever at King's College?'

§

A week later, I addressed the boys just before closing grace for lunch.

'We've had a second hand trampoline donated to hostel and we need to dig a hole for it this afternoon. I would like for some senior boys to come along and lend a hand.'

This suggestion brought a lot of murmuring and even a little hissing, making me wonder if the problem was worse than I imagined and that my trampoline idea might be a mistake.

'And it is compulsory for second formers.'

After school, I walked out to the backyard to discover that no seniors had pitched up. Ungrateful dogs, I thought. The second formers proceeded to dig, first removing the grass sods and afterwards the topsoil.

After half an hour, flushed red in the face, my fag, Galoob, dared to complain. 'Sir, this soil's getting harder and harder!'

'And?'

'Can't we get some of the others to help?'

'Damn, you're a miserable lot. I get you a trampoline and all you do is gripe!' I reproached, thinking how much stronger they would be if they did a few press-ups here and there. 'Here, give me that spade!'

I jumped into the hole, plunged the spade into the soil but it barely sank in. Oops! My fag was right. The soil was indeed hard. Nevertheless, I couldn't lose face, so I set about digging with all my might. But after 20 minutes of hard grovel and sweating like a pig in the hot sun, I asked my fag, 'Go and fetch me the hose pipe.'

Whilst 10 second formers continued to work the soil with their shovels, I aimed the hose spray directly into the hole which slowly filled with water and softened the soil. Soon it turned into a mud bath.

Behind me, the back door swung closed with a bang. I spontaneously turned to see who the culprit was and accidentally sprayed him.

'Hey, what the fuck are you spraying me for?' Zulu demanded,

253

walking towards the mud bath.

I would normally have apologised, but his tone did not warrant it.

'Just because nobody but these twits rocked up to help you with your precious trampoline doesn't give you the right to spray me!'

Pissed off and imbued with a new reckless attitude, I deposited the hose pipe into my fag's hand, grabbed Zulu around the ankles and hauled him over my back and plunged him into the mud bath, submerging him like a hippo in the brown goop. Zulu emerged looking brown from head to toe like his namesake, arms flailing, mouth spluttering. The second formers stared open mouthed. Zulu waddled over to me and, in a quick flash borne out of sporting skill, he rugby tackled me into the mud hole.

We surfaced, stared at each other, when I suddenly whooped out, 'Yes! That was good!'

The second formers broke into loud laughter, before they, too, rugby tackled anyone and everyone standing.

'Look what you've started!' I commented to Zulu with a smile.

'Oh, no! Not me! This is all your doing!' he responded, looking wide-eyed at the scene before our eyes.

The little devil in me prompted the question, 'How would you like to do the same to some of the others?'

'What do you mean?'

'Let's round up some of the other boys and dunk them in. Start with the prefects. Are you going to help?'

'Dunk the prefects!' Zulu shouted, his eyes lighting up. 'You bet!'

I turned to the mêlée in the mud, whistled and restored order. Whilst hosing them down with the spray I announced my intentions to disbelieving eyes and ears.

'Yahoo!' they responded in unison.

'I think we should start with Chief, after which he'll be on our side. And we'll need him to get to Eddie.'

Everyone agreed.

'But be careful, guys, Chief is crafty. He'll be in the air-raid shelter which he probably has booby trapped, if I know him, so be on your guard.'

We stripped to our underpants and snuck around to Chief's Pad.

'Zulu, you knock on the door and draw him out of the shelter. I'll come from behind the door and you guys jump him from the roof!'

All followed instructions crouching in their spots. Zulu knocked on the door.

'What's the password?' came the familiar drawl of Chief.

Zulu looked to me as if to say huh.

'Tyke!' I whispered.

'Huh!' Zulu responded with a confused look on his face.

'The password is Tyke!' I repeated.

Baffled, Zulu turned to the door and said authoritatively, 'Tyke!'

Chief opened the door and poked his nose out, looking highly suspicious. Zulu started backing off, attempting to lure Chief out of his shelter. So when Chief stayed put, Zulu spat on the ground and ran around in circles, acting out an urban legend that such behaviour in the wild west would anger an American Indian. At first Chief looked unsure, but the vision of Zulu trying to catch his tale in only his underpants overcame his hesitation and the deputy head prefect emerged from his pad.

'Now!' I shouted and jumped Chief from behind, wrapping my arm around his neck and hanging on for dear life.

Zulu quickly embraced his legs. But Chief was strong and wrestled like a titan.

Sensing the need for help I shouted to the second formers, 'Now, you idiots, now!' This prompted young boys to rain down from the air-raid shelter roof. At first they seemed a hindrance, but I advised them, 'Just lift him in the air, Zulu and I will do the rest.'

It worked. Without his legs on the ground for leverage, the twelve of us seemed to match Chief with just a little to spare. Like a Chinese Dragon we headed off to the trampoline mud bath and dunked Chief, the momentum dragging all of us back into the liquid puree. We surfaced. I looked around to see a horde of brown bodies sporting huge white eyes. All except for Chief.

Through slit eyes he glared at me and said, 'There're many rubs of foreskin juice in store for you!'

'Chief, we only did this to get you to help us do it to Eddie and Hog. This is fun!'

Chief's eyes slowly widened. He looked left, then right, then straight in my eyes and with lips pursed he drawled, 'Then what are we waiting for?'

'Who should we do next?' I asked.

'Spazz!' suggested Zulu.

'Er, I don't think you'll find him here. He's sure to be visiting Hoover!'

'Then how about Eddie!' Zulu proclaimed, his eyes lighting up.

'Hmm … best we leave him for last. Let him stew. Besides I think we should solicit Mutt's help to get Eddie, and the best way to get his help is to dunk him first! He'll be in the prep room.'

After much wailing, Mutt succumbed and added strength to our team.

'Hog next!' I declared. 'Galoob,' I addressed my fag, 'Go and tell Hog that matron is offering free cake in the kitchen.'

My fag scampered off but returned after five minutes to say that the door was locked and that Hog had said he wasn't as stupid as he looked.

'Then should we go up the drain pipe?' I asked Chief, always confident in his opinion.

Before Chief could answer, Eddie shouted from the prefects' dormitory, 'Not a chance!' and slammed the windows shut and locked them.

Damn!

'What now?' I said to no one in particular. Then turning to Chief I asked, 'Any ideas?'

Chief gave his Clint Eastwood look and said, 'Well, there is a trap door in the ceiling of the prefects' dormitory and another in the senior dormitory. So there is a way in.'

'We can't all go climbing in the ceiling!'

Chief gave a look of deep Chief type thought, before saying, 'Then we'll need to flush them out and ambush them.'

'Aay!' Mutt wailed, his eyes lighting up. 'Drop in a dog bog bomb!'

'Mutt, you dirty ol' dog!' I exclaimed excitedly. 'Good idea, but we haven't the time to make a bomb, but some dog bog will do the trick.'

I looked to my fag and said, 'Go to the matron and get a packet, then go down the lane across the road, second house on the left and offer to pick up their dog bog.'

My fag looked at me with bewildered eyes.

'Off you go!'

After 15 minutes my fag and his friend returned, chattering excitedly, then handed me the packet of dog bog.

'So who's going to drop it in?' I asked.

'You are!' Chief replied.

'But you're good at climbing. You spend all your time swinging in the trees!'

Chief just shook his head, then said, 'Nah! This is all your doing.'

'Mutt?'

'No way, man. I supplied the dog bog idea.'

With no option but to go myself, I set off for the trap door in the senior dormitory. From there I made my way through a minefield of rafters until I finally found the trap door of the prefects' dormitory. Lying across two beams, I carefully pulled the lid of the trap door to one side and immediately heard Eddie's voice.

'That Tyke's a cunt!' Eddie swore, walking up to the window that overlooked the backyard. 'I'll fucking kill him if they get hold of me!'

'Are they still there?' Hog asked, lying down reading a *Sad Sack* comic, picking his upturned nose.

'No, they've disappeared, but I don't trust him. He's up to something.'

Hog removed a blob of *Wicks* bubblegum from his mouth, stuck it on the bed frame behind his pillow, got up from his bed, opened the prefects' cake tin, the same tin whose buckled lid once took on the shape of Mutt's head, stuck his finger in his mouth, licked it, then used it to mop up the remaining crumbs of cake. That done, he opened my locker and took out an apple I had saved from breakfast that morning. He climbed back on his bed, propped up his legs, carried on reading his comic and scoffed my apple.

'Yuck!' Hog complained, between mouthfuls. 'This apple's rotten!'

Serves you right, you miserable shit. But he kept on eating it.

Time for the deed, I decided. I squeezed the paper packet and extruded a long ripe dog bog that landed on the floor with a thud.

'What did you say?' Eddie asked, eyes still peering through the window, aware of a sound.

'I didn't say anything,' Hog mumbled, head buried in his comic.

'Did you fart then?'

'I didn't fart!'

'But I heard you!'

'I didn't fart!' Hog said in an increased tone of voice, peeved at the accusation.

Suddenly Eddie turned around, blowing and waving his hand in front of his face. 'Are you still making that fart bomb!'

'It wasn't me!'

'Yuck, you stink, man! It smells like dog bog!'

'Hey, man, it's not me! That's not my brand!'

The stench rose up to the ceiling, through the crack in the trap door and crept right up my nose. I didn't know how much longer I could stand it. Nearly gassed, Eddie pinched his nose with one hand and unlocked and opened the door with the other to rid the dormitory of the ghastly smell. Suddenly Chief, Mutt and Zulu ambushed Eddie, the second formers went for Hog who let out a loud squeal and I started to climb out of the trap door to get in on the act.

'What's this commotion?' a voice bellowed from down the passage.

Uh, oh! Bum Lump!

The head boarder master marched down the corridor and into the prefects' dormitory, confronting a seething mass of near naked bodies. He looked up to see me half dangling from the trap door, a wild look on his face.

The air was tense as Bum Lump marched down the aisle in the dining room that evening, followed by the prefects.

'Before grace I have an announcement to make,' Bum Lump spoke curtly. 'For your unruly behaviour this afternoon, the whole hostel is gated for a month.' Bum Lump then looked to the prefects' table, nodded to Eddie and Hog and said, 'Except for you two.'

We were stunned. Instead of going home on Sundays for the next four weeks, everyone would have to stay at hostel. Hardly a word was spoken during supper. And for the first time since that onion soup on day one, I didn't feel like eating.

CHAPTER 59

Devastated, I went and lay on my bed. The prep bell rang, but I ignored it and stayed by myself in the prefects' dormitory, deep in thought, wondering how it was possible for one person to tear hostel apart, and what it would take to heal.

Knock! Knock!

'Come in!'

'Good evening, merry gentlemen,' came a softly spoken voice.

I sat up from my bed to see Giblet slowly enter the prefects' dormitory.

'You look like I feel,' I said to the gloomy-looking kid. 'What's eating you?

Giblet slowly walked to half way between my bed and the door.

'I thought with Scab expelled you'd have a grin from ear to ear, even with tonight's bad news. What's the matter?'

Still there was no reply. Suddenly I was concerned.

'Come on, what's bugging you.'

Giblet's chin started to quiver and tears welled up in his eyes. I felt at a loss, not used to dealing with such awkward situations.

'You can tell me anything,' I offered, 'or would you rather talk to the master on duty.'

Giblet shook his head, then started to mumble.

'Sir ...'

'Yes?'

'He, he, he ...'

'Scab!' I guessed.

Giblet nodded his head.

'What about him?'

'He ... he ... he ... bum ... bum ... bum ...'

'Oh, shit!' I whispered under my breath, knowing what was coming next, something I had feared for a long time. To help Giblet I added, 'Bum-rushed you!'

Giblet nodded his head.

Despite suspecting this to have happened, his confirmation sent shockwaves through me, but I knew I had to pacify him quickly. 'Just relax, he's not here anymore, so you're safe.'

Suddenly the boy melted in a flood of tears. I got up and closed the door and returned to my bed.

'Sit down,' I offered sympathetically.

Giblet looked confused.

'Sit. Sit on my bed.'

He sat down, rather warily.

'Calm down and tell me what happened. In your own time.'

After a moment's silence he proffered, 'I don't know what to say.'

Sensing his difficulty, I decided it would be easier if he answered questions.

'Um, did it happen more than once?'

He nodded his head.

I breathed in deeply, wondering what to ask him.

'Um, where did it happen?'

After a moment's silence, Giblet answered softly, 'The swimming pool.'

I nodded my head, then asked, 'Any other place?'

'The boiler room.'

'Uh-huh!'

'And in sickbay,' the boy said, in a barely audible voice.

After a moment's silence I asked, 'Did he force you to do this?'

Giblet nodded.

'What did he say to you if you didn't go with him?'

Tears welled up in his eyes again, but he answered bravely, 'He, he said he'd kill me.' There was a moment of silence before he added, 'He always had this big knife.'

'Is that why you've never told me this before?'

Giblet replied, 'Yes!' and suddenly he looked a little more relaxed.

Stunned, I wondered what to do.

'Listen, I'm going to have to tell Duke about this. You don't have to speak to him. Not now, anyway. But this is very serious.'

Giblet nodded his head.

'Um, what do you want to do now? You can go to your dorm or stay here if you want!'

'No, I'll go to prep!'

'Okay, but remember, Scab's gone now. It's all going to be okay.'

A faint flicker of a smile creased his face before he turned to go.

'Oh, er, do you know if Scab did this to anyone else?' I asked.

Giblet turned around and answered, 'I'm not sure.'

'Do you think he might have?'

'I'm not sure.'

Giblet stood at the door and hesitated.

'Anything else?' I asked.

'Um, just thanks for getting rid of him, sir!'

I just nodded my head and added, 'You did a brave thing yourself.

Without your help he would still be here, so thanks to you, too!'

'Thank you merry gentlemen!'

§

After Giblet left, I knelt on my bed, stuck my head out the window that overlooked the cemetery and stared out into the night air. The whole hostel gated, now Giblet. And I felt so responsible. Feeling sick and tired of the war, I closed my eyes and started singing in just a whisper, 'Knock, knock, knocking on heaven's door ...'

'Have you taken leave of your senses?' Duke blurted as he marched into the prefects' dormitory. 'I hope you are happy with your escapades!'

For a brief moment I carried on gazing out the window, still peeved that Duke had sided with Miss Simpson, still jealous that he had a relationship with her. Turning around, I looked Duke straight in his eyes, but said nothing.

'I'm not quite sure what transpired here this afternoon, but it's not the sort of behaviour we expect from the head prefect,' rebuked Duke. 'I supported your idea for the trampoline to build spirit, not to tear hostel apart by having all and sundry gated.'

'Sir, hostel was torn apart long before today. Even though Scab's been gone two weeks now, his hand has left an indelible mark of evil on Windsor House and today it reached out and touched us once more.'

'Was he here today?' Duke asked, his angry tone turning to one of concern.

'No, but his legacy lives on,' I said. 'I've just had Giblet, er Gilbert, come to me and tell me that he was, um, how do you say it, um, well, bum-rushed!'

Duke raised an eyebrow of confusion before replying, 'I take it you mean raped!'

'Well, um, I don't know. Can a male get raped?'

'Most definitely!' Duke replied, his face looking serious.

'Well then, yes, he was raped.'

'Oh, my word!' exclaimed Duke, his face assuming a look of despair. 'When? Where? How?'

I repeated the story to Duke.

'Oh, my word! This is serious. I'm obliged to hand this matter over to the headmaster and he will need to inform the boy's parents.'

'Just take it easy on the kid. He's on the very edge!'

'Of course!'

Duke and I just sat there staring at each other in a sombre mood.

'Just as well he's now gone,' consoled Duke.

'Too late! The damage has already been done!' I said in a subdued voice.

'Perhaps it's best we just pick up the pieces and make a new beginning,' Duke advised as he walked to the door to leave. There he turned around and said, 'Son, your instincts were spot on wanting him removed immediately. And how fortuitous that he could be expelled because of something so minor as stealing a few cents.' Then with just the faintest of mock suspicion on his face, he added, 'If I'm getting to know you, as I think I do, I wouldn't put it past you to have had a hand in his expulsion. I'm still puzzled by what took place that day!'

'You know, sir,' I said, quickly changing the subject, 'for the first time in years we had a bit of fun out there today. Not just me, but all of us. We had fun together.'

'Don't you think you went a bit too far?'

'Perhaps!' I agreed, before shrugging my shoulders. 'But I guess it was simply a release of years of pent up bitterness.'

Duke nodded his head in a way which suggested he had some understanding of what I meant.

'But this is going to kill us.'

'What do you mean?'

'Four weeks locked up here and they'll fester like a boil until they burst.'

'What do you suggest?'

'I dunno.'

Duke left the prefects' dormitory and once again my thoughts turned to Miss Simpson. I wondered what she would do.

CHAPTER 60

Desperate for direction, I sought the advice of Miss Simpson. After school the following afternoon her office door was ajar. I knocked softly.

'Come in.'

'Good afternoon, Miss,' I said, walking in.

'Hello, Tyrone,' Miss Simpson greeted in a welcoming voice. 'How can I help you? But just excuse me, please, because I'm in a little bit of a hurry and I need to pack these books away.'

'Miss, er, I was wondering if you could give me some advice about, um, leadership or something like that. I've gone and got the whole hostel gated and, I dunno, I'm at my wits end.'

'I've heard.'

'Huh!'

'Mr Dawkins seems to think that you've become a little paranoid, but for what it's worth I liked your trampoline idea,' Miss Simpson said, placing the last of a series of books on a shelf in a wooden cupboard.

'But it backfired.'

'Perhaps, but you were on the right track,' Miss Simpson said. Whilst rummaging in her cupboard looking for something she continued, 'I have a book on leadership and motivational skills that can help.'

My English teacher found the book, turned around, picked up her handbag, walked over to me and said, 'I must leave now but I promise I will make time for you sometime soon so we can discuss the problems at Windsor House. In the meantime, I want you to read this book, which I would like you to have, and I'm sure you'll find the strength to see it through.'

Miss Simpson handed the book to me, smiled, then leant forwards, pecked me on the forehead and walked out the door.

'Be sure to close the door and it will lock automatically. Bye now.'

§

That evening I placed Miss Simpson's book on my bedside table still mesmerized by her kiss that afternoon and the happiness that glowed from her face. And she had given me a gift. I suddenly wondered what I could give her. I looked in my locker, thought about giving her some money, but decided against that and speculated what a woman would want for a gift. Perfume? No chance of that in hostel. Soap? I looked at the basin in the prefects' dormitory and decided that it wouldn't be quite right to give Miss Simpson a block of red carbolic soap. What, I wondered, would be suitable and cheap? Flowers!

§

Feeling chipper for the first time in weeks, using the remnants from a jar of Prep shaving cream donated by Duke earlier that year, I carefully shaved some bumfluff off my face, all the while whistling *The Morning After*. Ending breakfast a little earlier than usual, I set off to school via Hoover's house where I leant over the front picket fence and picked a flower. A red flower to match the fire in my heart.

Clutching the flower in my right hand I marched off to school and waited outside Miss Simpson's office. I knocked on her door. No answer. I turned the door handle. No luck. So I waited. And waited.

More and more boys arrived at school so I hid the flower in the inside pocket of my blazer to avoid embarrassment. Still no Miss Simpson. Eventually the bell went for assembly. Damn! Having no prefect duty that week, I sat in assembly and wondered where Miss Simpson was. Her chair on the stage where the staff assembled lay empty. My mind drifted off to the teacher I loved.

Spazz nudged his elbow into my ribs.

'Hey!' I complained.

'A bummer about your chick, eh!'

'What chick?'

'Miss Simpson!'

'Yeah?'

'Didn't you hear? Batman's just said that she was killed in a car accident when driving home yesterday.'

'Huh!'

Devastated, I excused myself on the basis of feeling ill, left school and walked back to hostel and lay on my bed. Tears came to my eyes, but I forced them below the surface. I didn't want to let go of my feelings. I lay there a long time feeling numb.

Finally the words of a Bee Gees song came to mind, 'Oh my heart won't believe that you have left me ... Don't forget to remember me, my love,' setting me off. Turning over on my side, I curled my legs up and sobbed my heart out. Drained of energy, drained of emotion, I fell asleep.

When I woke up, I thought a lot about Miss Simpson. Our conversation the previous day. Her kiss. I thought of death and I wondered where she was. I reached out to my bedside table and recovered the book she gave me. Holding it to my heart for a moment made me feel closer to her. I opened the front cover, saw her name and rubbed my finger softly over her handwriting, 'H. Simpson'.

Duke knocked on the door and entered the prefect's dormitory, saying in a sympathetic tone, 'Matron says that you're not well.'

I remained quiet.

'What can the trouble be, son?'

'I'm okay,' I responded disconsolately, looking down at the floor.

'Is it hostel troubles again?'

I shook my head.

'What's this crumpled red hot poker doing on your bedside table?' Duke suddenly asked, looking slightly bewildered.

'What's her name, sir?'

'Whose name?'

'Miss Simpson's.'

'It's Hayley. Hayley Simpson. Why do you ask?'

After a few moments I responded, 'That's a pretty name.'

'Aah!' Duke exclaimed, nodding his head. 'I see what's eating you up.'

The master sat on the end of my bed.

'You have a bad dose of infatuation! I'm sorry, son, I should have known. Come to think of it, all the signs were there these last few weeks.'

Huh!

'Many a pupil has suffered this, though in your case it's more understandable, living in this unnatural environment!'

Duke took hold of my hand and squeezed.

'You're not the only one who's going to miss her. I've been visiting her quite a lot myself, getting counselling for my troubled love life.'

Huh! Suddenly I felt bad. Bad that I had been jealous of Duke for no good reason. Bad that I had been so shorttempered with him of late.

'And if it's any comfort to you, there is someone hurting a lot more than us. Her boyfriend.'

'Her *boyfriend*?'

'Yes, her boyfriend was going to propose to her yesterday. We staff could see it written all over her happy face. What a tragedy for him!'

Miss Simpson dying, falsely accusing Duke of being in the hunt for my girl, and then discovering that the love of my life had a boyfriend. I felt shattered.

Duke rose and started walking to the door, then just before leaving he turned around and said, 'Remember, son, time is a great healer.'

'Thanks, sir, for your help,' I said meekly.

'That's what I'm here for! For moments like these,' Duke said with a wry smile, knowing that I had questioned his reason for being at hostel.

I nodded acceptance.

'Now, you take it easy for the rest of the day. But you're going to have to pull yourself together because you're going to have to represent the boarding establishment at her funeral.'

I took a deep breath and closed my eyes. I was probably the last person she spoke to and thought to what she had said. After a few minutes I opened my eyes and turned to the first page of the book that was cradled in my hands and started to read it.

CHAPTER 61

That evening I barged into Duke's bedroom whilst he was getting ready to go out with Hotstuff.

'Sir, I know what to do to restore spirit at hostel!'

'Yes, son, and what may that be?' Duke said in a tone betraying a slight hint of, 'Oh, no! Here we go again!'

'The school has four houses for sport and so on. I propose that we, hostel, that is, make up a fifth house.'

'And what good would that do?' Duke asked, walking to the window to puff out his smoke.

'Don't you see! We would have a goal, something to rally behind. And that will unite us.'

'Don't be daft. With only 50 boys, hostel is far too small to make up a school house. We would be outnumbered two to one.'

'But we can make up for it in spirit!'

'What spirit? In the four and a bit years I have been here, hostel is at its lowest ebb ever.'

'But that's my point. If we do nothing, especially being gated, that festering boil I mentioned will burst sooner rather than later and then all hell will break loose. But the spirit is there. I saw it the other day when we ran amok dunking guys in the trampoline mud hole. True spirit! If only we can unite around something to lance the boil,' I said, and then an idea came to mind. 'That's it! Our interschool athletics meet is in a few weeks' time. If the boarder rats can focus on beating the day dogs, there may just be a chance that we can unite again.'

Duke cautioned, 'You do realize it could backfire! The hoi polloi are not exactly champing at the bit to take orders from either you or me. If our house were to get soundly beaten, morale would plunge even further and then we'll have a real riot on our hands.'

'Sir, there's no other way.'

Just as Duke was about to squirt *Right Guard* deodorant under his arms, he paused and nodded his head, realising my point.

'Hang on,' I said to him, 'let me into your deodorant shadow.' Quickly lining up behind him, I raised my arms, then said, 'Okay ... now!'

'Must you persist?' Duke asked as he sprayed, the excess spray wafting on to me.

'I thought you wanted me to be a little more cultured and use deodorant!'

Duke snapped the lid on the can of deodorant and offered it to me.

'No thanks! I only wanted to use what was going to waste.'

'So, it's not a matter of not having to pay for it.'

'No!' I said, before backing down. 'Well ... why pay hard-earned cash for deodorant that you can get for free!'

Duke walked into his walk-in wardrobe to fetch a fresh shirt, returned and said, 'There's a shirt for you, though goodness knows why you'd want it.'

'Too big? Too small?'

'No. Let's just say it's getting a little on the old side!'

'So will you at least discuss it with the headmaster. Please!'

Duke looked unconvinced.

'Please, sir. Hostel has been torn apart on my watch and I want to put it right,' I said. Then with pleading eyes I continued, 'It's my home and I want us all to come together again.'

'Alright, son, but I can't guarantee anything.'

'Tomorrow!'

'Tomorrow's fine. I can see it means a lot to you.'

§

The following morning Duke collared me after assembly.

'I think you should be in on your own request to the headmaster. Given my grave doubts, it may be more convincing if he sees that I have your backing.'

Tension grew the closer we got to the headmaster's office. Duke knocked on the door.

'Come in!' came an austere voice from inside.

My heart started beating wildly.

'Yes gentlemen?' the headmaster posed, still seated, peering over his glasses.

'Mr Windsor, um,' hesitated Duke, 'Tyrone has proposed a novel idea for the boarding establishment. I think it best if *he* presented it to you.'

'Huh!' I responded, flustered by the ball being placed into my court, 'Um, er, sir, I think that the school should have a fifth house, and that the hostel make up that fifth house.'

The headmaster peered over his glasses at me and simply stared. Dumbfounded. Come on, say something, I implored in my head.

'Sir,' I continued, to rescue the tense silence, 'I believe we can generate the spirit to match any dayboy house.' Laying it on thick, I added, 'We have the competitive drive that I'm sure will reap better results, and that can only advance the school.'

'Hmm!' the headmaster grunted as he turned his head sideways and looked out the window, placing two fingers under his large hawk nose.

He seemed unsure, so I quickly pushed the envelope by appealing to his vanity and said, 'You know, sir, we could name it Windsor House!'

Mr Windsor quickly turned his head back to look at me, stood up, walked around to our side of his desk, nodded his head and held out his hand saying, 'What a fine idea! I don't know why we hadn't thought of it sooner!'

'Thank you, sir!' I said, hardly believing it to be true.

'Thank you, Mr Windsor!' Duke said, a smile showing both joy and relief.

On leaving, as we neared the door Duke whispered to me, 'Ever thought of a career selling second-hand cars!'

'Gentlemen,' the headmaster stopped us dead in our tracks, 'The boarding establishment is in dire need of pulling itself together so make sure this works! Just remember, *my* name is at stake!'

As Duke closed the door he addressed me, 'Well done, son. But I hope you realise that you've just caught a tiger by the tail and that tiger is all yours. I wish you luck.'

CHAPTER 62

When I entered the prefects' dormitory later that afternoon, the radio playing *Yesterday Once More,* I interrupted Hog's fag breathing in his prefect's fart and blowing it out the window and ordered, 'Please go and ask Zulu to come and see me.'

'He's airing the dormitory!' Hog slobbered.

A steely glare shut the pig up before I nodded to his fag and said, 'Off you go!'

'Why do you want that miserable brown specimen fouling up our dormitory?' Eddie demanded, referring to Zulu.

I took a deep breath, then explained, 'Batman has agreed to Windsor House forming a fifth house at school and with the inter-house athletics meet coming soon, I'm making Zulu the captain.'

'You *what*!' Eddie cried out. 'You can't do that! He's only a fifth former!'

'I know.'

'No, no, no! Please, Tyke, if *you* don't want the job then give it to *me*.'

I looked at Eddie, the bane of my life for the last five years, yet now he depended on me.

'Please!' Eddie begged, his eyes looking desperate. 'You've been head prefect and … and this would give me a chance to shine. Just this once, I deserve it, man. I deserve it for breaking the school shot put record last year!'

Eddie put my conscience in a tight spot. I did feel somewhat guilty over Eddie. But with the pack having lost their leader, agitation had set in with a jostling for position and before one emerged I knew that it was vital that *I* had a say. The greater good for hostel depended on Zulu being made captain, so I shook my head.

'Aw, come on, Tyke!' Eddie complained. 'Don't be a shit all your life!'

Again I shook my head.

'You're fucking chicken. Scared that I'll show you up. That I'll be a better leader than you are!'

Eddie's eyes grew wild, but I stood by my decision.

'You're gonna live to regret this,' my archenemy threatened. 'You heard it here and now. You will regret this!'

Zulu knocked on the door.

'Come in!' I said.

'Good afternoon, merry gentlemen,' the fifth former mumbled.

'The headmaster has given the go ahead for hostel to form a new school house. Windsor House.'

Zulu looked at me with deadpan eyes.

'Our first competition is in four weeks' time, the inter-house athletics meet. I'm making you captain of Windsor House's team.'

'Captain! Me, captain!' Zulu said incredulously. 'Why me?'

'I've got to start studying for finals,' I said. 'You've got four weeks. In that time I want you to round up the boys, bust their backsides, knock the shit out of them and train them up till they drop. Whatever it takes, I want victory.'

Zulu appeared hesitant, but eventually nodded his head and said, 'Okay, I accept, but on one condition. I want everybody training every day. And now that we're gated, on weekends, too!'

'Zulu, you're the captain! You're the boss! You make the decision.'

'Then that means you, too!' he said to me. 'I want you training with all of us every day!'

'It's a deal' I answered, shaking his hand.

Zulu looked to Eddie.

'You're fucking mad!' Eddie shouted. 'I'm not gated. There's no way I'm staying on Sundays.'

I led Zulu to the door and quietly assured him, 'I'll make a plan. He'll be there!'

§

Whilst combing my hair that evening after my shower, Chief sidled up to me and said, 'Word around here is that you know how to get into the pantry!'

'Is that so?'

'Come on, don't eat with the flies. Share it with us.'

After asking the second form fags to leave, I told Chief how I would raid the pantry in fifth form.

'So a gown cord is the trick. That's sneaky. I like it!' Chief said, his eyes narrowing to slits.

'How can you be sure the fanlight window will be open?' Hog asked. 'Surely matron shuts it at night.'

'Uh-uh. I presume she leaves it open for ventilation, otherwise I guess the food would go stale.'

Hog and Eddie left the dormitory chattering at a high pitch.

'Thanks, Chief. I can just imagine Duke lecturing to them that prefects should set an example and therefore be judged at a higher standard when he gates them!'

'Hmm! You're getting sneaky like me.'

'Just learning from the master!'

§

The response was extraordinary. Mothers, with free time on Sundays, sewed banners and old boys of Windsor House composed an anthem.

On the day of the athletics meet, we gathered on the front steps of the hostel to march up to the school field.

Whilst sitting on the top step putting on my running shoes, I looked up at Zulu and said, 'This is it! This is the big one!'

Zulu nodded his head, turned to the boys and, like a drill sergeant, bellowed, 'Guys, are we ready?'

'Yes!'

'Ready to kick arse?'

'Yes!'

'Then let's kick arse!'

The boys punched the air and responded with a resounding, 'Kick arse! Kick arse! Kick arse!'

Just as we lined up two abreast to march to school, Duke walked down the stairs donned in a track suit, a scarf and a cap, all in Windsor House colours. I couldn't believe my eyes. I had never seen Duke dressed in anything but an autumn coloured suit and tie.

All the boys responded with a thunderous, 'Hooray, sir!' and a chanting of his nickname, 'Duke! Duke! Duke!' before breaking back to, 'Kick arse! Kick arse! Kick arse!'

We marched up to school bellowing our anthem, raucous, off key, but with great enthusiasm. With such spirit, each boy responded with more than duty called for.

We matched the day boys race for race until it came down to the last event, the open four by four hundred metre relay. Our team comprised Eddie, Chief, Mutt and me.

Moments before the race Zulu approached me. 'Tyke, is there any rule preventing me from running this race?'

'Huh!' I responded. 'I dunno. Why?'

'We're two points behind Drummond House which means that we *have* to win this race to win the competition.'

'And your point is?'

'We have to risk all to win and, er, I think I'm faster than Eddie.'

'You are?'

'Maybe not over 100 metres, but over 400 metres I think I could beat him. He's got fat this last year and I'm sure he's slowed up some, especially over the longer distances.'

'I probably agree!'

'So, is it possible?'

'I'm not sure. We'll have to find out.'

But just then the official announcer called us for the race.

'Come on, Tyke! We've gotta win!'

'Well, let's risk all and you run it anyway. If there's a problem we'll sort it out afterwards.'

Zulu accompanied us to the start.

'Eddie, you're out of the race. Zulu is taking your place.'

'Bullshit! He can't. This is an open age group race and he's only a fifth former!'

'Sorry. He's the captain and he's already decided.'

The announcer called the runners to take up starting positions. Eddie walked onto the track. I looked at Zulu and nodded for him to go and run.

Eddie turned and looked straight at Zulu and ordered, 'Fuck off!'

Just then Chief walked on the track, grabbed Eddie by the arm and marched him off. Not a word spoken.

The gun went and the runners set off for the first lap. Immediately Zulu lagged behind the others.

'See what you fuckers have done!' Eddie moaned. 'I'd have left them for dust!'

I kept quiet, concluding that Zulu's poor start was probably affected by the altercation. At the halfway stage he started to open up and amid a crescendo of hurrahs from Windsor House boys he caught the field after one lap.

Chief next.

'Well done!' I congratulated Zulu.

'I had a shit start!'

'Doesn't matter. You ended well!'

'Mutt!' Eddie said. 'Zulu's gone and fucked up the race. I'll take your place and make up!'

Mutt just wailed, but never budged.

Chief was fast, but being a little thickset, not quite in the class of the other athletes. As he passed the baton to Mutt, Windsor House lagged five paces behind Drummond.

The noise grew deafening as the two came down the straight. All I could see was Mutt's fly shit face bobbing down the track. I settled myself down to take the baton. As Mutt approached I started jogging, then built up pace. As the wailing voice approached, I reached out for the baton, felt it, tried to grab it and set off to run, but the terrier latched on to it as if it were a bone.

'Mutt!' I shouted, but to no avail.

Desperate, sensing my opponent tearing away, I slowed, punched Mutt in the face, the shock releasing the baton. Grabbing it, I set off in a wild chase around the field. All the years of cross country training came to the rescue as I narrowed the gap on my opponent. As we entered the straight, I was two metres behind but closing.

Sucking huge volumes of air, I ran desperately for the tape, so consumed that I lost all sense of sound and my vision blurred, as if I were running in a vacuum.

As I breasted the tape the whole school stood to its feet. I turned to my left and saw that my rival and I had dead heated. Damn! Damn! Damn! A dead heat meant that Drummond had won the day.

I came to a stop and fell to the ground, my whole world caving in under me. All the training. All the building up of spirit. Now we had lost. I punched the ground, desperately disappointed.

Just then an ecstatic trio of Zulu, Mutt and Chief came running to me, the captain patting me on the back and shouting above the din. 'Well done!'

'Huh!'

'We won! Drummond House was disqualified for holding on to the baton too long at the last change over.'

'What!' I said out aloud, elated. I looked at Mutt and said, 'Just as well I banged you one in the chops. Sorry about that!'

Mutt looked confused. 'Aay, man, what do you mean? I was the one who thumped you. I had to wake you up. You wouldn't take the fucker.'

'Oh, whatever!' I exclaimed, punching Mutt on the arm, jubilant with our victory. 'So we won!'

As Zulu walked up to the rostrum to receive the trophy, the hostel boys applauded in unison and I thought to myself that Zulu would surely be the head boarder prefect the next year.

'When I came up with the idea to form Windsor House only four weeks ago,' the headmaster announced, 'I never doubted you would rise to the occasion. For your brave effort I have asked Mr Sherman to give you a free night out this evening.'

'Yes!'

§

That evening after supper, I went to the prefects' dormitory and flopped on my bed, exhausted. Mutt entered the prefects' dormitory for the first time that year.

'Mutt, you're meant to say good evening merry gentlemen when you come in here!' scolded Eddie.

'Fuck off!'

The mongrel walked over to my bed.

'Tyke, I need your help.'

'Mmm.'

'I want you to help me fill in this application form.'

'Yeah, what for?'

'A scholarship to the Royal College of Art in London.'

'I thought you were going to sail around the world,' I teased, though barely managing to raise a smile due to fatigue.

'I am. I'm gonna sail to London. Their art programme only starts in eight months' time so I'll be building up my portfolio. Then after I get my diploma I'll join my family and hit the high spots doing portraits of nude chicks.'

'Okay. Just leave it with me and I'll sort it out for you.'

'Thanks, Tyke,' Mutt called as he walked to the door to leave the dormitory.

'Mutt, where are you going tonight?' Eddie asked, combing his hair.

'Fuck off!'

Eddie turned around looking bewildered, then whined, 'Hmmph! You'd think I'd stolen his bone!' Before returning to the mirror he asked, 'And you, Spazz? Where are you going?'

'Fuck off!' Spazz spat, tongue in cheek just to goad Eddie, before breaking into a giggle as he pulled on a pair of blue denim jeans. With his Hoover affair blossoming he simply replied, 'Need you ask!'

'And that leaves you, Tyke.'

I took in a deep breath, still exhausted, sighed and shrugged my shoulders.

'Aw, Tyke!' Eddie belittled me as he stopped combing his hair and turned to look at me. 'Got nowhere to go.'

Just then Chief walked in and asked, 'Wanna go and see *Dirty Harry* at the drive-in?'

'Thanks, Chief, but I'll think I will stay in tonight.'

'Gonna stay here and celebrate with a hand job!' Eddie teased.

§

After they left, I lay on my bed clutching to my chest the book Miss Simpson had given me and fell asleep from exhaustion whispering, 'Today's victory was for you, Miss Hayley Simpson!'

An hour later, I woke to the sound of someone jumping on the trampoline, went downstairs, through the back door, walked towards the trampoline and was surprised to see it was Zulu.

'Why haven't you gone out tonight?' I asked.

'I dunno. Just didn't feel like it!'

I nodded my head in understanding and joined him on the trampoline.

'You know, it all started here four weeks ago!'

CHAPTER 63

At lunch the following day, whilst sitting at the table and waiting for Babalas to do his thing, Eddie started humming Coca-Cola's advertising jingle, then broke into song, singing, 'I'd like to teach the world to screw!' causing a broad grin to appear across Hog's fleshy face.

'Why are you so upbeat?' Spazz asked.

'We saw this blue movie at my dad's army camp, *Deep Throat*,' Eddie informed, before humming the tune again.

'Yeah?' responded Spazz.

'You should have seen it, man. This woman goes to the doctor because she can't get it off. You know, she can't have an orgasm.'

'Yeah, I know what that means. Carry on.'

'Anyway, the doctor examines her and discovers that her clit is deep down her throat.'

'Huh!' I responded disbelievingly. 'You talk shit, Eddie! A clit can't be in someone's throat.'

All eyes looked disbelievingly at me.

Hog looked at me and said scornfully, 'Fuck you, Tyke! Her clit was in her throat! The doctor said so!'

All eyes looked disbelievingly at Hog.

Spazz turned to Eddie and simply said, 'Eddie?'

'Well, her clit wasn't really in her throat,' he informed, looking at Hog. 'That was just for the movie.'

'Carry on,' Spazz urged.

Eddie beamed and regaled, 'The doctor tells this woman that the only way she can have an orgasm is if she takes him in the mouth. And all the way. Fuck, his cock was nearly the size of mine and she sucked it down just like a vacuum cleaner!'

For a moment we all sat in silence, our imaginations running wild.

Just as Babalas brought a tray of plates of food, Eddie piped up, 'And what did you do last night, Tyke?'

The longer I remained silent, the bigger the smirk on Eddie's face grew.

'You never got to go out with Hoover's sister, did you? Well, guess what. I've got a little surprise for you. Our sixth form party is coming up soon and I don't suppose you have a date?'

I kept quiet, knowing that Eddie knew full well I hadn't.

'Then I'm gonna organise one for you!'

I felt a rush of adrenalin.

'A blind date!'

I wanted to decline for the last thing I wished was for my dating life to be in the hands of Eddie, but with no date of my own I had no option but to accept.

'Tyke, I'll organise you this mean bird,' Eddie suggested, a gleeful smile on his face. He turned to Hog, 'You remember Mona from the beach. Mean Mona. She's got legs coming out of her armpits they're so long. Just wait until she wraps them around you, she'll fucking crush you, and swallow you up.'

Mean Mona, I thought. I imagined this mean looking girl with arms dangling out of hairy armpits chasing me around the party hell-bent on crushing me with her legs to swallow me up! What an introduction to the fairer sex, I thought.

To share my inadequacy I suggested, 'What about the others?'

'Not me!' answered Spazz with a deadpan voice. 'Hoover!'

'Mutt,' I called the mongrel sitting at the table alongside the prefects' table. 'You want Eddie to organise you a blind date for the sixth form party?'

'Aay!' wailed Mutt. 'What's Idi Amin gonna get me, a sex change? No way, man! I'm not a fucking rabbit!'

Suddenly Eddie seemed reluctant, as if his reputation had bitten off more than it could chew, replying, 'I dunno, man!'

'Why, what's the problem, Eddie. You're always bragging that you know lots of chicks!' Spazz teased him.

'Hmmph! I don't go with chicks. Women! I'm attracted to women! Broads!'

'Tyke,' Mutt called out to me, 'tell Idi Amin we need five dates for this table!'

And all the time Chief said nothing. Sitting at the table, wearing a strange looking felt cloth navy blue blazer, a homemade job if he had a home, Chief kept eating and slurping away, every so often looking one way then the other, suspicious that someone might steal his food.

§

Whilst walking back to school after lunch, Chief joined me and said, 'Talking about parties, why don't we stay on after school finishes and have a party.'

'What do you mean stay on?'

'Who knows? A couple of days. Longer maybe. Let's just park off and pickle our brains!'

After school. That was the first time I had ever thought of life after

278

school. Twelve years of school were about to come to an end. Yeah, why not park off and mellow, I thought. 'Sounds good. What about some of the other guys? Spazz. Mutt.'

Chief nodded his head, then added, 'We've gotta stock up on ale. I've already got one vat of brew on the go, but we need more. Here's the deal. I'll brew some more ale and you ask Duke if we can stay on. All we need is my pad. Throw down a couple of mattresses and it's a party.'

'Okay. I'll ask him.'

'And one other thing, work out how many vats I must brew.'

'Huh!'

'You know, four dudes, one ale every half hour for a few days or maybe longer. That kind of thing. How many ales do we need to keep going.'

'Wow, what kind of party do you envision?'

Chief closed his eyes to slits, looked left, then right, then drawled, 'If it means I'm outta school, the mother of all parties!'

'Mutt!' I called to the mongrel up ahead of us. 'We're planning to stay on a couple of days after school closes. Party around a bit. Are you going to join us!'

'Aay!' wailed Mutt. 'You guys are bad, eh! It all depends on my old man. He's only gonna pick me up when his yacht is ready. Then I start growing my hair and we fucking set sail.' With that he swiped his fingers across his lips as if to say he'd be gone for good.

I left Chief and Mutt and joined Spazz on my way to class, asking if he'd like to join Chief's mother of all parties.

'Sure. I'm gonna shack up just across the road anyway. So I'll be around.'

'You're going to live with Hoover?' I asked, shocked.

'Sort of. Next year I'm renting a room above their garage while I go to university. My love nest you might call it! Mind you, the way things are going she might have to move in.'

'Why?'

'She's late this month!'

'Huh! Where's she going?'

Spazz looked at me with a degree of puzzlement. 'She's late with her period.'

'Oh, her period!' I exclaimed, the penny eventually dropping. 'How do you know? Does she tell you these things.'

'Fuck it, Tyke! I can't screw her when she's having her period! But that's the beauty of twins. Screw one, screw both.'

'You screw both?'

'Pammy or Tammy, half the time I don't know which Hoover is

which, or whether I'm coming or going!'

My mind still boggled, I asked, 'So what's the problem?'

'The problem is that I could become a fucking father!'

'Phew, Spazz!' I responded. Then added, 'Well, look on the bright side, you're not shooting blanks anymore!'

'Hmm! Too much, too often!' Spazz sighed, looking shagged out.

As we entered class, Eddie passed by and uttered with an evil glint in his eye, 'Mean Mona. She's gonna eat you alive!'

CHAPTER 64

I peered at the mirror past Chief and his near suicidal attempts with a cutthroat razor and combed my hair one more time, nervously waiting for six o'clock.

Eddie burst into the dormitory, and like an executioner announced, 'It's time, Tyke! Prepare to meet thy doom!'

Thanks, I thought sarcastically. That's all I needed.

As we all headed downstairs to the courtyard, passing Duke's bedroom, I poked my nose in and asked, somewhat sheepishly, 'Sir, may I use some of your deodorant?'

'I see, young man. Refinement is good enough when you need it to impress a young lady!' he teased.

'Yeah! Yeah!' I acknowledged, knowing I needed all the help I could muster.

I squirted a little under each arm, handed the can back to Duke and as I turned to leave, the master said, 'Son, go be the beau for the belle.'

Upon entering the courtyard, the back door of a station wagon opened, and one by one young nubile nymphs climbed out. Second to emerge from the basket of fruit was a short redhead number. Mutt wailed, and without a word spoken and no introduction needed, they partnered each other and scampered off to the air-raid shelter.

Last to untangle her long legs was Mona. She stood up, and up, and up, towering over me.

'Mona, this is Tyke!' Eddie introduced, a gleeful look on his face.

Oh, fuck it, Eddie! What have you done to me? I thought. Mean Mona! She looked like a tall glass of water. Wet, flowing and eager to spill herself.

'Hello, Tyke,' she said in a deep husky voice.

'Hello,' I said politely, nervously holding out my hand.

But she looked straight past me and sized up the talent, leaving my hand dangling like a spare part. I felt awkward. Whilst the others paired off with their lasses, Mona behaved like a slinky, bouncing her way this way then that. Damn it, Eddie! You laid a real trap for me and I've taken the bait hook, line and sinker.

We all headed off to the air-raid shelter, venue for the party.

Spazz saw me and introduced Hoover. 'This is Tyke. Apparently you've met before. Pammy.'

Wow! Grown up she looked just like the girl in the movie, *Trinity is Still My Name*. Except, instead of a long Quaker-like dress she wore a buttercup yellow tank top, denim hot pants and white, calf-length PVC go-go boots.

Hoover eyed me up and down, then said, 'Oh yes, you're the one who picked up the doggie do from my lawn!'

Shit! I felt an utter idiot, shrinking like an exposed dick in Siberia.

Perve put on *Nights in White Satin* and we all sat. I felt awkward. Mona sat on the bed opposite me, oozing. I decided to do the honourable thing, stood up, got a plate of chips and passed them around, always conscious of Mona. Eventually I made my way over to her. But just then Chief walked in as the song changed to, *You Are The Sunshine Of My Life.* In a flash, Mona jumped up, grabbed hold of Chief, whisked him to the centre of the floor, and said, 'Let's boogie!'

They let fly. Soon the rest joined in. I felt rejected and wondered where Chief's girl was. With no spare girl to dance with, I sat alone and assumed the role of disk jockey. Between nibbling chips and swigging Coca-Cola from a glass bottle, I put on oldies from when I was at junior school like *As Tears go By, Those Were The Days* and a favourite of mine *To Love Somebody,* to songs that were hits during my five year stay at hostel like *Put Your Hand In The Hand, Joy To The World* and *Song Sung Blue* to the very latest songs on the charts *Goodbye Yellow Brick Road, The Most Beautiful Girl* and *Sorrow.*

Sitting on one of the beds that lined the room, I gazed over to Eddie. You fucking shit, I swore under my breath. Then I saw his girl look at me and I wondered if she had smiled at me. It was the first time I had noticed her.

'Tyke!' Spazz called me. 'Put on something heavy so we can go wild.'

I thumbed through the 7" singles and selected *Smoke On The Water.*

Just then, Bum Lump charged in, snorted and said to Eddie, 'The missus says the mother of those bevy of ladies is on the phone and wants to talk with you!' Bum Lump stole a quick perve and before leaving he groused at me, 'Change the music, Tyrone! Put on something quieter!'

Sitting there, I managed to catch a glimpse of Eddie's girl through a mass of gyrating bodies and a thousand swirling mini lights reflected from a rotating mirrored ball.

Desperate to be part of the party, dying to have a girl, I agonized. I suddenly remembered Miss Simpson saying that I just needed to take that first step and all would be fine. Just then, Chief squinted his Clint Eastwood look and nodded in the direction of Eddie's girl. It got me up off the bed, but I had to do the rest. As I walked across the room, my heart started to thump in my chest, and adrenalin spiked through my body making me feel rigid.

'Would you like to dance?' I asked her, my heart beating like African drums, so loud I could scarcely hear myself.

I wondered if she had heard so I mustered up the courage to ask again.

'Er, would—'

'Sure!' she replied with a smile.

So she *did* hear me the first time, I deduced and there I was asking her again. What an idiot! It took a long time before I realized that she had accepted my offer to dance, at which point I just stood there and started to move on the spot.

'Come, let's go to the middle!' she suggested.

I followed her, feeling an abject fool. We danced, she with the grace of a swan, me like a robot with a short circuit. I kept on feeling like I was having an outer body experience, where I would withdraw from my body and observe myself from above, all the time criticising myself and wondering what the heck she thought of me! But instead she smiled, politely, I thought, waiting for Eddie to return.

The song stopped. We stood there. I felt the silence.

'Hi! I'm Tyrone, but everyone calls me Tyke' I said, remembering I had asked her to dance and not even introduced myself.

'I'm Julia!' she said with a smile.

The next song began, *Save the Last Dance for Me.* I started gyrating and found myself the only one doing so. It was a slow song and everyone else huddled and shuffled. My face burned red! But Julia just smiled and took my hands. We huddled and swayed, me hiding my blushing face.

Just then Eddie walked in. Uh-oh! He glared at me. But I felt good. At least for the rest of that song I would have Eddie's girl and he would have to wait. Serve the swine right for setting me up with Mean Mona!

The song was too short. Way too short! As it ended, I braced myself for the explosion. Eddie got up from the bed, his nostrils snorting. I started to walk away, but just then Julia put her arm around my waist. The feeling of her arm touching my lower back, of her standing there, quietly defiant and making her choice, sent warm waves of triumph through my veins. Choosing me over Eddie, the guy who had screwed a hundred and one women, including a sex change, fathered dozens of children, the one who boasted equipment for women to die for. Suddenly, Eddie in my life was worth it!

My adversary scowled at me and skulked off, never to be seen again that night. I took Julia's hand and never let go! After a few more dances, we sat on a bed in a subdued light.

'How old are you?' I asked, trying my luck at polite talk, 'Or is it not done to ask a lady her age!'

'Seventeen. And you?'

'Same.'

I looked into her enchanting blue eyes and urged myself to take the plunge! My heart beating wildly, I leant forwards, she came closer, and our lips met. In a moment I pulled away licking my lips, a frown creasing my face.

'It's just strawberry lip gloss!' Julia said with a smile.

'Then I'll have seconds!'

Our lips met again and it felt good. The pure bliss of that first kiss, a moment that sent champagne bubbles through my veins. A moment when the world could have blown up right then and there and I wouldn't have cared to look because I was already in heaven. A moment I would have liked to freeze on film or place in a time capsule to relive again and again. A moment I didn't want to end, knowing there would never be another first.

Embracing her, lips pressing against hers, I opened my mouth. It felt soft and warm, her tongue, my tongue, exploring, tentatively, then fervently. With each deep breath, I felt her breasts press against my chest, causing me to go hard down below. I felt giddy and couldn't have expressed it better than the Carpenters's song that played at that moment, *Top of the World*.

Eventually we came up for air, panting. I placed a hand to her face and stroked her short dark hair off her face behind her ear and caressed her cheek in my hand. Shit! This is easier than I thought! Just about to go for more, she suddenly pushed on the bed and sat up erect with her back against the wall. Damn! Is that all, I wondered, feeling slightly miffed.

'Come!' Julia said, beckoning me to join her.

I did, taking the opportunity to wrap my arm around her. Boob time, I decided. Pretending to watch the others dancing but concentrating heavily on the job at hand, I navigated a journey to her breast without looking, eventually found a soft island and dropped anchor. My face went smug. But to my dismay two bony fingers suddenly lifted them up, held them at bay, caught red-handed. Disappointed, I consoled myself that at least we were holding hands!

'Grub's up!' Galoob announced, my fag standing in the doorway.

'Hungry?' I asked.

'Hmm!' Julia replied. 'Depends on what you offer here at boarding school!'

'Normally the food is pretty lousy,' I said, wondering how she would react to Ma Coughball's special brew of vulture's sweat soup. Holding hands as we walked over to Bum Lump's house, the traditional venue for our sixth form party supper, I added, 'But you've chosen your visit well. Tonight Mrs Sherman will give us good grub!'

I didn't eat! There was too much of a buzz in my tummy.

Nearing the end of supper, Chief sidled up to me, placed a bunch of keys in my free hand and in his curtailed dialogue, mumbled through his clenched teeth and jutting jaw, 'My pad!'

'But what about you?'

'Nah!' he drawled. 'I've organised a bed in the box room! See ya!' Chief! What an enigma. Somehow he had a bed everywhere, even in the box room! About to disappear, he divulged, 'The new password is Duke!'

'Huh! Why do I need a password?' I asked, but my friend had already disappeared.

After supper, on the way back to the party, I said to Julia, 'Come!'

'Where're you taking me?' she asked, a touch of mock indignation in her voice. 'I heard your friend!'

'Then you know where I'm taking you!' I answered with a smile.

I dug into my pocket and hauled out the bunch of keys. In the subdued light I looked for the right key, but spotted something else. Confused at first, but then it dawned on me, a condom tin! I quickly hid it and opened the door.

'What is this place?' Julia asked.

'It's Chief's Pad. It's actually an old air-raid shelter, but my friend uses it for his studies. Well ...,' I laughed, 'For Chief type stuff!'

'What do you mean by that?'

'It's hard to say. He's kind of ...,' I shrugged my shoulders. 'It's hard ... gee ... he's Chief, from another time, another place, but a good guy!'

'I can see that. You seem to follow his advice.'

'More his instinct!' I said. Then nodding my head, I added, 'And what better time than the present!'

After lighting a candle I faced Julia, held my arms out and looked into her eyes.

'Are you okay here?'

She smiled, edged closer and we kissed. Then we lay on Chief's makeshift bed and continued kissing. Puss 'n boobs! Tried the one before supper, admittedly with no luck, now for the other! No sooner had my hand headed down under and touched her thigh, when Julia retracted and sat up.

Damn, I cursed myself. Too fast, I thought. Desperate not to lose her, I thought of what the sex book said. Foreplay! Hmm, I thought I *was* doing foreplay! Then I remembered the book saying something about talking as a way to foreplay.

'Sorry,' I said, surprising myself, but that simple word restored her trust in me.

'I understand you are the head prefect?' she posed, changing tack.

'Uh huh!' I responded, noting that she did want to talk. So the book *was* right!

'Why you?' asked Julia, then added rather guiltily, 'Oops! I don't mean it like that. I mean—'

'Yes! What *do* you mean?'

'Um! I—'

'What's with you and Eddie?' I suddenly shot at her.

'I beg your pardon.'

'Before I answer about me being head prefect, I've got to know how serious you two are?'

'We're not.'

'Are you dating?'

'No!' Julia replied emphatically. 'It was a blind date. I actually filled in for a friend of mine.'

'Does *she* date Eddie?'

'No she was also going on a blind date! What's with the inquisition?'

'Julia, you don't know how happy you've made me!'

'Oh! I thought I had somewhat disappointed you just now.'

'No! Not that!' I said with a smile. 'You see, ever since I came to hostel, Eddie has seen me as a threat. I don't know why, but—'

'Well, *you're* the head prefect!'

'Yes, but he … gee, where do I begin,' I said, gathering my thoughts. 'He's great at sport. First team rugby, first team cricket. He's stronger than me!'

'Has that counted?'

'Um, no,' I replied hesitatingly, 'No, we haven't fought. Goodness knows he's always threatened to. But he looms large!'

'Maybe he is all hot air with no substance. How have you avoided a physical confrontation?'

'I dunno. I guess I've had to outwit him at times.'

'Now that's a virtue. What's the use of physical strength against wit!'

'Julia, you don't understand. This place, it's a law unto itself. To be strong is to be somebody.'

'It's obviously not worked for him! *You're* the head prefect!'

'Yes, but …,' I sighed.

I looked into her eyes, placed a finger to her lips and said quietly, 'You've no idea what tonight means to me!'

Julia looked at me, searching for more.

'Five years ago, when we came here, Eddie was twice our size. Not only his body, but down below, too!'

Julia giggled.

'Seriously! He claimed he'd slept with, oh, I don't know, plenty of women, including, can you believe this, a sex change!'

We both laughed before Julia asked, 'Do you believe that?'

'No!' I said emphatically.

'Do you believe he slept with all those other women?'

'No, I suppose not!'

'Well?'

'Hmm! You're a tough case!'

'Do you suppose he's a compulsive liar?'

'No question. You must hear the stories he's told. Utter bullshit!' I said, then quickly apologised for my language, 'Sorry!'

Julia just smiled and said, 'Well?'

'It goes deeper than that. I get measured against his lie.'

'But why?'

'Well, you see, Julia,' I said hesitatingly, a wave of emotions swelling inside me. 'I've never been to bed with a chick!'

'A chick?'

'A girl.'

Julia placed her hand softly against my face and whispered, 'And I didn't help your cause!'

'No, you didn't!' I responded, wistfully. 'But that doesn't matter. Just me ending up with his date, Chief romping with Mean Mona, and Eddie skulking off, it's a dream come true! In one fell swoop his haunting spectre has vanished.'

We sat in a moment of silence.

'Now it's your turn,' I said, turning the tables. 'Why me?'

'Instinct!' she laughed, then teased, 'But how wrong I was. I imagined Eddie and not you to be this lecherous monster pawing at me but—'

'Hey! Hey! Hey!' I laughed, then asked, 'What about you? Are you a prefect?'

'No! I'm only in fifth form. I went to school a year late because we lived abroad. But I'm not so sure I want to be a prefect after what you've told me!'

'You seem so sure of what you want, like you've got your life mapped out for you?'

'It's discipline. I am a dancer!'

'And that's discipline?' I scoffed. 'Discipline is catching guys smoking and caning them, and—'

Julia laughed and said, 'You've been locked up too long. I'm talking of self-discipline, the kind you need to do ballet!'

'Ballet! Isn't that just a girl thing?'

'No it's not! But even if it were, what do you mean *just* a girl thing?'

'Did I say that?' I replied sheepishly, wary of her tone.

'Yes, and you'd better have a good answer for it.'

'Well,' I hesitated for a moment. 'You get girl things and you get guy things.'

'And in your mind guys are better than girls!'

'They're not equal, if that's what you're implying.'

'Oh yeah!' Julia cried out. 'You are aware that Billie Jean King recently *beat* a man in tennis?'

'Yeah, but he's old and decrepit.'

'But his point was that even an old man could beat the best woman player in the world. That was belittling and he had to eat his words. Now I want to see you eat yours.'

'Well, isn't ballet where girls go 'pit-a-patter' on their toes like fairies?'

'No! Some of the great ballet stars are men. Nijinsky, Nureyev, Baryshnikov!'

'But aren't they … er, er, er—'

'Yes!' she said sternly, raising an eyebrow.

Damn, I felt trapped and answered rather sheepishly, 'Pooftas!'

'Come!' she said and beckoned me to the centre of the floor.

In one swoop she fell to the floor, doing the splits. I looked down at her and all I could imagine was her pussy hugging the ground like a kitchen sink plunger! Like rebounding elastic, she sprung up and came for me so I backed off. But she meant business. Soon I had my back to the wall, cornered, and in a flash her right leg darted out and pinned me at the throat.

'Can you do this?' she asked sternly.

'Well, er …,' I hesitated. Despite my predicament, my eyes gravitated down her legs towards the magnetic allure that lay beyond, itching to see where they started. But her haunting eyes brought them back to her eye level. 'Er, … no! I can't!'

Her austere look broke into a smile as she let me go. I felt relieved.

'Teach me to dance!' I asked, shocking myself. 'I feel so spastic!'

'You dance fine!' Julia comforted, breaking into motion in rhythm to the song *Knock Three Times* from the air-raid shelter next door.

I stood flatfooted.

'I've got no rhythm!' I conceded, made worse by the fact that the song reminded me of Mango, since you were only supposed to knock twice.

She took my hands and said, 'Feel the beat. Feel it flow from me into you.'

And it did. And I felt graceful and stylish and one with Julia and the music.

Next door the music changed to *Under the Boardwalk*. We huddled together, stood in the same spot and swayed to the soft tune. Julia hung her head back and looked into my eyes. Neither of us spoke. Instead they were calm, warm moments.

With both hands on my chest, she tugged softly on my shirt and drew me onto the bed. As we lay down, we kissed passionately. At times I wondered if it were real. Her warmth and the sweetest scent I had smelled in years reminded me it was.

Time to explore. I noticed she had buttons on her blouse. Still kissing her, I started to undo them. Shit! The buttons were lined with cloth and had a mind of their own. The first button took forever. I twisted it this way then that, and then pop! Oh no! I had the blouse open, but the button remained in my hand. Feeling rather guilty, I quickly threw it to one side.

That ordeal over, I saw her bra in the subdued light and wondered how it worked. The last bra I had seen was the pre-war contraption of Ma Coughballs. Slipping my hands behind her back I fumbled for a buckle, all the while still kissing her, but it was nowhere to be found. Damn!

Without a word spoken, Julia sat up, undid the buckle between her breasts and the bra parted before my eyes. Boobs! They were small, not like the Playmate that Chief had ogled over, but they were real! Sitting there I gingerly lifted my hand and placed it on her left breast. It was soft and warm. Fuck it, I thought, I was touching a real boob!

I gently lay Julia onto the pillow, bent over and placed my lips on her one nipple. I ran my tongue around it, then over it. And it grew firm. And below it her skin puckered. And I reasoned she loved it, blissfully unaware that it could be irritating the shit out of her!

Done boobs, now to her pussy! I reached up to her and kissed her, placed my hand on her thigh and gently stroked up to her groin. Where her legs met, I felt her panties. Shit! So close, but I cautioned myself to go slowly. So I gently ran my hand around her bum and back down her thighs. She sighed. Good! On the return journey I slid my hand up her skirt, placed my hand on her tight, flat tummy, down to her panties, over the top, back up again, then ran my hand inside her panties. The land of forbidden fruits.

Wow! I felt her bird's nest. I had read about it in the 'sex book', vaguely seen it in the dark shadow of the valley between Scratch's' legs, but now my fingers spread through it. I was really there!

And still my hand explored, down between her legs, and my fingers felt for it. Huh! Quite expecting to feel a money box hole through which she spent her pennies, things seemed quite different. The Book! The Book! Oh yes! Inner lips. Outer lips. A clitoris. Oh, yes! That's what chicks like. So I just let my fingers meander around, not quite sure where, but extremely chuffed they were there.

Then it was time! Time to do the deed. Time to complete a momentous journey that started when my balls dropped, that built as hormones gathered momentum, but tormented with five years of living with 50 boys.

I got up, knelt between her legs, whipped my shirt off, unzipped my borrowed jeans and drew down my under-rods. In an instant my spring-loaded weapon stood to attention, a boner one could hang a large beach towel on. Julia spontaneously backed off but I gently took her by the hand, closed my eyes and placed her on me. For the first time a hand other than my own touched me there and it felt so, so good.

As I opened my eyes with a sigh, a somewhat startled look on Julia's face in the candle light prompted me to set aside my desires. Instead, I lay down next to her and hugged her. Tightly at first as she buried her head into the nape of my neck, clung to me and sobbed. Gradually her sobs faded and long moments of silence passed as we tenderly embraced each other. They were moments of pure bliss.

After awhile, Julia released herself and I looked into her eyes that glistened with tears.

'Are you okay?' I asked softly.

She nodded her head and placed a finger to my lips. I didn't know it at the time, but to Julia I had done something special.

A long time passed before she whispered to me, 'I'm dying for some coffee but I don't want to leave.'

'You don't have to. Chief has all the ingredients right here.'

'You get dressed,' I told her, zipping up my jeans, 'while I sort out the coffee.'

'Hey, what's this?' she asked.

I turned around to see Julia sitting, dressed except for the top of her blouse which lay open, holding a button in her hand.

Feeling sheepish I admitted, 'Er, it sort of came off when—'

'Butterfingers,' she said with a smile.

'Don't worry, I'll see what Chief can do for us.' I rummaged through his supply box, held up my find and announced triumphantly, 'Fishhook and gut! Let me prove my handiwork when not under pressure.'

Whilst Julia finished making the coffee, I stitched on her button.

'Not bad!' she exclaimed. 'Even looks strong enough to withstand another session of you pawing me!'

'Hey, hey, hey!'

Where only a few months ago Chief and I ogled a Playboy from opposite ends of the bed, Julia and I now sipped coffee and chatted. With me lying across the bed, legs crossed and resting on the table, Julia propped up against the end wall, legs resting over mine, and despite a bad case of blue balls, we talked late into the night.

§

Later, back in my own bed, I couldn't go to sleep. Sometimes I wondered if I had just woken from a dream. Maybe I hadn't exactly made love to her, but I had this good feeling that I'd be seeing Julia again.

The door opened and in the darkness I made out a body entering the dormitory and approaching me. Suddenly Chief jumped on the bed.

'Oh, no! Piss off, Chief!' I cried, thinking he wanted to rub his foreskin juice over me. 'Not now! Not tonight!'

'Nah, I just want to know how it went?' he asked with a grin.

'Let's put it this way. I surprised myself!'

Chief wore a satisfied look on his face, nodded his head with approval and said, 'Quite the Casanova, hey!'

As he started to leave I asked, 'Did you arrange that phone call for Eddie?'

'Well, pardner, I thought I owed you one for swiping Mona.'

CHAPTER 65

With two weeks left until my final exams, surmising that Spazz had bunked out to go and study at Hoover's house, I entered the box room to borrow a past exam paper from Eddie. Lying on the prefect's table was a half-jack of White Horse whisky and a plastic tumbler in Eddie's hand.

'Well, well, well!'

Eddie made no attempt to hide it. Instead he took a swig and for a few moments I just stood there, shocked.

'Where did you get that from?' I asked

After a few moments, on the same day an infamous president declared that he was not a crook, Eddie replied in a tone that showed little care, 'From the office. I stole it from the drawer in the office. It belongs to Mr Sherman.'

I looked at Eddie and thought to myself that he had grown to look more and more like Bum Lump. Even the same flushed red face. He cut a pathetic figure.

'You realise that you can get expelled for this?' I informed him.

'I suppose you'll blabber on me again like you did last year,' Eddie stated nonchalantly. 'If you hadn't squealed, you realise that I would have been head prefect. Both here and at school. My uncle told me that.'

I nodded my head.

Eddie, pouring himself another drink, added wistfully, 'And then my father would be off my case.'

There was a moment of silence.

'Ever since my parents divorced my dad wanted me to be just like him. First team rugby captain, head prefect, then join the army and become sergeant major. But you fucked that up for me.'

'Do you want to go to the army?' I asked.

Eddie looked into my eyes and answered, 'I *have* to go!'

'But do you *want* to go?'

'Tyke, you don't understand, man. I gotta do what my dad wants me to do!'

'But what do *you* want to do?'

'Be a farmer,' Eddie replied despondently.

'Eddie,' I implored, 'then it's time you stepped out of your father's shadow. Stand up to him.'

'It's not that easy,' Eddie complained. 'He's my dad!'

'Just wait here. I'll be back.'

I went and fetched Perve's tape recorder, plugged it in, popped in a cassette and pressed play. 'Listen to the words, Eddie. It's a song called *Father and Son.*'

When the tape finished, I continued, 'Your dad will always be your dad. But you're at a turning point in your life where you need to choose your own career. A career that will last you the rest of your life. If you go to army you'll forever be doing what your father wants you to do. And he will continue to see if you measure up to him. But if you choose to be a farmer you'll be doing what you want to do. And if you're any good at it he will be proud of you. My guess is that you will have a better relationship with your dad.'

'Aw, it's too late. I don't have a farm. The only way to get into farming is to go to university but I'll never get in. I've done bugger all studying.'

After a few moments of silence I said, 'Well, this may be news to you but with all the shit that's happened this year neither have I, and I'm in dire need of help. So I'm going to make you an offer. I'll forget this drinking episode if you agree for us to study together. And I mean study like Mutt studies. It's nearly impossible for me to work in the prefects' dormitory, but if I join you here every day we can join forces, help each other, push each other and, maybe, just maybe we can get through finals.'

'So you're not gonna tell Duke about this?'

'No,' I promised, then teased, 'because the flip side is that if we don't study together, there's a strong possibility that we will both be back here next year and I'm sure neither of us wants that!' I put the whisky bottle to my mouth took a swig and said, 'With this swig we make a pact. I promise not to tell, but you promise to work with me!'

IT'S GOODBYE, MY FRIENDS

CHAPTER 66

Late in the afternoon, three days after breakup day, I knocked on Duke's bedroom door.

'Come in!'

'Hi, sir!'

'You know you don't have to call me sir, anymore. I'm fully aware that you plebeians call me Duke. That's fine by me.'

'Whatever,' I responded, shrugging my shoulders. 'Chief and Mutt and Spazz and I want to know if you'd like to come with us to a restaurant?'

My ex-history teacher stopped fluffing up his pillows, looked up at me over his glasses and said, 'To one of those sordid topless bars for a pub lunch? Er, no thanks, son!'

'No!' I replied, somewhat surprised at Duke's comment, but after five years of bearing the brunt of my frugality, I did understand. Nevertheless, I decided to prick his conscience and milk the situation. 'In fact, we want to take you to one of those posh restaurants you go to so that you can teach us some good manners!'

'Oh, stop pulling my leg!' he said, brushing me off as he straightened his pillows.

I tried as best I could to mask a smile with a deadpan face, even pretended to be hurt.

'You're serious!' he said, his mood changing to surprise.

I nodded my head.

'Good gosh! Most certainly, son. I'll phone and make a booking right away.'

I walked back to Chief's pad chuckling away before knocking on his door.

'What's the password?'

'Duke!'

Chief opened the door to his domain. My three friends had already started to get dressed. Spazz as if he had slept in his clothes for a week, Mutt like a puppet and Chief in a Huckleberry Finn outfit.

'Guys, I think Duke's going to say that we have to get dressed in smart clothes!'

'But these *are* my smart clothes!' Chief countered.

'I know, but I mean Duke type smart! And I think I can help. Over the past year or so Duke has been giving me his castoffs. I think he feels sorry for me.'

'Aay!' Mutt wailed. 'Tyke you're a skinflint. Mooching clobber off a master!'

'Let's blow his mind and dress like him,' I suggested.

Spazz nodded his head and radiated his mischievous grin. 'Like I've said before, Tyke, you're wicked!'

We did. In a couple of minutes, the four of us transformed from schoolboy hooligans to Duke lookalikes. Well almost. No doubt our hair was still scruffy and, instead of fitting tailor-made, Duke's cast-offs had to drape over four decidedly different body shapes.

We met Duke at the entrance to the hostel.

'Good gosh!' the boarder master exclaimed, somewhat shaken, then slowly absorbing the picture, he nodded with approval, 'My old castoffs. I quite expected you to be dressed, er—'

'Yes?' I asked with a stern face.

'Not to worry!' Duke weaselled out of his predicament. 'Come gentlemen, the bus has arrived.'

We boarded the bus for the city centre, the five of us dressed in polyester longs, long sleeve cotton shirts with large collars and wide ties, all in autumn shades looking starched stiff and Duke-like.

On our arrival, we followed Duke to the entrance of *Jacque's Bistro*. He walked with spring in his step, met the maître d' and spoke restaurant talk. After some moments we sat down and, except for Duke, were somewhat bewildered. Tables with large and rather stiff white cloths on them stood on plush wine red carpets, and the walls were draped in heavy cream curtains. In one corner a violinist played Henry Mancini's *Love Theme* from *Romeo and Juliet*.

'Sir, why's it so dark in here?' Spazz asked.

'It's the ambience.'

A puzzled look on our faces prompted Duke to explain. 'They use a subdued lighting to create an atmosphere of, er, romance or—'

We cackled.

'Just what we need. A romantic evening between the five of us!' I exclaimed.

'What will you fellows have to drink?' Duke asked.

'I dunno. I guess a beer,' I said.

'Have they got any hard tack?' Mutt asked.

'Tequila!' Chief drawled, still looking very suspiciously at the restaurant.

'Why don't you fellows try some wine?' Duke suggested.

We nodded our heads.

'Hmm! Now what do I select that's suitable for all of us,' Duke wondered aloud, puzzled.

Whilst my ex-history teacher pondered the wine list, his ex-pupils drum rolled on the table with our fingers. A quick look of disapproval from Duke brought an abrupt end to that, so I whistled along with the violinist.

'Where do you know that piece from?' Duke suddenly asked.

'Huh!'

'The song you're whistling. Canon in D by Pachelbel. It's a classical piece.'

'I dunno,' I answered, feeling my face flush red as thoughts of Miss Simpson came to mind. 'I guess I must have heard it on one of your records.'

'So not quite the cat's chorus you've always suggested!' Duke exclaimed, with a nod of approval.

After some more restaurant gobbledygook to a stiff looking waiter, Duke tried to teach us by saying, 'Gentlemen, he is called the wine steward.'

We nodded our heads.

A waiter arrived at our table and gave us each a menu. Duke perused his as if reading his beloved history books. I took one look at the prices, looked up and noticed Mutt had seen them too.

Using the menu to shield myself from Duke, I leant over and whispered, 'It looks cheaper down this end. Go for that!'

I then turned to Duke and asked, 'How are we meant to know what we're ordering? It all looks Greek to me!'

'It's written in French.'

'That's dumb! We're English!'

'This is a French restaurant but you can always ask the maître d'.'

Duke nodded his head discreetly and the maître d' arrived at our table.

'Are you ready to order?' he asked in a heavy French accent, which was lost on us.

Duke interpreted.

The maître d' then proceeded to explain the specials of the day, which sounded like a lesson in language, a tossed salad of French, but meaning no more than Greek.

'Gentlemen? What will it be?'

'I'll have that one!' I said, pointing to the cheapest item on the menu.

'Oh! You're going for an hors d'oeuvre!' Duke commented.

'Mutt?'

'I'll have the same, sir!'

'Spazz?'

'Er, that one, too!'

'Chief?'

Chief nodded his head.

'I'm hungry,' I complained. 'Is there any chance of scoffing anything like some bread before our whorey dervey things come?'

'Hors d'oeuvre!' Duke corrected. 'That means a starter!'

'Starter?' I reacted with bewilderment.

'Your appetiser before your main meal!' Duke added.

'Oh, shit!' I whispered to Mutt, thinking of cost. 'We've ordered a course before our main meal!'

'Your snails!' Duke added.

'Snails?' we all bellowed out in unison, horrified.

'Escargot,' Duke said, 'You do know you've ordered snails!'

'Oh, yuck! I'd rather have matron's vulture's sweat soup than snails!'

'Then why did you order them?' Duke asked.

'Cheapest on the menu!'

'Gentlemen, you're not to worry about prices. You may have anything on the menu!' The quiet response prompted Duke, 'Am I sensing that you fellows think you're paying for your own meal? Because you can put that one to bed. *I* am—'

'Actually, sir, *we* are!' I said with a forthright tone. 'We are treating you to this meal.'

'Nonsense. I won't have any of that!'

'I beg your pardon, sir, but *we* invited *you*.'

'That may be so, young man, but I can't expect you to pay for a meal at an expensive restaurant like this!'

Though the temptation was great to let Duke pay, I resisted, and feigned, 'Sir, you're our guest. We'd be hurt if you paid!'

Duke looked at me suspiciously.

I milked the situation and said, 'Years ago you forced me to accept payment for cleaning your books—'

'That's different. I had authority over you,' said Duke.

'Well I have news for you. Now you don't have the authority to refuse!'

'Hmm! I see you're getting cheeky already!' my ex-master teased.

'Besides, you're supposed to be teaching us this manners thing!'

'Okay, fellows, I relent, but I'll pay for the drinks. Fair's fair.'

We agreed.

'So, any chance for some bread?' I asked.

'The waiter's bringing some right now!'

On cue, he placed a basket in the centre of the table and I quickly reached for a slice.

'Huh! Er, waiter, this bread is stale. Blimmin' thin, too!'

'No, no, no!' Duke hushed as the waiter scurried away. 'It's not bread, but Melba toast!'

'Toast! Looks like it's seen better days to me!' I complained.

Nevertheless, we ate the basketful in a matter of minutes so I put my hand up and clicked for the waiter to get some more.

'No, young man, you don't click your fingers at a restaurant!'

'But I need the waiter. Clicking always brought Babalas hopping along,'

'This is not hostel!' Duke replied with disdain.

'Well, how does one get a waiter in this place?'

'You wait until the right moment, catch him in the eye and nod your head. Then he'll discreetly come over.'

The waiter seemed to be avoiding us, but couldn't resist when all five of us caught his eye and nodded simultaneously.

'How about some more of that Melba toast,' I asked.

Just as the waiter left Spazz added, 'A basket each!'

'Yeah!' Chief and Mutt agreed.

The waiter looked somewhat puzzled but dutifully headed off.

'Goodness, how much do you fellows eat?' Duke questioned.

'Not much, tonight, it seems, with just a starter!'

'Why just a starter?'

'Er, with those prices we haven't enough cash!'

'I see. So that's why you chose a starter!'

'Uh-huh!'

'Well, gentlemen, you can't just eat a starter. Let me pay for the main meal!'

I shook my head slowly but emphatically, then added, 'We'll stock up on this toast stuff!'

'But, sir,' Spazz commented, 'If you're paying for the drinks, we'll knock back a few rounds before our snails arrive.'

'Aay!'

One waiter brought us a basket each of Melba toast, another a round of beers. We tucked in. After three rounds of bread and beer our snails arrived, each plate covered with a silver dome and brought by a separate waiter, toffee-noses aimed high, little fingers curled in the air like shrimps.

'They all look like Dukes!' Spazz whispered to me.

The maître d' snapped his fingers and on cue, voila, they each removed the silver dome.

'Huh! Not much snail stuff!' I whispered to Spazz. 'We'll need more

Melba.'

The wine steward arrived, removed the cork and poured what appeared like only a couple of drops in my glass.

'More!' I ordered him.

Duke butted in. 'You're supposed to taste the wine and if it's fine then he'll pour the rest.'

His explanation seemed odd, but I lifted the glass of wine to my mouth and swigged back the tot.

'Tastes like medicine to me! But I'll have some more.'

Duke nodded to the waiter, but instead of pouring more in my glass he went on to Spazz.

So I lifted my glass and stretched over to let him know, 'I said I'll have some more!'

'No, no, no!' Duke exclaimed. 'You can have more, but it's protocol to serve the rest of the table before the taster!'

'That sounds dumb!'

Duke then unwrapped a large crisp serviette and tucked one corner into his collar.

'Huh! You look like you're going to the barber!'

'It's etiquette, young man!'

We copied him. Five Dukes, starched to the hilt, stuffed full of Melba toast and tipsy on beer, dressed for a haircut but sitting in a posh restaurant slurping snails and swigging back wine. Well, the real Duke did not slurp.

As the last mouthful of snail slimed its way down it repeated, a bubble of gas emerging in my throat, ready for expulsion. Duke caught my preparatory action and shook his head vigorously.

With the bubble of gas still lodged in my throat, I croaked innocently, 'Not done?'

Duke shook his head.

I tried to expel it quietly as best I could, and succeeded. Duke nodded his head with satisfaction, as if that one moment of manners had made up for five years of indiscretion. As if all his teachings led to that one focal point. But I guess he knew better.

Chief *did* burp. A look of satisfaction creased his face. 'Time for a cigar!' he drawled.

I quickly looked to Duke. 'Hey, you haven't puffed on that vile weed of yours since school broke up!'

'No, I haven't!' he said proudly.

I patted him on the back as if to say, 'You're cured!'

The maître d' came around and he and Duke babbled some more restaurant talk, I guess telling the ol' bugger that we had had enough, prompting him to give us a rather strange look as we paid in masses of loose coins collected from five years of giving haircuts.

'Why'd you tip the waiter?' I asked as we left the table.

Duke responded, 'It may just be that I'd like to come back to this restaurant someday, say, in a decade or so!'

'Let's pub crawl!' Chief suggested.

Duke gave us a look of horror. But to his credit he joined in. Late that night a taxi spewed five bodies out onto the pavement just outside Windsor House, and we staggered down to Chief's pad.

Chief dug into his bottomless trunk, retrieved five enamel mugs and poured some witches brew from his vat.

'No, no, no!' slurred Duke, before falling over.

To my utter surprise, the hair on his head fell forwards.

'Blimmin' heck. You're bald!' I accused.

'I'm not bald!' Duke replied indignantly. 'Just thinning!'

'You're fucking bald!' I accused, then patted Duke on his bald patch. 'I was right. *That's* why you use a hair spray!'

Duke shoved my hand away but I resisted and started a slow motion scuffle. Friendly but sozzled, the five of us wrestled like sloths on a go-slow late into the night with the efficacy of a bunch of sumo wrestlers making love on a water bed.

The last I remembered that night was Chief mumbling, 'I'm gonna rub my foreskin juice over you!'

§

I woke the following morning with the sound of a large truck in the distance.

'Aay! He's here!' Mutt wailed, coming to, his eyes opening wide as he jumped out of bed.

'Who's here?' I asked from my pillow.

'My old man.'

Mutt jumped up from the mattress on the floor and peered over the high window that looked onto the road. Just then a loud hooter sounded from outside.

'See you!' Mutt said.

'You're *really* going?'

'My old man's yacht is outside. Time to set sail!'

I looked out the window and couldn't believe my eyes when I saw this large yacht perched on a truck just outside hostel. Mutt went to wake up Chief to say goodbye.

'He's still pissed! You'll never wake him up.'

'Say cheers for me. I'm off'

I walked outside with Mutt. Carrying his trunk, he climbed aboard the truck and sat next to his father, spitting images of each other, except that his father's hair was long, he had a beard that extended down to his chest and a pipe dangled out from yellow teeth.

'See you, Tyke!' Mutt called from the truck.

The dog's father revved up the engine and over the noise I called out aloud, 'How do I get in touch with you?'

'I dunno, man. We'll be out at sea! In six months' time I'll be at the Royal College of Art.' As Mutt, his lookalike father and hillbilly family rode off down the road in a truck carrying the yacht that nobody ever believed in, the last I heard my friend say was, 'Later!'

As I walked back to the air-raid shelter, Chief emerged, somewhat unsteadily and with a beer bottle in hand. Slurring his words he asked, 'Where's everyone?'

'Mutt's gone, eh!'

'Without saying goodbye! I'll rub my foreskin—'

'He said to say cheers!'

Just then I heard a grunt from the direction of Bum Lump's house. I turned around to see Bum Lump half stuck up the tree, Kit Kat just out of reach.

'Chief, Mrs Bum Lump will be calling for you soon,' I said with a laugh, pointing to the tree.

'Oh, Mrs Bum Lump wants me, eh. This time she can have it!' Chief slurred, then started to stagger over to Mrs Bum Lump's house, bottle in hand, and dressed only in a pair of underpants.

'Chief, you can't go in like that,' I cried out, grabbing hold of him. But I was still no match for Chief, even an inebriated one who wrestled free and mumbled, 'I'm gonna rub my foreskin juice on her!'

'Give that to me,' I said, rescuing the beer bottle from his hand.

With Bum Lump still grunting, stuck in the tree, Chief disappeared into the house and I stood alone on the tarmac holding an empty beer bottle, unsure what to do. Suddenly I heard a shriek from Mrs Bum Lump's kitchen. I ran inside to confront a very drunk Chief lurching after Bum Lump's wife.

'Chief,' I called, grabbing him by the hand.

'He looks ill!' commented Mrs Bum Lump. 'Let me get something for him.'

She returned, opened a bottle and said to Chief, 'Have a shot of whisky. That should make you feel better!'

Chief took one look at the bottle, slurred the word, 'Nah!' before his eyes rolled back and he passed out cold on Mrs Bum Lump's kitchen floor.

As I left Mrs Bum Lump's house singing, 'I'm comin' home, I've done my time,' from a hit song earlier that year, I bumped into Duke.

'Oh, Tyrone, there you are. Your father has just arrived.'

I fetched my trunk, put it in the car, turned to say goodbye to Duke and advised, 'You'd better make use of the break to replenish your batteries for next year!'

'There may not be a next year at this place,' Duke said with a smile.

'Huh!'

'I'm taking my lady friend abroad for a vacation to test the waters and—'

'You dirty ol' bugger!' I said, nodding my head. 'Way to go, sir!'

Duke nodded firmly and shook my hand vigorously, 'Keep in touch, son!'

'I'll do that!'

To counterbalance the concrete he had packed in the rusted front passenger door to preserve our Vauxhaul station wagon, my father, without wearing a formal hat for the first time, instructed me to sit directly behind him. As we drove up Windsor Road, passing the infamous tree and the school on the right, a lump grew in my throat as I thought of my home for the last five years. But the future was calling and there was no looking back.

I married Julia and, of course, attended to unfinished business. As for Eddie, I bumped into him a couple of times at university where he chose to read agricultural science. Years later, rumour had it that after a command for attention at a military parade his father fell down dead, flat on his face and Eddie bought a small farm with the inheritance.

But Chief, Spazz, Mutt and Duke, my friends of five years, I never saw, nor heard from them again. Gone, but not forgotten!

THE END